P9-DED-917

THE RETURN OF MERLIN

Also by **Deepak Chopra**

Creating Health

Return of the Rishi

Quantum Healing

Perfect Health

Unconditional Life

Ageless Body, Timeless Mind

Journey into Healing

Creating Affluence

Perfect Weight

Restful Sleep

The Seven Laws of Success

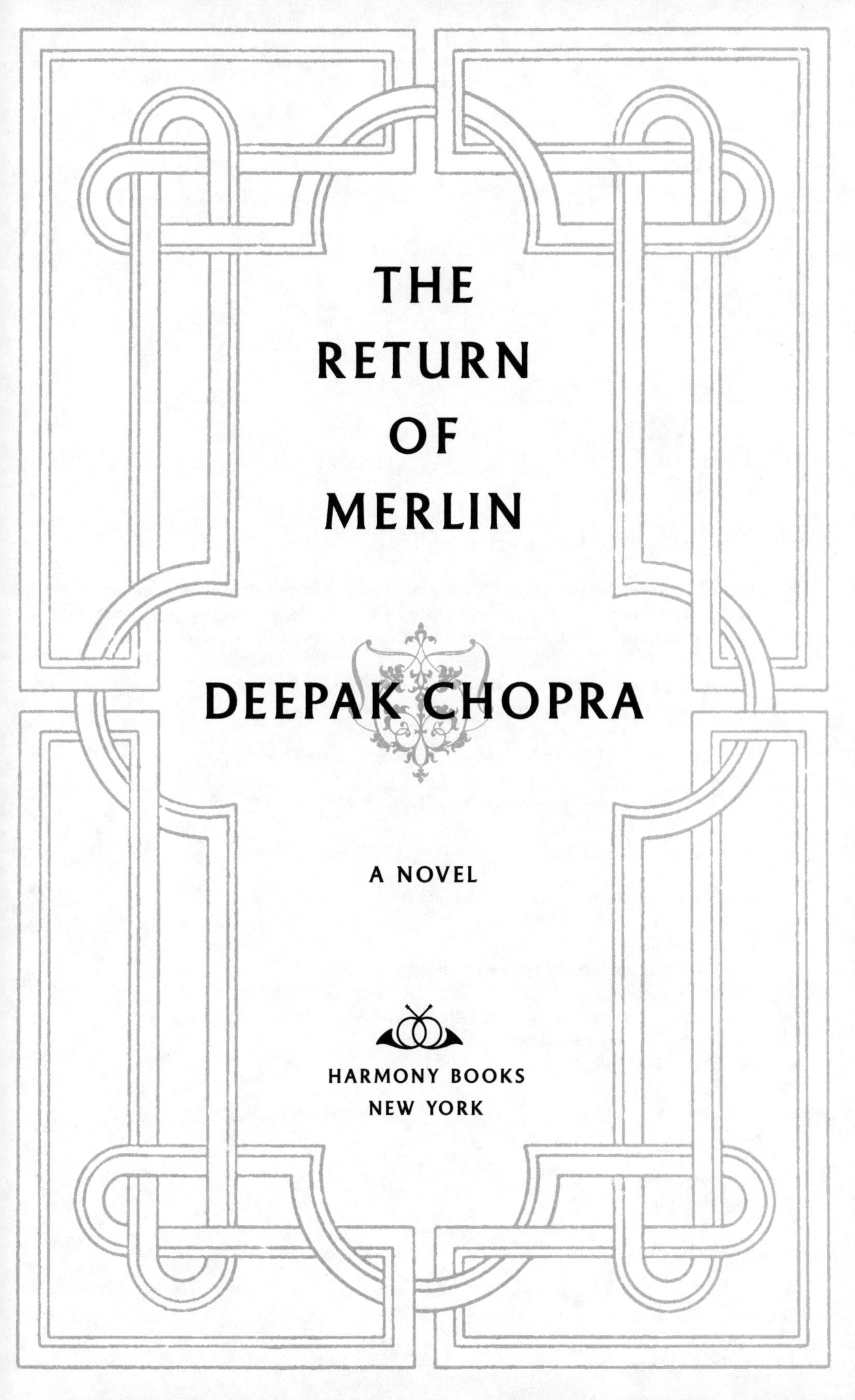

THE RETURN OF MERLIN

DEEPAK CHOPRA

A NOVEL

HARMONY BOOKS
NEW YORK

Published by Harmony Books, a division of Crown Publishers, Inc., 201 East 50th Street, New York, New York 10022. Member of the Crown Publishing Group.

Random House, Inc. New York, Toronto, London, Sydney, Auckland.

HARMONY and colophon are trademarks of Crown Publishers, Inc.

Manufactured in U.S.A.

Library of Congress Cataloging-in-Publication Data

Chopra, Deepak.
The return of Merlin / by Deepak Chopra.
p. cm.
1. Merlin (Legendary character)—Romances—Adaptations.
2. Arthurian romances—Adaptations. I. Title.
PS3553.H587R48 1995
813'.54—dc20

95-1824
CIP

ISBN 0-517-59849-3

10 9 8 7 6 5 4 3 2 1

First Edition

THE KEY TO MERLIN

MERLIN—THE NAME EVOKES IMAGES OF MYSTERY, MAGIC, adventure, wonder, and enchantment. The wizard is the central figure in one of the most enduring myths of our culture, the story of King Arthur and his kingdom, Camelot. In early versions of the legend, Merlin is the keeper of all knowledge; all-powerful, all-seeing, eternal. This version, *The Return of Merlin,* is about waking up the wizard that sleeps deep within all of us, so that we can reclaim the field of pure knowledge and dream a new world into reality, from the purity of our hearts.

What society thinks of as reality today is the hypnosis of social conditioning, an induced fiction in which we are all collectively participating. It is the melodrama of a humdrum existence, filled with trite obsessions and trivial pursuits, wherein our only fate is to be born, grow old, and die.

If we could just realize it, the keys to the miracle of life lie in our own consciousness.

Life will bestow miracles on us when we begin to see it as an expression of the miraculous. Life itself is a miracle. We are here and now—that is a miracle.

The wizard's tower is that sacred place inside us, where there are gods and goddesses in embryo; their only desire is to be born, to manifest into form.

The inner intelligence of the human body/mind is the ultimate and supreme genius, and it mirrors the wisdom of the universe. In this wisdom lies the power of transformation. Transformation opens up new realities, new worlds.

In the vast expanse of the wizard's consciousness, infinite worlds come and go; they are like motes of dust dancing in a beam of light. William Blake has said:

To see a world in a grain of sand
And heaven in a wildflower
To hold infinity in the palm of your hand
And eternity in an hour

We are led to believe a lie
When we see with and not through the eye
That was born in a night, to perish in a night
When the soul slept in beams of light.

As you read this book, I hope you will see in the characters of Arthur and Lady Guinevere, and Melchior and Merlin, and Mordred and all the others, the different roles you play as your soul sleeps in beams of light. It is our destiny to play an infinity of roles; we wear social masks in the drama of life, and it is in this sacrifice of the self for the self-image, the sacrifice of the spirit for the ego, that time is born.

This is the wizard's secret: the spirit is never overshadowed by the form or the phenomenon. The wizard knows that to be truly alive, she must die to the past in every moment. To be alive now is to be dead to the past. To be alive now is to have life-centered, present-moment awareness. If you have your attention on what is, see its fullness in every moment, you will discover the dance of the divine in every leaf, in every petal, in every blade of grass, in every rainbow, in every rushing stream, in every breath of every living being.

The wizard knows that beyond the burden of memory and judgment lies the ocean of universal consciousness. We are as ripples in this vast ocean, and we have access to the totality of its infinite knowledge.

The Chalice Well, the Sword, the Grail, the Stone, these are the tools we must use for this transformation. The Chalice Well is the wellspring of life within us, where we must return again and again to wash off our toxic experiences. The Sword is the power of love that can slay any dragon. The Grail is the state of grace, and the Stone represents pure knowledge, which is its own fulfillment, and has the infinite organizing power of the universal mind, which is orchestrating the diversity of existence.

As the story unfolds for you, I ask you to look at the characters and the incidents as symbols of your own life experiences, and, bit by bit, as you traverse the vast landscape of your own consciousness, you will awaken the Merlin inside you. But before you encounter Merlin—the spirit—you must go past the dark alleys, the secret passages, and the ghost-filled attics of your own mind.

You must confront your own Fairy Fay, your shadow self that accompanies you wherever you go. Fairy Fay exists in all of us; we are a conglomeration of ambiguities, an agglutination of different archetypal energies, where the sacred and the profane, the divine and the diabolical, the sinner and the saint all coexist.

There are so many personalities inside us all, competing for the use of this one body? It may be our destiny to play an infinity of roles, but we are *not* the roles we are playing. This is the first great realization of the wizard; there are many more in the story you are about to read. Here are a few insights that I hope will enhance that reading experience for you.

In "The Questing Wode" I ask you to peel the layers of your soul and discover ancient places and ancient times.

"Zigzag" is to remind you of the wisdom of unpredictability and uncertainty, so that you escape the prison of the known.

In "A Sleepless Night" discover your own discontent, and be grateful, for without divine discontent there would be no creative force.

In "Ashes to Ashes" discover hidden treasures in the rubble of devastation and destruction. In adversity lie the seeds of great opportunities for evolution.

In "Dreaming Time" see how the wizard escapes from the boundaries of time, and teaches us the following lessons:

- A wizard is not bound by the spell of time.
- There are infinite versions of every event, depending on the observer.
- We exist simultaneously in all times; the straight, narrow lines of time are threads of a web that extend into infinity.
- Every event reflects every other event; when an electron vibrates, the universe shakes. . . . A single event can shape our lives or change the course of history.
- Life is magical, mysterious, wondrous, and miraculous. Lose the magic, and you lose life. It becomes dull and joyless. When you have flashes of wonder, that is the wizard's touch. The worst curse to befall anyone is stagnation, a banal existence, the quiet desperation that comes out of a need for conformity.

"Seekers" points to the clues we must look for, on every step along the journey of our lives. There is hidden meaning in everyday events.

"Rider on the Hill" relates the eternal clash between the spirit and the ego. The spirit is carefree and lighthearted, and full of laughter. The ego is serious, arrogant, and contentious.

In one there is peace and harmony and love, in the other fear and hostility.

"The Furnace" examines the archetypal energies that stoke the fire of life in the basement of our souls.

"Gypsy Camp" explores the court of miracles, the sages, seers, geniuses, and drop-outs who have escaped the psychosis of the collective mind and might be our only clue to freedom.

"The Dark Earth" is our Mother, this gentle planet which is our womb and also our extended body. When we fear, she trembles and dragons are released.

"The Wedding Game" confronts the mirror of relationships, where we discover that those we love and those we hate are both mirrors of ourselves.

In "The Old Queen" Guinevere allows us to see the imprisonment of womanhood through the ages, first in caves and caverns, then in castles and convents, and now through corporate institutions. Now is the time to honor the feminine in ourselves, in our species, and in our world. The feminine intelligence of the universe can help us heal the psychosis of the collective mind, because the feminine is nourishing, contextual, relational, intuitive, and wise.

"Circle of Peace" is the world we can dream into actuality from the purity of our hearts. It is about the critical mass and coherent, collective consciousness, which is necessary to bring about a phase of transition in our civilization. It is about a return to Camelot.

This story, then, is meant to be understood on many levels. It is fantasy, but it is also a reminder that we are ancient souls from ancient places and ancient times. It is a reminder of the ambiguity of being human. It is a reminder that life is an open-ended horizon, and that we are magical beings. It is a reminder that in each of our lives, there are moments when we rise to a privileged place, where everyday acts take on mythical meaning. When humanity cannot make that ascent, we exalt it in legend, and that place is called Camelot.

PART ONE

THE RUINS OF MAGIC

1
THE WIZARD'S TOWER

THE OLD WOMEN OF CAMELOT WERE SURE THE WORLD WAS coming to an end. Toothless Megan lit a votive candle made of suet to say her prayers, and instantly a wind, as if coming through the castle walls, blew it out.

"Ten candles won't keep the devil away tonight," Gudrun the cook declared.

"God 'a mercy we don't all perish in our beds," old Megan replied, trembling. There were three sitting in the dark scullery—the two old women and a boy. "Boy," Megan ordered, "bring me another brick. My feet is cold." Ulwin took the cold brick from her hands and unwrapped its burlap covering. With a pair of tongs he pulled a new brick from the ashes and carefully placed it on the cloth.

"Hurry now," Megan grumbled.

"I *am* hurrying," Ulwin wanted to say, wondering why it was necessary to rush if the world was going to perish. Ill omens had been gathering thick and fast—rooks and vultures nested at sunset in the same tree, a hedgehog had been seen rolling on fire across the common fields, dark clouds swept the sky like wild horses in panic, and worst of all, a most foul eclipse cankered the face of the moon.

It was a night only a wizard could fathom, yet consulting his wizard was the very thing the king was pledged to avoid.

Arthur had sat for hours in his carved chair by the window in the great hall. His favorite supper, spiced boar with apricots, lay untouched on a salver beside him. As the day died in a dull gray glow, his face reflected the deepening gloom. "He already knows," Gudrun had said ominously when she returned from delivering the king's supper.

"Knows what?" Ulwin asked, but all he got for his curiosity was a dirty look.

Walking softly in the twilit halls, the queen came to coax Arthur to eat, yet even her loving voice, which had always roused him out of his moods, fell on deaf ears.

"I bid you take something, at least a morsel," she pleaded. Arthur only turned his clouded eyes upon her. They were tragic eyes, no longer courageous and calm as she had known them for so long. "Why do you grieve, my lord?" Guinevere asked. At any other time her heart would have burned to see him in such a plight; now a raw, new fear gripped her.

The king said nothing but averted his face to the window. "Call Merlin," he whispered—it was almost a croak. "I have seen the night of our ruin." The queen rushed from the great hall, pausing for an instant to kneel before the cross by the door. She hastily bade the newest page, who happened to be Ulwin, to run to the tower as fast as he could.

By the light of the half-eaten moon (in those days it was believed that an eclipse was caused by a black dragon devouring the moon), the king made out the shadowy form of Ulwin racing through the east barbican to the wizard's tower at the opposite end of the outer courtyard. It was a round tower made of massive gray fieldstone like the rest of the fortressed walls, but covered by wizardry with a shell of black obsidian, giving it a smooth, glassy appearance, as dark as the eye of a well.

When he gained the base of Merlin's retreat, the breathless page stopped. There was no door, and the only visible opening was a slit window very high up, facing west into the center of the royal enclosure. Ulwin knew that another window of exactly the same size was on the opposite, eastern side. Merlin liked to get up early and meditate on the morning star.

"Merlin, wizard potent and eminence dire, my lord the king commands your presence forthwith," Ulwin shouted in a loud voice. He wasn't sure if it was loud enough, for the wind howled loud enough to put out every votive candle on earth; the faint light that glimmered in the slit window failed to stir, however, and there was no reply. On such a foul night Ulwin felt unsafe outdoors without his garland of witch's bane, wolfbane, fleabane, leopard's-bane, and all the herbal charms used to ward off pestilent evils.

The boy worked up his courage and called again. "Merlin, wizard potent and eminence dire, my lord the king—"

He was cut off by the sight of an irascible face that peered suspiciously out the slit window high above. Merlin's eyes, which Ulwin's grandmother swore could turn boys into flying weasels, were screwed up tight as if he had been rudely woken. Ulwin rocked nervously from foot to foot, wishing he were back in the cellar where his warm straw bed was kept.

"Ulwin, is that you?" the wizard called crossly. "Blast it, what do you want? And don't blabber in that puffed-up way they taught you. Words aren't brains, you know."

If it weren't an emergency, the page would have felt hurt by Merlin's stinging rebuke. In truth he was just a Wessex farm lad recently promoted from slopping pigs to waiting on royalty at table. "'Is Majesty wants you to nip down quick," the boy stammered. "'Appens there may be trouble."

The wizard leaned farther out the window. His long forked white beard caught the wind and whipped out like a battle ensign before a fight. "You say the king summons Merlin, after these five tedious, long winters?"

"Indeed, 'tis troth," the page replied, regaining some of his newly acquired dignity.

"Yea verily?" the wizard mused.

"Sans doubt," the boy said.

"Forsooth," the wizard shot back.

"I'faith," the boy stammered, biting his lip. He did not relish being made fun of, yet he was anxious to bring good news back to the king. After a moment's hesitation, he piped up, "Well, are you comin' or nought?"

"Nought!" Merlin shouted, slamming the casement shut and disappearing into his chambers. A flash of errant lightning lit up Ulwin's frightened face as he rushed back into the safety of the castle keep.

Inside his tower cell, Merlin wheeled back from the slit window in anger, but as he slammed the shutters, he set up a swirl of dust—wizards are far too lofty to be tidy—blowing out the huge beeswax candle that stood upon the table in the middle of the room. "Blast!" Merlin grumbled. He peered around the gloom. Atop a high bookcase two yellow eyes opened wide, shining in the dark; Merlin recognized these as belonging to his favorite bird, an old gray horned owl that loomed as tall as a small child. (Rustics called such great owls Whistling Wills and blamed them for babies that disappeared in the night.) The owl spread its feathers almost silently, like silk sliding on silk, and gazed at the beamed ceiling, from which several small bats hung.

"If only those mice couldn't fly," the owl thought wistfully. Merlin could read the thoughts of birds and animals, but he had little interest in the minds of owls, since by and large they only think about mice and how to catch them. What interested Merlin at that moment was Melchior.

"Where is he?" he mumbled. "I reckon thee, appear this instant!" he roared, kicking the astrolabe to underline his impatience. A green-and-black scarab beetle, startled by the disturbance, scurried from its hiding place under a book. Merlin, who could see in the dark as well as any owl or cat, spied the insect and grabbed it up between thumb and forefinger. He put his bulbous nose close to the beetle. "Melchior, is that you?" he asked.

"No, master, I'm here," whispered a voice behind his back. Merlin whirled around. A figure was lighting a hazel switch—the wizard's equivalent of a safety match—in thin air and applying it to the candle on the table. In a moment a soft golden light filled the room, along with the warm, oily smell of burning beeswax.

7

"Where the devil have you been?" the wizard grumbled. He hated being surprised. The figure lighting the candle didn't flinch. Although most mortals were deathly afraid of Merlin's power, his young apprentice was not. This was one of those rare cases where familiarity breeds content—Melchior had been summoned to Merlin's side seven years earlier, when he was almost as young as Ulwin. Where he had been summoned from was impossible for anyone in Camelot to guess. Courtiers rarely set eyes upon him outside the wizard's tower. Sometimes on a hot July day of mowing hay grass, the peasants working the fields outside the castle walls would be lying on their backs under the giant oaks at the edge of the forest. Looking up, they would see Melchior outlined against the tower's battlements.

Tall and slim, he was always dressed in long flowing robes, which looked vaguely Moorish, like the attire of a Berber chief. His skin was almond brown, though, too pale for a Moor's. A white burnoose was wrapped around his head and drawn forward to cover his face, except for a pair of liquid brown eyes.

"Don't you ever look in them eyes," the peasants would say, nudging each other wisely. "Or you'll never look at nothing else neither." These same eyes now turned calmly toward Merlin, as gentle as brown quail chicks peeping out from under their mother's wing.

"You wish me?" Melchior asked.

"Wish you? Wish you?" the wizard repeated crossly. "The king wishes *me,* but I won't go. No, not this night."

"Then let's have a flying lesson," Melchior suggested hopefully. He raised his arms like swooping wings, which startled the hanging bats into nervous flutterings. Merlin shook his head, and all at once Melchior sensed that his master was terribly tired. He looked like an old wolf ready to burrow into the snow, ready to die. This thought made Melchior sad. He loved his master and was the only person since the departure of the young Arthur who understood the many layers wrapped around the wizard's heart. A wizard's heart is defended with triple-thick walls, like the king's castle, and only those who have the courage to breach the fortifications can discover the hidden treasure within.

"I sense extreme danger," Melchior said. "Will the kingdom last?"

Merlin was startled by this stroke of prescience. He shook his head and sat down on the edge of his low iron bed, as rude and uncomfortable as any monk's cot. "The kingdom does not deserve to last. The magic I gave them was good, but they were not good enough for it." He sighed as deeply as the sea when it plunges through a blowhole on the Cornish coast. "The peace is broken, and evil has smelled us out."

Melchior pulled off the old wizard's slippers, which were made of threadbare moleskin, and laid them respectfully at the foot of the bed. Merlin lay down, shutting his thick, hooded lids. He appeared to drift off to sleep as Melchior knelt on the floor nearby. All at once the old one stirred.

"If they want a fight—" Merlin growled; he fell silent. The warrior in him was calling out. But sleep seemed heavier than his fighting spirit. He yawned and stupor veiled his eyes. "Go seek them out, lad, in the deep wild woods where they blend into the shadows. Read their omens," he murmured. Melchior barely caught the words, but he was up in a flash. He tapped his toes and twisted his head like a wary crane, dancing a strange whirling step in the middle of the room. The next instant he vanished, while a huge black panther with green eyes appeared on the edge of the deep druidic forest. The beast looked up at the moon, which was eaten down to the smallest paring. Cautiously the panther chuffed and growled, loping silently into the woods.

The pleasant, shady woods of modern times are nothing like the forests of those days, which were alive, and not just with trees and squirrels, bracken, maidenhair, and sprouting acorns. The old green world was alive in its leafy soul. A forest then was one great breathing creature that felt everything. It felt the nervous tread of the royal stag that no one was permitted to hunt under the king's ban. It felt the hatching of a cuckoo egg and the pitiful cries of baby warblers when the cuckoo chick pitched them out of their nest. It even felt the slow creeping growth of the thick moss that carpeted every moist space like a velvety, verdant shawl.

But that night, as the black panther slipped into it, the forest felt profound fear. Ordinary fear was a grace compared to this. How can the ultimate anxiety be described? Imagine a poor wretch condemned to be hanged, and upon the midnight knell rough hands wake him from a terrified sleep. "Stand up," a brutal voice commands. A taper is struck, and in the ghastly light the prisoner sees his hangman. "Yes," the hangman surmises shrewdly, "I think five turns of the knot will hold you nicely." And the condemned man, alone again in the dark, feels his bowels turn to water. That's the kind of fear the forest felt, fear that its existence had been forgotten by God.

Pausing in his stride, Melchior sensed the forest's fatal anxiousness and knew that he was not the cause of it. But what was? The ministrations of his master had kept evil at bay for so long that Melchior hardly remembered its smell. The wind carried complex odors of spring—leaf mold, orris, harebell, and hemlock—but nothing rank. Yet there was something on the wind: "What is that pelting sound, like hail on a roof?" he wondered. Overhead he saw open sky with stars. It couldn't be hail. It was hoofbeats, pounding distantly, and they came from many horsemen, more than he had ever heard in the woods before. But who were these midnight riders? Arthur's knights stood asleep in their beds, and besides, what knight would hazard riding through these woods after dark?

Without making a conscious decision, the apprentice felt the panther's body turn, following the sound of the clattering horsemen; the vibration was so dim that it tested the very limits of the animal's hearing. With one bound the panther gained the branches of an ancient oak hung with mistletoe, surveying the scene.

That direction, over there—yes. His rippling black shoulders were poised; he dropped to the ground and ran swiftly into the darkness. Stalking on cushioned paws, Melchior prowled the underbrush, crouching low as the sound of hoofbeats grew louder. Fleeting panther thoughts crossed his mind, not as words but as keen sense impressions: scent of a hare, frightened, cowering beneath a pile of leaves; wetness of toadstools crushed beneath his feet; flicker of green fox fire from a rotting log.

Yet mixed with these animal impressions Melchior had his own human ones: "Where is the danger? It is all around me, but it also comes from some one place, and that place is very near." All at once a stallion caught the scent of panther and neighed in terror. "Down or I'll kill you," a voice hissed. Melchior stopped still as frozen air—the voice was almost on top of him. He parted the elder brush with his muzzle and saw the stamping, terrified horse, which madly wanted to escape. Its rider, a knight in armor, was whipping his mount mercilessly. "Stop it, you fool," the knight muttered through clenched teeth. He threw up his visor, panting for air, and Melchior saw his angry, sweaty face. Didn't he know that face from some dim past? Before he could decide, five more mounted knights rushed into the clearing.

"Have you got 'im? It's our heads if you don't," one of them said.

"Don't bark at me, dog. My mount is daft," the sweaty knight replied indignantly. Suddenly there was the sound of breaking twigs. Not ten feet away from them a huge white deer with enormous antlers broke its cover.

Melchior knew it at once—the royal stag.

"Get 'im!" a knight shouted, and all the cohort charged in pursuit. In the excitement of the hunt, even the terrified horse forgot its fright and plunged recklessly into the obscure forest. Melchior knew that no one would pay any attention to him now; they were up for blood. He ran after the pack in full view, barely fifty feet on their heels.

The royal stag had been gifted by Merlin with powers. The king's gamekeepers could post warnings on as many trees as they wanted; no mere decree could have kept the stag safe, since poachers would risk death to draw his blood and capture his huge rack. In ages past the entrance to the king's forest had been lined with gibbets strung with the corpses of poachers who had dared defy the royal ban. Arthur had given up this barbarism, relying on Merlin's spells to protect his white stag. By day it was invisible, and by night, when it fed on wild rosebuds and woolly thyme, the animal had such keen hearing that it would stop still if a mouse clipped a blade of grass a hundred yards away.

Little good did Merlin's spells avail it now. The hapless stag plunged through the thickest part of the forest, snagging its rack on fir branches and tearing its flanks with brambles. Glistening gouts of blood stained the wild roses he loved to eat. His huge, soft eyes were rolled back in terror; his breath came in torn sobs. Having no time to think, the stag never wondered why his protection had failed or how the horsemen managed to chase him so skillfully on a moonless night.

Did they have their own spells? The animal would never know, for as it paused to leap over an immense fallen log that had been pulled down by the last of the giants, the lead horseman strung his crossbow and fired. His arrow flew with deadly aim and pierced the heart of the gentle beast, who dropped dead instantly, the first victim of black magic in Camelot. A strangled death cry broke from its throat, all the more pitiful because the stag had kept a noble silence all its life. But there were no pitying ears to hear it.

"Clean kill!" the men shouted. "God save our master!"

"God save our filthy necks if you had missed," a more practical voice said. But this sentiment was lost in the melee. One after another the riders tumbled from their mounts, weapons drawn. They rushed on the carcass, stabbing its belly with sword and pike and knife, craving to kill the beast a second, third, fourth time. "Let Harry through," someone shouted, "he brought 'im down."

Another cried, "If the master despises guts, the liver and lights is mine."

"Nay, hold your hand, it isn't to be touched," the lead knight commanded. After a few minutes their heaving breaths began to slow, but still the men did not notice the wary black cat eyeing them from a nearby tree. Its nostrils quivered to drink in the blood scent, and Melchior had to strain his will to the utmost not to leap in fury on the pack of them. Strange conflicts tore his heart—despite the savagery of the panther's nature, he felt a warm flowing pity for the beautiful deer, now slashed and defiled. He watched the lead knight begin to sling the stag over his saddle. The other huntsmen, already mounted, circled impatiently.

"Hurry up, won't you? And don't spill n'more o' its blood. God, it looks a mess a'ready," a burly knight grumbled.

"Shut up, it wasn't me as stuck 'im with, was it?" said the one who was strapping down the carcass. Soon the job was done, and the grim horsemen galloped off into the darkness.

Merlin shifted uneasily in his sleep, or what would pass for sleep to mortal eyes. It was only his fleshy frame that rested; inside, a bright spiritual spark, like a knowing flame, was guiding his apprentice. The old wizard felt the anxiousness of the forest even more keenly than his pupil did. "Everything is strangely transformed here," he thought. There were no words for this transformation in the forest, yet the sense was unmistakable—it was like walking into your house and knowing, even before you turned on the light, that a felon was inside.

Merlin was baffled that he could not feel out the identity of the criminal who had usurped the heart of the woods. But a sacred refuge had been violated; nothing could be more certain. This forest of Camelot was where all the wizards took their pupils to train them, from as far back as the age of the giants when wizards were much valued as protectors of the humans who huddled in thatched huts on the fringe of the woods. By the time Arthur gained his throne, it was a different age; wizards and humans lived in deep suspicion of one another, almost as enemies.

"They are brazen enough to think that we are human like themselves," Merlin snorted more than once when taking Melchior through a shape-shifting lesson in the forest. "I cannot die in their world, and they will never live in mine." The apprentice did not grasp what this meant, for in many ways he felt as mortal now as the day he had arrived under Merlin's care. The secret of immortality, which wizards supposedly knew, had not been imparted to him yet. It was eminently clear, however, that the old friendship and cooperation between men and wizards had soured.

The clergy were the worst. One Sunday the bishop of Westminster had sent a fat priest named Father Alaric to the village. The local parish priest meekly surrendered his pulpit. "It's a blessing to see you," he said.

"No, it isn't," said Father Alaric scowling; his manner was fiercely suspicious. "I am here to examine the purity of your flock." The village priest felt humiliated, although he had no idea why. In the pulpit the bishop's emissary railed at the cowed congregation. "News is abroad that some of you may be worshipers of satanic magic. Who among you is a consort of evil?" The simple peasants quaked in their pews.

When word reached Merlin that he was considered a devil in Father Alaric's eyes, he laughed contemptuously. "Priest? He's a lard-stuffed nobody. What do I care if every mortal in England shuns me? They all smell like maggoty meat and have the brains of puddings." When his temper cooled, he said more wisely, "Man makes distinctions, God knows none."

Ill feeling ran high, however, after the bishop's lackey threatened eternal damnation to anyone who refused to rise up against witchcraft and sorcery. Hatred simmered in the village like thorn stew. Toothless old ninnies who had the misfortune to own a cat or to bear an odd-looking birthmark on their backs were suspected of attending unholy Sabbath in the woods. At the inn three drunken bricklayers shouted for the death of Merlin himself. "Do y'wonder we're kept down and stepped on? Wring his neck and let's have the sun shine again."

However, since a wizard cannot be killed, so far as humankind had ever discovered, this malicious wish never came true. Brawls and unrest spread. Hayricks caught fire in the middle of the night. It was rumored that the church had gained the support of powerful barons in the north, who were more than willing to save some souls if they might grab their land into the bargain.

The king was finally compelled to preserve the peace by decreeing special protection for his old master in the gleaming black tower. It was the saddest day of Arthur's life when he parted from Merlin. "I am suffering, old beloved, sick at heart to exile you like this. But at least you will be within my sight. Memory and a warm fire a'nights shall comfort us," he said. "Forgive me."

Merlin had looked up at the slit window high over their heads. Exile meant nothing to him; wizards by their nature are always alone. "You shouldn't let this wedge of fear gain entry," he cautioned.

Arthur found it hard to meet Merlin's gaze. "I am not afraid. You yourself set me a task, to rule with the power of peace. I am not sure that I yet understand my task, but at least I can give you shelter and safety from the violence while it still lurks in Camelot."

Merlin looked as proud as an eagle. "Safety?" he exclaimed. "Do you think that's why I'm staying here? I am safe enough from those cabbage-breath fools. I choose to remain in this tower because it affords a good view."

"To see what?" Arthur wanted to ask; he had his first premonition of last acts and falling curtains, but he was afraid to question Merlin further, fearing even more that his teacher no longer cared what happened to him. These events had befallen some five years before. Since then Camelot had breathed in uneasy peace, while Merlin remained aloof in his tower.

It had taken the foul portents and a black eclipse to stir Arthur. The king, Merlin knew, would be baffled by the surprise attack that the wizard could see in the fates, and Arthur's knights would naturally want to fight back. "Little do they reckon what lies in store for them," the wizard mused. He slept on, seemingly dead to the world, but in spirit he felt the blow that slew the royal stag. With a start he sat up in bed.

"Come back to me," he whispered. His apprentice either didn't hear him or was too fixed in his purpose. Merlin lifted his head as if testing the wind. His nose wrinkled and twitched like a connoisseur's—the smell of disaster was in the air, musty and tingling, like a storm about to break. That had been hanging about for a while, but from under a shroud another, secretive element peeked out, and he knew the worst. A power to rival his own, a black flame to extinguish his white, was advancing upon the castle.

2

BLOOD OF THE STAG

ON THE HOUR THE ROYAL STAG WAS MURDERED, A CIRCLE OF knights was sitting around a low campfire in the deep woods. Most were veterans of war, bearing long red scars on their faces from slashing swords. They grinned through gaps of missing teeth knocked out in jousts, and not a few had puckered holes where one eye should have been.

Some were talking in an undertone, trying to fight off the urge to sleep—but no one would sleep until the word was given. They were too afraid. There was one unanxious face in the group, and it happened to be the only unmarked one. A young nobleman sat closest to the fire—he looked like a golden apricot dropped in among crab apples. His hair was fair and curled; his pink cheeks gave his handsome face a boyishness just saved by a jaw that was molded for valor. By these points of appearance it was easy to spy the son of Arthur. But to read his heart, the royal bastard named Mordred knew he was his father's shame.

"Where is the prize?" Mordred asked softly, looking at a subaltern putting logs on the fire.

The soldier trembled. "It's coming, my lord. You've sent the captain out under the charm of the midnight eye. A dozen hunters cannot fail."

Mordred scowled. "I sent clods and rank idiots. A child could find the stag once its magic is stripped away. I am displeased." The soldier bowed his head, the cords in his neck shaking under the skin. Mordred's company were chained to his whims, and there were days when putting too much salt in the mutton meant death. "If they don't produce the prize soon, and I mean very soon," Mordred said in his lowest voice, "we shall examine your guts for an omen. How does that sound?"

The answer was an unintelligible croak. "You disagree with my judgment?" Mordred challenged. The subaltern tried to hide his fear; he hoped that his master was only playing one of his cruel games. One couldn't ever be sure.

Mordred stamped impatiently as he waited for the omen that would tell his success or doom. The march against Camelot had taken barely a week. His men knew the lay of the land—almost every one of them had served at Arthur's court and been banished in disgrace. Noble blood ran under the scars. Few of them suspected that their downfall—through cowardice or lust or deceit—had been contrived by Mordred. He planted his schemes deep and knew how to put the maddening scent of a lady's bed into a knight's dreams or to propel a sword into another man's back.

The invaders had crept up from the coast by night, encountering no resistance. This in itself made Mordred suspicious. He expected to fight scattered skirmishes before laying siege to the redoubt that housed the king. It would be a good way to weed out the weaklings in his army, and he was disgusted when one road after another lay open to his advances.

Mordred's march from the sea had cast a plague in all directions, destroying everything good in its path, blasting the apple blossoms in bud, smutting the stored wheat, blighting infants with crib sickness, deforming new calves with three legs or two heads, putting despair and hatred into the hearts of gentlefolk. The earth still holds the memory.

Now they were so close to the castle that Mordred could smell its cooking fires on the turn of the wind, and still none of Arthur's knights came to issue challenge. Was it a trick? Mordred had to consult an omen, and so he risked this last-minute pause before the onslaught.

"*He* looks restless," one knight on the edge of camp muttered. "That's dangerous."

"What isn't?" his companion remarked. "*His* blood is a curious poison, and that's sure." Human experience couldn't prepare them for a person like Mordred, who was fearfully and simply called *him.* He had learned black magic from his mother, a witch named Morgan le Fay. Her plans were laid deeper even than her offspring's. Years ago she had seduced the king (how many times no one dared guess) by evincing an overwhelming passion for him; his being her half brother only whetted Morgan's desire.

She could not cloak her identity forever, and the day came when Arthur recoiled to see who had shared his bed. He cursed her unlawful appetite, and she gave birth to the fruit of this curse. The very name *Mordred* that she gave the babe at his christening, which was performed with black goat's urine in place of holy water, combined *murder* and *dread.* Mordred was not the first child born under malefic planets, but Morgan le Fay, rare mother, was delighted by her baby's twisted ways. "Bite my nipple," she would murmur, relishing the pain.

The campfire of the banished knights guttered to a low glimmer that cast strange shadows on Mordred's band; some of them had risked falling asleep wrapped in their dirty horse blankets. But all came stark awake when the sound of hooves unknit the seamless dark.

"Quick, be up," Mordred commanded as he caught sight of his huntsmen through the woods. His heart pounded at the thought that the white stag was his, and he almost tore the carcass from its bonds with his bare hands. "Hang the beast from that tree," he ordered, "and rip out its heart." Following his directions, the hunting party strung up the stag from a scraggly low oak, slit its battered belly from neck to tail, and pulled out the still-warm heart. Catching its scent, rank and sweet in the night air, carrion birds roosting in the oak's upper branches rattled their feathers in their sleep.

The captain approached the fire where Mordred had now seated himself on a three-legged stool. More wood was thrown on the coals, making the fire blaze and crackle furiously. Mordred seemed lost in a trance, mumbling strange incantations in the ancient druid tongue. "Here it is," the captain whispered, holding out the stag's heart in his mailed hands. Mordred looked upon it, eyes veiled.

"Do you know what you have in your hands?" he asked hoarsely. "Verily, 'tis my father himself. This stag was his spirit. Now we shall determine the king's fate, if by the light of dawn he lives or no." Wrapping his two hands around the captain's fists, Mordred began to squeeze, harder and harder, until it was all the captain could do not to cry out. A thin stream of clear yellow liquid oozed from the heart, but it refused to bleed. Mordred's face clouded.

"Nay, nay," he growled, "this cannot be. You've tricked me." On the instant he manifested a thin silver dagger from the air and pressed it against the throat of the terrified captain. "You dare to bring me this!" The dagger's point drew blood.

Quailing, the captain shook his head. "My lord, you can see that this is the animal." Even as it swayed sickeningly from the tree like a burst barley sack, the stag's antlers were wide and glorious, like no other's. The point of Mordred's dagger wavered, drawing a thin line down the captain's neck, when all at once another knight pulled his arm away.

"Sire, look!" he exclaimed. Staring down at the captain's hands, Mordred saw that the omen had changed. The heart had turned dark, and black bile now flowed from it. Mordred gasped with joy; dipping a finger into the black ropes of poison, he tasted lightly. His face contorted in hideous delight. "The king will die," he whispered. The captain fell back, stanching his neck wound with a dirty handkerchief, faint with relief that he would not die that night.

Melchior could hardly control himself. The long claws that had been sheathed in the pads of his paws shot out like switchblades, and his spirit boiled. A predatory growl gathered in his chest.

While Mordred's blood ceremony was being performed down below, Melchior had been perched in the same tree from which the white stag's body hung. In human words vague urges drifted into his mind—The king lost, tell master—but these were drowned by the overpowering panther nature, which could barely be restrained.

Then the twin rivers of human and animal rage flowed together. He focused his eyes on the back of Mordred's head, feeling how the soft flesh of the neck would give beneath his claws. As if hearing a twig snap, Mordred looked around. Melchior held his breath. "I cannot kill this evil one," he realized. "His human shape is a disguise to be penetrated. If I tore him to pieces, he would still escape untouched."

It was fortunate for him that he had this glimmer of reason—it was quite correct. Mordred was as potent in spells as Merlin, and no beast, however fierce, could kill him. But the panther, true to its nature, could not be wholly guided by this inner voice, and its growl grew louder. The horses on the ground below began to stir, pulling at their tethers. Melchior had no choice. With a tremendous effort he pulled his mind away from the panther's blood instinct, willing himself into his own identity, and as he did so, his form changed into that of a robed young man.

He was now in great danger, since a wizard is at his weakest in the moment of transformation. Mordred could have destroyed Melchior's body as easily as crushing a moist new butterfly emerging from its chrysalis. Quietly the apprentice crept along the branch toward the oak's gnarled trunk and slowly climbed down. Mordred, having turned back to his bloody work, was too entranced to notice that shapes had been shifted in his presence. Melchior dropped softly to the ground and paused for a moment before creeping off through the underbrush on all fours. After some time the glimmering of the campfire could no longer be seen; Melchior felt safe enough to get up and run.

In two hours he saw the rampart fires of Camelot flickering beyond the forest rim. His heart was glad at the sight, until he remembered the omen. Could it really be that Arthur would not live to see the sunrise? Exhausted as he was, Melchior doubled his pace. His breath felt ragged and hot in his throat; his feet were like anvils being dragged along. Still he felt hope, the hope that the good magic would prevail. He broke out into the broad green commons outside the castle just as the first light of dawn rose over Glastonbury Hill. He plunged through the wheat fields sprouting with new shoots, fields that Arthur had reclaimed from the low marshes that had once existed throughout the West Country. The castle walls loomed very near, and Melchior looked anxiously at the high slit window where Merlin was wont to appear in the morning. This morning it was dark and empty.

Looking toward the moat, Melchior caught sight of something he could not believe. He stopped in wonder, his legs so weak that he could hardly stand. In the purple gloaming, a circle of visored knights surrounded the entire castle. They stood as quiet as priests waiting to pray. For a moment Melchior hoped that these were Arthur's knights rising to defend the kingdom, but he knew that couldn't be—they were Mordred's men, who had somehow outstripped him and reached the castle first. Melchior saw the captain sitting on his charger; around him a dozen archers were holding unstringed crossbows dangling by their sides while the steam of the horses' breath rose like mist over the band.

"Can this be?" Melchior thought. How could so many warriors—there must have been two hundred on horse alone—make their way here undetected, and with such speed? He knew that magic must be at work, but if so, it was far more powerful than he understood. He crouched low in the field, concentrating his mind on what to do next.

"I can't possibly reach the tower like this, in human form," he thought. His mind raced; he felt weak as a kitten from his exploits that night. He needed a long sleep before he would be able to manage another transformation, yet without doubt a transformation was his only hope. Tired to the bone, he drew his spirit inward and began to weave his spell.

The banished knights circling the castle began to awaken. They looked around in surprise, rubbing their eyes and muttering, "Where are we?" They had no memory of their journey from the deep woods to the moat, for Mordred had placed them under enchantment back at camp, then transplanted them by the aid of spirits whom mortal men would die to look upon. He had made a pact with Albrig, king of the elementals, to whisk every knight and his mount through the air to Camelot. It was a risky bargain, for magic given means magic owed. "A spell for a spell," Albrig hissed. That is the rule, and no amount of money would satisfy Albrig. The evidence of this unholy bargain was the raw claw marks on the horses' flanks, where the demons had grasped them for the flight.

Mordred's captain stirred uneasily in his saddle. Many times he had fought Saxons and the wild, hairy Welshmen from the green mountains, but he had never fought under enchantment before. "I feel strange," he thought. He reached for the long battle sword hanging by his side and pulled it forth. It felt light; he swung it round his head, and a fierce exhilaration ran through his arm—he suddenly had the strength of ten men. Mordred had given him this power, and he was glad of it. Twelve long years had passed since his banishment from Arthur's court as a thief. Once he had loved the king with all his heart, now he hated him just as strongly for shaming him.

"Men, draw your swords!" the captain shouted. At his command the other knights tested their weapons. They were just as amazed as he with their new power. A wondering murmur passed through the troop; blood began to run high. Mordred stood up in his saddle from his position on a hill overlooking the plain down below. Strangely, the dawn, which should have reached the hilltop first, still left it in shadow.

Standing in his stirrups, Mordred turned his face to the castle in the distance. He stared at it as if he could breach the fortifications with will alone. A low rumbling sound began in his gut, like the warning grunt of a bear. It moved to his stomach, growing louder and louder, then to his chest. Instinctively, as if hypnotized, the knights closest to him began imitating Mordred's sound; it spread from man to man, until the air shook with a single, loud war cry. It gathered force, first like tribal drums, then like thunder, until a shout broke from Mordred's throat louder than any shout a mortal could produce. It struck like iron against the walls of Camelot. Birds flying overhead dropped out of the sky, struck dead by the impact. With a great clap of thunder the drawbridge split in two, sending huge planks crashing down into the moat and across it.

Seeing this sight, the army milled in a frenzy, but Mordred had not given his command to charge. "I'm going up," the captain muttered to his second-in-command. He drove his horse up the slope toward the shadows, which seemed to move and swirl, more like smoke or black fog than any shadows he had ever seen.

When he returned, Mordred rode with him. The banished knights fell silent, out of fear and anticipation. "We are here to answer Arthur," Mordred shouted, "to fulfill the omen and reclaim what is mine. Each man of you has suffered foul disgrace at the hands of the king. Remember that injustice and show no mercy, for none was given to you. Do you wonder that no knights of the Round Table have dared to meet us? They are afraid. You were banished because you are the strongest fighters ever born. You are power; you are hate. Now strike with all your power and kill with all your hate. He who does not slay today, I promise you, will be slain by my own hand!"

With this dire threat Mordred's voice rose to a shrill frenzy. His eyes rolled up in his head, but he was not out of control, not by any means. He knew that he had to inspire the utmost fear and rage in his men, because they were not the most powerful of Arthur's knights: they were the weakest. They understood nothing of the grace that Camelot lived under. Evil as he was, Mordred was still Arthur's son, and he had touched the chords of truth, love, and honor. Much as he hated these things, he also comprehended their power.

It had taken him seven years to gather enough black magic to hope to defeat Arthur and the Round Table. He had fashioned effigies of the king out of bloodroot, stuck them with needles, and buried them in adders' nests. He had snared spells from Sycorax and Hecate, sleeping with the foul witches to gain their secrets and almost dying from the stench of their breath. Death was the only price Mordred would not have paid to defeat his father, and in the end, after all his discipline in black magic, death was no longer a possibility.

He had wakened one night to see the Evil One himself standing at the foot of his bed, glowing with weird green phosphorescence, like a dead shark washed up on shore. Terrible to tell what rites Mordred performed to gain the final favor of his master, but when the room dripped with gore and his ears were almost deafened by his own screams, Mordred knelt before the devil, who was well pleased.

"Grant me a boon," Mordred whispered through bloody lips. "I have served you faithfully all my life." The devil said nothing. He reached down, grasped Mordred's sword, and unsheathed it. Mordred held his breath, staring fixedly at the gleaming point.

"You dare to ask me for a boon?" the devil croaked, and with a swift plunge he thrust the weapon into Mordred's chest. Mordred heard his bones crack as the steel tore him open; like a bat's tongue greedily lapping nectar from the night jasmine, the sword's point reached for Mordred's heart and found it. That was all he remembered. Two hours later he woke up in his empty room. He looked around in amazement. The sword was lying beside him, yet there was no wound in his chest, and the devil's vassal knew that his lord had given him the wizard's gift of immortality. He was Merlin's equal.

As Mordred's shout cracked open the castle, a tumult arose from the banished knights when they saw that the way was open. Steed crowded upon steed to be the first to test the fallen bridge, and when the lead rider made it across the moat into the castle, the frenzy for battle overflowed like boiling pitch. The captain led the charge with upraised sword, and the hordes of evil began their attack. In all this confusion, no one noticed a small brown field mouse scurrying for its life under the horses' hooves, making its way desperately toward the wizard's tower at the far end of the enclosure.

When Mordred's shout broke the spell that protected Camelot, Merlin stirred in his bed. He did not want to wake up. Knowing that this day would come, he still did not wish to witness Arthur's ruin. Although he had been charged with Arthur's safety ever since he had taken the boy under his charge, the wizard did not feel pity for his old friend. What did he feel? If he could have told Arthur, making himself understood through that thick plate of mortal ignorance, he would have.

Merlin walked to the slit window that faced into the east barbican. The clang of iron horseshoes on cobblestone reached his ears. Peering down, he saw women and children scattering in fright, chickens and sheep running hither and thither, panicked for their lives. But strangely, Arthur's knights had not rushed out to defend themselves. Mordred's men were making quick and bloody work, killing everything in their reach. Merlin saw a small boy run at a mounted knight with a pitchfork—it was Ulwin the page. With a sharp cry the boy stuck the pitchfork into the horse's flank, causing it to scream and rear. The mounted knight swiped at Ulwin with his sword, missing him.

"Bloody brat!" he screamed. But Ulwin showed no fear. He ran at the horse again. Merlin shook his head and drew his black wizard's robe with its stars and runes closer about his shoulders. Three more horsemen rushed to the scene, swarming over Ulwin and hiding him from view. The wild melee of death continued. Merlin could not see the final moment of Ulwin's fate, but he was certain it had struck.

"So it is all lost," Merlin said to himself, sighing. He felt unfulfilled duty weighing on him. "The king will suppose that I failed him. So be it." In his mind's eye, he imagined himself when he was talking to Arthur in the crystalline cave years before.

"There may be good magic and bad magic," he was telling the boy, "but these are not the same as good and bad. Magic is attracted to good or bad and intensifies them. It fans the sparks that already lie in a man's character." To illustrate, he tossed a bunch of straw into the low fire at the cave's mouth, making the flame lick up sudden and fierce. The boy looked on, nodding his head.

"The common people are always superstitious," Merlin continued. "They are in awe of charms and spells, but the real power—I want you to remember this as king—lies in the silence of your heart." Here he thumped the boy on his chest with a gnarled knuckle. "If you are worthy of the good magic, it will come to you without fail, but if your worth falls, no spell or charm will avail you."

Arthur thoughtfully looked into the fire, then asked Merlin, "But what must I do to be good? A king is renowned for his exploits, and yet from what I see around me, these are just an excuse for killing people and taking their land."

Merlin nodded approvingly—the lad had observed the world well. In those days, the knights who roamed the countryside were little better than bandits, stealing wheat from the peasants and forcing their loyalty through fear. Their "exploits" consisted of burning down the hay barns of helpless farmers and poking swords through old men who were foolish enough to protest.

"There is nothing you need to do to be a good king," Merlin said, fixing his eyes on Arthur. The boy looked confused, but before he could question, the wizard leaned forward. "Think deeply on this, boy: A man's goodness is truly measured by what he is, not by what he does."

It had taken Arthur many years to fathom this sentence. He never did get Merlin to elaborate upon it, but he remembered it often and worked at a better understanding. In the end, Arthur built Camelot into a great kingdom on this simple lesson. It was not the heroic battles he won or the courage of his knights but the certainty that he was good in his heart that made Arthur a ruler. In that certainty he lost all his fear, and thus room was made in his heart for love. For the first time in history, men bowed to a ruler because they were inspired by his love, not terrified of his power. This was the secret of the Round Table's success.

Merlin stepped back from the slit window, sick of watching the slaughter below. "I must get some word to him anyway," he thought. "I cannot allow the king to die without wisdom about the meaning of this day." He went to the table in the middle of the room and began to write a note on a wrinkled piece of parchment. Absorbed in this task, he did not glance around when a small brown field mouse peeked timidly from a crack in the wall behind him.

"Back so soon?" Merlin muttered dryly, scratching his quill

across the paper. The mouse scurried to the table, and in less time than it takes to read these words, Melchior undid his transformation and stood beside his master, breathless with news.

"I've been to their camp. This is the army of Mordred, Arthur's lost son. He has killed the royal stag and foreseen the king's death in its blood. Now the castle is being taken, and we must do something," the apprentice blurted out in a rush.

Without lifting his head, Merlin said, "It is not very extraordinary to bring me the news that the castle is being attacked, given the fact that the selfsame attack is taking place beneath my window. One might easily deduce that Mordred is behind all this, given that the outer walls were breached by magic, and save you and me, I do not notice an oversupply of sorcerers in the immediate neighborhood. But then, seeing how feeble your report is, perhaps I should not be so hasty in including you among the ranks of sorcerers in the first place."

This speech quite deflated Melchior. He stood before his master, tears coming to his eyes. It was hard for him to bear the sight of so much evil and destruction. He had rushed to bring his message to Merlin, hoping that the wizard would save the innocents who were being killed. Yet the callous old man merely sat there, as cool as a cucumber, obviously unwilling to interfere.

"I don't understand you," Melchior stammered.

"I agree, you don't." Merlin glanced up for the first time to see that his indifference (which after all was only a pose, one of many that wizards use to test their initiates) had genuinely hurt Melchior. A softer expression came into Merlin's eyes; he reached his hand out to reassure the apprentice.

"I have told you that every moment in a wizard's life is a test," Merlin said. "This is the test of trust. Do not let your eyes be deceived by this show of treachery and killing. There is more here than you realize." He folded the note he had written and walked over to the slit window. "You must deliver this missive to the king," he ordered, but before the last word was out, Melchior groaned loudly. He clutched at his throat and fell to the floor in agony. Merlin knew at once what had happened; his eye had caught sight of the deadly arrow the instant it flew in the window, whizzing past his head by inches.

"Mordred!" he swore angrily—he knew that no ordinary marksman could find his target inside a sealed tower. Crossing the room, he knelt beside the agonized apprentice. Merlin smiled.

"Do you know what this is?" he asked in a cheerful voice. "This is a very lucky stroke for us." Before Melchior could wonder what in the world his master meant, Merlin touched the arrow with his forefinger, instantly changing it into a small but fierce-looking dappled bird. Melchior rubbed his eyes in amazement and sat up. The wound in his throat had disappeared. He watched silently as Merlin strapped the folded parchment to the bird's back with a leather thong.

"Take heed," the wizard said, walking lightly to the window with the bird in his hands. "This is the smallest of all the hunting falcons, a dauntless predator despite his size, a native of broad plains, unlike his larger relations, who prefer hilly to mountainous terrain." With this rather didactic speech the old conjurer tossed the little falcon onto the wind, whereupon it immediately set course for the castle keep. The wizard's sharp eyes followed his messenger to make sure that it alighted safely on the sill outside Arthur's window.

He turned to his apprentice. "I trust you know the name of such an unusual falcon," he quizzed.

Melchior nodded and replied, "I believe they call it a merlin."

Many myths shroud the end of Camelot. It came to be believed that Arthur died in hand-to-hand combat with Mordred, or that his dear Guinevere broke his heart by betraying him with Lancelot, or that Merlin went to sleep under Stonehenge, trapped by black magic to end his days in the cold earth. These myths arose because the truth was too deep for people to understand: When Mordred launched his furious assault, Arthur did nothing. He did nothing when the crack of doom shattered the castle walls; he did nothing when he heard the iron clang of death in the inner courtyard; he did nothing when, incredibly, he saw Merlin's tower begin to crack and sway under some invisible destructive force.

The king sat like a living corpse in his chair by the window when the merlin landed outside on the sill. Feverishly he opened the casement and reached for the message tied to the bird's back. He expected the falcon to strike at him, for hunting birds are loath to be touched, yet the messenger stood by meekly and allowed the parchment packet to be removed.

The unfolded note read, *Do not believe the illusion. Remember the teaching. I am here.*

Arthur read it with wonder. Illusion? His glance fell on the falcon, which was staring at him. The king bent forward, drawn to scrutinize the bird. Its eye glowed with blackness like a jet bead; all at once the king saw a scene mirrored on the polished surface. It was an image of battle. Mordred his son was in the midst of terrible carnage, swinging his sword in a frenzy of glee, dealing death in all directions. Anger rose up in Arthur's heart. He longed to slay his damned progeny, but as soon as he had that thought, Mordred laughed and grew bigger, like a demon in a nightmare. Arthur shuddered and felt trapped. How could he kill his own son? Wouldn't that make his own evil equal to Mordred's? Deep down, the king knew that the battle for his castle was somehow taking place inside himself.

He strode from the window, startling the falcon, who flew up into the rafters. Inside the great hall the knights of the Round Table were assembled. As the king approached, Lancelot sprang to his feet.

"Sire, we must fight! Just listen, the people are defenseless," he cried desperately. "Can we stand by and see them slaughtered?"

"Has killing ever stopped killing?" Arthur replied.

"My liege, this isn't a debate," Lancelot argued in great distress. "We are grievously outnumbered, but every man here will die for you."

"Has any man ever died for anyone?" the king replied.

Lancelot stared about in wild consternation. He felt like a rudderless ship in a storm. The other knights were just as bewildered—it was torture for them to sit uselessly in the hall hearing the clangor of arms outside the door.

Arthur shook his head. "That is not the way to win."

"What way do you suggest?" Lancelot asked grimly. The king fell silent.

"Steel for steel, I say," Sir Kay muttered. A few knights stood up, buckling their swords, the tendons in their necks straining with suppressed emotion. Like a swollen seed, the sentiment of violence was about to burst its shell. Arthur pondered. How could he tell these valiant champions that this battle was a deadly illusion, that whoever fought the mirage would become its victim?

"You must not fight," he commanded. "The purpose of this affair is shadowed. All is not as you see it." Arthur looked calm, but his heart knew, with sickening surety, that his knights would not be able to contain their rage. Above all else, Mordred counted on this.

"Merlin," Arthur whispered. A faint dappled light flickered across the floor, noticed by no one but the king. It was light filtered through wings overhead, shadow wings that crossed the floor as the king's glance followed them. They reached the far wall where a long table was placed, on it the remains of the last meal—tin cups, silver plate, crockery bowls smeared with stale gravy and bits of meat. One drinking cup was precariously balanced on top of the pile. When the winged light touched it, it fell with a clatter. Arthur stood up and strode across the room. He picked up the cup and held it aloft.

"My knights, true men and brave, place your trust in this." As mad as his words were, his face was radiant.

"Please, sire, do not abandon us!" Lancelot cried. The derangement of the king broke his heart, and his face crumpled in torment.

Arthur walked over to Lancelot and placed his hand on his shoulder. "You have been first among my champions. Be the first to accept this blessing. It is the Grail."

Lancelot hung his head. The other knights were stunned, and the younger ones could barely restrain themselves from seizing their arms. They had all heard of the Grail quest; many had suffered to pursue it and come back empty-handed if they came back at all. "Are you asking us to die with you?" Lancelot demanded desperately. Arthur slowly shook his head, staring with fixed attention upon the drinking cup, which all could see was just an ordinary cup, slightly battered around the rim and stained with the dried lees of yesterday's wine.

Suddenly there was a crash as the blade of a battle-ax splintered the bolted doors of the great hall. From the rafters a shrill cry broke from the merlin's throat. "Here is the moment," Arthur murmured to Lancelot. He could feel that the others would not be won. "Do not doubt that this is the Grail. Look in your heart." Before Lancelot could react, a second battle-ax shook the great doors, then a third, and with a dull clang the forged iron bolts fell apart.

All but a few windows of the hall had been hung with tapestries to keep out the early-spring chill. Now, as the doors burst open, a shaft of sunlight dazzled the eyes of everyone in the room, but soon the sight of Mordred's horde dawned. The banished knights were thirsty for slaughter; not one of them was free of innocent blood already. Yet the captain paused for one moment of courtesy.

"King Arthur, I come in the name of my lord Mordred, who lays gracious claim to this sceptered kingdom. Will you yield?"

Sir Kay let out an angry oath and spit on the floor; Sir Ector, his father, came to his side, drawing his blade. Arthur said nothing but calmly crossed over to the place where his scepter rested on a shelf against the wall. He took down the scepter and held it out. "Is this what you want?" The captain advanced, holding out his hand. When he was three paces away, Arthur raised his arm and flung the scepter with all his might. It wheeled through the air and clattered to the floor.

"Fetch," the king said, a wry smile on his face. He held up the battered wine cup and placed it on the shelf. The captain stared in bafflement. Even if he had understood this mysterious gesture, he could not have held his men back. They poured into the hall. The Round Table knights broke rank. Some, such as Percival and Galahad, stood like statues, respecting the king's order not to resist, allowing the enemy swords to slay them without a struggle. Kay, Ector, and Gawain could not refrain from drawing their weapons, but to no avail; fifty blades were against them—they were hacked to pieces before they knew they were dead. Seeing this, the younger knights panicked and fled, only to be stabbed in the back on the marble stairway.

As some of the enemy rushed up to the gallery, the shrieking of the queen's terrified ladies could be heard. Arthur looked up and saw them running along the tapestried gallery; in sheer terror one young gentlelady jumped over the railing to her death. All at once the queen appeared. Mordred's captain held her, a dagger point pressed against her throat.

"Behold the death of Guinevere!" he shouted. Arthur lost his resolve at that moment. His heart leapt up in hatred, and no one can tell what he might have done if he had not looked up to see that Guinevere had a smile upon her face. In ecstasy her eyes were fixed upon the cup on the shelf.

Arthur could not understand. Had Merlin given her to know this sign as well? There was no time to say anything, even if she could have heard him above the clamor. "God help you, my love," Arthur thought. With a wrench of her arms, the queen pulled free of the captain, running out of sight down the gallery. Arthur could not see her, and this for some reason was almost worse than seeing her slain before his eyes. He quaked inside with fear for her, and for the second time he started to fail. He ran to the stairs; it was littered with corpses blocking his way.

"Guinevere!" he shouted. But he never saw his queen more. From high above, the merlin shrieked again; this time it was clearly a warning. Arthur knew this before he wheeled around. Mordred had entered the hall. He stood in his armor, visor up so that his father could witness the hatred in his face.

"What do you want, my son?" Arthur cried. "Take my kingdom but leave me Guinevere." It was the only cowardly speech he had ever made, but he was helpless. With tears in his eyes, he ran to Mordred.

"Kneel," the evil one commanded. Arthur had begun to drop to the floor in humiliation when his courage returned. He trembled on the edge of defeat, and yet he could not give in. Dignity returned to his face, and with calmed gaze he looked at the Grail.

"Old man, do you think I crave a kingdom? You sired a bastard, not a fool," Mordred growled. He removed his mailed glove and reached for the chalice.

"Nay!" Arthur shouted. At that instant the merlin, poised in the rafters, dove from out of the blackness. The king looked up in amazement as the falcon transformed itself back into an arrow. In a split second it swished to its mark and impaled Mordred's hand to the wall, inches from the Grail. The evil wizard screamed in pain from his own charmed arrow. In a fury he tried to tear his hand from the wall; Arthur could hear the rip of tendons in Mordred's flesh, but the hand would not come free.

"My beloved Merlin," Arthur murmured gratefully. He recoiled as a splash of blood spattered against his face. Mordred swung at him with his arm, now a mutilated stump. The king was aghast; in his madness, Mordred had drawn a dagger and cut off his own hand, which hung against the wall dripping gore.

"Death!" Mordred screamed, knocking Arthur to the ground with a wild swing of his mutilated arm. The king's hand reached for a sword lying nearby—this was the third time he had lost his resolve. Beside him lay Lancelot, struck down with a wound to the throat. The most valiant of knights had only one breath remaining, but Arthur heard him whisper, "I faltered only a little. My faith is strong yet. Thank you, sire. We shall live by the Grail."

Creeping along the floor, Arthur's fingers wrapped themselves around the grip of the sword. He felt the jeweled inlay and knew for certain what he had—Excalibur. His son stood over him like an animal, a wolf ready for the kill. Arthur saw himself lifting Excalibur and plunging it into the softness of Mordred's belly. It was the king's last temptation to violence, but he refused. His hand went slack as he dropped the jeweled hilt. Mordred's poised weapon hung in the air above the king's neck. Arthur closed his eyes, and the last sound he remembered was his son's mocking laughter as he drove the steel to take the life he hated.

3

DRAGONFLYING

MELCHIOR WOKE UP WITH A DIM, DARKENED MIND. HE FELT hazy—or was it just a hazy day? Into his head a soft word entered like woodsmoke: Afire. He stirred sleepily, feeling too heavy to rouse himself. "This is a sleep I could sleep for ages," he half-spoke to himself. But the word-smoke seeped into another chamber of his brain: Afire.

Suddenly he was wide-awake. Trembling with anxiety, the apprentice knew what the word meant. *The tower is on fire.* Where had he been? He became aware that he was lying alone in a moist, grassy field. The morning sun was warm on his back. Brilliant points of light dazzled his eyes from a small blue pond nearby.

How did he get there? Hastily he looked around for Arthur's castle, only to find that looking around didn't work. His neck felt rigid and stiff; it wouldn't bend in any direction by as much as an inch, and his back was as immobile as if he had been tied to the rack. He fought the impulse to panic; instead, the same urgent thought returned, this time clamoring in his head like a brass bell:

The tower is on fire!

Using his stomach muscles, which seemed to be working, Melchior jerked around as hard as he could. He felt a stab of pain as his body twisted perhaps ten degrees, but it was enough. He now saw, hovering in the hazy distance, that his clamoring thought was true. A tower half a league away belched furious black smoke against the sky like a dying dragon.

"Master!" he thought in anguish. He was overwhelmed by an impulse to fly to the wizard's side. To his amazement, his wish came true. He found himself flying through the air, and not with the clumsy hops he was used to from his flying lessons, which as often as not dumped him into a prickly hedge of may or upside down in a pig ditch. He was truly flying, about ten feet off the ground, aimed straight and steady toward the burning tower.

Wherever it came from, Melchior was too anxious to appreciate the joy of his new accomplishment. "I must go to him or all is lost!" he told himself. "The battle must be over, since there are no soldiers in sight. But why is the tower standing all alone like that? There should be walls and buildings. Where are the pennants and guerdons to signal that the king is inside?"

Above all, however, he wondered why he felt so odd. His thoughts sounded uncommonly strange in his head. "What is this?" he wondered, and the *s* at the end of his thought turned into a long, droning *zzzz.* He began to wish that life wasn't full of so many emergencies piled one on top of the other. He could barely comprehend the last crisis before a new one pelted him on the head. Becoming a wizard required the passage of many trials, and he could confess moments when he only wanted to rejoin common mortals in their world.

"And do what?" Merlin would snort whenever he spotted Melchior in one of these sloughs. "Eat toast and get jam on your face? Remember, it's better to be afraid with me than to be happy with them." Melchior wasn't so sure. He had no time for reminiscence, yet in a fleeting image he recalled the face of his grandmother years ago, smiling and crying at the same time, the day she had smuggled him to the coast disguised in his flowing blue robes. "These folk do not know what you are, magical boy," she had whispered mysteriously. "It's not your family's fault. You are a strange, wonderful creature, yet they will turn you into a donkey, enslaved in the fields. Even your mother would, but I will never allow it."

He recalled the looming masts of the barkentine at harbor, his grandmother's trembling hands as she released him to the captain, finally to be alone, rocking in the dark as he tried not to cry out for his mother or his soft bed at home.

The Irish sea captain who had taken his grandmother's bribe would not permit the boy to come on deck for fear that the sailors, who were little better than pirates, would attack him. Melchior lay in the hold day after day, suffocating beneath a pile of moldy straw and jute. Once the ship's cook, rummaging for a barrel of salt pork, almost stepped on him, and others must have heard him sob in his sleep, for the crew began to whisper darkly of a ghost that climbed the mainmast and threw burning pitch on the heads of unsuspecting tars.

The stowaway grew sick and soon delirious. The captain held a dirty piece of mirror up to his face. "Look!" he whispered hoarsely. To his horror, Melchior saw that his skin had turned bright yellow, even the whites of his eyes. "Ye're turnin' jaundice on me," the captain muttered, vexed that he might lose the second half of his bribe if the boy died. That night he permitted Melchior to stagger out of the hold so he could stand in the cool sea breeze. The sky was spangled with a banquet of stars, which he already knew by their liquid Arabic names—Rigel, Betelgeuse, Althazzar—but gazing upon the distant beacons only made him feel more alone, coldly alone on the wide sea.

The next morning frightened the captain within an inch of his life. He crept down to bring Melchior a flagon of stale water. The boy was on his knees, looking up with a rapturous smile. A faint glow of peach-gold light was all around him. The captain turned as green as a sick parrot. "Gad! a mad faerie it is," he cried, throwing the flagon behind him as he rushed up the ladder. Melchior noticed nothing, for his grandmother had come to him in a vision. She smiled at him and blew the sacred breath, the baraka, gently in his face.

"You will learn many spells," she said, smiling, "but none greater than this, the spell of faith. Only the wisest know that it is no spell but life itself." From that moment the jaundice disappeared, and Melchior knew that he came from a sorcerer's line.

These recollections of the long-ago past were struggling slowly to rise in Melchior's brain, like bubbles caught in honey, when a horrible shudder shook his body. An irresistible terror flooded him, and in an instant, with the life-or-death reflexes of a rabbit feeling the fox's incisors raking his back, Melchior dove to his left in a sharp swoop. He was just in time. A huge, dark mass zoomed past him. Monstrous claws grazed his right side. Melchior expected to feel his heart bound out of his chest in fear, except for some reason he felt as if he didn't have a heart. Strange.

"Safety! I must find safety," he thought. With incredible speed he turned a somersault in midair, hovered for a second like a doubtful helicopter, then dove straight for a round green landing field immediately to his right. The shadow passed overhead. His ears were filled with a loud angry "Kraw!" that almost deafened him. Then as quickly as it had come the danger disappeared. The air fell quiet, and Melchior was clinging to the green landing field with all his might.

Terrified as he was, it began to dawn on the apprentice that he wasn't in human form. The buzzing in his head, his stiff neck, the feats of acrobatic flying that came by instinct—no, this wasn't him. What was he, then? If the village children had been there, they could have told him immediately—he was a devil's darning needle, the swift menace of all smaller midges, moths, bees, bluebottles, damselflies, yellow jackets, and the rest of the buzzing clan.

In plainer words, he was the first dragonfly of May. His brilliant bronze-green body dangled airily from a sycamore leaf as he slowly realized his strange predicament. The buzzing clan are not endowed with intellect, so it is no surprise that Melchior could not recall that this day was his birthday, the very morning he was born. He had crawled out of the small blue pond when the dawn light first slanted on it, wrapped in crumpled moist wings that feebly unfolded to dry in the breeze. (Before then, he had spent considerable time underwater as a ferocious dragonfly nymph, one of the terrors of pond life, hiding in the ooze among the reeds waiting with a greedy pincer mouth to gobble up a passing minnow, tadpole, or anything else. But of this Melchior remembered nothing.)

The apprentice had no way of guessing that he had been put under a protective spell by Merlin after the battle for Arthur's kingdom was lost, transforming him into a minute dragonfly egg with its seed of life sleeping inside. Heedful to kill all magic and smash it into ruins, Mordred had blasted the castle to rubble and wasted the surrounding fields with fire, yet the infinitesimal egg was borne safely over the terror on a breeze toward the river Severn, where it washed for miles downstream (narrowly missing being eaten by a hungry hook-jawed trout) before landing in the murky swamps that then circled in all directions.

And there Melchior slept through history. Sleep is a tricky business: when first you crack your eyelids to wake up again, you can't tell for certain how long you've been asleep. It could be twelve hours or twelve minutes or twelve years. In Melchior's case, the spell had lasted twelve full centuries, and two more, until he woke up in a different world, where even the ruins of magic left by Mordred had turned to unremembered dust. What he had spied as Merlin's burning tower was the smokestack of an iron-smelting plant, and the reason he couldn't see the battlements of Arthur's castle was that they had long ago crumbled to mossy rubble that peasants had gathered and taken away to build sheep pens.

At present, now that his maiden flight was over, he was still quite confused. Exhaustion filled his body, and although he hardly felt safe swaying on the underside of a leaf, the gentle rocking, added to the heat of the sun, soon put him to sleep. He had no idea what time it was when he came around, but long shafts of afternoon light reached under the foliage where he had hidden. Again the impulse to take off gripped him. *I must go to my master.* And despite his fear of the giant shadow, which was in point of fact an ordinary hungry crow, he took wing. Only this time he didn't get anywhere. The burning tower was still straight ahead, due east. Yet as hard as he beat his crisp, veined wings, he made no headway. If anything, he found himself falling backward, bounced head over heels by the hard air.

"I've got a beaut!" a thunderous voice called out. Melchior fought against what felt like an invisible stone wall. It did no good.

With a deafening clap the lid of a jelly jar slammed down over his head, and in two seconds he was a bottled insect, trapped by a gigantic little boy who peered at him curiously.

"Yeah, you are a beaut," the boy murmured, drawing his monstrous face right up to the side of the jar. "Do you fancy coming home with me?" The gigantic little boy who was Melchior's captor started to turn the jar over, admiring the bold black bars on Melchior's wings, whose tracery was as intricate as a cathedral window. The boy's huge pink face was so terrifying that the apprentice was sure he had dropped back in time, to the age of the giants that Merlin had vanquished as a boon to humans.

"Look here, Tommy, look what I've got," the booming boy's voice called. Melchior saw a second giant bend down toward the glass.

"Smashing," the one called Tommy said, and a smile as wide as a carriage road appeared on his face.

"Do you think you'd like to help me catch some more?" the first boy said rather shyly.

"No time for that now, Sis," Tommy boomed back. "There's something rocking up ahead."

"Where?"

"Just up the road. Didn't you hear the sirens?"

"No. Can I go with you?"

The second boy's voice was rushing away already: "It could be bloody ghastly if it's a wreck. Come if you like." Melchior felt jolted and tumbled as the boy called Sis ran after Tommy. A pudgy, rather short-legged boy of nine, he couldn't keep up with his older friend, but his curiosity was fired. Crossing the furrowed fields at a trot took concentration and balance; he barely considered the dragonfly being jounced roughly in the jar. Melchior was dazed senseless as Sis rounded a stone sheep pen and bounded onto the pavement of a motorway. Whirling blue lights filled the air. Vaguely, half-conscious, he heard the whish of car tires on wet pavement and the rumble of tractor trailers (they sounded to him like the giants' bellowing oxen). Overwhelmed by chaos, he struggled to order his mind, not to slip into the madness all around him.

"God," he heard a booming voice exclaim—it was the second boy, Tommy. "No, no, you stay back, Sis."

"Why should I? I don't have to," Sis whined irritably. "Is there blood? Let me see."

There was pushing and shoving. A man's voice roared, "You boys, clear out. I mean it." A new figure loomed over Melchior's head—a helmeted knight of some sort—and Sis drew back with a choking sound, as if he were trying to hold down a gag or a cry. "His neck's twisted all horrible." Sis was almost gasping.

"All right, lads, you've seen it. Now do yourselves a favor and go," the looming knight said. The bigger boy's face was pallid with disgust. "That's enough for me. Come on, Sis," he said grimly. The small, pudgy boy turned away from the scene, swinging his collecting bottle. Now Melchior could see what they had been looking at, could catch a glimpse of horror under the whirling blue lights and the gray, patchy twilight: a crumpled body lay by the side of the motorway.

The tower is afire. Find Merlin. The word-smoke crept softly into his brain again. Melchior froze. With fixed insect eyes he looked at the smashed old man with the twisted neck that the knights in their odd caps were picking up. A hole gaped in Melchior's belly as recognition sank in. The old man's closed eyes didn't look like a wizard's anymore, but the tangled white beard did. Desperately Melchior sent his spirit out, feeling for some sign of living magic, some life. Nothing. At first nothing, then a sickening reverberation, the dark, ravening vortex of evil. He had felt that before, perched on a branch above a fire in the woods. "Master, master," he sobbed, knowing now that he was alone.

"My dragonfly. I forgot all about him." Sis had noticed the faint buzzing. Still shaken from seeing the corpse, the little boy thrust his collecting jar into a grubby wool knapsack. Everything suddenly went dark around the apprentice, and his heart fell into terrifying depths that spiraled into a midnight of despair.

4

AKA MERLIN

"CHRIST, ARTHUR, WE CAN'T DO TWO JOBS AT ONCE. DO THEY expect us to look after him and keep these vultures at bay, too? You'd think the effing circus was in town." The exasperated policewoman glowered at the line of cars that had pulled up beside the motorway, then back into the ditch where the body lay. With a swipe she pushed back the ginger hair straggling over her eyes. "We need backup. They must know that, don't they?"

"It's on its way." Her partner, a younger constable in his twenties, climbed out of the squad car. He seemed relatively unperturbed. It was twilight, and in the revolving blue lights his form looked almost as alien and disembodied as the corpse. "I've just called in. They say to hold tight. For now it's just us."

The policewoman looked around in deeper annoyance. "It's getting way past shift change, and you know it's gonna rain. What chance do you think we'll have of finding tracks then? Do you have a cigarette on you?"

Her partner shook his head and took a few steps to the edge of the ditch. The old man's body lay a little more than halfway down the slope. It had been tossed, presumably on impact, about twenty feet from the roadway. The arms were thrown wide in a gesture of surprise, as if the old man had slipped on a scatter rug, and his left leg was bent back under him like a rag doll. The young constable said, "Shouldn't we cover him up, Katy? It doesn't seem decent."

"There should be a couple of blankets in the back somewhere. And could you fetch my mac? I want to clear out these ghouls. They're the ones that aren't decent." She glared again at the silent line of spectators that was gathering one or two cars at a time.

"Right," her partner muttered as she started toward the cars, waving her arms. "Look, I'm going over there. I see somebody else." He headed off down the road in the opposite direction.

It was the merest luck that they had arrived on the scene so fast. If they hadn't been driving the back roads, and if they hadn't chanced to turn on the dispatch radio after duty hours, somebody else would be handling this mess. Luck.

"Anybody available near Tavistock Road?" the radio had crackled.

Arthur had looked over at Katy, who shrugged. She took the mike: "PC Kilbride here. I'm with PC Callum. Shoot."

"We've got a report from a phone box located approximately two miles east of the Tavistock Road turnoff. Somebody thinks they saw a body in a ditch. Can you check it out?" A spring rainstorm was brewing, making the dispatcher's voice fade in and out.

Out of the corner of her eye Katy noticed her partner nod. "We'll take it." They had pulled up no more than five minutes later. When Katy got to the old man and lifted his head, it lolled and flopped to one side. "Broken neck, probably broken spine, too, from the feel of him," she said soberly. "Better leave him where he lies."

Arthur Callum had never seen a corpse before, but then violent death wasn't common in the country districts. "Would you check out the pockets? He might have ID," Katy said. Arthur obeyed, expecting to be revulsed. In fact he was more curious than anything else. He rummaged in the side pockets of the shabby brown overcoat the old man had been wearing, but there wasn't anything, not even a book of matches or a wadded pack of cigarettes. To get to the inside pockets, he had to push aside the man's long flowing white beard, which was almost luminescent in the gray half-light of dusk. "Did you notice? He's still warm under the coat. Whoever did it might still be on this road."

"Along with a thousand other bad drivers."

They both stood up, staring at the victim. The extraordinary beard, which billowed in waves from the old man's chin, was flecked with blood. Climbing out of the ditch, Katy had spied the first curious onlookers pulling out of traffic. Pale faces were pressed curiously against rolled-up windows, but nobody got out of their cars. When Arthur saw somebody else—two spectators on foot, it turned out—they were just two boys who'd happened to walk across the muddy fields. "I need to talk to you," he said. They hovered reluctantly. The younger one, who was short and pudgy, drew nervously for protection against the older boy, who was tall, blond, and well-framed, about fifteen years old.

Arthur walked up to them. "You live around here?" he asked casually.

Neither seemed eager to respond. Then the older one blurted out, "It looks like hit-and-run, but it could be a murder, too, couldn't it?"

"Who's to say? There has to be a proper investigation," Arthur said cautiously.

"Was there a lot of blood?"

"Not much if you must know. There's nothing to see now. What's your name, anyway?"

"Tommy Ashcroft," the older boy answered promptly, without fear.

Arthur had to give him credit for that. At fifteen he himself had shirked from the shadow of any policeman who came his way. "Well, Tommy, I'd consider it a favor if you'd lead our young friend back to town. Or do you need a ride? It's getting dark awfully quick. I could phone your parents from the car to fetch you."

The two boys looked at each other in alarm. "Don't let him, Tommy," the younger one pleaded.

Tommy placed a reassuring hand on his shoulder. "Don't worry, Sis, it's okay." Then to Arthur, "We don't have parents around here. We go to St. Justin's." He pointed into the distance where a massive pile of vaulted fieldstone could be seen, its windows lit with a feeble yellowish glow. "We'd appreciate it if you didn't—"

"Sure." Arthur squatted down to be at eye level with the younger boy. "You sure you can take care of yourself—what's the name?"

"Sisley."

"But they call you Sis?" The boy hung his head—obviously he could have wished for a better nickname, but there it was. "I think you saw what was down there, didn't you, Sis?" The boy bit his lip and clutched his knapsack tighter to his chest. "Well, I don't blame you if you find it upsetting. I've never seen anything like that myself. I'm new in this district, and even though it's my job, it makes me very sad to see something like that."

"Me, too," Sis replied almost too softly to be heard.

"Good lad. Now try to forget it, okay?"

Sis nodded doubtfully as Tommy pulled him away. In a moment they had melted away into the fast-closing night. Arthur turned around and started walking back. He could see that Katy had made headway with the accident vultures; most of the cars were gone. The weather turned, starting to drizzle, and the wind picked up.

"I'm going down to keep him company," Arthur announced. Katy pulled up the collar of her mac against the wet and nodded. He took the blanket she held out. The grass was rain-slippery on the way down the ditch. When he got to the body, the old man's beard was sodden and pathetic looking, tangled around itself in ropy knots. Arthur crouched down and, without thinking, carefully undid the strands. Doing his best to smooth them out, he felt no revulsion; his hands moved almost in a caress. For some reason faint memories of childhood, of bedtime stories about wizards and warlocks, flickered through dim mental recesses.

"Looks familiar, doesn't he?" Katy's voice came from above. Arthur swiveled around as she came down beside him.

"What?" he mumbled, startled at having his mind read.

"That one. He reminds me of Merlin or somebody like that. Medieval. Sorry, I didn't mean to intrude." Arthur looked up, surprised that she'd noticed his reaction. "One of the old pubs around here is called the Orb and Merlin. I should show it to you sometime.

There's a picture over the saloon bar fits our bloke to a tee, not counting the pointed cap. You're not from Gramercy, of course."

"No, I am, or was. I went away to school for a long while."

Katy nodded. His gentle voice, so much not a policeman's, gave her pleasure. She kept it to herself. "We should call this the Merlin case," she said, half-musing. "'Deceased anonymous elderly gentleman, aka Merlin.'"

Arthur didn't answer. The wind was strong now, and the drizzle hit his face like needles. He hunched over, pulling the blanket over the corpse and using his body to shield it from the elements. A strange act of compassion, but it happened to make it easier to hear the words when they came.

Please—help—you are needed.

The shock threw him bolt upright. "You okay?" Katy asked, thinking maybe he was going to be sick.

"You didn't say anything just now, did you?"

"Me? No."

"Katy, listen to me, I think he might be alive." Arthur took off his cap and leaned close to the yellowish, waxen face. He listened intently. "There could be a breath, just maybe, I'm not sure," he said anxiously.

Katy grunted. "That's a bit barmy, you know. His neck's broken."

"Hush," Arthur warned, trying to shut out the noise of the wind. He cradled the old man's head gently with two hands, but he couldn't see any movement of eyelids or lips. The growing darkness was enough to dim the face. "This may sound loony, but I just heard him talk. He asked for help."

"I'm sorry, laddie, but this one's rather beyond help, don't you think? Look, they're coming."

She was right. In the near distance a siren whooped once, twice. Arthur looked up. He could see the bob and weave of bright ambulance lights bearing down on them through the traffic. Katy stormed up the embankment. Two patrol cars peeled out of the traffic flow and parked by the ditch behind the ambulance. "Over here, sir," she called, waving her arm. Westlake, the senior inspector from CID, was getting out of the lead car.

"What is it, hit-and-run?" He came up, looking rumpled and weary.

"Yes, sir, appears to be."

"Do we know who it is?"

"No papers or ID on the body. By the looks of him, I'd say he was a vagrant."

Westlake's eyes narrowed speculatively. "We can't be sure. Check the Gramercy geriatrics infirmary. Maybe one of their patients wandered away. It's nearly two miles, and I don't fancy how he made it this far, but he could have been off his nut. You never know."

"Right, sir, I'll check with them." Katy closed up her notepad.

"Anything else? You've called a scene-of-crime officer?"

She nodded. "Nothing else. Naturally we'd like to get the bastard that hit our bloke and left him here like this. It's routine except for the fact that he started talking after he died."

"What's that?" Westlake didn't look amused.

"Well, we found him dead as doorknobs, flung off the motorway, sir. Broken neck, probably broken spine as well. But my partner here—"

Westlake turned toward Arthur, who had come up to the squad cars. "You're new?" Westlake demanded brusquely.

The young constable could feel himself blush in the dark. "Yes, sir. Assigned to the district a week ago Tuesday. I did hear him talk, plain as anything, even if his neck does look broken. He said, 'Help me.' It was quite clear. I thought maybe PC Kilbride spoke, but it wasn't a woman's voice." Arthur stopped, realizing that he was practically babbling. He blushed twice as deeply, grateful that no one could see him well in the dark.

"Usually I find that being dead inhibits the power of speech considerably," Westlake remarked dryly.

"I'm not saying I can explain it, sir. I'm sure if you'd been there, you'd have heard him, too."

Westlake frowned. "You're not on traffic duty?" Junior officers in neon green safety vests were out on the motorway now, easing the congested flow of cars.

"No sir. My partner and I were heading home along a byway when radio dispatch caught us. We knew it was a matter for CID once we saw the nature of the crime."

"You might have submitted a report and waited until morning before calling me."

"The rain would have wiped out a lot by morning."

Westlake gave the young policeman a quick look. Fiftyish, built like a professional wrestler past his prime, Westlake loomed over Arthur as if he were contemplating a hammerlock.

Arthur said, "I know the state of the body makes it unlikely—"

"Unlikely? Was his neck broken or wasn't it? If you're starting out in detective work, it's rather fun to get at least some of these details right," Westlake snapped. He clambered down into the ditch. Reaching the body, he bent down and rocked the old man's head back and forth in his beefy hands. It moved with sickening ease. Westlake plucked lightly at the skin over the elbow, flexed the fingers once or twice.

"Give me your impressions," he said abruptly.

"Impressions, sir? Just what I told you," Katy replied, puzzled. "If you mean are there any tire tracks around or like that, we haven't spotted any."

A pair of ambulance attendants, bored and chilly in their white coats, emerged from the darkness and hovered nearby. The senior inspector stood up and shook off the raindrops leaking down the back of his collar. "You can take him, lads," he ordered, turning away and climbing heavily back up the ditch. He paused at the top. "What's your name?"

"Callum, sir, PC Arthur Callum." Lifting his hand, Westlake beckoned with a flick of authority. Arthur scrambled up and joined him next to the lead squad car. "Did you want Katy—Police Constable Kilbride—up here, too?"

"Did PC Kilbride hear your dead man talk?"

"No, sir."

"Then I don't want her up here, too. Besides, I'm sure you think she's a bit of a local oaf, you being a Londoner and all." Westlake had a good ear for accents.

"I don't think that at all, begging the inspector's pardon. I'm originally a local oaf, too."

"Hm." A long silence hung in the air. "You are aware, of course, that the body was almost cold when I touched it? Cold enough so that death probably occurred at least an hour ago."

The tone of the comment made Arthur angry. "I know what I heard, sir."

Westlake went on, unheeding, "And the disposition of the body leaves no doubt that death was instantaneous." The two men stared at each other. "Are you still sure of what you heard?" Arthur bit his lip. "Well, we're getting off to a beautiful relationship, aren't we?" Westlake opened the door and sat in the driver's seat.

"You didn't ask me about my impressions, sir."

"What?" Westlake turned back heavily.

"Back there. You asked for our impressions, and I didn't give you mine."

"Go on."

"I don't mean to contradict my partner, but I don't think it was hit-and-run. The condition of the body doesn't lend itself to that conclusion. A car striking a person hard enough to throw him that distance from the road, about twenty feet, would have left gravel and tar embedded in hair and skin. The clothes would be torn, but the victim's trousers and cardigan weren't. I saw no contusions on the skin, either."

When Arthur was through, Westlake whistled. It could have been irony or appreciation. "Are you prepared to go further?"

"Further, sir?"

"If it wasn't hit-and-run, what was it?"

"Murder, I think."

"Ah." Westlake raised his eyebrows. "And you were doing so splendidly. I can say yes to it not being hit-and-run, but murder doesn't sit so well with me. Don't you see? Sufficient facts may be at hand to negate one hypothesis without adequately supporting another. We'll talk about it tomorrow." Arthur looked down, crest-fallen. Then Westlake muttered, as if to himself, "Good show all the same."

"I hope you don't think I'm crazy, sir."

"You're observant and probably clever. I'll rule out crazy for the time being."

They saw Katy come up, looking impatient. "Medics need you to sign a form, sir, to release the body for autopsy. Unless you want us to call the pathologist away from his dinner."

"Bloody forms," Westlake grumbled. He rose out of the driver's seat like a bear standing on its hind legs and walked Katy and Arthur back to the ambulance just as the two attendants were swinging the rear doors shut. Westlake signed in triplicate, nodded curtly to no one in particular, and left.

Katy grinned. "Well, aren't you going to thank me for putting you forward?"

"Fat lot of good you did me," Arthur said, but without rancor. He felt oddly good. The events of the evening had intrigued him.

The ambulance driver started the engine as the other medic locked the rear doors. "See you at the pub, Katy?" he asked. Arthur looked surprised. Katy frowned and shook her head. "Well, toodle-oo," the medic replied, not the least put off. The ambulance moved off into the anonymous stream of headlights.

"You keep time with him?" Arthur asked.

"No, I don't. We're cousins, not of the kissing kind."

"Sorry. You sound cross."

"I'm not. I just hate being out in the damp. And I need a cigarette." Arthur noticed a softening of her tone. It came naturally, despite her attempts at being officially brusque.

The two said very little after they were back on the road in their car. Arthur was grateful for the respite. It needed pondering, what had happened. He wasn't shaken about the voice he had heard, or the least bit uncertain about hearing it, but things had to be precise. If a person in distress had been calling out, he would have said, "Help me." But the words had been different: "Please help, you are needed." Now that he looked back on it, Arthur realized what the words were hinting at—a mission. What else could "you are needed" mean?

He turned to Katy. "Look, I should tell you something. I'm sorry, but I notified Westlake I didn't think it was hit-and-run."

"Mm." He'd expected a gruff reaction or even a flare-up. She sounded unperturbed.

"I mean, I didn't want you to think I pulled the rug out from under you. My instinct just told me that our Merlin wasn't bumped off by a passing car. Nothing that simple."

The lights of a pub showed up through the rain. "You want to go in? We could share a pint." Katy's voice had softened even more, well out of official police range.

Arthur looked over, surprised. "Sure."

They pulled up. "Or better yet," she said, "maybe I could run in and have them pack us some sandwiches. I've got beer at the house." She was staring fixedly straight ahead.

Arthur felt embarrassed. "Katy." He made an awkward effort to sound gentle.

"What?"

"I really appreciate your asking me. But, I mean, we haven't been partners long and—" She had started the car again. He stopped, at a loss.

Her eyes opened wide, and she burst out laughing. "Oh, no. You think I was coming on to you. Don't be beamish, I'm just hungry. And you don't have to look so damned relieved." But she still hadn't looked at him.

"I'm not relieved. I was just going to say that I'm expected at home. My mother waits dinner."

"Good for her. I'll drop you off." Katy's voice wasn't soft anymore.

"Look, let me run inside and grab you a sandwich." He felt stupid placating her like that, but when she didn't reply, Arthur got out and dashed into the pub.

Katy looked at the soft indentation in the upholstery where his body had been. Unself-consciously she placed her hand there; it was warm. "Oh, Katy me girl," she half-sang. In the rearview mirror she caught a glimpse of her pale, plump face. It was pleasant, policewomanly. She thought about the fringes of dark, curly hair that cropped out of the back of Arthur's cap and his wide-set gray eyes. "I must tell him to get a haircut; he's not regulation," she thought.

Inside, the barman was just passing over a brown bag to Arthur with two sausage rolls when Katy ran in, excited and breathless. "Pay up, quick."

"I already have. What's the matter?"

She tugged him out of earshot of the barman, who tried not to look inquisitive. "It's a bloody wonder. He's escaped."

"Who?"

"Our Merlin. They brought him round to the hospital, and when they opened up the back, he was gone. Poof, now you see him, now you don't." Katy turned on her heels and headed back for the car.

Arthur followed, stupefied. "What should we do?"

"Nothing. We should have gone off duty three hours ago. Unless you're volunteering. Are you?"

Arthur wished he could say yes. He sighed. "We're both tired. I'm due back on in the morning. Let me drop you off."

Katy nodded. Her excitement was waning, and in the aftermath of adrenaline she felt a dull fatigue. She wanted to ask Arthur if he felt the same, but he clearly wasn't in the mood for chitchat. Hearing voices was one thing, but having a dead man prance off in the night was another. She began to munch the sausage rolls. They were greasy and savory, the kind of food she couldn't resist, guilt be damned.

Grisly accidents were just the kind of thing adults stared at with morbid relish, Tommy Ashcroft thought. But then, to make themselves feel respectable, they tell boys not to. If he had been by himself, he would have looked anyway. The instant he and Sis had witnessed the body, Tommy wanted to run down into the ditch, and even now he was almost too excited to take the little boy back as the police had ordered him to.

"We can't tell anyone," Tommy said aloud. "Can you keep a secret? We'll make a pact." Sis nodded, out of breath. They were plodding back across the muddy plowed fields, just sprouting in mustard and rye, taking a shortcut to St. Justin's. Although the rain had abated, the sky lowered with darker clouds moving in from the north.

"A blood pact?" Sis asked.

Tommy considered it. "No, I don't think that's necessary. You have to swear brotherhood for that. Although a killing should be almost as good. Let me think about it."

The two boys reached the murky stream at the boundary of the fields and followed it toward school. Discarded tires and rusted pieces of farm machinery littered the banks. Fresh grass grew up, not yet tall enough to mask the naked ugliness of the refuse that tumbled down to the water.

"It wasn't an accident, was it?" Sis gasped as they ran. The older boy grimly shook his head. "I hope it's a mad herd."

Tommy wheeled upon him. "Don't say that. This isn't a joke or a bloody Hardy boys, you know."

"What do you care what I say?" Sis retorted hotly. "If it's sewer pipe or mad herd, it's no skin off your nose." A lonely boy with few friends, Sis had invented his own private language. *Sewer pipe,* Tommy guessed, stood for suicide, *mud herd* for murder.

"Just come on if you're coming," Tommy replied, and continued on a trot. He felt guilty resenting Sis, and after a few moments he confessed to himself that he wouldn't have stayed to gawk with the accident vultures even if he had been alone. He slowed down to make it easier for Sis to keep up, and the smaller boy knew he was forgiven. They were real friends, like the brothers neither had, despite the enormous gap of six years that separated them, at least as the other boys saw it.

The school's streaked black walls could be seen over the rise as they climbed the bank of the stream. Sis pulled himself up the slope by clutching on to tangled hazel bushes. By the time he came over the top of the rise, Tommy had disappeared around a corner of the main building.

St. Justin's had once been the rectory of a Gothic church with an attached convent. Ages ago, when it was abandoned to the swallows and rats, someone had the idea of putting the moldering hulk to use by imprisoning boys there for educational purposes. The enterprise had caught on. Smaller buildings had cropped up here and there, each one striving to outdo its elders in ugliness, until finally the original sacred edifice was surrounded by a maze of added-on dorms, kitchens, latrines, tool sheds, and rickety structures no one had any use for.

Sis was faintly afraid of the empty staring windows, although he walked under them every day. Narrow alleyways ran all through the grounds, used by the boys, with their natural instinct for secrecy, as hiding places for furtive deeds. Running after Tommy, Sis peered into nooks and entryways where he had often smelled cigarettes or heard the rustling of forbidden magazines. He was too young to be admitted into these activities. A Maginot Line separated lower-school boys and upper-school boys—except for Tommy, of course, and Sis didn't entirely comprehend why his friend had crossed the line and risked the scorn of the others.

"Tommy?" he called softly. Above his head many of the iron-barred windows were lighted, meaning that the boarding students were at their books before supper. The day boys had all gone home. Sis was about to call again when a warm, strong hand grabbed his shoulder. "Don't make a racket," Tommy's voice came reassuringly in the darkness, "I hear someone that way." Three or four dark alleys branched off ahead, like a musty rabbit warren. Tommy picked his way surely down the narrowest one. Dimly, Sis could hear a repeated thunking sound ahead.

They rounded a corner, and in the faint light of a bare bulb swinging over the alley, a boy was kicking a soccer ball against a wall. "Who is it?" Tommy demanded softly. The boy under the swinging light gave the ball a vicious kick, slamming it into a wall. It ricocheted wildly around the narrow alley. Sis didn't wait for an answer but ran up breathlessly. "Want to see a murder?"

"Get off with it," the other boy said, annoyed.

"No, it's true. Give me your seedcake tomorrow and I'll take you to the body." The boy with the soccer ball turned his pale face toward them and scowled.

Sis felt Tommy's hand on his shoulder again. "Cool your jets, Sis. Edgerton's been sent to Coventry."

The little boy's eyes grew wide. He himself was habitually ignored by the older boys, and when someone as kind as Tommy

Ashcroft wasn't around, they had sometimes pelted him with mud balls or thrown his knapsack over the fence into the headmaster's yard of prize fowls. But he had never known any boy who was totally ignored, frozen out as if he didn't exist. Even so, being sent to Coventry was a punishment probably as old as the English public school.

Edgerton's eyes were coal black under the swinging light. He was tall and skinny, and his lanky, unkempt hair hung down over his brow. Against his pale cheeks his lips stood out, a vivid pink slash. "Hullo, Sissy," he said mockingly. "Did your baby-sitter let you murder someone?"

The pudgy boy turned red.

Tommy was already backing away. He was a brave boy, but not brave enough to go against the will of a hundred schoolmates. Sis felt strange. He knew it was weak of him to pity Edgerton. "Sis!" Tommy warned in a fierce undertone. The little boy shuffled his feet, undecided. He had an overpowering urge to blurt out everything. What had Edgerton done to deserve this, anyway? He couldn't remember.

His emotions got the better of him. "It wasn't me. I only kill insects, and that doesn't count. It was an old man," he blurted out, "and you better watch out it wasn't your filthy mates who bashed him." Edgerton reacted to this taunt with a harsh laugh. Tommy clenched his jaw and turned away. "We're not speaking to you," Sis said, rather lamely, as he ran after his friend.

Edgerton picked up the soccer ball and hurled it violently at their retreating backs. With a loud thwack it hit Sis in the neck, making him cry out. "Be quiet, can't you?" Tommy hissed angrily as the younger boy, never adept physically, stumbled. His wool knapsack hit the cobblestones with a muffled sound of breaking glass.

Sis's chin began to quiver. "What's the bother now?" Tommy asked. He picked up the sack. Bits of broken glass fell out, and he could feel more jagged edges poking through the fabric.

"That's mine. Gimme!" Sis cried. He made a grab for the knapsack, which Tommy held up out of reach, trying to protect Sis from cutting himself. Suddenly a sharp buzz was in the air. Tommy felt a sting on his cheek. He yelped and dropped the sack as Edgerton's mocking laughter pursued them.

"Shut it," Tommy whispered furiously. He grabbed at the dragonfly still suspended in front of his face. It barely avoided him, wavering feebly to and fro. It seemed to have little strength to fly. As if blinded by the swinging lightbulb, it ran into one side of the alley with a click and clung to the rough-plastered wall, slowly waving its stiff, sheer wings.

"He's mine, don't touch him!" Sis shrieked, now beside himself.

"Hold on, hold on." Tommy was still angry, but he knew he had to calm his frightened companion.

"How can you murder someone if you won't hurt a fly?" Edgerton taunted. He fetched his soccer ball and yelled, "Look, Sissy!" He threw the ball at the spot on the wall where the dragonfly clung.

Several things happened all at once. The soccer ball slammed into the wall. Simultaneously, out of the darkness flapping black wings brushed Sis's face, and he cried out in fright. No one had time to notice whether the ball had hit its mark.

"It's a vampire bat, coming to bite you," Edgerton taunted. Sis screamed and clung to Tommy with all his might.

"Come on, buck up, it can't hurt you—it's just a bird," Tommy said. A large black crow swooped down again. Sis was too afraid to look, but in the stark glow of the hanging bulb, it could be seen that the crow had caught the dragonfly in its beak. With a rattle of pinion feathers the bird shot up into the air and was gone. Everything fell quiet, except for Sis's breathless panting. Edgerton disappeared into the shadows, leaving Tommy to take care of the ridiculous crybaby.

5

"ALIVE AND YET NOT ALIVE"

MELCHIOR WONDERED IF HE WAS DEAD YET. HE WASN'T SURE. When the crow swooped down and plucked him off the wall, its beak should have crushed his shell instantly, but he could still feel its grip around his middle. Black wings beat steadily overhead, invisible against the night sky and almost silent except for the metallic clicking of the long flight feathers.

"He's clever and cruel," Melchior thought with a shudder. "He's keeping me alive until he decides whether to snap me in two or shove me down the throats of his horrible brood."

This thought didn't devastate the hapless apprentice. He'd be glad enough to die, given what he'd seen that night. Everyone else in his world seemed to be dead anyway. With a pang he saw Merlin's face in his mind's eye and realized that he would never see him again.

"Don't be so certain," the crow said, somewhat condescendingly.

Melchior almost jumped out of the crow's beak with amazement. "What?" he exclaimed.

"I said don't be so certain. The one you despair over is alive and yet not alive," the crow replied cryptically. Melchior didn't know which was more astonishing, that crows spoke in riddles or that they could read minds.

"*They* can't read minds," the crow said. "I can." The horny edges of the bird's beak closed around the dragonfly a trifle harder.

"You're squeezing," Melchior protested. There was no reply. He thought this must all be a dreadful nightmare, but then the beak's pressure relented a little. Melchior's urgency was too strong to be checked by fear. "What do you mean by 'alive and yet not alive'? Is my master near?" he pressed on hopefully.

"Your master is everywhere, nowhere, and somewhere." This time the bird sounded unmistakably pleased with itself, and Melchior became fully aware that their entire conversation was being conducted in his head. This made sense, given that dragonflies lack the power of speech, not to mention that the crow's beak was occupied with gripping its prey. Melchior felt extremely uncomfortable thinking of himself as prey.

"Who are you?" he asked in an effort to simplify matters.

"Your only friend."

Melchior grew frustrated; apparently speaking in conundrums was the bird's only means of communication. "Let me go," he said, writhing to escape. This request was acknowledged with no words, only a firm shake of the bird's head. The apprentice decided to submit. As he did, he became more aware of his surroundings. The night was thick, and the crow was flying low, perhaps fifty feet above the treetops. Its body swayed with every rise and fall of its wings; Melchior felt vaguely seasick.

Abruptly, with a sharp clatter of wings, they landed in the top of a tall ash tree on the edge of a field. Melchior couldn't tell whether the land was farm or waste ground. He wondered if the crow had reached its nest, where the horrible brood might be, when an impatient voice said, "Surveillance." This apparently explained why they had paused in the trees. The next instant the bird took off and landed in a small yew tree. With bright black eyes it searched the night, cocking its head as if listening for invisible threats. Finally the crow appeared satisfied. Taking wing, it hovered briefly in midair before plunging headfirst into the ground. If Melchior had had enough time, he would have panicked, but the crow shot straight for the earth, popping into a camouflaged hole that the apprentice couldn't even see.

"Here we are," the crow announced, as with a flick he dropped Melchior onto a soft pile of rabbit fur.

Where is here? Melchior wondered. He had gotten used to the fact that the crow could read his mind, so he wasn't shocked when the bird responded, "Here is home, my safe burrow."

"I've never heard of crows living in burrows." Melchior distinctly smelled rabbit, not to mention the bit of fur he was perched on.

"Have you heard of everything?" the crow grumbled. "Have you heard, for instance, that crows can eat rabbits and adopt their homes as a provision against danger? Wait until you are an eagle before you claim to know everything."

Melchior fell silent. It was pitch-black in the burrow, and for the moment he was content not to explore his surroundings. Apparently the crow did not intend to eat him, at least not immediately, and he was too disoriented to plan an escape just yet.

"Make yourself comfortable," the crow said placatingly. "Hungry? I don't have any flies handy, unless maggots have collected on the rabbit bones in the lower chamber. I could check if you like," he offered obligingly.

"Don't bother," Melchior hastily replied. "I'm sure I won't be a dragonfly for long. I'm a wizard, you know. Or I was a wizard, when there were such as we."

"Tut and bosh. You're merely an apprentice, if we stick to the letter of the truth, and you may be a dragonfly longer than you think, given that you didn't assume this shape of your own power to begin with."

Melchior was flabbergasted and thoroughly embarrassed. The old crow was proving himself a very knowing creature. It could read minds. It knew all about him, it had rescued him in near-darkness just when he was about to be killed, and to top it off he understood wizardry as it existed God knew how many centuries before.

"Can we begin at the beginning?" Melchior asked in a respectful voice, his consternation subsiding.

"Haven't you learned anything?" the crow snorted. "There is no beginning. And some beginnings are endings anyway."

"Is that a riddle, like saying that Merlin is alive and yet not alive?"

"Riddles are for chicks. I'm simply telling you the truth."

Melchior fell silent. He had few solid facts to go on, but it seemed to him that he had survived the calamity of Camelot due to a spell; therefore he must be in the future. The landscape, though extremely altered, nonetheless reminded him of England, and the people looked English. He had seen Merlin's body, which was undoubtedly from the past, but that was through a distorted glass, and besides, he had been confused and upset.

"That wasn't Merlin's body," the crow interjected, having followed this train of thought.

"It wasn't?" Melchior's insect heart, although only a shriveled speck, gave a thump. "He really isn't dead?" he asked timidly.

"Bright lad, you're coming round," the crow replied with mock approval. "But I'm sleepy."

"No, you have to answer my questions."

The crow rattled his wings rather menacingly and brought his curved razor beak an inch closer to the pile of rabbit fur. "*Have to,* young one? I doubt it," he growled. Abruptly the crow's head disappeared under its wing, which Melchior took to mean that no more questions would be answered that night.

DC Hamish McPhee thought like a policeman, acted like a policeman, felt like a policeman. Anyone less hell-bent on being a walking stereotype of the English constabulary might have responded to a dead man's disappearance with wonder. Bewilderment should have played some part in his reaction. It didn't. Hamish was simply furious, fuming with righteous indignation as if a wily criminal had slipped the collar.

"It's outrageous, cutting capers like that," he fumed. "If I ever get my hands on him . . ."

"What would you do?" Arthur asked. "He's already dead."

"That's not the point."

"It isn't?"

Hamish scowled and said nothing more. It was a few hours before dawn, and Arthur was working the second of his back-to-back shifts. "We're sending DC McPhee to look for evidence. Go with him and point out what you saw," the desk sergeant had said. The two men began by retracing the ambulance route from the scene of the crime to the hospital. McPhee had turned on the spotlight, directing it along the roadside. The trimming crews had cut the grass and weeds short for ten feet on either side; there was no place for a body to hide.

"Maybe someone took him," Arthur offered.

"Going sixty miles an hour? Not bloody likely."

"Where do you think he is, then?"

"How do I know? If he had any sense, he'd be in the morgue."

The night's rain had given way to ground fog that floated in and out of their spotlight in ghostly patches. Arthur fell silent. He didn't feel wonder or astonishment anymore, but something much more unreasonable—acceptance. The old man's disappearance was just the next thing that had to happen.

"Shouldn't we be searching the ditches?" Arthur asked.

"That would be pretty careless of old Merlin. Getting thrown into two ditches in one night."

For some reason Arthur found this inane remark wildly funny. He started laughing and couldn't stop. When he did finally stop, McPhee was staring. Arthur said, "You don't really think we're going to find him, do you?"

"Dead man on the loose, may be armed and dangerous," McPhee quipped. "Just hold your horses. We're almost to the hospital." McPhee had a dogged sense of duty; it was a predictable part of him, like his cigs and bitters. They pulled into the hospital's circular drive. Several ambulances stood under the portico at the entrance, lights off. Arthur didn't see the medics who had helped them, however. "I'd better check inside," McPhee said, climbing out of the driver's seat.

"I'll wait."

A few moments passed and McPhee was back again. "No luck,"

he said glumly. "They do shifts on and off for thirty-six hours—the ambulance crews—and our lot is off until Wednesday. We'll have to pop round where they live or come back." He put the car in gear; they rolled smoothly around the circular drive and out into traffic again. Several miles later the motorway made a sharp bend around a sheep pen with high stone walls. Fog was gathering. Two dark shadows appeared against the gray mist. Arthur craned forward to make out what they were. Horses. Two horses were standing on the verge not five feet from Arthur's window. One of them reared up and started to dash across the road.

"Watch it!" Arthur cried. McPhee had already slammed on the brakes. The headlights swept wildly across the slick pavement as the car spun in a half-circle and came to a halt, tires screeching.

"Jesus, what a fright," McPhee exclaimed. He wiped his face with his hand; his body sagged as if he had taken a gut punch.

"You all right?"

"Me? Absolutely. I just need a year or two to catch my breath."

Arthur nodded and stepped out on his side. The horses had gone. "Let me just take a quick look." He walked over to where the animals had appeared. The fog had filled in a large ditch, and it was a moment before he realized that the spot was almost exactly where the old man had met his end. Arthur's spine tingled lightly, yet he mostly felt the same calm acceptance as before. Having remembered to bring a flashlight from the car, he shone it into the ditch where the body had been.

Arthur felt terror empty his chest with a cold gush. Someone, an indistinct figure, was caught in the beam. The patchy mist drifted and thinned; it was the old man, sitting on the ground as if waiting for Arthur. "I've had quite a time," the old man said, looking up. "You can't imagine." He had spread his droopy cardigan out to sit on so that he wouldn't get muddy. Arthur's hand began to shake, causing the light from his flashlight to veer this way and that. The bright beam lit up the old man's beard when it passed over it.

The old man shook his head. "They're all scattered, sire." He didn't pause for Arthur's reaction but kept muttering, as if to himself. "I seem to have lost the queen, and wandering in limbo is no picnic, if such be her fate. Since you were my pupil, that made you easier to find. But it took time, it took time."

Oh, God. Arthur tried to call out. His mouth had gone dry—it felt as if moth wings filled his mouth. "You're alive," he whispered.

"Well, yes and no," the old man said thoughtfully. "Do we have time to go into that right now?" Arthur's feet felt dull and heavy. He couldn't turn away; he couldn't find the will to move at all. The old man looked irked. "It's very tedious, I must say, to have you stand there gawping like that. You knew you were coming back; you knew I'd be here. The plan has worked well. Why go in for melodramatics?" He raised his hand in a beckoning gesture.

Like a well-behaved marionette, Arthur's legs started to carry him down the slope. He felt a fist squeezing his heart, and sounds came to his brain as if through a furry thickness. *People die from shocks like this,* he thought. "That's good," the old man said more gently. "The web of time has gathered us in again. I never doubted it, sire, despite everything." He seemed to presume an intimate relationship with Arthur. It was bewildering, in addition to being uncanny.

"Let me go," Arthur managed to utter.

Sadness tinged the old man's expression. "Go where? Do you mean back to your partner? Never fear. The oaf will find his nap very refreshing." Arthur remembered that Westlake had used the word *oaf* just a few hours earlier.

"I just mean let me go," Arthur said, although he kept advancing until he stood directly in front of the old man, who remained seated.

"I'm not a cheap stage hypnotist. You're free to go anytime you like. You are not exhibiting your wonted courtesy, I must tell you that. Forgive me for not getting up. It's better when you raise the dead to let them gather energy from the earth. An hour or two is enough. I've had about an hour and a half already. Very nurturing."

"Raise the dead? Who are you?"

"Merlin. You know that. You've been calling me that all evening. It just happens that you're right."

Arthur heard himself laugh. In a bad movie he was supposed to say, "You're just a figment of my imagination, aren't you? You'll go away as soon as I wake up." No one ever really says that, Arthur thought. They just quietly go on believing their hallucinations until their lives fall apart and they get put in places where everyone eats with plastic spoons.

"You're delirious," Merlin pointed out casually.

"Thank you," Arthur said, surprised to find his self-possession returning. "That's the sanest thing I've heard in a while." He was amazed that he could venture a witticism when his mind was falling apart.

"I don't mean entirely delirious. Just temporarily. Here, I'll help." Merlin stood up and pressed his right hand on Arthur's chest directly above his breastbone. With an explosive gasp Arthur came to his senses. The fist that had gripped his heart loosened its hold, replaced by a warm, flowing feeling. It was a delicious liquid, as if his heart could taste sweetness. "That's nectar," Merlin remarked matter-of-factly.

"It's wonderful," Arthur murmured, swallowed up in the delicious feeling. He wished it would go on forever.

"Don't thank me. The gods make it."

Arthur couldn't understand why the ground wasn't swaying. Without warning, reality was washing over him with tremendous velocity, as if he was lashed to the bow of a ship in pounding seas. Disaster might crash over his head any moment, but his only choice was to hang on.

"Will you answer my questions? Please." The old man nodded. "You were dead. I saw the corpse, broken neck and all. Then I heard a voice saying I was needed, I don't know what for. Was that your voice? If so, what do you want, and how did you raise the dead, as you put it, and why, above all, why me?"

"A lot of questions."

"I only stopped because I ran out of breath." Arthur was struck by the absurdity of the whole insane evening. Merlin reached out to touch his chest. "No, thanks, not again. I mean, it was great, but I'd like to approach this thing without the joy juice, if you don't mind."

Merlin scrutinized him closely. "You've changed. But it's all right." His eyes deepened, and before Arthur could react, the old man's mood began to undergo a momentous shift. The mask of the slightly cracked gentleman vanished. In its place, a mantle of wisdom and authority descended. "I will speak to you in this wise once and only once. You reckon not what grave peril I have placed myself in. This is not my body but the body of a poor wretch who was murdered because he had the misfortune of being too curious. His death was not natural, and I was able to intervene to occupy his mortal frame for a while. God grant we may restore him to it one day. That is why I am alive and yet not alive."

Arthur knew all at once that he had to run away, instantly, or be lost. The vortex of unreason was pulling at him, and his power of rationality flickered like a guttering candle in the wind.

"No," Merlin commanded. "Stay and hear. Then decide." Arthur found himself unable to resist. In the whole unbelievable business that would follow, this was the only time the wizard deprived him of his free will. He was transfixed, frozen in captive attention. His fear was held at bay for the next few minutes; his mind was clear as never before in his life.

Merlin went on: "There is a battle being waged that concerns your fate and those of all you love. It is not certain which side will win. You once held great power for one side, which is of the light. That is why you are needed. The dark army knows that you are the key. Why else did it take me so long to find you? Mordred, their commander, has the fell ability to tear open the fabric of time. He did so and threw you far, far away. And in his malice he must have thrown Guinevere along a far more devious path; I have yet to rescue her.

"But I will, with your help. You do not know who you are, but I do. It is no mere compulsion that I reveal myself to you or anyone else, but I took on a responsibility and must fulfill it. A few who are dear to me are lost in this dreadful time and place. We are trapped in the worst, the cruelest of ages. I thought long and hard before venturing here.

"The whole situation is fraught with danger. At any moment *he* could sniff you out. From the oppression of the air, I feel his force. It will take all our wits to survive. I cannot safely impart more. Every bit of nonsense you may think I am saying serves to protect you. Every particle of sense you can understand only puts you in graver peril. Mordred knows the rebels by their thoughts, so thank God for now that you are still a fool."

The old man had finished. As quickly as the air of authority had been assumed, it dropped away. The old man seemed to grow smaller, and the fire in his eyes faded. Arthur, released from his transfixed state, held out his arm as if reaching for something to lean on. He slowly sank to the ground, falling on his knees next to Merlin. It could have been the gesture of someone overcome by awe or confusion. Arthur leaned close to Merlin's ear and whispered, like one conspirator to another, "I have been a better pupil than you reckon. The fool has survived a long time, hiding from the enemy. You cannot imagine how long I have waited for you."

The two looked at each other with new understanding, tears brimming in their eyes. For a brief moment they were meeting outside the tumult of history, each knowing that he would be called back on time's stage in a matter of moments. They were reluctant to put on their costumes again, which is always the case when pure spirit shines through the disguise of flesh. Arthur sighed. "Safety above all else," he said somberly. "Weave the charm of forgetfulness around me again." Merlin nodded.

It only took a second. Arthur stood up, looking puzzled. A momentary blankness seemed to be clearing from his head. He knew that he had seen someone in the ditch and come down to investigate. He held up his flashlight, whose beam fell on a bedraggled stranger. "You shouldn't be out here, you know," Arthur said. "It's cold."

"I know. Thanks for your help. I must have been wandering." The old man stood up, moving just out of the flashlight's beam.

Arthur spotted something on the ground; he leaned over and

picked up a soft brown kid glove that had dropped in the mud. "This yours?" The other man was walking away.

"No, you keep it," the man said casually. "I think you'll be needing it."

"Really? Why?"

The man had climbed the slope of the ditch and was about to vanish from sight. He looked over his shoulder. "Because there's been a murder, and that, my friend, is your only clue."

6

A MURDER OF CROWS

"BREAKFAST?" THE CROW ASKED IN A COAXING VOICE. "A FEW grubs make a nice pick-me-up."

"No, please." Melchior shuddered, declining as politely as possible.

"Earwig, then? I can see you want something." Like a head-waiter passing a tray of canapés, the crow eased a tiny wriggling thing across the burrow floor with his foot.

"I mustn't," Melchior pleaded, but at the same time he couldn't help noticing that his dragonfly mandibles clacked greedily and his stomach sac quivered. This was by far the most unpleasant shape he had ever assumed. The crow noticed his reactions and began to laugh. Melchior stirred his wings as a crack of morning sun seeped in from above. "Can I question you now?" he asked cautiously. "You puzzled me last night about quite a few things."

"Puzzled you? Concerning what?" the crow asked, cocking his head. This was the first time Melchior had regarded him in the light, and he now noticed that the bird must be very old. The feathers on his head had turned almost completely gray, and here and there bald patches shone through his thinning neck plumage.

"I cannot understand why you won't say whether my master is

alive or not. It can't be that unclear. Who was that corpse by the road? It certainly appeared to be my master."

"Passing resemblance," the crow muttered dolefully, "with fatal consequences. You were not the only one who imagined that Merlin might be among us."

Melchior's blood skipped a beat. "Then he isn't? Or is he?" he stammered.

"It's not healthy to dwell on this subject. Let us say that you are on the right path," the crow answered ponderously. Melchior's segmented carapace creaked with impatience, and if it weren't for the fact that the grizzled bird was sixty times larger than he was, he would have bit him with frustration. Wisdom told him, however, to be silent and wait. "I am not a mystificator," the crow continued slowly, "but your friend in need, your only true friend as yet."

"I know," Melchior admitted apologetically, "I appreciate that you rescued me from certain annihilation."

"Not quite that. Who's to say if you would have died or merely transformed again? Quite a lot of that sort of business may lie ahead for you. But I am, as I say, your only friend here. Doesn't that make you ask *why* I am your friend and *how* I knew you would arrive?" Without pausing for reply the bird answered his own questions. "To help you understand, my kind are not just crows but the crows of Dolbadarn Castle, emissaries of kings. We have nested in these islands for two thousand years. You have never seen our castle in its vale of lakes, circled by snowcapped peaks. It lies many leagues to the west of Camelot."

"In Wales. Merlin once took me to that land."

"That is no matter," the crow said irritably. "Just listen—I am a messenger, not a foolish old carrion-picker, and in my message is the possibility of saving many lives, including yours, if not the whole kingdom." Amazed at this admonition, Melchior fell silent. "At the time when our castle tower was raised by Llywelyn the Great," the crow resumed, "the kingdom of Wales was in peril. The English invaders were fiercely opposed by the rebels; green valleys ran with blood from the Severn to Holyhead, and the outnumbered Welsh had much need of wizard's work to aid their cause."

"This was in Merlin's time?"

"No such thing. This was the thirteenth century, in the reign of Edward Longshanks, fully seven hundred years after the fall of Camelot. You missed it all, I believe. But Merlin's name held great power in Wales, and when Llywelyn gathered his exhausted forces at the crest of Llanberis Pass, his eye was caught by the sight of two crows circling and crying over his head. 'This is where our fortress shall be built. Merlin has sent an omen,' he declared. And so my ancestors took roost the day the castle tower was finished."

"Did Merlin send the birds? Was he still alive seven hundred years later?"

The crow shook his head. "I see that Merlin left a considerable bit out of your education." Melchior felt abashed, but the crow's rasping voice took on a kinder note. "I was merely pointing out that certain matters had not yet been revealed to you," he intoned. "Firstly, my kind are messengers by right and duty. Before my ancestors in Wales, there were the royal French corbeaus of the Valois, and before them generation upon generation whose task is always the same—to know. What Merlin wished to pass on as vital knowledge, we have preserved until the moment is ripe."

Melchior reflected a second. "Then Merlin saw into the future and passed this particular omen on through your kind," he ventured. The crow nodded. "But if that's so, then your ancestors themselves had to live seven hundred years. Come to think of it, if you were told to rescue me, you must be—" Here the apprentice faltered in his reckoning. It dawned on him that he had no idea how many centuries had passed since he last saw Merlin. He suddenly wished desperately that the pontificating crow would simply tell him straight out where his master was.

"I *am* telling you as straight out as anyone can," the crow rejoined, his feathers ruffled. Melchior kept forgetting that his only true friend could read minds. "The fact is," the crow continued, "that birds are not burdened with individual identity. You noticed perhaps that I have not introduced myself by name, because I do not need one. It's not a fault of impoliteness. Crows have been slandered as coarse, cruel birds, simply because we kill to eat, but the dauphin of France did the same, did he not? The Medici popes were known to enjoy a platter of roast squab. Bearing this beautiful black color on our backs, we are branded with baleful suspicion, and whereas you folk say a gaggle of geese, a flock of pigeons, or an exaltation of larks, how are we called? *A murder of crows!* Outrage!"

The old bird's disgusted voice had risen to a hoarse shriek, but Melchior didn't dare remind him that he was digressing. The crow shook his head. "Where was I? Oh, yes. It is not necessary for my kind to live hundreds of years. All of us carry the same ancestral memories, and when one of us suffers his last molt, the totality of his knowledge enters into the stream of crow memory. The stream flows forever, which is why I told you last night that there is no beginning and no ending, and some endings are beginnings in disguise. I myself am not old by so much as half a century, yet I can tell you precisely what happened on the day Camelot fell."

Melchior buzzed frantically. "Tell me," he implored.

The crow fell silent and fixed Melchior with a withering gaze. "My God, what a fool I can be. I'm talking to a dragonfly."

"But I am a very intelligent dragonfly," Melchior protested, and at once felt the ludicrousness of his remark. He sensed that the bird was about to lapse into another long silence and keep him forever dangling within arm's reach of the things he most anxiously needed to know.

"No offense," the crow said dryly, "but the most intelligent dragonfly is stupider than a dung beetle, which is not impressively smarter than dung." And with that insult, he snapped up the stupefied apprentice in his beak, exited the burrow with two quick hops, and took flight.

"I can't stand it any longer!" Melchior's mind cried. "Where is he? Where is my master?"

"Don't be such a fool," the crow croaked. "Feel his presence."

"What do you think I've been doing, you pompous old fraud!" Melchior cried. "He's not here—there is no wizard in this land, our magic is in shambles, and your beak is about to crush me!"

The crow apparently did not relish being insulted, as he gave Melchior's slim, needlelike middle an extra hard squeeze before he eased up. "Just stop panicking," he ordered, "and feel again, not for the Merlin you knew but for the one you have to find."

The apprentice hadn't the slightest idea what the bird was talking about. He squirmed and writhed, but after a few minutes of futile struggle, he did as he was told. His panic was ebbing, and with calmer mind he sent his subtle spirit out to comb the green-and-brown patchwork of fields racing beneath them. Nothing.

He directed his awareness toward the surrounding hills, farmhouses, even the smokestack that still belched smoke like a dying dragon. No answering vibration came; his body trembled in emptiness. With a thump the crow shook the dragonfly, pointing it toward the gray, dreary town lying a few miles off. "Feel!" he hissed insistently.

A faint tremor of recognition stirred in Melchior. "You're right," he whispered. "There is something. It's very faint and vague, it's not my Merlin, but it's, it's—" He was at a loss for words.

"It's faintly wizardly," the crow finished for him. "No doubt of it," he repeated, pleased with his phraseology, "there's something faintly wizardly in the air. That's why it calls to you." The next second he swooped down toward a two-lane asphalt road, tracked it for half a mile, and came to rest on a weathered wooden fencepost. Melchior was too agitated to pay attention. "But the sensation came from that dismal gray town. It's a total wasteland, a graveyard of magic—how can I find anything there?"

With the assuredness of a feathered Houdini, the crow only murmured, "All will be revealed."

After Tommy had led Sis sniffling into the darkness, Edgerton paced the maze of St. Justin's alleyways alone. The night turned cold. Edgerton felt angry and alone. If he had gone home again with the other day boys, maybe all the trouble wouldn't have started—no, it would have. He was hated too much to begin with.

The incident that had sent him to Coventry savored of the bizarre. One morning the school mascot, an old spaniel named Chips, was heard howling in his kennel and running frantically in circles. His tail had been set on fire, reduced to painful, naked pink flesh. The animal went into shock and was barely saved after being rushed to the veterinary hospital. Mr. Phelps, the headmaster, had been livid.

"Find whoever did this beastly thing; use the cane if you have to," he told the masters in the common room that afternoon. The masters had passed the word down the line to the prefects, who put intense pressure on the other boys to spy or confess or rat out on someone. The upshot of overturning every locker and mattress in the school was meager: no matches, no oil-soaked rags, no fuel cans, although the smell of kerosene lingered on the forlorn Chips for days.

Although no one actually saw Edgerton do it, whispered rumors centered on him, and his habit of playing with matches, dating from early childhood. It had gotten him into trouble before. "He's a real altar boy," they said about Edgerton. Altar boys were one notch short of being socially disposable. Either they had run afoul of the police so many times that the magistrate's court wanted to dump them into detention and throw away the key, or else the boys had been left to roam the streets by their parents.

The reason they wound up at St. Justin's was the church. In some extreme cases, if the court deemed a boy salvageable, the church would exercise its Christian duty and take custody of said offender. After a delousing bath and a new outfit of gray flannel pants and a white shirt, they entered the ranks of St. Justin's.

The night he met Tommy and Sis, Edgerton had been out by himself for hours in the rain. Technically he lived at home, but he felt like a stranger there, too. His dark hair was matted against his forehead; cold droplets slid down the back of his neck, soaking the collar of his white school shirt.

Edgerton refused to believe that Sis and Tommy had actually witnessed a murder, but as he kicked his soccer ball down the alley, he mulled the news over. He imagined a bloody corpse by the motorway, and for a while the thought distracted him from the scenes of revenge that usually filled his mind.

"Bugger," he muttered, "I should just run away from this hell-hole and let it all slide." He gave the soccer ball a hard kick. It caromed off a wall, then he heard the smash of glass. Edgerton peered into the shadows. A broken window, less than waist high, was baring its jagged teeth. The ball had disappeared.

He swore again. It had not been easy to shoplift that ball from Whiteside's Sport. Peering into the window, he could see very little. The school had strung feeble lights here and there among the buildings, and in their light he could just barely make out the basement lumber room. Scraps of timber lay about moldering as if they had been there for a thousand years. A wheezy furnace throbbed somewhere not too far off.

He tried to climb through the window, but it was no good—too much broken glass. If he could hear a furnace, the boy reasoned, there had to be a door or at least a coal chute close by. He hesitated, wondering what to do next, then a glimmer of light spread across the room. "Joey?" he whispered, thinking maybe the Jamaican furnaceman had come in. No answer. The light glimmered again, stronger, moving in soft waves across the gray planks of lumber. The glow couldn't have been from the furnace, because it changed color, from flowing pink-gold waves to opalescent blues and greens. It was like undersea flame, like fairy gold sparkling in an ocean grotto.

But marvelous as that was, it wasn't the color that seemed so extraordinary, but the *feeling* that the light gave off. It beckoned; it was like soft, loving arms that wanted to wrap around the boy and make him safe.

I will see you through the fire.

Did the light speak? Edgerton jerked back, noticing the cold air on the back of his neck. He shivered and shook his lanky, damp hair. How long had he stood there? He pulled up the collar of his worn denim jacket. An upstairs window lit up across the alley, and a boarding-school boy leaned out. "Who's there?" he called in an unfriendly voice.

Edgerton slipped into the shadows. "Prefect, come here, there's an escapee," the voice from the window called ironically. Some other boys laughed noisily. They'd be rousing the security cops in half a second if Edgerton wasn't careful. A quick glance told him that the light was waning in the lumber room. Should he go or stay? How long would it take to find a door?

With all the rubbish lying about and St. Justin's crazy-quilt of disused alleys and false starts, he could have searched for hours, but instinctively he seemed to make the right turns. A rusty doorknob appeared beneath his hand, and with a quick turn he opened a door to confront some stairs descending into darkness. Behind him more voices were talking now; it sounded as if the first boy's alarm wasn't being taken seriously. Edgerton eased himself down the stairs, leaving the door ajar for what little light might seep its way inside.

He walked more by touch than by sight. His fingers slid along a crumbling wooden rail until it abruptly ended, practically pitching him over. He reached out with the other hand and hit a cold, mossy wall. Leaning on it, he followed the stairs down to a landing, which ended on a dirt floor.

"Damn," he said. Rats and other vermin scuttered in the dark, disturbed for the first time in a century, he imagined. Getting past the piles of lumber wouldn't be easy, and he had no idea what direction he was facing. After a moment, his eyes adjusted. He heard the whoosh of a furnace firing up—it was behind him in an adjoining room, not the way he wanted to go. In the opposite direction he caught sight of the broken window his ball had smashed.

Something was happening. This time the light was twice as powerful as before. Waves of gold, blue, and green swept down the walls like a waterfall. Edgerton looked down and saw rippling iridescence playing seductively over his clothes. He turned up his palms, and they seemed to catch fire, but ever so softly. He wanted to follow the light, but there wasn't any place to go, for in the glow he saw that the basement was piled high with broken desks, wardrobes, cracked mirrors, and furniture that only a mad miser would think to store instead of throwing into the stove. Then he stopped looking around. The light absorbed him completely—the light *loved him.*

After a few moments that the boy hoped would never end, the

light started to swirl, quite slowly. It formed a vortex, and without thinking, Edgerton reached toward the ceiling, as if waiting to be whirled up and out of the world. The vortex glowed brighter, like mother-of-pearl caught in the full moon. Gradually he became aware that the vortex was centered at a spot about twenty feet ahead. He walked toward it, wanting to stand inside it. Inexplicably, this mattered very much. With each step the speed of the whirling increased, and the light's intensity burned brighter, now like a bonfire of opals.

"Here I am," he thought, "you've found me." These weren't words he willed; they expressed his innermost feelings of—what?—of not being lost anymore, of not having to be worried, ever again. Perhaps the light pulsated in reply, it wasn't clear. Now he was scrambling over damp lumber, splinters stuck into his palm. An hour later his hand would ache with pain, but at that moment he felt nothing. A few more timbers thrown aside and he was there at the center of the vortex.

He started as his heart seized up. The light was changing again. Fading! No, please, it couldn't, mustn't fade. Desperately he waved his arms, as if to harvest more light before it was extinguished. He felt like an emptiness being drained of life; his insides were a cave of freezing air. He wanted to panic. It would be unbearable to be this empty; rather full of resentment and grievances, the way he had been before, than to be void. The light understood and briefly stayed itself from fading.

Edgerton caught himself holding his breath and released a shuddering sigh. It was over. The fading light was no more. He wanted to cry and didn't care who witnessed his shame. The emptiness lingered in him; fortunately it was more bearable now. The errant soccer ball rolled against his foot, stirred by a jostled timber.

"In there, sir, I'm certain I heard a racket in there." Some boys' voices were calling outside the window. They must have been attracted by all the noise he'd made. He backed into the shadows just as the beam of a flashlight scanned the room. "What do you see?" "Can I look?" "You're shoving," the boys' voices came again.

"No, it's just the lumber room. Damned firetrap, like the rest of this place," a master's voice said irritably. "You boys there, get back inside. We'll have Jenkins haul out this rubbish later. Do as I say." The flashlight poked around the basement one last time, then footsteps retreated down the cobbled alleyway, fading into the distance.

Then Edgerton realized that he had been mistaken. Whatever was happening to him, it wasn't over, not entirely. The light had disappeared, but his hand had landed in the dark on something else. He felt the sharpened edge running down like silken death and the leather-wrapped hilt, and in his mind's eye he saw jewels on the guard. But that part was hard to tell. Only in the light of day could he be certain about the jewels. They were secondary, for the important thing was unmistakable, joyously unmistakable. There was a blade, a hilt, a guard. He had found his sword.

7
THE CHALICE WELL

As they settled to earth from their flight, the old crow set Melchior down on a weathered fencepost and looked around. "Quite a few improvements about the place," he remarked, not altogether approvingly. "But I believe what we want is still here." Melchior didn't know which was worse, the bewilderment he had been kept in so long or the hunger gnawing his vitals.

"Down you go, follow me," the crow ordered. With a swift flip of his wings he sailed over a short stretch of neatly mown lawn bordered with small trees and roses. The roses weren't in bloom yet, but a tender green foliage covered their thorns. The crow's claws clicked onto a flagstone pavement encircling a garden fountain or a natural spring of some kind. Melchior flew after him and alighted beside the water, which bubbled up in a clear jet, tumbling over three tiers of red-brown stone.

"Where are we?"

"At the Chalice Well," the crow replied, as if imparting the most ordinary piece of information.

"The Chalice Well?" the apprentice repeated hollowly.

"That seemed a logical place to go, if you need a miracle," the crow said calmly. Melchior turned around, taking in the low stone buildings, the suburban garden, the traffic noise on the two-lane road beyond the fence.

"If we need a miracle?" He was repeating the crow's words again, idiotically.

"That's what I came up with. If you had the power to transform yourself into a proper shape instead of remaining a ridiculous dragonfly, we would have gotten down to business much more rapidly." The crow paused for a moment. "Do dragonflies pray?"

"No."

"Why did I need to ask?" the crow said dryly. "Well, as far as I can tell, if you aren't going to pray, you should just jump into the water." Melchior felt his body instinctively draw back. "I'll drown," he protested.

"That's right, I guess you will." The crow paused. "Well? Go ahead." He cocked a bright, beady eye expectantly.

What kind of absurdity was this? "I don't believe there's any chalice in this well," Melchior babbled, stalling for time. "Merlin took me to that place. It was the deepest well in Camelot, surrounded by impenetrable forests. A ring of faerie power protected it from unbelief, four angelic swords were planted at the points of the compass. The holy light perpetually danced above it—my master taught me to see the light there. And drowning myself is the furthest thing—"

"Times change," the crow retorted tartly, and before Melchior could protest again, the bird summarily picked him up, squeezing him tight in his claws, and plunged him under the water that pooled around the clear jet.

"No, please no!" Melchior begged helplessly. The pool was very cold, even in the warm spring sunshine, and he could feel it seep, smothering and heavy, into his carapace as the crow's claws broke through to his soft innards. Panic tore at him, an unbearable pressure stifled his spirit. With a horrible crunch he felt his whole body crack, realizing at last that the crow had intended to do away with him all along.

How strange, at that mortal moment, that he thought not of Merlin or his grandmother or God Himself but of Mordred. The bastard's handsome golden-ringed face was poised over him, gloating with hatred. The image was uncannily clear. Melchior gasped and struggled, but while his body violently resisted death, his amazing clarity of vision continued. He saw Mordred pass his hands in weird incantation. The four angelic swords around the well—why hadn't he noticed them before?—turned into Judas trees and withered before his eyes. Mordred's face showed keen pleasure. He barked a command, and his lieutenants, dressed in bloody chain mail, lit a circle of bonfires over the perimeter of the faerie ring.

"Hie, hie!" the soldiers shouted. They were driving horses into the bonfires, and the horses screamed. Blades slashed at their flanks—they had no choice but to exchange the death behind them for the death ahead. One by one they plunged into the fire, and Melchior saw in the terrible light whose they were—the mounts of Lancelot, Galahad, Kay, Percival. He turned his eyes away, too afraid to look for the king's steed.

"More!" screamed Mordred's voice. Multitudes of hunched dwarfs had materialized from the ground, dragging huge, gray boulders through the solid earth. Melchior recognized them as elementals ruled by Albrig. Monstrous-faced, like pug-nosed, hairless moles, they dragged their stones to the well and threw them in. At first the boulders disappeared in bottomless silence, but soon Melchior heard faint splashes. Gradually the holy light faded overhead.

Mordred summoned a particularly fat, loathsome dwarf to his side. "Look to see if your work is going as I ordered," he said. The dwarf hesitated, then looked over the edge. "It goes well, my lord," he tried to say, but before his words were out, Mordred had cut off his head and sent it crashing down into the darkness. Twice as fearful, the remaining host brought even larger boulders. Melchior was too sickened to wait for the end. "Thank you, God," he prayed, "for letting me perish before surviving in such a world."

"Nonsense," the crow's voice said. "All you've seen is from the past. In the present we've got some very pressing appointments." Instantly Melchior was standing beside the pool, shaking droplets of water off his feathers. He was damp right through, and his natural reaction to this discomfort was to stretch his wings and fluff his plumage. This told him that he was not dead, indeed that he was not a dragonfly anymore but some kind of bird. He peered at his reflection in the pool—a crow.

"Rather satisfactory for a short-order miracle," the old crow said. "You are clothed in a much more agreeable shape, but then, I'm biased." He laughed raucously as Melchior stretched his wings again. What a relief! He felt the strength of his new body, so much more congenial than an insect's. His neck worked! His mind wasn't buzzing anymore. In fact when he stopped to think about it, when he pushed his awareness gently into that crow mind—

"Ah, I know things," he gasped.

"Just let it sink in," the old crow commanded. Melchior had never felt such a sensation. His awareness was floating on the stream of crow wisdom; he absorbed its knowing, and veils started to part. As the old crow had promised, he now knew everything about the day Camelot fell. He saw Mordred laying waste to the land. The Grail had eluded his grasp, driving him into excesses of fury such as even he had never felt. Knowing that Merlin had found the cup for Arthur in the Chalice Well—such is the story still passed down from that time—Mordred desecrated the place beyond redemption. Or so he thought.

The crow mind held centuries of time compressed into revelatory moments. Melchior witnessed an age of barren waste when the Chalice Well remained dry, apparently forevermore. Then one day the faintest moisture appeared among the stone ruins scattered over the ground; a faint trickle gathered, and slowly the spring started to bubble again, not with the overwhelming grace of its former depth, but not vanquished either. He saw the amazed peasants finding the trickle of clear water, saw it gather force little by little as the humble faithful prayed beside it.

Healings followed, and the approval of the Church. Then the stream of crow wisdom told him something else, something far more pressing. "What am I doing sitting here?" Melchior cawed sharply. "The king is not dead, and the business with Mordred is about to resume. I've got to get to my master before it's too late. Don't you know that?"

"We all know that," the old crow replied. Melchior flew up above the trees, his tutor rising after. Though shaped like a crow, he was still Melchior, too: a lingering wizardly awareness lodged inside his feathered body. But it was muffled, like a baby wrapped in thick velvet christening robes. His single will was feeble compared to the powerful current of the crow mind, which tossed his individuality aside like a cork on the flood.

"I've got to regain myself," he thought desperately. If he could pull his own mind out from the rest, he would be able to think, to reason a way out of his predicament. An idea struck him. If turning into a crow was the result of a miracle, perhaps he should pray for a countermiracle. Did such a thing exist? Words of his own now began to softly surface: "O God, loving Father in heaven, save this humble penitent who beseeches Thy boundless mercy from his lowly station at the foot of Thy throne." (If this seems like a flowery supplication, remember that being medieval, Melchior could invent a formidable prayer ad lib.)

However, as soon as Melchior had regained himself to the point that he could utter his plea, he forgot how to operate his bird's body. The grip of the crow mind unraveled, and he started to plummet from the sky like a rock.

Don't resist. Trust.

The crow mind brought him this useful admonition just in time—or perhaps it was actually God's reply to his prayer. In any case, Melchior nearly blacked out in free fall, which was squeezing his heart into a tight knot of terror. Only seconds before impact he forgot where he was, which fortunately allowed the crow mind to take charge again. With a deft flip of his pinion feathers he righted himself, and for the remainder of his flight, Melchior lulled his mind into nonresistance.

It was really very pleasant not to resist. He floated into deeper and deeper silence, and while the May wind rushed through his wings, a warm welling-up inside him began to expand into knowledge. The river of crow awareness wasn't just hurtling him along like a stray leaf; he was being inducted into the mysterious presence that the old crow understood so deeply. The birds had woven their lives into the suffering and turmoil of humankind. Eyes were pecked out of vanquished Saxons lying in burning rye fields ages past. Harsh caws of warning saved a Celtic king who forgot to look behind him when he took his ambitious nobles on a hunt. In whispered remembrance the crows absorbed runes imprinted by wizards and messages imparted by kings.

In the unfurling scroll of time, Merlin and Arthur flashed by, and for an instant Melchior tried to leap after them—but they were only bubbles, images dissolving like foam on the crest of a wave. So much emotion welled up in him that sorrow and gladness clashed and canceled each other out. Epochs were extinguished like brief candles; great fiefdoms were broken and thrown away like straws.

While all of this was happening in his mind, the green Somerset fields sliding below Melchior gave way to townscape. Grassy knolls turned to stone dwellings dotted with half-blind windows. He was flying up the High Street of Gramercy, the dirty rooftops of St. Justin's visible over the rise above the stream. The High Street was full of cars and people. They looked ordinary, yet at the same time different. As if he had eyes behind his eyes, the milling crowd took on the appearance of walking clouds of energy. Fogs of feeling, emotional vapors. Geysers of anger and bubbling mud pots of resentment. A ghastly landscape of lives at a slow boil beneath the pleasant humdrum of shopping and strolling.

"That woman has just lost her baby in the crowd and is frantic to find her," Melchior thought. "That man surrounded by grayness is sick with a growth inside his chest. The old woman next to him doesn't want to admit to herself that he is dying, but she knows."

These impressions filled his mind, not so much as thoughts but as direct perceptions. What a curious way to see people, as if they were not wearing masks. Every emotion that was guiltily tucked inside had been laid open for him to inspect like organs laid open for a surgeon's detached examination.

Melchior was fascinated by the lesson being imparted through the crow mind, but at the same time he didn't want to look. A person on the street would have noticed only that Gramercy was a dull market town thirty miles from the Welsh border, lined with rows of groceries, shoe shops, stationer's stands, and a post office. Potholed streets radiated from a dingy town square clogged with buses and cabs. To the wizard's apprentice, Gramercy's population wandered in numb sleep, barely emitting enough energy to remain alive.

Something new appeared, an energy that wasn't sickly gray but a shy ray of coral dawn. Melchior quickly found the source. "A young couple in love." So it was not hopeless. The young couple radiated life, but they were only a flicker in that gray landscape.

Melchior was shaken by the scene. "Camelot, Camelot," he mourned. But the crow mind was wiser. Having witnessed so much bleakness for the many centuries since Mordred won his fell victory, it didn't flinch.

Look, remember. Consider why you are here.

Melchior wanted to heed the lesson, but it confused him. "I don't know why I'm here," he thought, trying to address the crow mind. "What good is it for me to look at this horror and not be able to do anything about it?" He was suddenly wracked by the pain of a loving spirit that cannot close itself to other people's devastation.

Your pain is the key to your healing, the crow mind whispered mysteriously. Before he could absorb this idea, the apprentice felt his wings take a swift tack up and out of the High Street, and in a moment he was far above the town, wheeling in circles. At that height the air was cool, clean of human misery; for the first time he was glad that a larger will was guiding him; the numbness of humans had almost anesthetized him. "All right, I will observe and learn," he told the crow mind, and as he looked over his shoulder, he saw that he was not alone: he was leading an entire black formation toward the heart of town, a veritable murder of crows.

"Three of Swords, Ace of Cups, the World, the Fool reversed." A man's voice was calling the cards as they turned up. From across the dimmed room a woman's voice interrupted him: "Whatever you do, don't give me the Hanged Man."

The supple gentleman who dubbed himself Master Ambrosius

looked up in annoyance. "You know I don't have a choice about what cards come out." He disliked clients interrupting.

"Yes, but the Hanged Man is too disturbing. Sometimes I think I should hide it before we start." The woman sitting on the window seat turned to look outside. She was nervous when the cards were being spread, even after so many years.

"Hide a card? Most irregular. Besides, I daresay you aren't in for a Hanged Man today. The vibration is totally contradicted. There, what did I tell you? The Empress. Come and see for yourself." Master Ambrosius was sitting at a small folding table, its tea things pushed aside. He relaxed his body in the chair languorously. His raven black hair was carefully smoothed back over his scalp. The expression on his face was that of someone who had licked the creamer clean and sneaked half the sugar cubes into his pockets.

Peg Callum continued to gaze out onto the street scene below. Really, it was almost too nice a day for a reading, one of those spring days when the promise of summer swelled a thousand buds in defiance of the chill north wind.

"You look like you're waiting for someone," Master Ambrosius remarked. He was getting impatient.

"No, not someone. Just a spot of sun. And there it is. The wish is father to the deed." A patch of sunlight was moving down the High Street, propelled by a sweep of fleecy clouds. A middle-aged woman with loosely gathered dark hair, Peg Callum sat in the second-floor window of her brick house on Fellgate Lane in Gramercy. She wore a plain blue housedress and an apron she invariably forgot to remove when her guest arrived. Her face betrayed lines of care, still faintly etched at her age but nevermore to be erased. A perpetually mild expression marked her face, as if being the meek of the earth came naturally. But a lively quality shone in her eyes, a merriness that could still make her appear childlike.

"Well, turn your back if you like," Master Ambrosius said peevishly. "I suppose no one likes this first one, the Three of Swords." Peg didn't move; she loved the sun, though God knew it greeted her stingily enough. Today was generosity itself, however. A large pool of sunlight appeared, and the streets of Gramercy lit up for a moment, if one could say that grimy, soot-stained cobblestones ever light up.

Master Ambrosius had run out of patience. He stared at the five cards arranged in the shape of a squat pyramid on the spotted damask napkin. "The Three of Swords signifies conflict, distress, coming trials." He put a fleshy finger on the card, which lay at the bottom of the pyramid. It depicted a scarlet red heart pierced through with three swords. "Beware difficulties in relationships."

Peg at last got up and crossed over to the table. "Relationships? Strange thing to tell a widow. Or do you mean Arthur?"

"It could be him. Has anything happened between you?"

Peg shook her head. "It's such a dreadful card. Can't you go on?"

Master Ambrosius moved his finger one position to the right on the bottom row. "Ah, Ace of Cups—an upsurge of emotions, new relationships from an unexpected quarter. The pattern is revealing itself." He indicated the next card. "Strength, in the position of desire. Whether you know it consciously or not, you desire a man of strength. I see him coming. He may not be someone you know, or he may be someone you know whose inner nature is hidden to you."

"I won't fancy him if he looks like that. Too brutish." Peg had picked up the card of Strength. It showed a muscular giant strangling a lion with his bare hands. He was stripped to the waist; below he was girded with animal skins. His hair was long and matted. "I don't want a Hercules. I'm used to gentleness. I mean, I was." Peg stopped, disconcerted; she felt a wave of loneliness. Master Ambrosius regarded her intently. The subject of gentleness did not evoke any words from him.

Peg turned away and returned to her window seat. "Thank you for coming, but I'm not really quite myself today." No more patches of sun were traveling down the High Street anymore. She gazed out over the rooftops at the belching smokestack in the distance. How dreary and ugly it all looked, even after twenty years. Master Ambrosius said, "We do not have to finish. But it bodes ill to leave the crown of the pyramid empty. Let me put down the master card—aha!"

Whatever dramatic flourish he had in mind, it was cut short by a tap at the door. Arthur Callum stepped into the room dressed in his policeman's uniform. "Hullo, Mum, just checking in. I went into the kitchen for a spot of lunch."

"You remember Master Ambrosius, don't you, dear?"

Arthur nodded curtly; his quick glance at the tea table betrayed his distaste. "I didn't know he made house calls."

"Oh, he's just leaving."

Belying Peg's words, the cartomancer kept his seat. "You are not a student of tarot?" he asked blandly. Arthur made no reply. "Tarot is the greatest of occult mysteries, a gift of Hermes himself. It magnetizes energies according to the soul vibration of whoever touches it. Gamblers have been led to the brink of hell, the pure of heart to the gates of paradise. Exaltation, destruction, desire, whim—tarot is nothing less than the world of fate. Is the tea still warm?"

"Oh yes, forgive me, let me pour," Peg said hurriedly.

"Just an inch."

Smiling, Master Ambrosius allowed her to pour a small amount of Earl Grey. He sipped and then set the cup over the card he had just placed at the apex of the pyramid. He stood up slowly, a touch of arrogance in his deliberate movements.

"Ambrosius—if I may ask, how does someone like you acquire that sort of name?" Arthur remarked.

"Arthur, you're being rude," his mother warned.

"No, no, quite all right," Master Ambrosius said. "My name has deep significance for me. Do you recognize it?" Arthur shook his head. "Ah, pity. If you understood my name, you'd know a great deal about me."

"I'm not sure I want to," Arthur rejoined with dead quiet.

Flustered, his mother began to make weak flapping motions with her hands. Master Ambrosius tilted his head in mock courtesy. "I'll be going now," he said.

"Not on account of me, I hope," Arthur replied. But the master had found his coat, a beautifully tailored lamb's-wool overcoat absurdly too warm for the weather. He swathed himself in it and turned up the collar, which made a dramatic frame for his high, stark cheekbones. "Let me escort you out," Peg said, timidly pointing the way.

"I hope it won't make you nervous, but the police are waiting downstairs," said Arthur. Master Ambrosius did look vaguely nervous, or at least nonplussed.

"That's really too much," Peg protested.

Arthur laughed. "Sorry, Mum, I'm just teasing." Through the thin floorboards, rustling sounds from the kitchen could be heard. "Katy joined me for lunch; she's just doing a little washing up."

Master Ambrosius had resumed gliding down the carpeted stairs. Arthur and his mother followed. In the kitchen Katy Kilbride was at the sink, wiping her hands on a tea towel. "Done," she announced. The appearance of the warmly dressed stranger caught her off guard.

"This is my partner," Arthur said, "PC Kilbride."

"You look familiar," Katy remarked. Master Ambrosius ignored her and marched for the front door with Peg in tow. "Odd fellow," Katy remarked.

"Sly fellow, you mean. My mum's lonely, but attracting that type is a bad sign."

"I don't know. He's rather dashing."

Arthur shook his head. "He bears some looking into. I wonder if he doesn't have a sheet. Maybe I'll check him out."

"Quite suspicious, are we? Or a trifle jealous?" Katy seemed amused at Arthur's discomfort.

After a moment his mother returned to the kitchen alone. "I don't understand why you dislike him so," she told Arthur.

"Got to run," he said noncommittally, giving her a peck.

"Well, if you don't mind, I'm just running upstairs again. I forgot to bring down the tea things." They heard Peg tread lightly back to her room and shut the door.

Arthur said, "Listen, Katy, I'm going to ask Westlake to put me on the case full-time if he will."

Katy looked surprised. "The Merlin case? But nobody ever found him, unless there's a flash I've missed. You don't have a case when there's no stiff and no evidence of foul play."

"A broken neck could be construed as evidence of foul play."

"Can you produce the neck in court?"

"In this case the disappearance of the body is our strongest clue."

"Immaterial. In fact, most immaterial, given that you have nothing to show."

"You're a walking brief for the defense, I see," Arthur said, not quite joking anymore. Katy poised her hand threateningly over the sink, ready to splash him. "No, no," he said, "I ironed this shirt myself."

"Very impressive."

"But in point of fact, there is that glove I found at the bottom of the ditch."

"Is that really significant?"

"Well, assuming that it belonged to the old man, where's the other one? He wasn't wearing it, and besides, he was dressed too poorly for such a glove."

"Maybe he lost it on the way to the ball."

Arthur turned unexpectedly grave. "If it was hit-and-run, we need to find the culprit; if it was foul play, then all the more reason to keep at it. I just have a feeling about this one."

"I don't think Westlake buys into feelings much."

Arthur shook his head. "You're right, of course. Yesterday he told me that he was dead set against the supernatural."

"Did the supernatural come up?"

Arthur shook his head. "Not exactly, but the disappearance of a corpse from a moving ambulance couldn't be kept under wraps. The local papers picked it up, and now I believe the London rags are chewing on it. I'm a minor celebrity, in fact."

"What for?" She smiled. "Helping to lose your man?"

Arthur flinched. "That's not fair."

Katy took off her apron. "Well, I'm ready if you are."

"Right, back to work."

A few moments later they emerged onto the stoop. "Look at all those birds," Katy said absently. "Crows, aren't they?"

Arthur looked up, shielding his eyes with his hand. "I'm never sure. Crows or ravens or maybe rooks. I should know, but somehow birding was never my thing. There seem to be an awful lot of them."

Katy nodded. "You go ahead for a sec, will you? I forgot to freshen up."

Arthur looked at her. "Are you sure?"

Katy nodded and stepped back inside. She shut the door and leaned against it. A feeling of doom had hit her quite suddenly and hard, as if she'd had a telegram about a death in the family. She breathed softly, not moving. Upstairs she heard his mother's footsteps, then a chair being moved. "Get hold of yourself," she said, then opened the door again. Arthur had already set off down the street; she followed a dozen yards behind, waiting for her strange emotion to pass.

The birds that thickened the gray sky continued to circle at a distance, except for two particularly large specimens who approached the house and landed directly on the windowsill outside the second-floor bedroom. They peered inside. The window was shut, but the curtains were not drawn. Peg was bent over her tea table, intently staring. She had cleared the spotted damask napkin and put almost all the tea things on the tray, except for one cup. Lifting it, she saw a card. "The Hanged Man," it read in Gothic black letter. The splayed corpse of a naked man was depicted, suspended upside down from a high rock. A large bird of prey was hovering over it with sharpened beak.

Peg's hand came to her mouth. What had Master Ambrosius said? *It bodes ill to leave the crown of the pyramid empty.* She looked at the swooping bird; the card was too small to make out the expression on the hanged man's face. Worried, Peg didn't look up to see the two crows outside her window. The pair hadn't flown away or even budged. Their bodies were as intently motionless as hers—for all the world one would have thought that they, too, were students of tarot.

When Arthur and Katy reached the station, he left her in the squad room and headed directly for Chief Inspector Westlake's office. "Ah, Callum, come in," the inspector greeted him. "Monstrously stupid, this tabloid rot. 'Where Is Merlin? Wizard Pulls Disappearing Act.' No doubt the ambulance drivers clued them in on that ridiculous name. But we let ourselves in for it, I suppose," he sighed.

"Actually, I think there may be something to this Merlin business, sir."

Westlake looked at Arthur with irritation. "You have a lightning bolt, Callum?" he asked ironically.

"I'm not sure. I just had the notion that our man's appearance might not be just an eccentricity. Do you know about druids, sir?" Westlake raised his eyebrows. "A lot of them look like our missing man. I mean the ones you see on television."

"You are a regular viewer of druids on television?" Westlake muttered.

"I'm sorry, sir, let me explain. Every year at midsummer's eve the people who call themselves druids show up at Stonehenge. It's a kind of cult. They wear white robes and quite a few sport long white beards. No one knows what druids—I mean the real ones—looked like, but in the popular mind, one thinks of them looking like Merlin. Or vice versa. Merlin, I believe, is often considered to be a druid. Our dead man conceivably could be associated with these people. With your permission, sir, I'd like to check up on it."

Westlake greeted this speech without comment. He was holding his chin in his hand, open-eyed, as if he were a scientist examining a rare specimen. "Is there more?" he asked dryly.

Arthur took a breath. "My mother has a relative named Derek Rees—Sir Derek Rees, actually—who knows a great deal about this druid business. It wouldn't be any trouble to contact him, in an unofficial capacity if you prefer—" Arthur stopped abruptly as Westlake stood up.

"Good day, Callum," he said, turning toward the window and putting his back to the young constable.

"Um, do you want me to pursue this line of inquiry, sir?" Arthur asked uneasily.

Westlake glanced over his shoulder. "As far as I can gather, everything you've said has been in the vein of personal conjecture. What you do with your time is your own business." He picked up a pair of binoculars lying on the windowsill and began to intently examine the fauna in a large yew tree across the lawn. As an afterthought he said, "You've proved yourself to be not altogether stupid. I told you at the crime scene that I didn't think it was murder, but I didn't tell you why. Exoticism. The whole thing is too exotic. When a detective is starting out green, as you are, it's appealing to come up with complicated explanations for unexplained events. But these twisted hypotheses hardly ever pan out. Our man, I warrant, was hit by a car, and even though he wound up too far from the road, what's to prevent a frightened driver from stopping and pushing the body into the ditch? It would be cruel and cowardly and a bit unusual, I admit, but it would also be simple. Do you understand?"

Arthur nodded doubtfully. Westlake examined him for a moment, picking up the younger man's frustration and deciding how to respond to it. "Look, if you happen to hit upon a credible line of investigation, I shall be here. But don't expect me to accompany you down every twist in the lane." He raised his binoculars again to scrutinize a mantled ground squirrel. The interview was over.

8

A BOY AND HIS SWORD

WHEN EDGERTON WOKE UP THE NEXT MORNING, HE KNEW THE sword must have been a dream. He curled on his side, squeezing his eyes shut to pretend that the sun wasn't up. He seemed to have slept a long time. There was a sharp rap on the door.

"Squirm," a voice said cheerfully from the other side. Edgerton waited for it to go away. "C'mon, Squirm, join the human race, it's almost nine." His sister Winnie burst into the room. "Why aren't you up? It's a school day." She was twenty-two and thought she could treat him like his mother.

"This is my bloody room, and you have no right to be in it," Edgerton said hostilely.

Winnie looked unperturbed. "That still doesn't explain why you're in bed so long."

"I'm sick."

"Do you have glands or something?" His sister looked skeptical. "Hurry up. Better late than never." Edgerton buried himself under the covers and grunted. "Look, I've got to pop round to the stationers for a sec. You want anything?" Edgerton shook his head under the blanket. "Come on, Hamish has the morning off. We could walk you partway to school."

With a jerk Winnie pulled the covers from the bed and tossed them against the closet door. Edgerton was about to yell when he saw a glint of steel glimmering under the box springs. *It's true!* His breath caught in his throat, and he knew Winnie mustn't see the sword. "Okay, I'll come. Just wait while I wash up." He stumbled over to the basin in the corner of the room. "Alone," he added with a glare.

"Oh, the maiden blush," Winnie mocked, slamming the door behind her. Edgerton heard her clumping down the stairs. Muffled voices could be heard, followed by laughter. He jumped out of bed and pulled on some rumpled clothes. Standing at the uncleaned basin with its familiar hairline crack running from rim to drain, the boy splashed cold water on his face, rubbed it dry with a dirty jersey from the floor, and ran back over to the bed.

It was there. The blade lay like a tense thoroughbred restless to leap into action. Edgerton pulled it out from under the bed. Where was the scabbard? Searching with his fingers, he found it under the mattress, too, just where he dreamed he had left it. Pearls of sunlight rolled off the blade's edge—it was so beautiful. He could kill anybody with this. Impetuously, he grabbed the hilt, his arm swung high, and the shifted weight of the sword pitched him over. With an effort he managed to right himself without dropping the weapon. Ashamed, he wondered if he was too little to wield the blade.

It was just a matter of balance, he thought. He seized the hilt with both hands and raised it over his head. Yes, that was better.

"Dear?" a voice said on the other side of the door. He hadn't even heard Mum come upstairs. Panicked, he dropped the weapon, which plunged six inches into the mattress, ripping a gash in the bottom sheet and feather bed. A puff of pinfeathers filled the air. "Are you there?" their mum asked a little louder, but still timidly. "I've got a nice cup of mocha here for you." She wasn't the kind to enter without knocking. With a tug Edgerton wrenched the sword out of the mattress, spraying more feathers around, and shoved it under the bed.

"Come in, won't you? Didn't you hear me say come in?"

"Why, no, I'm sorry," Edie Edgerton said, placing the thick

white crockery cup on the bedside table. She had filled it too much; brown splotches of mocha spilled onto the night table and dribbled over the edge. Ignoring this, she noticed the feathers and picked up a handful. "Feathers," she murmured distractedly. She stared at them as if they might have migrated in through the window. You never knew what was going on in Mum's head sometimes.

She let the feathers fall from her hand and brushed her skirt. "Oh, good, you're dressed for school. Are they treating you nicer there? I know it's tempting to hide sometimes, but your dad and I think it's important. We only wish we had had your opportunity." He glared at her and didn't reply. "Give it time," she said in feeble reassurance. "Boys hold a hard grudge, but they'll come around, you'll see. I know you don't have it easy, the Edgertons never do."

Edie shook her head wistfully, touched his cheek, and padded away. Her fingers seemed to leave a burning mark behind. "Just leave me alone," he thought. He finished putting on his school tie and rushed downstairs. The Haggis was standing at the bottom of the stairs. His real name, Hamish McPhee, was Scottish. He was a copper, several years older than Winnie.

"Hullo," the Haggis said cheerfully. "She's waitin' for us." Edgerton brushed by without comment.

Winnie was sitting on the stoop looking at the sky. Their house, on one of the poorer streets, Mogg Street, was three blocks from the Callums on Fellgate Lane. To one side of the stoop Edie Edgerton was absorbed in a clump of seedy chrysanthemums she had wintered over under a bushel basket. "Good as new," she said brightly, poking at the clump of dead brown stems. *Welcome to the loony bin,* Edgerton thought. His sister and her boyfriend started heading toward Wink Hill, in the direction of school. He followed. "Look," Edgerton said, "was there a murder on the motorway yesterday afternoon or not?" Winnie flinched and the Haggis looked annoyed.

"Oh, so Tommy Ashcroft blabbed to you," the policeman said, his lips pressed tight. "It's a body so far, lad, not a murder."

"Did his brains drip out of his nose and everything?" Edgerton asked.

The Haggis ignored this provocation. "That's the strange bit," he said, addressing his reply to Winnie. "There was not a scratch on the body despite the broken neck. Pathology probably don't believe the report. Fortunately, the chief was there and saw it with his own eyes." The press had covered the events in such detail that Hamish McPhee felt free to open up, within limits. "We don't know as yet who the poor bloke was. I thought maybe he was an old duff who wandered into the road from the local geriatrics infirmary, but they said he wasn't one of theirs. And now God knows where he is."

"Burning in hell for all I care," Edgerton muttered.

The Haggis turned on him. "What's eating you?"

"He's just at that age," Winnie said.

Edgerton ignored her. "Was his money gone?"

The Haggis shook his head. "No more now," he said firmly. "Here's your turnoff for school."

"If they don't find him, will you be demoted?" Edgerton pressed. "Since you lost him."

"I said not now. And it wasn't me that lost him."

"That's right. A meter maid wouldn't have that kind of responsibility."

"That's the limit," Winnie burst out. "No wonder nobody will have anything to do with you. I've never seen such a horrid little—!" She was so vexed she looked about to cry.

"Say you're sorry," McPhee ordered, his voice cold.

"She's a cow."

"Now say you're doubly sorry," McPhee demanded. He was going red.

"Make me."

"God already made you, and a sorry excuse of a job that was," McPhee shot back. Edgerton broke away and ran in the opposite direction. "Hey," McPhee called after him. "School's that way." Edgerton kept going into the park. He dashed past two twin toddlers in rompers who were dipping their hands in a dirty pond rimmed with a concrete retaining wall. Their mother tried to pull them away and they screamed.

I could kill you now if I wanted to, was all he could think. *You shouldn't even be around our dad and mum and me. If anyone would marry you, you wouldn't be in the house.* He ran out of the park around the corner into the High Street and lapped the block before doubling back toward Mogg Street. He didn't want anyone to track where he was heading, although for the life of him, he didn't know why.

The front door was open and their mum was shaking out a filthy rag rug on the stoop. "Forget something?" she murmured as he ran past her. He rushed upstairs, slammed the door, and stood there panting in the middle of his room. The whole house was quiet. He couldn't hear any sign of their dad, who always slept late. Father and son had that desire in common. Only their dad had more chance to sleep in since the accident that smashed his foot. "The king rises last," he liked to say, although the loss of his job was a grim business that had thrown the family into near-poverty.

Winnie hates it because our dad is more like me, Edgerton thought. Their family seemed to have no center and hadn't for three years now. Their dad refused to retrain for a job that would keep him off his feet; he was waiting for his rights, he said, expecting the print shop where he was injured to pay him off in huge damages. A shyster kept this fantasy alive while he spent his days brooding about the failure of the courts to give him justice.

Edgerton felt renewed anger washing over him, blotting out his hidden fear. Their dad was contemptuous of the school where his son went. "We weren't charity cases before this 'appened, and we shouldn't be now," he maintained.

Edgerton crossed his room and pulled out the sword from under the bed. He blew off a few stray feathers. Somehow it felt lighter this time and more suited to his grip. He had large hands for a thirteen-year-old, big enough to grasp a soccer ball securely. He examined his prize. Yes, there were jewels on the hilt; smoky topazes laced in French curves and between them knobby tourmalines that kept his grip secure. He liked the heavy swing of the blade; his body swayed as he learned its rhythm, making the sword go left and right just so, not enough to topple him, but wide past his hips.

He went into himself and smiled at his power. *I could kill them all now.* The thought stopped him in midswing; he realized that it was the third time that day he had considered killing. Why did the voice keep coming back to that? Yet how natural the voice seemed, how easily he turned toward violence when it beckoned.

Edgerton's hands grew hot gripping the hilt, and he felt a sharp throbbing in his wrists; sinewy bands stood out on his forearms. The blade's weight was making his fingers ache, and he knew he would have to practice alone like this, secretly, before he struck. *If* he decided to strike. Now it was his decision; they didn't have the power anymore.

That's right. There's plenty of time. There's plenty of ways to make them pay.

The voice was like a stranger who dropped into your sitting room one Sunday, informing you it was your friend. You didn't remember having a friend like that, but since he wouldn't leave, you had no choice—the stranger became a friend.

And the stranger told Edgerton what he wanted to hear, that he wasn't the only bad one. For such a long time that was his deepest fear, that in all the world he had been cursed to be the bad one. *They're as bad as you are. They're dirty inside. The best of them is filthy dirty, don't you know that? They don't want to admit it; they're too weak. So they chose you to punish. Hurt them, and they won't be able to hurt you anymore. Show them how bad you can be.*

Then the stranger's voice said the most seductive thing of all: *Hurt them enough, and then you'll know they can't hurt you.*

Now the stranger's voice sounded as if it was outside his head. The sword dropped from his grip; his chest was heaving hard, then harder. Only crazy people heard voices. Oh God, he mustn't start crying. If he was crazy—

You're not crazy. They just want to make you crazy. Be strong. That's why you have to punish them, so you won't be crazy anymore.

His knees went weak, and he turned to see himself in the mirror. A dark, shadowy aura surrounded his body. He couldn't see it straight on, but he could catch it at a glance as he turned toward the glass. The aura was elusive. It darted out of sight the instant he knew he had seen it. Black and dirty-transparent, like a bat's webbed wing-skin, it clung to his head and flowed down around his body. Seeing this was too much. Edgerton bolted from the room and ran downstairs. Bursting through the swinging doors from the dining room, he saw his father reaching up from his wheelchair, half-standing; he was putting a bottle back on the shelf.

"What's with you?" his father grumbled. He wiped his mouth with the back of his hand as the whiskey smell reached the boy from across the room. Edgerton shrank back. "What in hell's that thing in your hand? Where's the pageant?" his father mocked. The boy looked down. He had dragged the sword with him downstairs.

"Uh, I got it at school," Edgerton mumbled. He started to back out of the room.

His father sank back into the wheelchair and pulled a blanket over his legs. "Why aren't you in school?" he asked irritably. "If we're layin' out three quid for that fancy tie, you needn't fool around wearin' it at home. Nobody's impressed, I can tell you." He started to roll toward the boy. Edgerton backed into the dining room.

"Come here," their dad said menacingly. "I've got somethin' to show you." The boy hesitated, not knowing whether to stand his ground or run upstairs.

This is the time. Kill him, the stranger's voice commanded. The boy saw himself in the pier glass hanging in the hallway opposite the stairs. The dark aura was still there; he trembled anxiously. The voice had never commanded him to act before.

"Give me that thing." His father was in front of the boy now, holding his hand out. Edgerton glanced down at the sword. He shook his head and slowly, carefully, raised the blade. It was amazingly light, as if his arms had never been tired. They felt twice as strong as he had ever felt them. Like a man's. And all he wanted was to be a man. His father's eyes grew wide, undecided between amazement and fear. The two stood frozen for a second. "Give it me," his father muttered, raising his hand to strike the boy.

The next sequence of events became blurred. The door opened. "Paddy, you should be resting," a voice said—it was their mum.

"Restin', hell!" their dad replied, scowling at her. He had turned his back, and the boy raised the blade higher.

Strike!

Edgerton was no longer in control. In sudden fear he wanted to warn his father, but no words came out, and he felt himself rearing the sword to smash it into his father's spine when an old man touched his hand.

"Don't do this," the old man said softly. Edgerton's eyes grew wild. He whipped around toward the mirror—the dark aura was gone.

"What's wrong?" their mum asked.

"Leave him be, he's trainin' for a ridiculous pageant," their dad said. They didn't seem to see the old man in the room. A shudder coursed through the boy's body, the sword dropped with a clatter, and the old man's arms went out to catch him from falling.

"Remember this," he whispered. "This is the evil you were born to resist. You will not find me easily again, but try, you must try." And then he said the most amazing thing of all: "I will see you through the fire." A burst of loving light glowed around the boy, shimmering blue and green like the sea, and the last thing he remembered as the light engulfed him was the wizard's white beard, luxuriant against his robe of moons and stars.

Arthur's car turned into the driveway leading to his uncle's house. He had never actually set eyes on Emrys Hall. Judging by the entrance, it would be awesomely grand. Row after row of ancestral beech trees lined the way like a hushed honor guard. The manor house itself was hidden around a bend. Whoever planted this alley over two centuries ago must have wanted just this effect of slowly drawing aside a curtain, and it was worth waiting for. As Arthur's black Ford compact turned the corner, the greenery parted, exposing a magnificent three-story manse wrought in huge blocks of golden Bath stone.

"What am I doing here?" Arthur asked himself. He wasn't exactly sure of a welcome, and he wished that he hadn't been so bold about telling Westlake that the house's owner, Sir Derek Rees, was his relation. In a court of law the claim would have stood up. Forty years ago his mother's half sister, Penelope, had left home to marry the rising young luminary Derek Rees, but after that there had been no contact with Arthur's side of the family. The two sisters had been born almost fifteen years apart and barely lived in the same world, even before Penelope left home.

"Go on, up to the front door," the young constable encouraged himself. He couldn't help but notice that the gravel crunching beneath the car's tires was also golden, in perfect harmony with the stone walls of the house. But then you were meant to notice. His rumpled coat and coffee-stained tie felt suddenly rather shabby. His car hadn't been washed in a fortnight, and the little Ford had several dents in its side that he hadn't bothered to have the body shop knock out. Ah, well, poor relations.

Arthur had been ten years old before he learned of the family link between his mother and one of the richest families in the county. "You shouldn't have married for love, Peg," his father had said one morning over Sunday scones and jam. "I'm ashamed to say that I've made you domestically disadvantaged."

His mother was clearing the table. "What do you mean, dear?" she asked mildly.

He shoved a copy of the *Observer* across the checkered oilcloth. "Look how your sister's improved her lot." The rotogravure section sported a gushing article on county gentry, and the centerpiece was a color photo of Emrys Hall. The house was fronted by an army of blazing yellow daffodils that seemed to take spring by storm.

"How astonishing," his mother said admiringly. "It must be the largest house in Somerset, don't you think?"

"Don't take a fancy to it, I can't give you one," Frederick Callum replied. He was a writer of advanced novels, which Arthur found out, even at ten years old, meant novels that didn't sell. Being wildly unsuccessful seemed to suit his father. He was the kind of man who would rather dwell in proud obscurity than give an inch to public taste.

Sitting at the breakfast table, Arthur had glanced curiously at the picture of the overweening house and the middle-aged couple standing tweedily before it.

"That's your uncle, technically speaking," his father said. "Uncle Derek and Aunt Penelope."

"We used to be called Peg and Pen," his mother said. "When I was four and saw a pigpen at a farm, my sister said it was named after us." She laughed, but Arthur remembered a tinge of distant sadness in her voice.

"Technically speaking? What does that mean?" Arthur asked.

"It means they don't talk to us, but we'll be obliged to dress uncomfortably and attend their funerals," his father replied. Peg gave him a look. Undaunted, he pointed to the pair in the picture. "Perhaps we will survive the whole lot and inherit this great swag of a place. Nobility is notoriously prone to rot—drunken lords falling downstairs and all that. If you're lucky, you might get the hulk for a few hundred thousand in inheritance duties. But I should warn you, it takes real cash to maintain these leviathans. That's what tells. Upkeep." Arthur and his mother were both entertained by this bit of breakfast rhetoric, but the boy never heard of Uncle Derek or Aunt Penelope again.

Pondering these faint blood connections, Arthur pulled up to the looming facade of the house, glowing in the sun like a banker's smile, and got out. Upkeep. There was no doubt that someone attended to it here. The topmost windows of the maids' garret shone as brightly as the French doors on the ground story; the massive matched oak doors loomed before him. Arthur put his finger to the polished doorbell, which looked to be made of gold, and waited. The butler, when he slowly opened the portal, revealed an endless stretch of marble in his wake.

"Police," Arthur announced, a shade too gruffly. "I'm here on an unofficial call. Is Sir Derek at home?"

For some reason the butler seemed to flinch. "Are you expected?" he asked, shifting his body to make it apparent that police visits, even if unofficial, were not welcome. Arthur wondered why.

"There's been a crime committed in the vicinity, and I'd like to ask your master a few questions."

The butler's expression was as blank as the gray marble that covered the walls, floors, and ceiling behind him. "By all means, come in. I will announce you if you would be so kind as to identify yourself."

"The duke of Windsor," Arthur said, but only in his mind. He rummaged in his wallet and handed over one of his new cards. "I'll need that back, by the way," he remarked as the butler put the card on a small silver tray and marched off.

Arthur's father had once commented, "The extinction of the English butler—the real article, not these jump-ups pretending to be stuffed auks—occurred more swiftly than that of the dodo. There were fully three thousand privately employed butlers in this country during the decade before World War Two and no more than eighty in the decade that followed. Interesting, to say the least."

"Is that true?" his mother had asked, impressed.

"Statistics are always true unless you personally know who made them up," Frederick Callum replied. Arthur's father intensely disapproved of the existence of any kind of serving class. Arthur never saw him go to a bootblack, and no cleaning women were allowed in the house.

"You don't look like the police. You're too young."

Arthur turned to confront a woman, presumably Penelope Rees, descending a curved staircase in the near distance. She was squinting fiercely at his police card, as if she intended to burn a hole through it.

"I'm Police Constable Callum," Arthur said uneasily.

"Bosh. You're Arthur, Peg's boy. Peg and Pen. I'm not old enough to forget that."

Lady Penelope must have been approaching sixty. She was tall and willowy, not gaunt but a touch too thin to be considered elegant. She wore a black dressing gown of brocaded silk and matching slippers with green dragons embroidered on them. Her hair was black and pulled back in a knot, except for an unruly streak of white in the middle. This sprang up, refusing to be tamed. Her eyes were dark and witchy.

"I'm very glad to meet you at last. Mum—Mother would be delighted to see you, too," Arthur said tentatively. "Am I intruding?"

Penelope Rees's face remained masklike as she appraised her

nephew. "You must be frightfully new at policeman's work. I've never heard a more soothing introduction. I'm not being arrested for eighty-five unpaid parking tickets, then?"

"No."

The witchy look disappeared from her eyes. "If the town can't put parking spaces where I need them, is it my fault?" Lady Penelope smiled, and the sudden change startled him. It was like seeing a Roman bust crack. Arthur reached out his hand, which was grasped warmly. "Pardon my attire. I've been studying the books of mysteries all morning. Rather in your line of work, Police Constable. Tea?"

Arthur shook his head. "I'm here on official business." It wasn't a bright response.

"I thought Jasper told me this was an unofficial call. And since when does police business preclude the drinking of tea?"

Arthur glanced around. "You're right, it is an unofficial call, but the subject is official."

"How odd. Let's have tea anyway. It's very fine Assam and will calm your nerves." His aunt's voice sounded extremely tolerant now.

Arthur relaxed. You needn't be so defensive, he told himself. There was no reason to believe that Penelope Rees, even if she had never written or called in thirty years, would turn out to be a threat. He followed her into the main drawing room, where Jasper the butler had already set tea. On a tufted settee silver pots jostled Limoges cups as thin as eggshells. The tea service looked out over extensive gardens. They were models of upkeep, too, but in the English landscape style, where infinite care is taken to make everything appear spontaneous. The near vista was populated with blowsy tapestry hedges that must have been two hundred years old.

"I should warn you, I'm cracked," Lady Penelope remarked as she poured a limpid stream of delectable-smelling tea into his cup.

"Pardon?"

"Cracked. Funny in the head. It's been an interesting experience, and the only thing I've been able to do about it is to delve into the books of mystery. Divine madness and insanity are closely related, as you know. You would know, I mean, as a dedicated reader of my husband's books." Arthur didn't know if she was joking or probing. He had been aware ever since he was a boy that Derek Rees was a famous expert in the lore of ancient Britain. For as many years as Arthur could remember, as soon as a new Rees volume was published, a copy would arrive in the post "compliments of the author."

The glossy volumes on Celtic wizardry and druid sacrifices stood on a shelf in the Callum home, not to be touched. "They're dumped on us like orphaned children, dropping through the slot," his father would grumble. Arthur had to sneak the books down whenever he was tempted to gaze at the wonderful ghastly pictures. These were pure melodrama. In one, a wild-eyed priest brandished an obsidian dagger, while a terrified maiden (her milky breast exposed through a flimsy shift) cringed before her death blow. When he was ten, Arthur had actually torn that one out and kept it under his pillow. He knew it pained his father that Derek Rees was immensely popular: "History? It's conjecture and fairy tales slicked up into rubbish." When a knighthood was bestowed on Rees, the Callum family permitted the event to pass without comment.

Arthur changed the subject. "Why do you say you're cracked?"

"Because extraordinary things have been happening to me lately. The only rational explanation is that I've lost my wits. Unless, of course, one chooses to toss out rationality altogether. I'm considering that course if all else fails."

"What kinds of extraordinary things?"

"Strangely enough, things that are not so very different from your situation. I read the papers, you know. The Merlin case and all that. You would think the druids are back."

"That's exactly what I've come to talk to you about. How amazing."

His aunt nodded. "That's another novel aspect of being cracked. I knew that you were coming and why. We've never met, but I had a feeling you'd want my husband's advice."

Arthur set down his teacup. "How did you know?"

She shook her head. "It's quite uncanny. So is the disappearance of my husband the day before last, not to mention the inexplicable object he left behind. It's all so uncanny that sometimes I wake up at night in semihysterics."

Penelope Rees stood up and crossed the room; when she returned, she had a black velveteen bag in her hands. "I'm willing to talk candidly to you about absolutely everything, but first I must show you this." She placed the bag down on the tea tray and slowly removed its contents. "What do you think of that?"

Arthur's gaze was pulled down to a flat, round stone on the table. It was hardly an extraordinary sight at first. He looked blankly at his aunt, then glanced down again at the round stone, large enough so that he couldn't span it with one hand. He picked it up, finding that the stone was almost a perfect disk, worn smooth by centuries of water running over it. "I don't think anything about it. Should I?" he asked.

A look crossed Lady Penelope's face, her eccentricity replaced by graveness. "This stone was delivered to me when my husband disappeared. One quite ordinary evening he walked out the door, saying that he was going to fetch some pipe tobacco in the village. As usual he set out on foot. My husband was fond of walking. We have not seen him since. That night, on the verge of calling the police, I ventured outside after I saw a shadowy figure I couldn't make out lurking near the maze."

Arthur looked confused.

"We have an old maze, you see, planted even before this house was built. When I saw this figure, I should have called out; I should have been frightened. I wasn't. The figure strode into the maze, and I decided to follow. Our maze is still original, made of yew trees so thick you can't pass three fingers through them. Try as I might, I found no one inside. All I found was this." She pointed to the stone, now replaced on the table.

"Are you implying that your husband might have delivered this to you? That's who the shadowy figure was?"

"You listen well. I approve. Yes, I simply had a feeling—for it was much too dark to see—that he had come back."

"Why didn't he stay or at least speak to you?"

"Call it another uncanny moment. I know you are wondering why I never reported my husband's absence. If you'll humor me, I can explain that, and several other things as well. What you need to accept now, if you can, is that this stone is a more important clue to your Merlin case than the druids, though they may also figure into it before all is said and done."

During this unexpected and baffling speech, neither Arthur nor Penelope looked out the windows facing the garden. Therefore they missed the gathering of crows sitting silently in one of the ancestral copper beeches, as thick as black fruit on a giant fig tree. Lady Penelope gestured to the stone. "Turn it over. See anything?"

At first Arthur couldn't. The rock was commonplace. Minute cracks ran here and there over its surface. It seemed only a little odd that one side of the stone wasn't quite as smooth as the other. Arthur got up and walked over to the window to get better light.

"Oh, I see what you mean. There's writing in and among the cracks. Someone's scratched a name or words on it. I can't really make it out too well. Here we go—'Clas Myrddin.' Yes, that's what it says."

He looked over at his aunt, who had changed dramatically. Her face was white, and when she managed to speak, she said, "So you see the words? Thank God. I'm tremendously glad, my dear, but I have bad news. You're cracked, too." Arthur felt a wave of premonition tingle across his skin. The tall woman with the witchy eyes seemed to feel it at the same time. She was on the verge of tears; quietly she said, "We could be going through quite a lot together. You had better start calling me Pen."

9
CLAS MYRDDIN

"ARE YOU AWAKE?" THE OLD CROW ASKED.

"Yes," Melchior replied. "I'm too restless to nap."

"Restless? I'm feeling a bit of that myself. Perhaps you've infected me. I've never been restless before," the old crow mused. "Do hold on to that branch a little tighter."

Melchior just caught himself from toppling as a gust of wind came up. The copper beech that they were perched in swayed to one side like a tipsy dancer. Although the flock was mostly asleep in the warm afternoon sun, all the other crows instinctively tightened their grip; it was a reflex Melchior would have to practice. But how does one practice anything asleep?

"The truth is, I'm feeling altogether queer," the old crow confessed. He looked around nervously. "I have a suspicion that I'm entertaining notions. And frankly, if you can keep a secret, I don't think the others are having them." The birds that were dozing nearby slumbered peacefully, untroubled by bad dreams.

"I suppose that's the drawback of sharing everybody else's mind," Melchior said. "You can't have your own thoughts without feeling that you're a traitor."

"Yes, something like that," the old crow said hastily. "Don't talk so loudly if you please." A few crows shuffled uneasily; there were faint caws of distress from the treetops. An outbreak of free will had never occurred among their kind, and the merest hint of one was disturbing.

"What sort of notions were you having?" Melchior asked softly.

"Don't laugh, but I can't stop seeing humans as plucked angels."

"Plucked?"

"Featherless. Wingless, too. I've never actually witnessed a human when it hatches—perhaps they wear pinfeathers then. But naked they certainly are. Put them in the sun and they die of heatstroke; stick them in the snow and they die of frost. I can easily punch a claw through their soft hide, and their idea of flying is to huddle inside giant metal tubes in abject fear of crashing. Pathetic."

Melchior wanted to protest, but the old crow cut him short. "It's almost ludicrous that a race as superior as crows should have to mind after them. And they take a deal of minding, I can tell you. Look at that deluded pair." The old crow nodded toward Arthur and his aunt, who could be glimpsed through the French doors on the garden side of Emrys Hall. "Inexcusable. Standing on the brink of disaster and barely suspecting that the predator's talons could rake their backs at any moment. No wonder they need omens."

"There will be talons soon enough," Melchior agreed. He glanced up at the dark leaves rustling overhead. All at once their brownish purple hue made them look stained with dried blood.

The old crow put on a wise look and said, "Best to wish yourself clean of the whole lot. I'm amazed that I've even started to think about them."

"But you have anyway. So have I."

"Ah, perhaps it is you that has infected me. In that case, I'd just as soon go back to sleep." The old crow fluffed himself up into a round, black ball and closed his eyes.

"Don't fall asleep. You shouldn't ignore your notions. They may be valuable." The old bird emitted a counterfeit snore. "My fate is tied up with these humans. Are they angels, even plucked ones?"

The old crow, who had a liking for metaphysics, propped one eyelid open and said, "Any sensible creature would call them devils. Puffballs of vanity when they're not being absurdly violent; wretchedly unhappy in their mental prisons and too stubborn to open the door and escape. They are a total waste of spirit, by and large." Melchior pondered this dismal judgment. "The problem with you is that you're tenderhearted," the old crow continued. "You'd save them if you could, wouldn't you? Well, if you try, they will tear you to pieces. Fat lot of consideration they ever showed you to begin with. The best of you wizards has been trivialized and shunned. You're an extinct race, as far as *they're* concerned. Almost extinct, I suppose, given that you showed up. I wonder why."

The grizzled bird fixed a beady accusatory eye upon the apprentice. Melchior looked anxious and said, "I feel the gathering of a great evil. An unfinished battle is going to be rejoined. Do you sense it?"

"Of course. So do we all. Rather rich pickings in these combats, carrion-wise," the old crow remarked calmly. Using his beak like a surgeon's forceps, he delicately picked a flea from his breast plumage and nibbled at it.

Melchior felt the strangest sensations. He wanted to help Arthur in the struggle to come, yet the prospect of fresh corpses to pick at—split skulls and eye sockets to probe daintily, finger joints to crack like lobster claws—made him incredibly hungry. "Shouldn't we warn somebody?" he burst out.

"And miss a feast? We're here to wait. There may be messages to carry. Perhaps we'll be needed as portents of catastrophe. Our role is to accept our role, as always."

Melchior subsided; the old crow's fit of free will had clearly passed. For his part, Melchior was growing unhappy with the murder of crows. They had been patiently following Arthur for hours, trailing him from town to country. The crow clan didn't rush things. They had a saying, "We will know when we know." By contrast, Melchior felt a compulsive curiosity, an urge to pierce the veil of the future. This urge seemed as pointless to the crow mind as compassion.

It dawned on Melchior that a common thread was running through his life. Whether he was an apprentice in a tower or a crow in a tree, he was constantly being misunderstood. But why? Why couldn't his mind settle into the grooves that made other lives run so smoothly? Why, to begin with, was he set apart as not quite human and yet not quite a wizard?

He was on the verge of sinking into melancholy when he noticed something new. The slant of the waning sun had made it difficult to see into the room where Arthur stood; now he was no more than a vaguely familiar outline. Now the light shifted, revealing the room's deeper recesses, and a thrill of recognition ran through Melchior. "The stone! They have it," he gasped. Impatience leapt up in him like a bolting horse. "I'm going down there," he announced loudly. "Will you come with me?" He glanced over at the old crow, who looked too drowsy to move. A shady canopy of leaves shielded away the heat and protected him from attacks by His Lordship the Eagle (such attacks were the old crow's obsession, although eagles had long since abandoned Britain and flown elsewhere).

"Please come with me," Melchior implored once more. "You said you were my only friend. We're needed down there." He knew that he was being studiously ignored, so he drew up on his wiry black legs, poised for flight.

"Down there? Why bother?" the old crow muttered. "Go to sleep. Events will summon us when need be. Race ahead of a chariot and it might crush you under its wheels." At just this moment Arthur stepped closer to the window, holding the round, flat stone up to the light.

"Do you see that?" Melchior exclaimed, almost beside himself.

"The stone, you mean? Nothing has been imparted to us about that."

"It's the Alkahest, don't you see? It's the most precious object in the world," Melchior blurted out.

"I doubt that," the old bird said coldly. "It's a larger than average river rock." A glint entered his eye. "Alkahest? I do recall, let me see." He pondered deeply. "Yes, now I'm quite sure. There was an old word of the sort you refer to—I'm not sure you speak it quite right—but the stone is valueless. We have journeyed in the train of kings. As I recall, no *diamant,* sapphire, or smergadine goes by that name."

"Ah, so you don't see," Melchior said regretfully. "I may be the only one who does. You said these humans are a waste of spirit. I almost believed you, but the stone proves you're wrong. I have to go down there."

"Don't be absurd. What will you find that we won't soon know all together?"

"I have a clue. If my master is not here, or if I can't find him, then the Alkahest is the best I can do," Melchior said breathlessly.

"Your tender heart will be roasted on a spit."

Melchior didn't heed the old crow—he had already swooped down and alighted on a golden cornice above the drawing room. An overwhelming urge made him want to rush in and touch the stone or, if he could, release its powers.

The sharp clatter of wings against the glass startled Arthur. "How extraordinary," he said. "Did you see that?"

"It's coming back," Pen said. The large crow backed away from the French doors for a second, then once more launched its body full force against the panes.

"It's going to hurt itself."

"I'll call Jasper." Pen went to an old-fashioned tassle pull-rope and rang. The impetuous bird persisted in its assaults. It was not heavy enough to break it, yet every time its beak smashed directly into the window, a veined crack spread across the glazing like jagged lightning. Arthur knew that glass was essentially invisible to birds. As a small child he had chanced across dead sparrows beneath the shubbery after they had smashed themselves against a window. The first time it happened, he had carried the crumpled feathery heap around in his pocket, desperate to coax it back to life.

But this crow wasn't a hapless victim. It seemed to be deliberately trying to force entry, and when his aunt waved her arms to spook it away, the bird only beat its wings harder. A moment later Jasper was dispatched to handle the disturbance. Unexpectedly the crow ceased its onslaught and flew out of sight; it must have become exhausted.

"I don't see it anymore. You're not superstitious, are you?" Pen asked. Arthur shook his head. “Pity,” Pen murmured. “I’ve been forced to rely on superstition just to survive. This event means something. It’s another piece of the puzzle, a clue to the mystery we’re living through.” Arthur looked perplexed. “Oh yes, we’re not detectives,” Pen continued. “Despite your uniform, which I’m very grateful you dispensed with today, our job isn’t to solve mysteries. It’s to live them. I just hope we’re not so stupid that we miss the vital clues.” She stopped abruptly and retreated into a private, impenetrable space. After an awkward silence Arthur decided to pick up the thread where they had left it.

“I’m still awfully confused. These words etched into the rock don’t mean anything to me. Why did you say I was cracked?”

“Because, my dear, no one besides myself seems to see them. Until your visit. To ordinary sight, those are just random fissures and jumbled cracks in the stone.”

“I’m sorry, but I find that hard to believe.”

“I assure you, in the last two days since this curious object came into my possession, I have approached various of Derek’s colleagues. Without telling them that he has disappeared, I’ve asked them to interpret the stone. I was as astonished as you that not a one could decipher any engraved letters. In fact they looked at me sideways for just suggesting that I had found Clas Myrddin, which was long ago relegated to myth, pure myth.”

“Are the words so significant?”

“Immensely. They are the first clue. The first thing to note is the second word—*Myrddin*—which is the Welsh name for Merlin. The two *d*’s are soft, pronouned like the *th* in *whither.* So it sounds like *mer-then,* more or less.”

“Mer-then,” Arthur repeated softly.

“Exactly. But what about Myrddin? That’s revealed by the first word. *Clas* is an enclosure; therefore the meaning of the phrase is ‘Merlin’s enclosure.’ All of Britain was under the protection of Merlin, hence Merlin’s enclosure was a very old name for England itself.”

“Oh.”

“Wait, that is only the obvious meaning. There’s actually something of import here. You see—”

Arthur's aunt stopped short, her gaze riveted by what was happening outside. Unnoticed by them inside, the crow must have returned, for Jasper was trying to do more than shoo it away—he had knocked it to the ground and was poised with a coal shovel, ready to crush the bird to death. "No, stop!" Pen shouted. She was too late. The butler brought the shovel down with a clang. Arthur and his aunt rushed to the French doors and flung them open.

"What's going on? What do you think you're doing?" Pen asked angrily.

"Bashing it," Jasper replied sullenly. "Only I missed." Semiconscious, the bird had managed to flutter a foot out of harm's way. The butler raised the shovel to strike again. Arthur stepped out quickly onto the terrace and seized the tool by the handle. Jasper glared at him and growled, "Let go!"

Pen turned on Jasper angrily. "What's gotten into you? You're acting like a brute." She turned to Arthur. "Jasper here is usually the mildest of men. I can't understand his behavior."

This rebuke had an immediate and dramatic effect on the butler; his arms went slack and a passive expression came over him. "I'm sorry, madam," he murmured apologetically. "I went too far." The man seemed to be in a daze, Arthur noted.

"Go back inside and take that lethal implement with you," Pen said, still angry. She stooped to examine the bird, which was lying motionless on the ground. "I think it's in shock. What should we do?"

Arthur said, "It needs warmth. We could wrap it in a blanket." His aunt agreed. She gently lifted the bird in two hands and carried it into the drawing room. In her jet silk kimono, she resembled a crow herself. Pen wrapped the injured bird in a faded afghan; it remained conscious but still, faintly shivering.

"How peculiar," Pen said. "I was in the process of unpacking a mystery, and then along came this bizarre interruption. We've had our omen, of that I'm certain." Although half-unconscious, the crow's shiny black eye seemed to watch her with peculiar recognition.

"You need to know more about the stone," Pen said after a

moment. "It goes much deeper than you suspect. There's a mystery connected with the phrase *Clas Myrddin,* as there often is with runes and glyphs and other extremely old words. To the ancients words were concrete things, not abstractions. Words could enfold magical power. A particularly powerful word could fell a tree or frighten the soul out of your enemy."

"And how did one unlock this power?"

Pen shook her head. "I haven't learned that yet. Words cover secrets like trapdoors over underground passages. To find out their true import, you have to be willing to explore." She fell silent.

"Do you believe Merlin was real?"

"For a long time I didn't. He lay beyond my powers of personal belief. Until I found this stone." Pen ran her hand over the etched rock. "If we can find Merlin, I'm sure we will find my husband. You see my reluctance to seek the help of the police, don't you?" Arthur looked at the stone, and for a second he could see nothing. Meandering lines flowed in tantalizing confusion, and then, like a memory emerging from the fog of forgetfulness, the words reappeared. Pen replaced the stone in its velveteen bag. "We have had a remarkable encounter," she said, "but I have entirely forgotten what you came to talk to me about."

"It was about druids. But now I'd rather ask you something else. Did your husband own a pair of brown kid gloves?"

"I never noticed, he may have."

"It was chilly the night before last, wasn't it, the night Sir Derek failed to return? It's likely, isn't it, that he wore gloves?"

"I'm sorry, I just don't know. I didn't see him go out. Did you find gloves at the crime scene?"

"A glove, yes."

Pen looked thoughtful. "I don't see how that leads us to Derek. I can assure you that my husband didn't have a beard, much less a long flowing white beard."

"Yes, of course." Arthur stood up. "It's getting late, and I've taken up too much of your time." The two of them walked toward the marbled hallway leading to the foyer. Jasper was nowhere in sight, and Pen opened the massive oak portal herself. "We will talk again, I'm sure," she said. Arthur nodded gratefully and got into his car.

The golden gravel of Emrys Hall crunched beneath the black Ford. Arthur drove slowly. Streams of late-afternoon light lit the house with a burnished radiance; he had the feeling of departing an enchanted castle. Off to either side the alley of beech trees that must have been saplings in the reign of George III reared their imposing crowns into the dusky atmosphere. From one magisterial tree a flock of birds arose, swirling like a living cloud. Crows. Arthur had a vague sense of this whole day being spent with crows somewhere in the middle distance. The black cloud wheeled against the sun, took an unexpected tack in midair, and headed his way. He braked the car to watch. Suddenly he remembered the injured crow in Penelope Rees's drawing room.

Arthur glanced in the rearview mirror. The entry to Emrys Hall was framed in it; the massive doors opened, and his aunt appeared, waving her arms. She appeared to be shouting, though her voice did not carry that far. Looking over his shoulder, Arthur threw the car into reverse. When he reached the house, Pen rushed up in a state of agitation. "Quick, come and see," she said breathlessly, and without another word hurried back inside.

When Arthur entered, he heard running steps off the hallway. His aunt had not waited for him; Arthur followed the steps to the drawing room. It was dark. Since his departure the thick brocade drapes had been pulled. Pen was crouched in the corner, almost indistinct in the shadows. She was transfixed by something. Arthur approached, his eyes adjusting to the gloom.

"What is it?"

Pen moved aside to reveal an impossible sight. Two long, pale hands seemed to be extended toward him, beseeching in mysterious need. They were suspended near the floor, just in front of his aunt. No body or arms were attached to them. In his first shocked glimpse, Arthur imagined that they were severed hands, evidence of a hideous crime. His mind raced for explanations. What kind of violence had taken place in the few seconds since he had left?

But then he saw that the hands were not dead at all. They were quivering. Arthur staggered backward. "Steady," Pen warned. The hands were clutching the air as if begging or praying. They almost had a voice, and Arthur saw that they weren't severed from a body nor hanging in the air like Marley's ghost. They were attached to a solid blackness whose shape was barely discernible in the dim light of the drawing room. The crow. Two hands were emerging from the extended wings of the crow.

"Turn on a light, but be quiet," Pen said in an undertone. Arthur flicked the switch on a ginger-jar lamp nearby. He returned and knelt by his aunt. The hands quivered more violently, as if crying out. Now wrists started to emerge, slowly. Someone was being born out of the crow. Forearms followed. With a massive effort, Arthur stifled a wave of panic. Words flashed through his mind, familiar words that yet had no source in memory: *Please—help—you are needed.*

It was the second time he had been summoned. With total certainty Arthur realized that the creature who was struggling to be born in front of his eyes was speaking to him. "We have to help," he said aloud.

Pen looked confused. "How?"

Arthur was still too shaken to think clearly, yet in the strangeness beyond strangeness he had to do something for the creature.

The crow's body twitched and its wings drew up to the ceiling. The birth pangs should have torn it apart, yet still the process continued. Arthur was by the bird's side now. He put his hands to still the wings from their trembling; the instant he touched them, his feelings changed. Horror fell away, replaced by something secure, without shuddering or fear. It was a solicitous love. Yes, he was the midwife, the mother of this birthing in the dark. He had never felt such a thing before. A warmth was in his chest, and he knew that he badly wanted to see the creature's face when it finally arrived in the world. The bird sensed that he was there; it was totally quiescent.

"Are you afraid?" Arthur asked.

His aunt had moved into an armchair and sat with her face in her hands. She shook her head. "It was a shock at first, but I'm getting hold of myself. Thank God you were still here." She got up and came closer. Now they were on either side of the crow. Uncannily, the hands knew this; they reached out. A gentleness overcame Arthur. He took the offered hand in his own; more timidly, Lady Penelope followed his example. The pale hands gripped with fierce tightness.

"No, wait," Pen gasped. But there was no waiting. The process had accelerated a hundredfold. Quicker than their eyes could follow, the upper arms, head, and shoulders were born into the light. The head was slumped and dark and they could see no face yet—a glistening film covered everything, like a caul. Even if they could have made out a face, the process was too swift. In a matter of seconds a young man's naked body lay curled on the floor. He was sleek and almond-skinned; long hair flowed down his back.

"What should we do? Should we touch him?" Pen asked. Arthur shook his head. They waited a second while the glistening caul melted away of its own accord. Now the face was revealed. Even in exhaustion it was a remarkable face, as if etched from immortal materials. Pen took off her dressing gown to cover the youth; in his naked helplessness, he looked like time's orphan. Her heart was deeply stirred, and for the first time in two days, its sorrowful longing for her husband faded. "He's conscious, I think," she murmured. Arthur nodded. Looking over his shoulder, he saw someone in the doorway. It was Jasper.

"Quick, bring blankets and some clothes," Arthur ordered. He cut himself short, realizing his presumptuousness. He was a stranger in the house, although he felt as if he had been there forever. His aunt spoke up: "Do as he says." Jasper hurried out into the hall, heading for the stairs. In a few minutes he returned with the things asked for. The curtains had been parted to let in more light. The young man sat silently in a chair, staring around him.

"We're friends. Can you tell me who you are?" Arthur asked. The young man cocked his head without saying anything. His movements had a lingering birdlike quality. Utterly expressionless, more a dumb creature than a person, he seemed to be figuring out language for the first time. He had extraordinary large brown eyes that combined innocence and great depth; at the moment, however, they looked bewildered and exhausted. He obviously needed food and drink. Arthur spoke quietly to his aunt. "I think I'd better go to the pantry and fetch the food myself. You might want to keep Jasper away."

"Why?"

"Did you see the expression on his face when he first showed up at the door?"

Pen shook her head. "I'm sure he looked shocked like the two of us."

"No. It was dark, and I can't exactly be sure, but for some reason I don't think Jasper was shocked at all. He made me feel something quite different—much less benign."

"All right. You go and tell him to take the rest of the day off. It's late anyway."

Arthur nodded and left. He came back with tea and scones and set them down in front of the young stranger. "This is all I could manage to find. I couldn't find the cook or maid."

"There's just Jasper and me. I let the others go, to spare local gossip. I preferred to face all this alone. Until you came." Arthur put his hand in Pen's and kept it there.

The young man was looking at them, ignoring the food in front of him. He seemed as startled as they when he spoke: "Master."

Pen looked at Arthur, then asked, "Can you tell me your master's name? Can you tell us your name?"

The young man gazed at her mutely, then pointed to the stone, which had been left out beside its black velveteen bag. He didn't speak again but only traced with his index finger the letters that only the two mortals had been able to read before.

"He knows," Arthur said, and Pen nodded. "What do we do now?"

The young man had slumped back in his chair, paying no more attention to them; his eyes were fixed on the stone as if mesmerized.

"I think that much is clear enough," Pen replied. "We wait to be astonished again."

10
FAIRY FAY

AS SOON AS HE GOT TO HIS ROOM AND LAY DOWN, JASPER'S stomach started to churn. He didn't exactly know what he'd seen downstairs in the drawing room. The lighting had been dim, and it was against his code to look. Discretion is an iron law among good butlers. "It doesn't matter what I saw. I saw too much," he thought. She would want to know everything now; he had no choice.

"Who's there?" he asked, startled.

The floorboards in his room had creaked slightly. Jasper sat up in his bed. It was a fine antique bed made of mahogany, heavy as iron on its ball-and-claw feet. A simple, sturdy nightstand stood beside it with an open Bible on top. "Go away. I don't need anything. Really," he called out. To whom? His voice sounded hollow and afraid.

When the young constable had come into the pantry to get some food, he had sent Jasper straight upstairs. "As if he has any right to order me about," the butler thought resentfully. But Jasper hadn't gone upstairs. He had lingered at the top landing instead. He had waited a long time, his knees growing stiff, his head starting to ache.

Finally Her Ladyship had come out of the drawing room into the entrance hall. She had the young constable with her but not the bird-thing that had appeared. Perhaps the bird-thing was gone. No, they were talking about it. It had fallen asleep in a chair by the fire. "Let's just leave him there," Her Ladyship said. "It'll be a greater kindness than putting him to bed. He's totally exhausted."

Arthur said, "I wish I could stay over, it would put my mind at ease, but I'm afraid my mother is alone."

"No, no, I wouldn't think of keeping you. We're quite safe here. There's Jasper to look out for us, after all."

The young constable frowned and made a remark—Jasper missed the exact words as their muffled voices passed under the stairway. He risked stepping out of the shadows to lean over the marble railing. They were too engrossed to notice.

The front door opened; Arthur stood irresolutely on the threshold. "Well, I won't feel right unless you call me first thing in the morning. At home, not the station. Promise?"

Her Ladyship nodded absently, then put a hand on his arm. "There's something I haven't told you yet," she said, an anxious tone in her voice. "Our astonishing friend seems very lost, and I think he has pinned his hopes on finding his master again."

She looked out the door into the darkness. "My heart tells me that his hopes will be dashed. You see, there's something else about the stone—the last layer of the Clas Myrddin riddle." Her voice faded—they must have stepped outdoors. Jasper leaned farther out into space, risking discovery.

Standing on the portico, Her Ladyship said, "The old lore holds that Merlin had one besetting weakness. Not surprisingly it was love—romance was the poisoned rose in the garland of Camelot. It ruined many noble knights. In her passion for Lancelot, it ruined Queen Guinevere, and eventually it ruined the king himself. Death and betrayal were committed in the name of love. But I'll leave that aside. We're referring to Merlin for the moment.

"The old wizard was on a journey abroad to do King Arthur's bidding when he became enchanted by a lady named Vyvyen. It wasn't that she was beautiful. Merlin, remember, could have summoned Cleopatra to darn his stockings if he had so desired. It took something special to weaken him, and Vyvyen had it. She was a powerful witch in her own right and intensely curious to know Merlin's most cherished secrets. Her black arts gave her the means to worm them out of him. Foolish, fond old man, he probably wanted them wormed out anyway."

"Why?"

A wistful look crossed Pen's face. Sad recollections seemed to play for a moment on a darkened stage in her mind. "Don't bother about that. One night while Merlin was fast asleep in their bed, Vyvyen turned one of his own spells against him. She had learned that a wizard cannot be killed; the only way to vanquish Merlin was to enclose him within four stone walls and bury the vault deep within the earth. Merlin had foolishly revealed this knowledge to her, and Vyvyen lost no time clapping him into a secret chamber known as Merlin's Enclosure."

"Clas Myrddin."

"Precisely. That's why everyone scoffed when I said that I'd found it."

"And this stone may be, for all intents and purposes, a kind of tombstone?"

"I don't know. A powerful spell may be wrapped around it that you and I certainly aren't about to undo. Perhaps our young friend can; time will tell. If we were superstitious, we might fear being dragged down by the spell."

"Are you afraid?"

Pen shook her head. "We're living a smashing mystery, but I'm too tired to think straight. There hasn't been much sleep for me since Derek left."

Jasper had withdrawn quickly from his listening post; Her Ladyship would be coming upstairs any minute. He heard a few parting murmurs, then the heavy clunk of the doors closing like a drawbridge for the night.

Lying in bed Jasper felt exhausted and dreadfully alert at the same time. His throat had tightened with fear. Water. He reached out for the white china pitcher kept beside the bed. The floorboards creaked again. He started to pour, but his hand was wrenched violently. The pitcher went flying across the room, hit the opposite wall, and shattered. Jasper lay back and closed his eyes in the dark.

"Darling, what's this mess? You're just a mucky pup. Let me help you."

She was back; she always kept her promises. Jasper opened his eyes. The light had been turned on. A young woman was in the room, her body bent over to pick up the broken pieces of china. Even when you couldn't see her face, you knew that she was young and beautiful.

"You don't have to do that," Jasper said. "I'll tend to it later."

Smiling, the young woman replied, "No bother, it'll just be a jiff." Jasper turned away. Keeping up the game seemed pointless; they both knew very well that she had snatched the pitcher from his hands. "You look far too tired. They needn't work you so hard, darling. You do the job of three servants as it is. Anyway, what happened to the concept of a gentleman's gentleman? Sir Derek should be more considerate of your feelings." She liked prattling on in an easy, caring, domestic way. Frightening.

Lady Penelope's words about the curse of love—the blighted rose of Camelot—came back to Jasper. The churning in his stomach grew worse; he started to cry, softly and to himself. For two weeks, love had been his precious secret.

He had managed to fall in love without the two parlor maids who lived in garret rooms next to his suspecting a thing. The walls were thick, and anyway, Ivy and Vi were getting on. You could shoot rabbits in the gallery and they'd never hear it. When he met the girl in the village grocer's, it was love at first sight. Miraculously, when she caught his glance, she had returned it. She asked him to help carry her market basket home, and things grew from there.

Her name was Fay.

The first time, he felt guilty about bringing the girl to his room for the night. "Don't be such a worrywart. If you love me, they will, too," Fay had reassured him. In his butler's pin-striped waistcoat and starched dickey, Jasper looked mature, but in fact he was still a young man, a very inexperienced one.

She wiped away his timidity quickly. For the first time in his life, he luxuriated in the season of passion that being young is made for. His desire for her ripened every night like swollen peaches and burst with sweetness.

When she looked around his room, Fay immediately noticed the narrow shelf of hardbacks over his dresser, filled with Derek Rees's works. "Oh, you must read to me," she exclaimed, and he did, for hours on end. Jasper loved his master and passionately devoured his writings.

Fay took to opening the books and staring at the pictures on her own. *Enchanted Albion* was her favorite, with its pastels of Titania besotted with Bottom in his ass's head and Robin Goodfellow peeking up the milkmaid's skirts. "It's all rather silly," Jasper said, "but the master makes it come alive."

In books Jasper first read about the unseen world of fairies and elves, wizards and warlocks. Jasper had always been practical. His life was as dull as a halibut's, but he knew about things: how to store the Spode between layers of tissue paper and polish the silver in one direction to minimize streaks. Useful, safe things to know, not like this frightful—what do you call it? "Arcana," Fay had told him. Oh yes, *arcana.* Fay was thrilled by the whole business of banshees digging up their lovers' bones and ghosts shooting green fire from their eyes.

Emrys Hall had been the most peaceful place to live that Jasper could imagine. He had been truly happy there, and once he had brought in Fay—who cared what name she gave now, in or out of hell?—it was blissful to dream about introducing her to Sir Derek and his wife. Unexpectedly, she turned shy about meeting them. "Let's just keep to ourselves for a while," she suggested, "until we're sure."

Fay came and went a few times a week but preferred that he never call her at home—stuffy landlady, she said. Being away from her tore Jasper apart; being with her was paradise regained. One time he had followed her back to her lodgings, a large rooming house off the High Street. It was evening, and after she went inside, he peered over the wall to see if a light came on in an upstairs window.

"Can I help you?" a voice behind him had asked brusquely. Jasper whipped around to confront a dark-haired man in an oversize wool greatcoat.

Jasper was at a loss. "I have a friend who lives here," he stammered.

The man eyed him suspiciously. "Friend? What's her name?"

"How do you know it's a her?" Jasper mumbled.

"Because I own the place. My name is Amberside. Shall we walk in, my good fellow, and find your friend?" The man took a step closer, and the fact that he kept his hands in his greatcoat pockets added to his menace. Jasper was already sidling away down the street; it was a hundred yards before he worked up the nerve to look over his shoulder in case the man was after him. The sidewalk was empty, to his relief. After stopping for a whiskey to settle his nerves, the butler wondered why Fay had said she had a landlady. Perhaps Amberside was married.

This embarrassing incident was soon forgotten, although Jasper found himself avoiding the neighborhood. Then Sir Derek disappeared; Fay had not come to Jasper that night. The house had been quiet all the next day; Her Ladyship asked Jasper not to tell anyone. It was the next night when Fay appeared again. After they made love, she got up out of bed and walked over to the open window. Not bothering to put on anything, she leaned out and held her hands up to the moonlight, for all the world like a fairy worshiping the goddess. Fairy Fay.

"I could watch you forever like that," Jasper said from the bed. She seemed to blush and covered her breasts with her hands.

"I won't look at you if you don't like it," he said timidly.

She shook her head. "No, it's nice. Only I'm getting a little chilly." He got up and draped one of his butler's jackets around her shoulders. "What's that?" she asked, pointing down into the gardens. A smell of lilac and lemon balm drifted up from them.

"That? The maze. It dates from Queen Anne's day. Their idea of a playground, nymphs chasing satyrs, all that sort of nonsense."

She wasn't listening. Her eyes focused hard on the maze. "I want to go down there," she said suddenly.

He was astonished. "What? At this time of night—it's impossible." He felt abandoned, then caught himself and laughed. Maybe she was just being coy; maybe she wanted to be chased through the maze. They tiptoed downstairs, semidressed. The house was dark except for a light in the study where Her Ladyship was reading and one over the portico in case Sir Derek returned on foot. They hadn't started seriously worrying about him, or at least the servants hadn't been alerted.

Once outside, Fay's excitement became frantic. "Hurry," she whispered, gripping his arm fiercely. The green walls of the maze were like black barricades, even under the moon. He stumbled, but she drew him on. It was uncanny that she could find her way. The north entrance was closest. They rushed toward it; Jasper grew more uneasy. "Come on," she urged. Somehow, it didn't seem like a game anymore. Over his shoulder Jasper caught a glimpse of a flashlight wavering in the dark. He pulled back.

"I think it's my lady, we'd better wait."

"No."

"Then let's just go back." As he reached out in the gloom to find Fay's face, she growled, low and menacing. Jasper's heart nearly leapt out of his body. The growl sounded unnatural, menacing. With all his might he pretended he hadn't heard it. "It's dark. Let me touch you," he whispered, as he reached out for her cheek again. It was, he realized, the bravest thing he had ever done. What did he touch in that awful darkness? Bristles? Scales? It was gone so quickly, he might have imagined it. She had disappeared noiselessly into the depths of the maze.

Jasper tried to stagger out the way they had come in. In a gap between the yews, he thought he saw the flashlight go by. After a moment it was apparent that he was lost. Panic took over. He stumbled about recklessly, badly scratching his face and hands. It was only the grace of God that got him out of there. Seeing the open lawn ahead, he ran pell-mell toward the lighted portico. He had collapsed in bed, catching his breath in ragged gasps; he felt strangely clearheaded, however, as if he were witness to someone else's terror.

By the time she came back, he was numb. "You're still up," she remarked casually. It was impossible to read her mood. Had she succeeded in her purpose, whatever it was? "Can you help me with this?" she asked; she had her arms up around her neck, trying to unfasten the hook of the blouse she had thrown on. Fay was standing in front of the mirror when he came behind her and fumbled with the hook at the back of her neck. Somehow he knew not to look at her reflection. "You silly," she said, laughing darkly. "What do you think you're going to see, that I'll have a hedgehog's face—that would be rather pretty—or snakes for hair? Perhaps a forked tongue?" She stuck her tongue out. It was pretty and pink as ever. Her eyes were twinkling.

"I, uh—" He couldn't speak. She pushed his fingers away and undid the snap herself. Gazing into the mirror, she sighed. "Arrangements are going to have to change a little, darling. We've lost something precious, despite my best efforts." So she had failed. Fay pointed. "Here, take a look." It was an order. Jasper looked over her shoulder into the pier glass hanging on the wall, but Fay's face wasn't there. He saw through her body as if she were only a shadow. Then she made some kind of guttural wheeze (he remembered Sir Derek's books claiming that spells were cast in backward Latin), but the sound came to him from a million miles away. With a bang the mirror exploded, sending glass everywhere. He had no time to duck. A flying splinter pierced his forehead just above the nose. His eyes rolled up and he passed out.

When he woke up, he had been in bed with strong morning light coming through the window. "Who's there?" he asked.

"Just us. Don't move, it'll be all right," a voice said. It was Lady Penelope. Jasper was groggy, but when he heard Fay's voice, his heart sank.

"He looks very weak. Should I change the bandage?" Fay asked. The two women conferred. He could hear the snip of scissors; cool hands touched his forehead. He felt his stiff, sticky bandage being unwound. "Leave me alone," he protested.

"Please hold still," Fay said. "The accident wasn't as bad as it looked. There was a lot of blood, but I don't think you're hurt badly." She sounded worried and tender. He wanted to vomit.

"I just want to say that you needn't fret about having brought Fay here," Lady Penelope told him. "I'm sure you were going to tell us soon. I'm very happy for you. She's lovely." A soft hand squeezed his. Gradually the room came into focus, and he saw a glass tumbler in front of his face. Her Ladyship hovered just above the glass. "Take some. It's just hot water with whiskey and honey. You'll feel better," she said. Jasper knew that his dream of happiness had fled forever. He turned his face to the wall and prepared to die.

Since then, Her Ladyship had seemed delighted when Fay came to the house. She hadn't shown up today when the bird-thing happened, but then, the night was her time, and it was just getting dark. Jasper knew now why he had had the impulse to stop on the stairs and spy. It wasn't a grievous lapse in his butler's discretion. He was afraid to go back to his room.

These thoughts took only a moment, although Jasper felt that he had been pulled far away by them. He opened his eyes, hoping against hope that Fay would be gone. Instead she was standing by his bed, her hands filled with the broken china fragments. "I know you prefer to be alone, but I couldn't just stay away. I thought you'd want me," she said, putting the pieces of china aside. He shook his head, and she laughed. "No? Well, I know you better than you know yourself. That's what it means to be loved." She traced a fingernail lightly across his chest, and he felt fire in the wake of her touch.

"You haven't got a right to do this," he mumbled.

"Do what? What you've always desired?" she said, a slight mockery in her voice. Her mouth was luscious, her eyes soft and innocent. He had never even imagined such skin, like a lily kept under glass, smooth and fragrant. Even now, Jasper couldn't help but be dazzled by her. She started to undo his tie; he put up a hand to stop her: "Not tonight." She smiled more sweetly and started slowly peeling off her stockings. It seemed old-fashioned that she wore them. But sheer nylon stockings were just what he had wished for, like everything else about her. "You have a very good body for a butler. Aren't I lovely, too?" she murmured. Taking his ears in her hands, Fay made his head nod like a puppet's. She was feeling playful. It frightened him. "You saw something today, didn't you, darling?" she asked. "But you didn't kill it, and you haven't got the stone yet, have you? Naughty." She twisted his ears harder. "Pay attention now."

"Get the stone yourself," he gasped, wincing with pain.

"Oh, I could, only it's so much more fun to use you. It makes us alike, the way we should be, the way lovers are." Jasper shuddered. She was excited, and he had begun to notice that strong emotions made her smell of decayed mushrooms and mouse droppings.

"Tell me what you saw." She was whispering in his ear and nibbling at it.

"Just a lost bird. I tried to kill it. You put the idea into my head, I suppose."

She didn't answer; she didn't need to. It was part of the nightmare that she could be inside his head or out, just as she could pass through locked doors and enter his room anytime she wished. "Would you do me a little favor?" Fay asked.

"Put a bullet in my brain?"

"No, silly. Just watch the stranger." He knew she meant the bird-thing. "It would be impolite for me to intrude, but I'm ever so curious."

"You're afraid of him."

She laughed lightly. "We don't know fear. But it's good to be a little cautious. When he's out, fetch the stone. That's all."

"I'll only do it if you promise to leave me alone."

"I could never leave you alone," Fay murmured. She kissed him full on the mouth. Jasper felt himself weakening. The decayed smell that she faintly exuded didn't matter anymore. Enchanted as he was, she represented everything Jasper had dreamed about.

"Yes," he mumbled, wanting her. She seemed to melt in his arms, moaning with pleasure. But the rush of passion failed to hide a lingering suspicion. Why did he have to be seduced? Why didn't she just invade his mind and make him her slave? It was worth pondering.

11

THE QUESTING WODE

"TOMMY, WAKE UP. I'VE SEEN HIM AGAIN." SIS HAD TO WHISPER; HIS face was pressed close to the paneled door that separated the lower-school dormitory from the upper-school's. "Tommy?"

No answer. Sis didn't dare try the squeaky doorknob. Waking up everybody would spoil everything. At least Tommy Ashcroft's bed was the nearest one to the door on the other side. Sis bent down to the keyhole, through which he could see almost the whole room. It had eight beds in it. On the one that was Tommy's there was a twisted pile of bedclothes and underneath that was a lump, which didn't move.

"*Psst.* It's the mud herd man. I'll give you three seconds to wake up or I'm going after him myself," Sis whispered, a notch louder this time. Now he could discern long arms and legs sticking out of a tangle of sheets. Tommy looked like Houdini trapped in a particularly difficult straitjacket.

The lump heaved a little as Tommy stretched and sat up. *"Psst,"* Sis hissed. Tommy looked in the wrong direction, then wobbled out of bed and padded across the floor, heading for the radiator. Sis groaned. "It's not the bloody radiator. It's me, Sis, at the door," he said aloud. He couldn't tell if Tommy heard him or not. In one of the other beds a boy sat up.

"What's the matter?" he whined. "It's bloody four A.M."

"Don't wet your pajamas, Giles. I'm just turning down the heat," Tommy mumbled, reaching for the radiator knob.

"Heat? They could use this place for a mackerel locker. I think you're sneaking out."

Tommy stared at the boy coldly. "Don't be snarky. Go back to sleep like a good boy."

"What if I rat?"

Tommy shrugged. "I'll put razor blades in your porridge and you'll die." The other boy gave a twisted grin and, shivering, burrowed molelike back under his blankets. *Come on,* Sis urged mentally. He was about to jump out of his skin with exasperation. But Tommy was just being cautious. He waited for the other boy to let out a ragged snore before crossing out of sight to a battered wardrobe in the far corner of the room. Sis heard the muffled sounds of drawers opening; clothes were being slipped from hangers. In fifteen seconds Tommy was opening the window whose hinges he had oiled for just this purpose.

"Giles was right. It is bloody four A.M.," Tommy said when he joined Sis in the courtyard below. "I can't believe you're up."

"The moon woke me up. It must have been the moon, because I was suddenly awake for no reason. I looked outside, and then I saw him."

"Who?"

"The mud herd man, the one who escaped. He came into the courtyard, right where we're standing, and he looked up at me."

"You're sure?"

"He wanted me to follow him—wanted us to, I mean."

Tommy yawned and stretched his arms wide. "Well, the moon didn't wake me up. I was sleeping like potatoes in the ground. Set off a bomb next time." Sis laughed softly. "I don't fancy taking a stroll across the fields again. It's almighty damp."

"I don't care. We could be the ones who track the mud herd man down, but now he's getting away." Sis's face looked up expectantly. "You don't have to go."

Tommy looked around at the empty courtyard. "I imagine it was just a commonplace ghost. Was he floating?"

"Don't tease. Just come on, or we'll lose him." Sis wasn't sure the older boy believed him, but he headed across the courtyard anyway into the maze of alleys that lay beyond. The buckling walls of St. Justin's seemed to lean inward with dark disapproval. Sis looked over his shoulder; to his relief Tommy was following. Sounds could be heard up ahead, and the little boy stopped.

"What's the matter?" Tommy asked when he caught up.

"I have a feeling he's there."

Tommy peered into the unrevealing gloom. "You mean the murdered man?" Tommy considered for a moment. This was Edgerton's territory, where the altar boys lay in wait, holding their secret meetings or dragging off younger boys to torture them with pranks. "Look, better let me take a gander. If I find the old man, I'll come back for you." Sis looked dubious but relieved. "Hold tight here or go back, whatever you like."

The little boy found a knocked-over rain barrel and sat down. "I'm not going back without you. The doors are locked."

Tommy nodded and set off. After two minutes he wondered where he was. The endless crumbling paths kept leading nowhere, running into dead ends and collapsed walls. The atmosphere was eerie and dank. He was ready to turn back, discouraged, when he heard a faint whistle. He looked up without making out what it was. Then he spotted it, fifty feet in front of him, a peculiar light flickering faintly across the path. It looked as if it was coming from a low window.

The boy moved forward. The window, he could see now, had recently been broken. Smashed glass lay strewn under his feet, and a patch of thick cardboard was taped over the jagged opening.

Tommy looked around to make sure he wasn't being spied on, not that anyone but a rat catcher would wander this deep into the maze. He wrapped his fingers around one corner of the cardboard patch and peered through the crack. The window looked down on a basement, which was too dark to see into. He bent the cardboard farther to widen the crack.

"Welcome back," a voice said.

Tommy straightened up in alarm. "Who's there?" he demanded, before he realized that the voice had come from the basement—he must have been seen from the other side. Heavy clumping steps came up the stairs, and then Joey Jenkins, the furnaceman, appeared in the doorway with a load of lumber in his arms.

"I'm lost."

Joey laughed skeptically. "You're not lost. You're reconnoitering." Being a Jamaican and the only black man at school, Joey intimidated many of the boys. He rarely spoke, and almost everyone, including the masters, acted as if he were invisible.

He stood steadily regarding Tommy, balancing a jumbled pile of stained desktops, cracked mirrors, and empty windowpanes in his muscular arms. Even in the morning chill he was starting to sweat. "I'm busy clearin' this here rubbish out. You lookin' for somethin'?"

"No, well, maybe." Tommy was too nervous to contemplate why anyone was hauling lumber at four in the morning.

"Whatever you be lookin' for, it didn't get lost breakin' that precious window, did it?"

Tommy shook his head. Joey sighed. "Well, no reason you should part with the truth for nothin'." He tossed the armful of lumber into a rubbish bin and without warning produced a soccer ball, tossing it in a hard, straight shot at the boy. Tommy caught it on his stomach, too surprised to clench his lax muscles. He made a supreme effort not to flinch.

"You strong boy," Joey remarked, amused. He raised his own dirty red jersey and exposed rippling stomach muscles under shiny ebony skin. "You going to be as strong as Joey one day?" The furnaceman smiled, showing a gap between his front teeth.

Tommy looked at the ball in bewilderment, then remembered seeing one just like it before. *Edgerton—he thinks I'm Edgerton coming back for his ball.* "Thanks, man," he said aloud. "Look, I don't mean to clear off, but—"

The black man frowned. "But you're not so sure Joey is safe? Not as safe as running away, that's for certain."

"I'm not running away," Tommy protested weakly.

"What's your name?"

"Tommy."

"I got friend back in the islands named Tommy. Good marlin fisherman, quick with a gaff. Plenty fish." The black man clinched his fingers into hooks and raked them a few inches from the boy's face. "You know someone named Arthur? I be lookin' for him everywhere." Tommy shook his head. "I hear Arthur be king around here, you know," Joey went on to nobody in particular. "Kings is of interest to Joey, they are. I wonder where the pearly king gets his pearls. Does the kingfisher ever catch kings when he goes fishin'? Joey comes from Kingston, too, you know? Back where Joey comes from, we've heard of Arthur, oh yes, we have."

Listening to him ramble, Tommy wondered if Joey wasn't a little crazy. "Look, I'll catch it if I don't get back." He could hear the tinge of panic in his voice. Without warning, the furnaceman reached out and grabbed Tommy's hand.

"Let go!" the boy said, startled, but he was held in an irresistible grip.

"Don't fight so, Joey not hurt you," the black man said; his voice was sober and soft. He opened Tommy's palm and drew a line across it with his index finger. It left behind a streak of sky blue pigment. "There, you remember that." Joey released his grip.

"I can't stay, I just can't," Tommy stammered. Backing away, the boy nearly stumbled; he regained his footing, turned, and ran down the alley. Behind him he heard the faint amused words, "Joey don't mind, everybody run from him," before he rounded the corner.

As luck would have it, the boy made it out of the maze with no wrong turns. He stopped running and caught his breath. If he was right, the rain barrel with Sis on it should be just ahead. But when Tommy got there, the little boy was gone.

"Sis," he called.

As if by magic, his friend rushed into view from the courtyard end of the alley. He was pale and excited. "You're back. Quick, I've spotted him again," Sis exclaimed.

"But I thought you said he went that way." Tommy pointed

back into the maze. "It's nothing but dead ends in there. How did he get out?"

"I don't know, but it's nearly five. The track team comes out for practice about this time. If we don't get away now, we'll never catch him."

Tommy reluctantly allowed himself to be pulled into the courtyard. He had serious doubts that he wanted to catch anyone. He looked out beyond the edge of the bricked enclosure. Cracked pavement extended until its crumbling edge blurred into grass and weeds where St. Justin's hill dropped off. The air was chilly in the feeble first sunlight; even the crickets felt too cold to chirp.

"Blimey," he muttered. Sis tugged at his sleeve. "Right," Tommy said. Something was definitely moving out there; he had seen it. The boys set off together, walking fast. The elusive movement darted in and out of sight. A lip of orange light was widening now on the horizon. Tommy could see that they weren't chasing some fugitive shape; it was a man. He moved ahead of them as if he was leading the boys on. The gummy mud of the fields stuck to their shoes; they had to stop every hundred yards to scrape an inch of it off to keep from being weighed down. The man-shape, still indistinct, didn't stop for this procedure, but it didn't widen the distance between them, either.

The sun's disk ventured a slightly bolder peek over the horizon, as if deciding whether the day would be safe. "You're right," Tommy said when the light became bright enough. "It's him." The boys recognized the baggy coat and brown cardigan from two nights before, and above all the banner of white beard. Excited as they were, there wasn't much to say. It was the old man's game, wherever he was taking them. The fields were coming to woods now. The old man hesitated, unsure whether to melt into the screen of trees. Being newly leaved, the thin maples and sycamore saplings afforded little cover. Farm machinery had knocked down a good deal of the smallest brush, but fifty feet ahead, where the machinery couldn't go, the thickets were dense.

"Maybe he's letting us catch up to him," Sis said, panting from exertion.

"Do we really want to catch up?" Tommy asked. "I'm not scared, but he's supposed to be dead."

"Let's ask him."

"You can't ask a dead person anything, if he's really dead," Tommy said, somewhat redundantly.

"You can't chase a dead person through the mud, either, and I'm getting too tired to keep it up." Sis stopped in his tracks and cupped his hands around his mouth. "Hey, mister," he called. "Are you dead?"

The old man turned his head and looked at them over his shoulder. He appeared to be considering the question. "God, this is weird enough," Tommy muttered.

"We have to know." Sis called again, "Are you dead?"

The old man moved his mouth. *Why do you ask if you won't like the answer?*

The two boys jumped. Although the old man was thirty yards ahead of them, his voice was right there between them.

"This is getting strange," Sis said.

"News flash, huh?" Tommy replied. "I vote for clearing off." The old man must have heard this, too.

Don't go, and don't be afraid.

Again his voice was right there between them. Turning back toward the woods, the old man stepped into them with a decisive tread. "Why doesn't he wait for us?" Sis asked.

"I think he wants to lead us," Tommy said reflectively, "but at the same time he's giving us a choice. He's not trying to scare us, and he's not forcing anything. Let's give it a chance." They didn't have time for any more discussion; the old man had all but vanished into the thick brush. Crossing the last of the fields, the boys entered after him, allowing themselves to be swallowed up by the undergrowth. For the next fifteen minutes the going was tough. Brambles snagged their pants, nettles left stinging trails on their arms. "Keep your hands up in front of your eyes," Tommy warned. Sis nodded grimly. As he raised his own hands, Tommy noticed that the streak of blue pigment was gone.

They plunged on. The trees closed in overhead, casting a carpet of thick shadows everywhere. Tommy stopped and looked around. "Wait a sec. I need to listen." The old man couldn't be seen, which wasn't unusual; he had slipped in and out of sight several times. But he had always made some sound to keep them going, and now that had disappeared, too.

"Where is he?" Sis asked, the beginnings of a whine in his voice.

"I don't know. Can you hear anything?"

Sis shook his head. "Are we lost?"

Tommy looked around. These were the same woods he had tramped many times, but yet they somehow weren't. They seemed wilder and thicker than he remembered, and no open clearings appeared in them. Even without a map Tommy knew that the woods couldn't be more than half a mile wide. "No, we're not lost," he said slowly. "The road's pretty close, I reckon. Let's keep going. I think I hear cars."

"I don't hear a thing," Sis said stubbornly. He was beginning to feel agitated from exhaustion and hunger.

"Well, that's just because we're in a low spot. Don't worry." Tommy pulled aside a thick screen of brambles and urged Sis through. Better to keep on than to panic. They walked another half hour. The trees seemed older and taller the farther they went. A hush had settled over the world; the warblers and jays sounded high and far away, as if nesting on cliffs rather than branches.

"I can't see the sun. We're lost, and I want to go home." Sis slumped in his tracks, sitting down on a gigantic fallen log. "Tell the truth. Do you know the way back?" he asked hopelessly.

Tommy looked at him. "Are you thirsty?" he asked, evading the question. Sis nodded miserably. "Well, this ground slopes down, which means there's bound to be a stream at the bottom. We just have to follow the lay of the land. And where there's a stream, there's usually berries."

Sis looked slightly encouraged. Tommy reached out a hand and pulled him up. They followed the steep slope of the hill. Exhausted as they were, it felt good to let gravity and their feet pull them along. Sometimes rocks and roots tripped them up, but the boys were beyond caring. "Don't give up," Tommy muttered; he knew that the next time they stopped would be the last. Sis would simply collapse.

What time was it, anyway? The treetops were so thickly woven they formed a sort of roof. You couldn't tell the sun's position, and the difference between night and day was just degrees of gloominess. Better not to think about night. The prospect of sleeping out in the cold made Tommy shiver. He remembered the two chocolate bars stashed under his pillow at school and thought what a fool he was not to have brought them. *Stop torturing yourself.* It was hard not to think about the candy, though. Sis mumbled something.

"What's up?" Tommy asked.

"Nothing. I just hate that old man," Sis grumbled. "We're going to die because of him."

"Don't talk rubbish. Your head's just muddled. Once we get some water, you'll feel better. Then we'll make a plan."

"What plan? Nobody's going to find us. We don't have matches for a fire, and besides, I think there isn't any stream," Sis said despairingly. Tommy looked around; the soft hush of the woods would have been beautiful if they weren't in trouble. The mossy rocks looked invitingly plush, and the pillared forest itself was a cathedral of peace. *Just don't tell yourself it's a nice place to die,* Tommy thought.

"Nicer place than I had," a clear voice remarked. "Filthy motorway."

The old man! Tommy whipped his head around, and there he was, sitting on a rock beside a clear running stream they had somehow overlooked. Tommy felt his heart jump in his throat. With a yelp, Sis stumbled the last few steps down the embankment and ended up in the old man's arms. He burst into tears.

"There, there," the old man said reassuringly. "I've been watching. You only thought you were lost." He made a beckoning gesture to Tommy, who stood his ground on the upper slope.

Tommy eyed the old man doubtfully. "You may say that you died by the motorway, but clearly you didn't. Why have you been leading us? Where are we?"

"Come, come, rest awhile," the old man said mildly. He lifted

Sis's face. "How do you feel, lad?" he asked, patting the boy, who was doing his best to stop his tears, although he had been far more frightened than he had let on, even to himself. "You have a habit of directing questions that are harder than you think," the old man told Tommy. "First you ask me if I'm dead. If you must know, I'm as dead as I have to be. In general, I do not prefer being dead—it limits my enjoyment at mealtimes—but exceptions had to be made. Speaking of mealtimes, aren't you the least bit hungry?"

"You know we're starving. We've been following you for hours," Tommy said. "I'm grateful that you found us, I have to give you your due, but the police are looking for your corpse. You may be in a deal of trouble."

"Thank you for considering my welfare, but the people interested in me can be left to their own devices. As for where we are, welcome to my woods." The old man made a sweeping gesture around him.

"I've been in these woods for years, and I've never heard that they were yours," Tommy said.

"True, but let's be frank. You've already figured out that these are not the woods you're familiar with. Mine are the heart of the original green world that once existed, will always exist, and yet has been destroyed by men. Is that helpful?"

These remarkably unhelpful answers delighted the old man, who leaned back, shaking with quiet amusement. Tommy felt his ears burn. "Let me ask an easier question, then. What's your name?"

"That depends on events that haven't unfolded yet. I may turn out to be this or I may turn out to be that."

"The newspapers call you Merlin."

"That will do. It's a fanciful name, and yet Merlin is as unlikely to be alive as I am. It's all a matter of belief. But my own belief is that right now you both need reviving." The old man pointed to the sparkling stream like someone who really did own it.

Sis, who had listened wide-eyed to everything that was being said, realized that he was parched. He ran to the water's edge and cupped a drink in his hands. "Tommy, it's ever so sweet." The older boy hesitated.

"Come, eh?" the old man coaxed. "Only don't cross the stream unless I tell you, for the other side is very different. There lies the Questing Wode."

"It looks the same from here." Tommy couldn't deny that he was thirsty, so sidling cautiously past the old man, he took a sip from the cold, clear rivulet. Perhaps because he was so tired, it tasted incredibly good. Looking up, he saw bushes heavy with wild raspberries (he didn't wonder how berries could be ripe in May).

"By great good fortune, I struggled out of that unfortunate ditch with a supply of Cheshire cheese and water biscuits packed in my overcoat pockets." As the old man spoke, he was spreading these things out on a large handkerchief. In a matter of moments the boys were lying on their backs, sleepy and well fed. For a dead man, Tommy conceded, this one was exceedingly hospitable.

"What happens when someone crosses the stream?" Sis asked curiously.

"Into the Wode? If he is truly questing, then he finds what he seeks or loses all," the old man said rather gravely.

"We don't want to do either," Tommy quickly interjected. "If these really are your woods, you can lead us out, can't you? I'd like to get back as soon as possible."

"You sound rather fainthearted."

Tommy sat up. "No, really. I have Sis to look after, and we'll be missed soon, if we aren't already. And besides, we have nothing to quest for."

The old man had ceased to pay attention. "Your father died in a car accident five years ago, didn't he?" he said musingly.

Tommy glared at him. "What of it?"

The old man held up his hand. "I'm not accusing you of anything. It's not your fault, you know. In my time, I've witnessed many tragedies happen to good people. Have you ever wondered why?"

"Does there have to be a reason?" Tommy said uncomfortably.

"Well, yes. Whatever happens shapes our lives. The real question is, who is in charge of the shaping? In your case a single event has made you different from other boys. For one thing, you've wound up a charity boy at school, haven't you?"

"I didn't know that," said Sis in surprise.

The old man went on, "And I can see you holding a pillow to your face to muffle the sound of your mother's crying at night. Why is fate so cruel that it wants to acquaint someone so young with grief? Was there a reason? You did decide to become strong from that moment on, didn't you?"

Tommy jumped to his feet. "C'mon, Sis, we'll get back on our own."

"I don't want to. We'll just get lost again," Sis protested, his voice trembling.

Tommy looked angry. "Just get up and follow me."

Sis glanced from the old man to Tommy with troubled eyes. "Merlin," he pleaded, "Tommy doesn't like you to talk this way."

"Doesn't he? I need someone strong like you, Tommy, but you have to be really strong, not just tough in order to hide a secret sadness."

"You're stepping out of bounds," Tommy warned, jerking Sis's arm to make him get to his feet.

"Ow," the little boy cried.

The old man went on, unruffled, "A boy like you is too young to have secrets, but there you are. Secrets develop so early nowadays. If my mother had to take in boarders to support her family—"

At this Tommy raised his fist. "How dare you humiliate me?" he yelled.

The old man regarded him steadily. "What's humiliating about love? Your mother loves you and wants you to go to that school because her own days are dwindling by slow degrees. Your life is the hope she would give anything to fulfill. I'm sure you know that."

The rage that had flushed into Tommy's face drained; his color went pale, and he seemed unsteady on his feet.

"What's the matter, Tommy?" Sis cried.

"Truth," replied the old man. "Mortals are never humiliated so much as when their shell of secrets is cracked and sweet truth enters in." A low murmuring sound rose in the old man's chest, amused and yet understanding.

Tommy, who was almost in shock, felt tears in his eyes. "Don't do this to me, old man," he whispered.

"Call me Merlin, like the newspapers. If you're so strong, why does it hurt to be loved?" With a stricken look, Tommy hung his head. "You don't know, do you? When you do, you will be strong in truth, not in grief. Would you like that, Tommy Ashcroft?" The murmur in Merlin's chest rose again, like a cooing dove, developing into a chuckle, then (once it reached his throat) a chortle, and finally saw the light of day as an indescribable sound. Wise laughter is impossible to depict or imitate, but when it comes from a true source, acceptance and love are blended with sympathy for all things human. The boys had never heard such a laugh; in their hearts they drank it in.

"Are you all right, Tommy?" Sis asked.

"He's all right, lad. We're just starting to be friends. I need friends who can stand the truth." The old man had risen to his feet. "Events are about to overtake us. I should get ready." He took off his shabby overcoat and threw it with a dramatic flourish into the stream, followed by his brown cardigan. The garments billowed out like brown stains on the water and swiftly floated away. "Now, if you'll back off just slightly, I believe you'll be out of harm's way."

Holding up his arm, Merlin directed the boys to stand behind two trees. "Whatever you see, don't allow yourselves to be seen." He took his place behind an ancient English oak a few yards off. Its low sweeping branches were so thick that even his beard didn't glimmer through. "I believe that we're in exactly the right place at the right time," he called. "But be prepared. Unpredictability is the one thing you can always count on."

Tommy, who had emerged from his state of dismay, wondered how anyone could plan on the unpredictable, but what happened next snatched away any leisure to ponder. From the distance a crashing sound could be heard, mixed with muffled pounding. Sis grabbed his tree with both arms. The pounding shook the ground harder and harder. The two boys pressed their bodies out of sight. "Merlin, we should run, shouldn't we?" Tommy shouted.

The old man shook his head. "Run? Where to? We're not exactly here. Of course, we're not exactly there, either. Quiet."

The crashing sound had drawn deafeningly near. The boys held their breath as a huge white stag, blood streaming from its sides, leapt out of the undergrowth, soared over their heads, and cleared the stream in one bound. Instantly the pounding grew even louder, and a dozen mounted riders shot out of the woods. Running flat out, the horses raced by, their flanks close enough to touch, sending a wall of muddy water spewing from the stream. In three seconds the apparition was over, leaving behind only the rank smell of sweat and fear hanging in the damp forest air.

"What was that?" Sis gasped.

But the old man had jumped into the stream and was puffing across, sending up his own small splashes of muddy water. "That? That's something no boy in his right mind could bear not to follow," he called out.

"Come on," Tommy urged, more excited than he'd ever been in his life. "It's the king's white stag, and if we don't hurry, it's going to be killed."

Sis was amazed. "What's happened to you? How do you know that?"

Tommy stared at him. "Beats me. We just have to save it. Besides, don't ask silly questions. You know what the royal stag is yourself."

Sis hesitated. He didn't feel like the same boy who had crept out of the dorm that chilly morning. That boy was small and afraid and had absolutely no idea what was going on. His new self, whoever it was, had blood in its veins that raced at the prospect of heroism, grace, hope, and love. How peculiar.

Tommy and Merlin were across the stream already. "Decide!" Tommy shouted.

Sis didn't have to. He jumped into the water, his nose pointed toward the future, throwing his old shabby identity behind like another brown, billowing coat for the stream to sweep away.

12

ZIGZAG

TOMMY AND MERLIN DIDN'T WAIT FOR SIS TO MAKE IT ACROSS the stream, roiled and muddied by the crashing horsemen. The little boy had hesitated only a few seconds, but it was a few too many. The hunters and hunted had already merged into the thick forest, dissolving before their eyes like a dream.

"Hurry up!" Tommy shouted. He ran after the pursuit party, following the smashed brier and alder brush left in their wake. Fire was in his brain and unbelievable power in his legs.

Despite his age, Merlin kept up with Tommy pace for pace, and Sis lagged behind by only a few strides. The fleetest man afoot cannot outstrip a galloping horse, but somehow they seemed to be gaining. The pounding of hooves grew louder. A flash of the stag's white haunches appeared in a gap through the trees.

"Look!" Tommy pointed in wild excitement. He had kept his eyes glued to the trail. Tripping and breaking a leg would be a disaster in these woods. A patch of boulders lay ahead half-buried in fallen leaves. Tommy tensed, preparing to leap over them, then suddenly he felt himself being seized from behind.

"No!" he cried, falling off-balance, certain that one of the hunters had stayed behind to trap them. But when he spun around, the hand holding his collar was Merlin's. Tommy's chest heaved like leather bellows, and he wrenched himself out of the old man's grasp. "What? Let me go."

Merlin shot him a warning look and put a finger to his lips. Sis caught up and stopped in bewilderment. He bent over, wheezing and wincing from the stitches in his sides. In despair he saw the fleeing stag vanish. The clamor of pursuit died away into leaf-muffled quiet.

The old wizard released Tommy and lifted his nose to the wind. He was scarcely drawing a breath and seemed preternaturally alert. Whatever he was trying to detect seemed to be eluding him, however. After a few moments he set off again. "Wait. Why did you stop?" Tommy shouted. Merlin didn't look over his shoulder; the boys had no choice but to follow.

Tommy had never seen anyone run so peculiarly, sometimes bounding over the terrain like a jackrabbit, other times jerking to a halt without warning to cock an ear windward. Trampled earth and broken branches marked where the fear-crazed stag had been chased, but the old man, ignoring these obvious signs, veered off on a different tack.

"No, they're ahead, over there," Tommy called several times. Merlin would shake his head vehemently and, as before, put his finger to his lips. What a peculiar game! Every time the wizard spied a hoofprint or snapped twig, he did an about-face and ran exactly the wrong way. This went on for fifteen minutes, until Tommy lost all hope of saving the stag, which after all was what Merlin must have wanted.

"Isn't he just running us in circles?" Sis muttered. Grimly, Tommy noted the prints of tennis shoes in the soft earth. They were his own tracks, so the old one must have doubled back over ground they had already covered.

Tommy was certain that they were totally lost. Merlin dashed over to a massive oak bearded with mistletoe. Merlin leaned forward, as if consulting with a senior counselor. He gestured for the boys to join him. Crouching down, he gathered them close. "This tree has agreed to guard us for a moment, at great peril to itself. You can't imagine how horrible it is to be burned alive when you don't have legs to run away."

"What are we being protected from? The riders are up ahead," Tommy said, imitating Merlin's cautious whisper.

"Don't worry about that. Just tell me one thing: Is *he* listening?"

Tommy exchanged bewildered looks with Sis.

"Is he?" Merlin repeated, this time with such intensity that he hissed.

Without knowing how, Tommy tried to listen acutely, with full alertness, the way Merlin had; he shook his head. "No, I don't think *he's* listening," he replied softly.

Quick as a wink, the old man darted to his feet. "Very good," he said in a low undertone. "Now don't think, don't talk. Just stay with me." Without further ado, Merlin tucked his beard into his shirt (a beard already decked out with brambles, burrs, nettles, thorns, prickles, and stickles, not to mention enough windblown seeds to start a cottage garden) and set off again at full tilt.

Tommy hung back. It was all he could do not to run where the trail of muddied tracks led. The instinct of a born hunter was in him; he didn't know what kind of transformation had come over him when he leapt the stream, but it gave him a sixth sense for where the stag was headed. He could feel the beast's heart pounding in his chest. His senses were sharpened by approaching death, just as the noble beast's were.

"He said to stay with him," Sis whispered fiercely as he passed Tommy on the run and veered to follow the old man, who was now zigzagging across the trail like a confused spaniel. Tommy reluctantly decided to fall in line.

The dappled light grew dimmer. The pillared forest had thinned out a little, yet somewhere in the shadows Merlin disappeared. The boys had lost their guide. They cast about for a few frantic minutes, not daring to call out. Merlin seemed to have vanished into thin air. One brilliant beam of sunlight pierced a hole in the green roof overhead. Sis ran toward it.

"Oh!" With a startled cry he almost went down. It had been

impossible to spy Merlin, crouched in the ferns and bracken, until the last second.

"Easy does it, my boy," he whispered, reaching up a gnarled hand to keep Sis from toppling. Tommy spotted them and came over. Merlin had put his ears to the bed of pine needles blanketing the forest floor.

Is he listening?

The words seemed to come from nowhere—Merlin was projecting his voice in the uncanny way he'd employed earlier. This time the boys weren't surprised; they even expected the question, strangely, and although they still had no idea who *he* was, an answer came unthinkingly to their lips: "No, nobody's listening."

Crouched in the short bracken, Tommy's hand brushed against a patch of white eglantine casting its sweet scent to the breeze. Some of the buds were streaked red on one side, and his palm felt wet. "Look, it's blood," he whispered. "It's smeared on the right side of the bush. If we want to catch them, we should turn here."

Merlin took the boy's hand and smelled the blood. He smiled. "Well done," he declared in a startlingly loud voice, "I think we can stop now." The boys couldn't have been more surprised if lightning had struck.

"I think you're crazy," Sis exclaimed.

Merlin seated himself on a large lichen-covered boulder. "Well, that's better than hating me, which you did only an hour ago," he said amiably. "I didn't mean to eavesdrop, but the Wode tells me things." The boys' consternation seemed to amuse him richly.

Tommy and Sis sank down exhausted on a thick bed of pine needles that had drifted like snow against a tree. Red rays of sunset penetrated almost horizontally through the forest now. The boys were fiercely hungry, and the prospect of not returning home began to gnaw at their stomachs.

"I'm going to try to get us out of here," Tommy muttered, cupping his hand close to Sis's ear. When he brought his hand away, he saw something new, a streak of blue around his wrist, just where the wizard had grabbed it when he sniffed the stag's blood. It looked exactly like the blue pigment Joey had left that morning.

"Merlin!"

The shout from the old man made the boys jump. He was on his feet, staring intently around him.

"Merlin!" he shouted again, this time squaring off a quarter turn to the right like a soldier on parade. His shout seemed to carry far away; Tommy thought he could hear it echo from unseen canyons or cliffs. Twice more the ritual was executed, until "Merlin!" had been shouted to the four points of the compass.

As quickly as he had jumped into action, the old man relaxed like a cat lounging back onto his boulder. "Sorry to interrupt," he said casually. "Carry on with your alarm."

"I'm twice as alarmed now," Tommy declared. "Why were you shouting? Aren't you Merlin?"

"That's what I want *him* to ask. Hearing my name will prove irresistible, I imagine, particularly because he thinks he already knows where I am. We're playing a very risky game, but his attention only has to falter for an instant. The stag has superb instincts. It will escape through any opening, however small."

Tommy was thoroughly agitated. He thrust his hand into the wizard's face. "And what's this blue streak?"

Their guide scrutinized the mark. "That's a clue. Definitely a clue. Do you mind if I make myself more comfortable?" Without further warning, the old man began to peel off his white beard. The effect might have been less disturbing if he had taken it off slowly, giving the bewildered mind a second or two to make sense of it. But there was no time for adjustment. With one snatch he pulled off the entire right side of the beard and started to rub cosmetic gum off his cheek.

"Sticky," he muttered.

The boys were beyond being perturbed. "You can't do that, you're supposed to be a wizard," Sis exclaimed.

Tommy sank to the ground, holding his head in his hands. "We're following a fraud," he moaned. By this time the old man had snatched off the left side of his beard, too, and was holding the bedraggled thing up for inspection.

"You wouldn't begrudge me if you had to wear this filthy lot of prickles."

Sis slumped to earth next to Tommy. "What's this charade you've been running us through?" Tommy demanded angrily.

"No charade, lad. It's a hunt, and I'm trying to make sure that we are the ones who are being hunted."

"Hunted? Are you aiming to get us killed?" Sis cried.

The old man shook his head. "I'm trying to offer *him* a decoy, but on my word, I'll do all in my power to make sure that we're not killed. *He* doesn't treat his victims very nicely."

"For heaven's sakes, who is *he*?" Tommy asked.

"A wizard, Mordred by name. He's keenly interested in the outcome of this hunt, and he desperately needs a kill. Those clods on horseback could never capture the king's stag, who can slip through a crack slicker than mercury, if Mordred weren't guiding them. Can you feel him? His attention is everywhere in the forest. That's what the stag cannot run from. So we've been throwing in a little interference—crossing the trail, doubling back, leading a merry chase to nowhere. It's the one thing *he* might not suspect."

This long speech made Sis grow wide-eyed, and for the first time in hours he looked like a timid little boy again. "And that's why you came to the woods, to fool *him.* But why do you need us? Aren't you a wizard, too?"

"In a manner of speaking, yes. I haven't returned totally as myself, though. It's hard to explain. There was this man named Derek Rees, you've no doubt never heard of him. He made the mistake of attracting Mordred's attention. This fake beard and the blue pigment left on your hand were two things connected with that. This chap Rees came across an object that was precious to Mordred—and to Merlin as well. If he'd gotten away with the object, he'd be alive today. But Mordred caught him in the act and murdered him. Alas, I was a fraction of a second too late to prevent it."

"That doesn't sound very reassuring," Tommy said anxiously.

"I really wish you had kept your beard on," Sis added. "I trusted you in that."

"I realize how peculiar all this seems, but you must trust me still. You boys are needed, far more than you can guess. Things are going to happen very fast, assuming that Mordred has overheard us. We're running a risk that he is hearing our words now, except that I've taken the precaution of leading us into a sacred grove. He cannot hold sway here. If we're ever separated, try to find this grove again. Mark it with your eyes."

The two boys gazed around. At first everything looked the same. The red warmth of sunset was sinking into purple afterglow, darkening ancestral trees, which would soon merge with the night. But on closer examination, Tommy could discern that these trees were not randomly scattered. They formed a ring of evenly spaced trunks, like sentinels. And the atmosphere was not quite the same as elsewhere in the Questing Wode. A deeper peace prevailed here; the whole place conveyed the feeling of sanctuary.

"Good," the old man said. "Now I have to warn you about something that may or may not happen. I could well start acting strange—well, more strange—and if I cease to be myself, you are on your own. Try not to worry, but when I said that I am a wizard only in a matter of speaking, I told the truth."

Tommy was on the verge of launching a hundred troubled questions when some faculty he never suspected he possessed—an inner eye or ear—caught a flicker of a sensation. He glanced at Sis, who seemed to be holding his breath. A definite change had occurred; a chilled shift in the atmosphere touched his veins.

Someone's listening.

Beyond reason, he knew that they were being overheard. But how? Emptiness surrounded them in all directions. "Ah, you've caught on," the unbearded wizard said. Tommy nodded. "Now you must sit extremely still," Merlin cautioned. The boys obeyed, waiting. Nothing seemed to happen. The silence in the grove was as deep as before, except for their own irregular breathing. Perhaps the faintest distant noise made itself heard against the tapestry of quietude.

Merlin frowned. "I didn't count on this," he muttered. "Mordred's baffled—we did well there—but the stag is coming back. He thinks I'm going to protect him. Poor beast. He's the only way Mordred could ever penetrate this place." True as his word, the sound of hooves increased, and in seconds a crashing of branches announced the arrival of the stag, which bounded into the grove and reared as if beseeching Merlin to save him. Exhausted, its sides heaving, the animal stopped, spellbound. Merlin shook his head. "If only it had stayed away. Coming here has spoiled the decoy."

"What can we do?" Sis asked.

Hearing voices, the stag snorted; its eyes rolled in panic at the sound of the approaching hunters. "What we can do we've already done. Hide yourselves. Now we can only observe," Merlin said regretfully.

Tommy jumped up. "That's not good enough," he declared, striding toward the stag. Seeing him, the alarmed animal leaped to his left. There was enough strength in his weary limbs to carry him only three or four feet, but that was enough. An arrow flew from nowhere, and in a heartbeat the stag was pierced through the chest.

"Oh my God, I've killed him!" Tommy thought. He ran toward the stag, but the hunters were fast upon it. They cried out in blood-lust, drawing their swords to hack at the fallen beast. Its death cry pealed forth, freezing Tommy in his tracks. The lead horseman sprang out of the brush. Jumping from his mount, he rushed in and grabbed the king's stag by the throat. Tommy began to run.

"No!" Merlin shouted.

"Who the bloody hell?" the hunter said, but the boy was already on his back, violently tearing at his head. Being in chain mail, the knight was clumsy and unable to use his greater strength to tear the boy off his back. Three other hunters burst onto the scene.

"Help me, fools!" their leader called. With a powerful jerk of the shoulders he threw Tommy off, but in his fall the desperate boy grabbed at the quiver slung on the knight's back. *"Agh,"* the man gurgled in agony as Tommy pulled out an arrow and plunged it into the bulging neck exposed beneath his foe's helmet.

Merlin was on his feet, approaching the melee. "Come back," he called. Blood was spraying from the stag's wound. Panicking at the smell, several horses nearly threw their riders. Tommy and the lead knight were lost in a blur of men and animals. The boy's hand was raised, ready to plunge the arrow into the knight's neck again, when everything stopped.

In dreamlike slow motion the boy glanced up and caught the wizard's gaze. "What's happening?" he asked. Merlin was still advancing toward him, but no one else was moving at all. Both men and beasts were a frozen image of chaotic violence. The stag's eyes were rolled up, lifeless and dull. Tommy saw this with stricken heart. He wanted to rush to the animal, but he couldn't stir by so much as an eyelash.

Merlin was by his side now. "You don't realize what you've done," he said severely. "I told you not to be seen. Now you can't leave the woods, even with my help. You have tangled yourself into the weave of events." Tommy still couldn't move, but the wizard seemed to understand the jumbled alarm in his mind. Merlin cautioned in a softer tone, "We haven't saved the stag. Mordred has won there, but we must do what we can to disguise our presence." With a quick gesture he brushed his fingers against the neck of the lead knight. The streaming blood vanished, and the wound inflicted by the arrow closed up.

"That will have to do. Now, listen to me. I can only hold time's web apart for a few seconds. When I nod, run after me for all your life, and mind you bring the arrow with you."

Tommy nodded, and at that instant he found himself able to move, and the scene of chaos erupted anew. The lead knight was on his feet, shouting. The other hunters had leapt onto the dead carcass of the stag, stabbing at it gleefully with knives and swords.

Run!

Faster than the mind could think, Tommy was racing away. He knew now that it was imperative that no one see him. The hunters' blind lust for killing was his best hope. Merlin was already into the woods. Tommy saw Sis ahead, a fleet shadow among the trees, and pumped his legs furiously. At any moment he expected to feel steel slashing into his back, but there was no time to look over his shoulder. Only running mattered.

Low branches whipped against the boy's face, cutting him. His red-hot lungs wanted to explode, but still he willed his legs to pound forward. He was alone now—Merlin and Sis must have zigzagged to mislead *him.* Tommy decided to follow suit. His fear made him want to keep straight on, so that he could put as much distance as possible between himself and the hunters. But his reason said that they were not the real enemy. He forced himself to cross back and forth, doubling back on his own trail, as he had been taught.

The diversion took time, but after a while he felt safe enough to stop. The hunters were not after him, that he could sense. So he had run well. It was a miracle that he hadn't tripped in the dark. Unexpectedly, he caught sight of a light. Fire. For a moment he was gripped with fear—maybe he had actually run back toward the hunters, who had camped for the night. Slowly the boy dropped to his hands and knees. He crawled cautiously away from the firelight. It seemed to take hours before the glow faded, and once he thought he felt the presence of a huge animal prowling past him.

Then very close to him, a voice said, "Bury the arrow." Tommy looked up to see Merlin not ten feet away; Sis was by his side in the pale light of the moon, looking silent and grave. Tommy clenched his fist, the stolen arrow still held tight in his grip. He dug his hands into the forest floor, scraping aside layers of leaf mold, getting down to black loam.

Merlin made a twisting motion with his hands, and Tommy nodded. Holding his breath, he broke the arrow in two. The snap ripped like a gunshot through the deserted woods. Carefully he placed the twin pieces of the arrow in the hole and started to cover them up. It only took a few seconds. The last glimpse he had of the arrow's point was a shiny glint, like a secret wink between conspirators. There were no traces of blood. The man he had attacked should have no memory of foul play. On the other hand, there was *him* to consider. Mordred was sensitive beyond mortal measure, and though his knights would return with their prize, the hateful glee their master would feel wouldn't last forever. Once Mordred cooled down, he might realize that a single thing—a lost arrow—had been ripped from the web of time. If he discovered that, he would come for them. Oh yes, that was as certain as death, even without taxes.

It must have been the streak of blue that tripped his memory. Derek Rees dimly saw his body race through the forest, like watching a movie projected through a flickering bulb. At first the picture was silent. "Sound, sound," he felt like yelling, impatient with the projectionist.

Then he began to feel a sensation—his feet springing off the pine needles that cushioned the ground. He'd always loved the feeling of needles and tanbark—that memory must have been the second thing that pulled Derek in. All at once it hit him.

"I'm not dead."

A small boy, running beside him, looked up in surprise. "What did you say?"

Derek Rees gazed in bewilderment at the spectral woods, colorless and hollow in the inadequate moonlight. He tilted his head to see where the moon was, and like a fool he ran smack into a tree. The impact knocked him off his feet.

"Merlin, are you all right? Are we near the cave?" the boy was asking him. Derek felt warm breath near his face; he must have passed out for an instant. Two pairs of hands reached out and helped him into a sitting position.

"Much obliged," he mumbled blearily. "Are you scouts?" There were definitely two boys now, and they were staring intently at him. "Is your troop camped out in this cave you're talking about? I'd like to speak to your—whatever you call him—your scoutmaster." Derek stopped, aware that he was almost speaking gibberish.

"Merlin?" the younger boy said.

"I'm sorry, give me a minute, will you? I seem to be a bit disoriented." Derek drew several deep breaths, and as he did, things started to clarify. He must still be on his walk near home. He'd told Pen he was going to the tobacconist, but then something else happened.

"Merlin told us this might happen," the older boy remarked.

"What's that? Why do you keep saying Merlin?"

The boys seemed troubled and kept staring at him. Oh, yes, it must be that silly beard and the blue facepaint. He touched his chin; the beard wasn't there. Putting his hands down into his coat pockets, Derek came up with another surprise. "I don't have my coat on. Where is it?"

"You threw it into the stream, don't you remember?" the little boy asked.

The older one shook his head. "Don't bother. Merlin said that if this happened we were on our own. Let's clear out. I think Mordred's got him."

He pulled the little boy to his feet, but the younger one resisted. "He doesn't sound that dangerous. I don't think Mordred's got him."

Derek wobbled to his feet. "Dangerous? Of course I'm not dangerous. If you would kindly find your scoutmaster—"

"We haven't got a scoutmaster. Are you Merlin or not?" the older boy asked, a note of desperation growing in his voice. Derek shook his head. "Then I suppose you don't know where the cave is, either, the one Merlin was leading us to?"

"I really can't answer any more questions just now. It's very odd that you refer to me as Merlin. My name is Derek Rees."

"Yes, Merlin said that would be your name," the older boy remarked.

Matters were so tangled that Derek let this pass. "I left my house about a few hours ago. I live at Emrys Hall, which is in that direction." He pointed straight ahead. "No, that might not be right. The moon rises in the east, and—" He stopped again, bewildered. "To tell the truth, you'll have to direct me."

"We can't. We're lost, too," the older boy said grimly.

"I knew he shouldn't have taken off the beard," the little one lamented.

The older boy went on, "Do you know that this is the Questing Wode?" Derek nodded. "You do?"

"Yes, I read it in books, while doing research, you know. The Wode disappeared at least five hundred years ago."

The older boy shook his head. "No, it didn't. That's where we are right now. These are Merlin's woods, and until a minute ago you were Merlin, and you were leading us to shelter in a cave for the night. You look completely surprised, so I can't imagine that you're any kind of wizard anymore. A wizard would know all that already."

Derek didn't find this long speech very enlightening. "You've said some amazing things, but if you don't mind, it would be helpful to know your names."

"I'm Tommy, and this is Sis. We're from St. Justin's." The boy kicked a rock in frustration and stood there, waiting for something to happen. Sis started turning around in slow circles, wondering which way to head.

Derek assumed a greater calmness than he felt. "I'm glad to know you both. It's not clear to me what we will do, but the brightest sign, and I'm speaking strictly personally, is that I'm not dead."

"Congratulations, but that's the least of our worries," Tommy rejoined.

Sis had stopped circling aimlessly and was on the alert. "Do you notice anything?"

Tommy was about to say no, when something caught his attention, too. "You're right. *He's* not listening anymore." The little boy nodded.

Derek cocked his ear windward, exactly as Merlin used to do. "If you mean Mordred, I think this is only temporary. His attention has been drawn away."

Tommy's jaw all but fell open. "You mean, you know about Mordred?"

"Yes. That's how this all started. I encountered him, although why it happened is beyond me. He isn't just in this Wode; his plans are on a much wider scale."

"But where does that leave us?" asked Tommy.

Derek was thinking. "I don't know," he said speculatively. "You say Merlin wanted you to find a cave? I might know where it is. I was raised in this county and have tramped it since I was smaller than either of you. The lay of the land might lead us to the cave. I remember some limestone formations lining the stream at the bottom of St. Justin's Hill."

"Then that must be the stream Merlin stopped by, the one that bounds the Questing Wode," Tommy said. "I don't think we can find it at night."

"Perhaps not, but I can just make out the brow of a hill over there," Derek said, pointing. "The moon is setting, and a bit has been chewed off the bottom. It's run into a hill, you see, and the only sizable hill in the west is St. Justin's." The two boys were looking at him in admiration. "Well, shall we give it a try? I don't fancy straying in the open until *he* sniffs us out."

"We haven't got much of a choice, have we?" Tommy responded.

"Will you ever turn back into Merlin again?" Sis asked plaintively. The three of them had already set off toward the moon-biting hill.

Derek shook his head. "I really can't say. I'm afraid that until Merlin does return, I am all you've got, and you are all I've got. On the other hand, given what you've been through, you must be exceptionally brave boys. I consider myself to have fallen into a rather lucky bargain."

13
A SLEEPLESS NIGHT

THE MOON LAID DOWN A TRAIL OF BLUE LIGHT ACROSS THE FLAGstone floor like a ghostly snail. Pen had been sitting up in bed watching it approach. But the main bedchamber at Emrys Hall was vast ("We could stable oxen in here if it weren't for the smell," Derek used to say), and it seemed to take hours before the moonlight crawled, quiet as a church usher, to the edge of her bed.

Pen felt intensely worried. In times of trouble she had always consulted her husband, but that night, when she reached across the bed to make sure he was beside her, her hand touched only cold linen. *God, where is he?* He might be dead or wandering lost and alone. Fending for himself would be hard. Derek wasn't the sort of man who had ever wanted to have much to do with the world. Being born in it was almost the limit. "Don't you wish we could just be pulled up by a moonbeam?" he once said. "Up and out of this place."

The bedchamber was getting cold. Knowing that sleep was hopeless, Pen got up and threw on a faded flannel robe. She walked over to close the shutters, wanting to banish all light. The window was a quaint affair, specially designed by Derek, inlaid with ruby and azure glass facets in the shape of a mythical beast. Running her fingers over the panes, Pen found it hard not to cry.

She noticed an acrid smell, drifting in from outside. She glanced toward town. A dull-glowing red eye seemed to be staring at her from the horizon. The next moment she realized what it was: a fire was burning in the night, coming from somewhere in Gramercy. The wind had carried the smell of smoke, but Pen couldn't discern what was burning. It was big enough to be a house; the flames waved and flickered like wind-greedy banners. The sound of sirens could be heard, faint, faraway wails that made her shudder.

"Your Ladyship?" a muffled voice called from the other side of the door. Pen turned her head. It was Jasper. He'd never woken her in the middle of the night before. Pen pulled her wrapper tight and opened the door. A puzzling sight greeted her. Jasper was dressed in his waistcoat and creased gray trousers, a black cravat neatly knotted at his throat as if he were announcing dinner.

"Did the fire wake you up?" It was a silly question, she realized, given that even Jasper's utmost dedication wouldn't drive him to get out of bed and put on his uniform.

"No, ma'am," Jasper mumbled. "I just wanted to say that I'm leaving."

"Leaving? Now? What do you mean?"

"Giving notice, ma'am. I'm no longer able to serve."

"Why not? Has something happened?"

Jasper's face was contorted and his eyes refused to meet hers. "It's not the jackdaw, ma'am, if that's what you mean. I saw—things—but they are forgotten."

"All right." She kept her voice steady, despite the faint absurdity of his words.

"I had planned to give two weeks' notice, as per usual in service, but, um, things have changed beyond my control." At that moment Jasper's obvious effort to maintain his composure gave way; his voice broke with the strain.

Seeing his distress, Pen said, "Couldn't you at least wait until morning, Bert? This is so hasty. We could talk it over."

He looked startled at her use of his Christian name. For a split second he seemed uncertain, but then he shook his head, turned away without another word, and fled down the corridor. Pen heard the thumping of his heavy carpetbag against the stairs. Since Jasper didn't have a car, she mused, it would be a long trip to the road, much less to town.

Sighing, she turned back into her room. Out the window the banner of flames still waved. She couldn't think about Jasper; her eyes remained fixed on the fire. It had to be a house, she thought. Added to everything else that had happened, the fire deeply unsettled her. She was alone now except for the sleeping stranger downstairs. This didn't frighten her; if anything, she wanted to confide in him and ask for his help.

When she had looked in on him before going to bed, he had called her close to his chair by the fire. "I didn't tell you my name—Melchior."

"Are you a wizard?" She didn't wait for his nod or his distinction between a full-fledged wizard and an apprentice. A wave of relief made her want to burst out laughing, grateful that she wasn't cracked after all. It wasn't a coincidence that the last thing Derek had talked about before vanishing was wizards.

Pen had found Derek wandering about the scullery, staring at the huge old black cauldrons that belonged in a monastery or walled fortress. He was in a philosophical mood, the kind that often gestated a new book.

"Whether we know their names or not," he mused, "whether Merlin was the first or the last or just one of the most famous, wizards have always been among us. They are not a luxury but a necessity."

"Why?" Pen asked.

"Because we humans find life far too baffling and treacherous. Our own puny weakness is intolerable. A power must exist that can rescue us from calamity."

"I don't feel I've been rescued."

"That's a modern person speaking. You are in the habit of assuming that there are no monsters outside your door, no demons or dragons or mischievous fairy folk lying in wait. Until very recently, however, these menaces prowled the landscape, infesting every bosk and dell. You couldn't walk outside into your garden to pull carrots without danger of being made into a griffin's lunchmeat or vivisected by a giant's halberd." Derek paused, relishing the exotic vocabulary his readers expected.

"But the fairies are gone and the wizards with them, I suppose. Why?"

"Time, my dear, the tragedy of time. Everyone remembers a time when they were guarded from harm by omnipotent magic—their childhood. That's when we're imprinted with the image of beings who have all the power in the world. We called them father and mother. Their magical protection lasted only so long before we outgrew it. Think back—by the time you were ten or eleven, you had outgrown your household gods, who were reduced to the size of a mere father and mother with bills to pay and questions they couldn't answer. Poor deposed gods. Losing them is a terrible shock."

"Which is why, according to you, we have no magic anymore?"

"The whole world outgrew it, or is about to. Wizards didn't so much leave as wither away." Pen looked saddened. "I wish they were back. Life hasn't become more bearable for banishing them."

Standing at her window, Pen now noticed something that hadn't happened. The massive front doors of Emrys Hall hadn't banged shut when Jasper left. Without pausing to consider, she moved out into the corridor and made her way to the landing. "Jasper?" she called over the railing. When there was no reply, she hurried downstairs. The overhead light in the foyer was off. The vaulted marble space was dimly lit by two wrought-iron table lamps. She called again and thought she heard rustling from the direction of the drawing room. No light shone from the room, although the door was open. She advanced toward it.

The fire in the grate had subsided, but by the glow of the embers she could just make out a standing figure. The bulk of a carpetbag told her that it was Jasper, staring down where she had left the young stranger sleeping. The butler set his bag down and swayed from side to side, drunkenly or madly, it was hard to tell which. Pen took a step closer; he didn't look up. Now she saw that the curtains were pulled open and one set of French doors left ajar.

Jasper made a sudden lunge to his left. His hands reached out, as if clutching for a throat that wasn't there; he grunted in frustration and spun around.

"No, you don't," he growled, addressing thin air. "It's cats and rats, is it? I'll find you." Suddenly she knew what was going on—the butler was fighting an invisible opponent. She looked at the armchair where she had left Melchior; it was empty. There was a crashing sound as Jasper knocked over a side table with his next swing, and as he thrashed about, a large Chinese vase went over, smashing to bits.

"Stop, or I'll call the police." Pen made her threat as loud and firm as she could. Jasper whipped around as she turned on a lamp. "You've no right to be here. I'm not asking questions. Just go." Her heart was in her throat, but not because of Jasper. In the lamplight she saw something. Melchior, if he was Jasper's opponent, was no longer invisible. He stood, leaning against the mantel, no more than a foot from Jasper's side.

"Look out!" she cried.

At that instant Jasper spotted Melchior and swiped at his head with a vicious side-hand blow. "Ow," he bellowed as his hand smashed into the mantelpiece. He had missed Melchior's face by a foot—and yet how could that be? His opponent was standing exactly where he had been. He hadn't moved, at least not perceptibly.

Jasper was too enraged to clear out, despite the threat of the police. "Face me, you bloody coward," he said grimly. He drew back a fist and slammed it into Melchior's chest. The crack of bone against marble made Pen wince. Jasper screamed and put his fist to his mouth—he had missed his opponent again, by no more than inches. Pen watched in silent amazement. Melchior wasn't dodging the blows; he simply wasn't where he seemed to be.

The fight ended quickly. Hurt and humiliated, Jasper lost his rage for combat. "Who are you?" he mumbled.

Instead of answering, Melchior pointed to the open French doors. "You don't belong here," he said in a calm voice. "I won't harm you as long as you take your anger away. And tell *him* not to send you again."

"Him?" Jasper repeated in a confused voice. He gave a slow,

drugged nod, like a sleepwalker, and headed for the door. Pen noticed that the carpetbag was still sitting on the floor. "Wait," she said, and Jasper halted until the bag was placed in his hand. He clutched it absently and padded away into the night.

"What was he trying to do?"

"Steal the stone. But I was keeping it." Melchior patted the cushion of the armchair.

"Did he have a reason?"

"He had orders. He was under the influence of a power too strong to resist."

Pen looked at the apprentice, appreciating that his powers went further than transforming his shape. Although Melchior was much slighter than the butler, their struggle had not left him winded in the least. Before she could comment, however, he said, "I couldn't sleep. I've been lying awake thinking about humans."

She was startled. "But you're human, aren't you?"

"In some ways, yes. But in other ways I'm a stranger to your kind. I have a friend who calls you plucked angels, and he claims that you are a total waste of spirit. Do you ever think like that?"

"Of course, in honest moments. But I can be just as honest and think that we aren't a spiritual waste but a spiritual potential waiting to grow."

Neither of them said anything for a while.

"I need your help," the apprentice began again, "but I am afraid of you. I don't mean to be harsh, but if it were up to me, I would not have had you see anything. There is much humiliation in having a mortal witness us when we shift shapes. But that was only my weakness."

"I don't want you to be afraid. I'd like to understand you," Pen said simply.

Melchior nodded. "I assumed as much, or the stone wouldn't have fallen into your hands. That's part of the teaching."

"Merlin's teaching?" It was the first time they had acknowledged the name that had hovered around every strange event in the past three days. "Was it Merlin who said that humans are a waste of spirit?"

"No," Melchior admitted, and he laughed, relieved. "Master would never be that cynical. He only said that people live their whole lives shut in by walls. Reality stands before them, yet they don't see it, because what you call real is just the mirror image of your expectations. You project the same images everywhere you go. They blind you; they keep you chained to the past, but your greatest fear is that one day the mirror will show you reality. Master had compassion for that."

"I think I understand. But how do we find out what is real?"

Melchior looked at her. "Reality is simply what is; reality is the thing right in front of your nose, pressing so close that there is no room to miss it. But you do miss it, because all you see is what you think should be there."

Suddenly Pen smiled. "That's how you fought just then, wasn't it? You were right in front of your opponent's nose, but he couldn't find you. I thought you were invisible."

Melchior shook his head. "It takes a great deal of concentration to turn invisible. I'm not that good yet." He sounded a bit embarrassed. "But there's an easier way. I just stood where he didn't expect me to be. If you know where your opponent thinks you're going to be, then it is simple to stand somewhere else."

"So you read his mind?"

"No, I'm not that good, either. His eyes told me enough." Melchior reached under a cushion and pulled out the black velveteen bag that the butler had failed to steal. He withdrew Merlin's stone and held it up in front of Pen's face. "Do you feel anything?" he asked softly.

She wasn't sure. The stone looked the same; the same faint words were scratched on its surface. Melchior shook his head, as if directing her attention somewhere else. But where?

"I feel a swirling sensation," Pen said hesitantly. "A kind of swirling energy. It's very faint."

Approvingly Melchior said, "You are meant to learn from Merlin's stone. Do you know what the sensation is?"

"It feels like the stone is drawing me in."

He nodded. "At first it was like that for me, too. But Master told me that the stone was not doing anything. Nothing is doing anything, because there is only perfect peace and order. But Master told me that it takes many lifetimes to realize that. For the moment, this energy is your own mind beginning to pay attention. When attention is perfect, it is a point, like a diamond."

"And what does that do?"

"Something simple and yet extremely difficult—it allows you to see what is in front of you all along. The journey towards the point feels like a swirl because you are drawing your mind together from confusion to clarity, ever moving towards the point."

"I still don't know what you want me to do," Pen murmured. "You're lost; my intuition tells me that. Is that why you need my help?"

"I don't know. I've been looking for clues—that's why the stone made me come here. I was amazed that you had it, but I've been pondering. What's really amazing is that *he* doesn't have it."

"The one who now wants to steal it?"

"Yes. His name is Mordred. He's not an ordinary enemy. To even find him, you will have to look into secret places where he already rules. In your own heart are the ashes of the houses he has burned." Pen saw that tears were standing in the apprentice's eyes. Melchior walked to the French doors and gazed at the distant fire. She had forgotten about it, and now it was almost gone, reduced to a dull glow no brighter than one of the coals in the grate.

"See that?" he said. "Imagine someone who could burn down every dwelling in this town with a wave of his hand and just as easily burn hope and happiness. Would you be prepared to confront an evil such as that? The amount of misery he has inflicted is all around you; you call it ordinary life." Pen saw a look of sweetness tinged with pain cross the young stranger's face, and in the recesses of her mind a voice said, *Remember that look. It is compassion.*

Then in her own heart a gentle, silent weeping unexpectedly began; it swelled quickly, straining against the gates of grief. She hung her head, and Melchior's voice said near her ear, "Let it begin. Cry for what he has done to you."

The floodgates opened. All the sorrow of being human seemed

to pour out at once. Pen didn't feel just for herself. She was the mother of sons lost in war but also the sons; she was a baby dying of famine but at the same time the greed that caused the famine. The rage born of unreasoning fear burned in her, and yet the light that would quell the rage was hated and pushed away. Wracked with sobs, she could still hear Melchior's voice: "Good, you are strong enough to learn."

After a few moments the pain ebbed. She knew that she had only experienced the edge of a single wave, and it frightened her. "What happened? Why did it stop?"

"You are given a choice. It isn't fair to ask you to join me if you don't choose freely. So you had a taste." She gave him a look of fear and anticipation. "There is more to it than what you've just felt," Melchior said, wanting to reassure her. "I was very afraid at the beginning, until Master told me that pain isn't the truth; it's what you have to get through in order to find the truth."

The overwhelming feelings were almost gone from her heart. "It's all right. I want to understand."

He replied, not looking up, "It would be unbearable to hurt you, and where we will go is very different from these surroundings." His eyes swept the drawing room and its gilt fixtures. When he looked at her again, the sweet, pained expression was in his face. "If you want, I will tell you a story, one that Master told me."

"Yes, please."

"There once lived a king of India who was visited by a wandering holy man. To show his respect, the king lavished the holy man with every kind of rich food and drink. His begging bowl and staff were taken away, and fresh robes of silk were draped over his body. He was given a feather bed to sleep on and numerous attendants to carry out his slightest wish. One day at banquet before the assembled court the king announced that he was going to make the holy man his prime minister.

"'Oh, but I cannot accept,' the holy man said.

"'Why not?' the king asked. 'You will be the most powerful man in the kingdom, excepting only myself.'

"The holy man replied, 'But I am more powerful than you

already.' At this effrontery the court buzzed like wasps. 'I do not mean to offend Your Highness,' the holy man continued. 'To show you how touched I am by your offer, I will gladly give you all my power. Follow me.' The holy man rose and called for his begging bowl and staff. Without another word he walked away from the court.

"The king could not decide if he was more curious or angry with the old beggar's boldness, but in the end curiosity won out. He dressed in traveling clothes and followed the holy man on foot. It was a beautiful morning, and the king enjoyed the journey, which lasted until nightfall. The two weary travelers slept by a stream under the full moon and were up by dawn.

"'Do we have much farther to go?' the king asked somewhat anxiously. He was tired, and in the night he had begun to think of his enemies back home. The holy man said nothing but kept walking. Thus they continued for two days. On the third day they reached the frontier of the kingdom.

"'Stop,' the king commanded. 'I must turn back.'

"'Why?' the holy man asked. 'What I want to show you is only a step away.'

"The king retorted, 'I can go no farther. If I cross the frontier, my throne will be seized by my enemies.'

"The holy man nodded. 'I said that I have power you can only dream of, and here it is: I can walk away from this kingdom while you, its ruler, cannot. If you want my power, just follow me.'

"But the king would not. With a smile the holy man strode over the frontier, a free spirit, leaving the dejected king to return to his palace."

As Melchior's voice died away, Pen did not speak for a while. She felt very quiet inside, and she noticed that an empty space existed in her chest. The apprentice leaned over and gently touched the spot where her breastbone lay beneath the skin.

"There," he said, "is the frontier."

Pen trembled. If her heart had exploded or unfolded like a rose, neither would have surprised her. Instead, a warm fluid feeling of joy flowed into her chest. It came in waves, one cascading over the other. Sweetness gave way to ecstasy as she imagined that arrows of golden light were about to pierce her. In the intensity of it she had no words to express the power of her bliss. And then she must have gone away, across the invisible frontier.

When she came back, the afghan was draped over her. She was sitting in the armchair by the fireplace, squinting at the glare of a bright dawn.

"Are you ready?" Melchior asked.

He was squatting on the floor like an African guide on safari. Pen sat up, drowsy and confused. Her head buzzed. It wasn't clear what had happened that night, if anything.

"I'm sorry," she mumbled. "Ready for what?"

"We have to leave this house, and we have to leave it like strangers who never expect to return. Your servant—"

"Jasper."

"Yes. He will expose us. He doesn't want to, which is why he ran away, but Mordred will give him no other choice. It's only a matter of time before an accident would happen. You would be killed or made to disappear." Pen was taking this in, her face uncertain. Melchior gave her a look of clinical appraisal. "You have had a moment of opening. It was true, it happened, but in order to survive from now on, you must forget everything and anticipate nothing. Master wants you to know that."

"Master?" Pen looked around bewildered. There was no one else in the room, yet there *was* someone else. She could feel a presence surrounding her.

Melchior spoke, but this time the words were not his own. "Welcome, daughter. You are the first open heart I've found. Let this be our secret, and come. Come out of the circle of fear and into the circle of love." It felt like centuries since Pen had heard such words. But she was as certain as age rolled upon age that she had heard them before, and this was only a reminder. She stood up and said to Melchior, "I'm ready."

14
ASHES TO ASHES

By the time the local fire brigade arrived on the scene, the blazing house was beyond salvage. Tongues of fire had stripped the walls and roof, shingles and clapboards down to a black, hollowed skeleton.

"It's arson, Tom. I'm sure of it," was the first thing out of the chief's mouth. Chief Officer Cochran didn't speak loudly in the din, but Leading Firefighter Hopkins heard him and nodded. It looked like any other fire born from a tipped skillet of bacon grease or a mouse biting through some old wiring. But something about the flames was malicious; veteran firefighters could feel it in their bones.

This was a terrible, greedy fire, ready to swallow the neighborhood in one gulp. In controlled fury Cochran barked out his orders: "Simpson! Let's get two units on the left and right, try to flank it. What's holding up crowd control, Tom? Push those people back behind the barricades, we've got to get water on the roof in two seconds or we'll lose it." He was driven by the knowledge that the cheap semidetached dwellings up and down the street could go off like tinder, creating a firestorm in minutes.

"Is everybody clear, Tom? Do we have the family out?" he shouted.

Leading Firefighter Hopkins passed the question along to a smoke-begrimed fireman staggering out of what used to be a front door. The fireman pulled off his canvas helmet and visor. Streaks of soot and sweat covered his face; he gasped from the intolerable heat. "I can't tell how many was in there to begin with, but if anybody's left, they've met God."

Hopkins nodded and cupped his hands. "Chief, we've got all we're going to get." Cochran gave the signal, and arcing spews of water hit the roof. The fire hissed in rage, spitting smoke and steam.

Someone said, "I know the family. Their name's Edgerton. I can try to gather them up for a count."

Cochran turned and shook his head. "Better wait for the police, who must be taking their lazy sweet time." He was confronted by a young man in sneakers and jeans who had thrown his T-shirt on backward in his haste to get to the scene.

"I *am* the police," the young man said, moving toward the barricade.

The fire chief pulled him back. "Where's your identification?"

"I left my badge at home, but I'm okay. My name is Callum. You can call in and ask for Chief Inspector Westlake, CID. He's my boss."

At that moment an explosion ripped off one whole side of the house. The impact rocked Cochran, almost throwing him off his feet.

"Didn't I tell you to shut off the damn mains?" he shouted. He ran toward the source of the explosion.

By his side Leading Firefighter Hopkins shouted, "We did shut 'em, Chief. I think it's residual gas in the pipes or the water heater."

Arthur Callum, the young man in jeans, didn't wait on anyone else's authority. He slipped between sawhorse barricades and began searching the faces in the crowd. He figured that Winnie and her mother—and Paddy Edgerton if he made it out in his wheelchair—would be together. The crowd was staring in awe at the flames, as if at a pagan rite, their faces flickering orange and black.

"Winnie!" Arthur shouted. "Winnie!" He ran from person to person, surprised at how difficult it was to recognize people he knew well by daylight. Suddenly he thought he saw the Edgerton boy standing in an opening between three or four milling bodies. He was dressed in pajamas with a man's overcoat thrown over them, his arms wrapped tight around his chest. Arthur waved and shouted, but his voice died in the booming racket caused by falling beams, crumbling brickwork, and the fire's roar. The boy seemed peculiarly unmoved by the sight of his home being wiped out. Arthur moved toward him, jostling spectators out of the way.

What was the name of Paddy Edgerton's boy? Arthur didn't know the family that well; his mother read tea leaves mostly for Winnie, the plump daughter. Gerald. That was it. "Jerry," he shouted. Hearing his name, the boy looked over his shoulder. "Where is everybody? Did your family get out?" Arthur cried.

"The fire will take one but save many," said a woman very close by. Ignoring her, Arthur stumbled in the dark. His shins barked against some bundles on the ground. "Let the boy go," a woman's voice said.

"What?" Arthur replied, trying not to lose sight of Jerry Edgerton.

"You're not listening. I must leave to help with the fire, but it's important that you listen."

"Look, I can't, I'm on police business. They don't need your help with the fire. Keep clear and don't get into trouble."

The woman laughed with strange certainty. "The firemen can't do enough. It's me, me and the others, that's keeping this fire from spreading. We'd call on you, but you're too green just yet."

Impatient as he was to get away, Arthur paused to look at her. With an investigator's eye he quickly gathered in the relevant details—small build, stocky, fortyish, a green felt hat covering a mass of black hair, and a matching coat. Everything about her was shabby genteel. The bundles on the ground apparently belonged to her, too. She had to be homeless or perhaps a slightly deranged spinster attracted to disasters.

"I think you'd be better off not hanging around fires," he said sternly.

"Ah, do you, sire?"

Arthur was startled. Crazy as the archaic word sounded, it struck a fathomless chord. The woman in the felt hat laughed again. He tried to make his way around her, but she skillfully blocked him with the bulk of her body.

"We'll be at court, just inquire for the court of miracles. Can you remember? Oh, you seem so distracted," she mumbled.

"I must get by, you'll have to stand aside," Arthur said forcefully. She made a space for him to pass and said, "If you can listen at all, just remember. When you look in the ashes, look well."

"All right, all right, I will," he replied, straining with impatience. He peered over her head and was relieved to see that Jerry Edgerton hadn't moved; he stood rapt before the flames, just where he'd been. "Jerry, hey!" Arthur shouted, catching the boy's attention at last. He didn't expect Jerry to bolt, but he did, sliding between two spectators with a furtive twist of his body.

"Wait," Arthur called, pushing past the crazy woman. Jerry Edgerton looked over his shoulder, a flash of bitter resentment captured by the glare of the flames. Then he was gone.

Feeling deflated and tired, Arthur looked around to see a police car pulling up. The bulky figure of Hamish McPhee stepped out. Arthur trotted over. "Have you seen Winnie?" McPhee asked, worried.

Arthur shook his head. "Something's amiss. I can't find the family except for the boy, Jerry, and he ran away as soon as he saw me."

"Probably set the blaze himself," McPhee remarked grimly. When he saw the look on Arthur's face, he added, "Sorry, it's just that I'm too well acquainted with his likes. They're not all angels, you know." He scanned the crowd. "I'm going to use the horn." He picked up the car's microphone from its cradle and flicked a switch. His booming voice carried over the crowd: "If you have any information about the survivors, please come to the police car. Help us find the survivors, please." At first there was no response. The crowd milled aimlessly; the firemen rushed about with disciplined haste, totally absorbed in their work. Then Arthur saw a man approaching with a woman on his arm; she was bent over, almost collapsed.

"I believe I have someone for you," the man said. He had to lift up the woman's face—it was the mother, Edie. Her features were crumpled with grief and shock.

Arthur placed his hand on her shoulder. "Mrs. Edgerton, can you talk? Is everyone all right?" She trembled, unable to comprehend. "We need to lie her down in the back of the car. Do you have a coat or blanket to cover her?"

McPhee nodded and with the help of the man who was holding her eased the frightened woman into the police car. She slumped across the backseat, numbly letting herself be covered with a blue police blanket from the emergency kit.

"Mrs. Edgerton, we know you've had a shock. There's an ambulance coming straightaway, but can you tell me anything about the others?" Arthur asked. Edie shook her head. "I've seen Jerry." She looked at Arthur with glazed eyes. "He's all right. I can't bring him to you yet, but he's all right, I promise."

"All right?" she mumbled. "He would be."

It was a strange comment, even under the circumstances. McPhee frowned. "We'd better nick him as quick as we can," he said direly.

Arthur stood up. "I'll comb the crowd again." As he spoke, they saw another figure walking unsteadily out of the crowd. McPhee recognized Winnie and rushed over to help her. When he reached her side, she burst into tears and sobbed on his shoulder. "Now, now," he said, "you're safe. We've found almost everybody in the family."

She looked up with stricken eyes. "It's Dad, Hamish, I'm sure he was trapped."

He hugged her close and looked over his shoulder at Arthur, who shook his head. "Did you see his chair?"

Burying her face in the breast of McPhee's jacket, Winnie shook her head. "You know he can't walk, Hamish, you know he can't," she said, weeping feebly.

By this time Arthur was circling around the back of the barricades. The flames looked almost as ferocious as before, but the firefighters had turned the tide, and much of the tension had leaked out of the onlooking crowd. Fire hoses had soaked all the neighboring roofs, and no other structures were in danger. Sleepy bystanders had begun drifting away, passing Arthur in the dark.

"Jerry," he called. Some boys were in the crowd, but they didn't respond. It was peculiar, he thought, that none of the neighbors had helped the Edgerton family to safety or offered support. Something told him that the Edgertons had set themselves apart, either by their hostility or strangeness. The cordoned-off street was clogged with fire trucks and police cars. Passing by, the people on foot looked drained and exhausted as they drifted back into the waiting houses of the town.

Against this slow-moving backdrop, a sudden burst of activity under a streetlight some fifty feet away caught Arthur's eye. He made out two figures, one tall, the other short, who appeared to be arguing. As he approached them, the short figure cried out in a boy's voice. Now he could see that the taller figure was a thin, dark-haired man, who had collared the boy and was shaking him hard; the boy kicked at him wildly, trying to get away.

"Police!" Arthur shouted, breaking into a trot. He could make out the pale face of the boy now—it was Jerry Edgerton—but the man who had hold of him was turned away, not recognizable. The boy doubled his struggle, then broke free and ran off, leaving the man with a torn shirt collar in his hands. Arthur came up. "Who are you? What are you doing?" he accosted the man angrily.

"I'm trying to help you. Didn't you say you wanted that boy for starting the fire?"

Arthur shook his head. "Nothing like that. I wanted to see him back with his family. Besides, how do you know anything about it?"

The man gave a crooked smile. "You can see how much he wants to be with his family."

"You have no business handling the boy that way. He's in shock."

"I very much doubt it," the man said blandly. Despite his controlled manner, Arthur could sense an animal frustration in the man, like a cat that has lost its prey. Arthur had calmed down enough to recognize that this was the same man who had brought Edie Edgerton to the police car when she was in near collapse.

Arthur hesitated when another association clicked in. "If you don't mind my asking, what's your name?"

"You know my name very well. It's Ambrosius," the man retorted coldly.

Arthur was rattled. Why hadn't he recognized his mother's tarot "master" straight off? He had spotted him twice that evening, yet somehow the familiar features—slicked black hair, thick eyebrows, long neck, and supercilious smile—hadn't come into focus until just then. "I still don't know why you're here," Arthur said sharply.

Ambrosius looked unruffled. "The same reason you are—curiosity. I must say that I have ample reason to be on the scene, given that my house is at the bottom of the street. I was concerned about its safety." He pointed languidly to a large brick structure a hundred feet away.

"I wasn't here out of curiosity. I don't have to remind you that police are needed at an emergency." In fact the night patrol were perfectly capable of lending a police presence. It was a strong sense of premonition that had pulled Arthur to the scene, not his but his mother's. All his life they had been closely attuned. He had woken with a vague sense of unease and going into the hall had seen his mother standing in her bedroom doorway dressed in a bathrobe and street shoes.

"What's the matter? You're not going out like that, are you?" Arthur asked.

His mother looked distracted. "I don't know. There's a fire," she said uncertainly. Behind her he could see flames and smoke through her bay window.

"It can't spread this far, Mum. You can see that it's blocks away."

She shook her head anxiously. "It's not that."

"Then what is it?"

"I just feel I should be there." She stopped, as if wanting to say more but unable to. Arthur didn't succeed in getting a more coherent explanation, and in the end she'd agreed to stay home only if he would go. Along the way, Arthur realized that he wasn't just coddling her. He had a sense of premonition as well.

"Can you tell me why you were struggling with the Edgerton boy?" he now demanded of Ambrosius.

Ambrosius seemed to consider this request for a second. "It's not as if I have to answer your questions, you know, but as it happens, I believe that he might have set the fire himself."

"His own home? With his family inside and a crippled dad? I don't believe it."

Ambrosius shrugged. "Unfortunately, he is known to be a troubled boy. You do not seem to be aware that Gerald has been suspected of fire-starting before, since he was quite small in fact." Arthur shook his head. "Well, I'm not one to spread tales, but my residence has been in this neighborhood for more than fifteen years. As a child Gerald was caught playing with matches in the coal chute of that selfsame house. The fire spread to a nearby rotted wall, and the whole dwelling almost went up. Most distressing. I believe it is a psychological truism that children start fires when there is trouble at home. The modern term is *abuse,* if I'm not mistaken, but of course there was no proof, not real proof."

Ambrosius's voice had taken on a singsong quality, both mocking and insinuating, that revolted Arthur. He wanted to stop this oily stream of insinuation, but it had a seductive quality.

"Do you know Miss Clinch?" Ambrosius asked. "A most upright female, unmarried, who serves as dietitian at St. Justin's. There was an exceedingly nasty incident there recently. It had to do with the school mascot. The poor creature is an aging spaniel named Chips. Miss Clinch avers that no one quite knows how a grizzled old hunting dog ever got picked as a mascot—apparently it was the whim of a rich benefactor. But I tarry.

"Someone maliciously tried to set dear Chips on fire, not exactly the treatment a mascot deserves. The culprit couldn't be found. Then the upright Miss Clinch remembered the Edgerton boy's history. He was called in and interrogated. Naturally he confessed nothing. The court of opinion, it grieves me to say, is harsh, however. Gerald was sent to Coventry. Miss Clinch believes that he is guilty. But she is very suspicious of the male sex; I'm sure her entire experience of us is that she lets in the gas man to read the meter once a month. In any event, if you don't believe my little narrative, you can oblige yourself by checking it out."

"I will, don't worry," Arthur retorted, his jaw set. Ambrosius gave him an ironical bow, turned on his heels, and departed in the direction of his house. It seemed to Arthur that they had been engaged for no more than a minute, but it must have been five or ten. He looked around, hoping that Jerry Edgerton might have returned, but he was nowhere in sight. The street was deserted, and Arthur realized that he had wasted precious time stopping to talk to Ambrosius. He shouldn't have taken the insolent bait the man threw out.

The police cars had left, escorting the ambulance with Edie and Winnie in it. The firemen were beginning to unhook their hoses and reload the trucks. Arthur approached the chief. "Excuse me, but have you ever been called to this house before?"

"And what would you know about that?" Cochran's face was slack with exhaustion.

"The police have a file, I'm sure, but this is just a personal inquiry."

"Well, yes, we have been here before," the chief said reluctantly. "A neighbor happened to see a wisp of smoke out the side of the coal chute and phoned in the alarm. Lucky for them the house didn't go up that time."

"Which was how long ago?"

"About five, no, six years back."

"That's fairly long ago, but even so, two alarms from the same house. Might lead one to suspect a firebug, wouldn't it?" The fire chief nodded. "Is the boy under suspicion?"

"Not yet. I don't want to speculate. Word was that he started the first one. We never got him to say so. He's a bit of a tough nut."

Arthur frowned. "Tough? He must have been about seven back then, no more than nine. You couldn't break down his story?"

The fire chief shook his head. "We'll investigate and should report the results by week's end."

Ten minutes later the rest of the fire equipment had been reeled in. Most of the exhausted firemen were already dozing off in the cabs of the trucks while some hung on to the sides, apparently asleep while gripping the lashed-on ladders. Arthur watched them, reluctant to leave the scene. The Edgerton house gave off smoldering heat like an overactive compost pile. He walked closer. A few faint muffled explosions went off under the rubble. Beer cans, he thought, and was reminded of Paddy Edgerton, the one who didn't get out. Arthur supposed that one of the first things the investigators would recover in the morning would be the cripple's twisted wheelchair.

A pang of sorrow ran through Arthur. The Edgertons were unremarkable folk. Paddy was not the only worker ever injured on the job and retired with a miserable pension. His wife wasn't the only woman pretending to respect a useless man around the house. Troubled children, veiled despair, snatched moments of happiness clutched like chips in greasy newspaper. Staring at the burned-down house, Arthur wondered all at once why every house in town didn't burst into flames.

Perhaps they will.

The horribleness of the threat hit him with great force. Like cracked walls groaning under an unbearable weight, his ordinary optimism collapsed. A cold mudslide of hopelessness hit him, and he saw in an instant the flimsy protection people rely upon. So little, so little kept things from turning into a disaster. Women who chatted over the butcher counter could turn into wolves preying on one another; happy families could explode with hatred; despair could stop traffic, every driver paralyzed, his hands clutching the wheel.

The wonder was that these things didn't happen all the time. Arthur felt terribly confused. He put his hand up to his heart in a vague gesture, wishing he could reach inside and repair the delicate tissue of hope that had torn. But he couldn't reach inside, and the fabric was not repairable. With dull eyes he looked down at his feet. Unconsciously he had walked into the rubble; his shoes were covered with gray, water-soaked ashes, ruined.

The woman in the green felt hat had told him to search the ashes well. He decided to do so. Knowing that he looked like a crazy, he dug his hands into the black char and began to stir around. Sweeping right and left, he felt like a blind man groping for a lost treasure. Chunks of brick and wood scraped his fingers; he broke a nail on a jutting floorboard. In a matter of minutes his forearms were exhausted from moving so much debris, but he kept squatting, moving forward an inch at a time.

There was absolutely nothing he expected to find. Arson wasn't at issue—the fire investigators would uncover oily rags or a twisted can of white kerosene in the ashes. *The kinds of things kids find around the house.* He pushed the thought to the back of his mind. His T-shirt and jeans were no doubt ruined by now. Suddenly his hands were in front of his face holding something. They had grabbed it without his knowing, and now, like trusty hunting dogs, his hands presented the prize for his inspection. It was a long, thin object, heavy, metallic. His fingertips brushed one edge; it had straps made of leather.

A scabbard. The instant he recognized it, he knew that he had been looking for just this thing. But his mind had no chance to study the situation. Another realization hit him. The sword was back! He scrabbled out furiously, looking for the blade that fit the scabbard—it wasn't to be found. Despite his disappointment, the very fact that the sword was back filled him with elation, although his rational mind had no idea why.

Arthur staggered to his feet and started wading out of the rubble. Covered with ashes, he looked charred and primeval. Nobody was about, but he still tried his best to wipe his clothes off. The whole while, his mind raced, thinking about the sword. It wasn't nearby—he was certain of that. Somewhere, someone must have told him that a sword had been lost. The calamity was beyond measure, yet this burning house had changed things.

The fire will take one but save many.

Remembering her words, he half-expected the lady in the green felt hat to pop out of the ashes—nothing could surprise him anymore. Something had shifted in Arthur. It was pointless to think of her as crazy now. She was prophetic, and that's how things would be from now on. Not ordinary and easily explained but—what?

Symbolic, knotted with hidden patterns and meanings. There really wasn't a single word adequate to describe it.

Arthur thought back to those optical illusions that look like an everyday tree and underneath bear the caption, "Can you find the ten children hiding in the branches?" He had entered a similar world. Trees he had walked past without seeing anything would have secrets hiding in their branches. Wells would have fairies in the bottom, staring at him when he gazed at his reflection. Chance words from strangers on the bus would open coded chapters written in invisible ink.

So the fire must have its riddle hidden in it. He stared dumbly at the scabbard. Clues, clues. *Can you find the ten children hiding in the branches?*

It all came clear. The blaze had been a distraction. What had really been happening was a struggle over the sword. The firemen hadn't suspected, nor had he or any of the mesmerized bystanders. The woman in the felt hat was certainly right: Arthur was much too green. He was like a baby crawling around a stage, having no idea that all around him cues were being thrown and caught. Jerry Edgerton had been acting his part, like the woman in the hat, Ambrosius, and perhaps even his mother. She had had her premonitions. Arthur examined the empty scabbard and threw it back into the smoldering pile.

Deep in thought, he missed the turn where Fellgate Lane met Mogg Street. He retraced his steps, and the damp night raised goose flesh on his exposed arms. The sound of his footsteps was unnaturally loud on the cobblestones. He imagined that he could hear birds stirring in their sleepy nests and even worms burrowing underground. It was this combination of extreme alertness and near-to-bursting excitement that kept his nerves on edge.

His own street, lined with houses and trees he had known since boyhood, appeared totally foreign. It took an effort of will to find the darkened porch of his mother's house; he felt for the handrail like someone who had never entered the place before. His hand reached for the doorknob, but he couldn't turn it. The idea of going to bed after such a remarkable day was impossible. It would be like dying back into the ordinary world he had fit into before but never would again.

Arthur sat down on the dew-moistened wooden steps and looked up. He didn't know it yet, but he had entered into a silent compact with people he had never met—a woman in a felt hat, two boys lost in a woods, a murdered author who flickered in and out of being a wizard, a woman escaping into the unknown with a magical apprentice. The bonds holding them together were invisible, but that night they all looked up at the same moonlit sky and felt completely alone. In fact, the web of time was drawing them inexorably toward a center. Providence, however, protected them from sensing the clawed foot that patiently tested the outskirts of the web, waiting for the right moment to pounce.

15
LONELY HOUSE

"When I was a little girl," Peg Callum recalled, "Gypsies would come right down the High Street in their painted wagons, and the lady Gypsies would set up a tent to read palms and tea leaves. I knew I'd read leaves one day, too, in that funny way children sometimes know. Of course my father thought the Gypsies were totally disreputable, but my mother put great store by them. She said they could tell when a baby would get scarlatina or a house catch on fire."

"They were the ones who set the houses on fire, so people claim," Arthur said.

"Well, I would have forgiven them anything. The Gypsies had such beautiful clothes—all fancy patches of yellow and red silk with enormous hoops in their ears. The Gypsy men rode black ponies with their babies tied on the side, and you would see grandmothers who looked eight thousand years old sitting on the backs of the wagons smoking cigars. I'm sorry they left. No one knows where they went to. They simply melted away. It was long before you were born."

Arthur's mother sat at the kitchen table musing over a plate of half-eaten eggs and toast. He had found her there, waiting for him with his breakfast, when he came down the morning after the fire.

"I don't think Gypsies set that fire last night," he said.

"Then who did, Edie's boy?"

"It's hard not to suspect him, now that he's run away."

Peg shook her head. "I can't believe it. He'd have to be a regular psychopath to try to burn his family up alive and stand by watching."

"Psychopaths start somewhere."

"I'm sorry, but you sound so cynical."

"Professional cynicism, Mum, that's all."

"That's the worst kind, in my opinion." Peg cast a look of mild reproof at him, and Arthur wondered, for the thousandth time, whether she was extremely naive or something altogether different. The truth was hard to pin down. His mother's total inability to think evil of anyone was a peculiar trait. In an age of faith it would have been a mark of sainthood; nowadays it was a questionable form of denial.

"What do you really know about this man Ambrosius?"

The sudden change of topic startled Peg. "I realize you don't like him, dear."

"It's not a matter of dislike, though he does fancy himself to a disgusting degree. I met him last night at the fire acting peculiarly."

"Well, I'm sure that's open to interpretation. You take after your father. He would have loathed Master Ambrosius." For some reason, this observation made her smile.

"I phoned up Westlake first thing this morning to tell him that I wanted to run a background check on Mr. Amberside. That's his real name, you know—Terence Amberside. He must have a taste for esoterica—the name Ambrosius, I found out, is Latin for Merlin."

"You make such a funny policeman. I rather thought you'd turn out a painter or a dancer." Arthur grimaced. "You shouldn't turn your back on your sensitive side. It's not unmasculine to be gentle."

"You're doing an excellent job of distracting me, Mum, but I wish you'd just listen. Your precious master isn't in danger of arrest."

"Good."

In fact, when Arthur had phoned the station, Westlake had regarded his request as improper. "You can't go on a personal witchhunt against this man, even if you think he's a charlatan."

"He's more than that. The fire was deliberately set."

"That's pure speculation on your part. We can't assume arson when we don't even have a preliminary report in our hands."

"Sir, is it asking too much to make sure if Ambrosius is on the up-and-up? It seems routine to me."

"If you had a case, yes. I sympathize with the fact that your Merlin remains unavailable. But to haul in an irrelevant house fire and propose to harass this—what does he call himself?"

"Ambrosius."

"Preposterous. Sounds like a Christmas pudding."

"I'm pretty sure it can't be his real name."

"It isn't."

"What? You know about him?" Arthur was caught completely off guard. He sensed Westlake's quiet pleasure at the other end of the line.

"You weren't even born then. But I remember Terry Amberside from my childhood—he was several grades behind me in school. His father peddled antiques; Terry worked beside him in the old shop on Tremont Street before leaving town for several years. He returned to settle the estate once his parents died. There was a bit of money piled up over the years, and the rather grand house he occupies was his inheritance."

"Does he have a record?"

"Nothing that's crossed our desks. Probably the most evil thing he's ever done is to underreport his taxes to the Inland Revenue in order to keep that house going. I am somewhat at a loss why you find this man so sinister. He may be offering solace to old maids at a price and reading mumbo jumbo into a pasteboard deck, but none of his clients has ever lodged a formal complaint."

"I saw him roughing up Jerry Edgerton."

"From what I gather, the boy is a hooligan. Whatever you say to the contrary, Master Ambrosius is a semirespectable citizen in society's eyes, except for the chapel Methodists. They think he's Satan."

"Why's that?"

"I don't know. Bigotry would be my guess."

"Or it could be something else. He makes me uneasy. He goes about playing Jack the lad, ridiculously full of himself, but he's deeper than he looks." Arthur regretted his words almost before they came out. Westlake growled skeptically and hung up.

Afterward, while his mother waited breakfast, Arthur had his wash. As he was shaving, he suddenly remembered his promise to call Emrys Hall. How had it slipped away? The fantastic scene in the drawing room, all but a hallucination now, must have tricked his mind into filing it away under dreams.

Leaving flecks of lather on his cheeks, Arthur phoned but got no answer. Troubled, he dressed hurriedly, and when he came down to breakfast, it was all he could do to sit still and eat.

"You're just pushing that poached egg around on your plate," his mother observed. He knew she wanted him to confide in her. His cursory remarks about the Edgerton fire had not been sufficient. But the attack on Ambrosius—he was sure she saw it as an attack—had turned her quiet and subdued.

"Mum, I'm not bringing up Ambrosius to upset you." He reached across the table for her hand. "I'm trying to get to the heart of a game that somebody's playing, and I don't want you to be hurt."

"Hurt?" She looked genuinely surprised.

"It's too vague to explain yet. I went to see Aunt Pen, you know, and it seems that Derek may have disappeared. We aren't certain about that—most missing persons return after a day or two. Until I had definite news, I didn't want to bother you."

Her attention had started to wander. "You used to play with your eggs as a child."

There she goes, he thought, pulling her gambit of retreating at the first hint of unpleasantness. Arthur hesitated. "Maybe I should have told you before going over there. Look, I think Pen would really like to see you. I know you haven't spoken for lo these many years, but I'm going round there before reporting at the station. You could come along."

His mother looked uncertain. "Shouldn't we call first?"

"I tried already, but I didn't get any answer."

"And you're worried?"

Arthur was taken aback by her sudden prescience. "Yes, maybe. The servants have all been let go. Aunt Pen wanted to be alone to think through this whole situation with Derek."

His mother regarded him with unexpected shrewdness. "There must be more to it if the servants have been dismissed. There's something Pen doesn't want them to see."

"You're right." When Arthur didn't elaborate, Peg narrowed her eyes. Remarkably, his mother seemed to be on the verge of interrogating him, but she made a visible effort to suppress her curiosity.

"If Pen wants to be alone, I shouldn't be surprised. Why don't we leave it to her about seeing me? We've left it to her long enough as it is." Peg stood up from the table and kissed her son on the cheek. "I'm sorry about the breakfast. I knew you didn't want any." That, Arthur knew, was her way of thanking him for revealing more than he wanted to.

When he came out of the house, Katy Kilbride was leaning against the patrol car, smoking a cigarette. "You look chipper," she commented. Arthur had circles under his eyes, and a patch of hair sticking out sideways where he had lain on it wrong.

"Not much sleep," he replied curtly.

"I thought a lad like you always slept well." The faint innuendo made him uneasy. He resolved that this was going to be one of their "professional" mornings. Silently Arthur climbed into the driver's seat. They alternated days at the wheel, and Katy never forgot which day was hers. As she got in, Arthur sensed that she was embarrassed for coming on strong. It was an easy thing to forgive.

"I'd like to make a short detour to the Rees place," Arthur said. "The people there are sort of long-lost relations, and I promised to look in. Actually, it's been three days since Sir Derek was last seen by his wife—that's my aunt."

If she was surprised, Katy didn't show it. She nodded and looked out the window. She was in a strange mood, he thought. "How are you feeling, anyway?" he asked.

Her head turned with deliberate slowness. "That's an odd question, isn't it?"

"It is?"

"If you consider the source." The bitterness in her voice snagged his conscience like a burr. He regarded Katy's plain face. Her nose was prematurely starting to redden, and her ginger hair bristled where it should have flowed. She had good eyes, however, clear and blue as a tidal pool. But he couldn't strike a spark of feeling for her, and they both knew it, despite having never exchanged a word on the subject, at least not directly.

He had never encouraged her, but there were times when her feelings for him couldn't be buried so easily. "Being in love is a tragedy," Arthur remembered from a book somewhere, "because one person always loves more than the other." And Arthur didn't even begin to be in love with Katy, which made it all the worse for her.

They drove in silence for the next few miles before turning into the tree-lined drive to Emrys Hall. "Gloomy place," Katy remarked. Arthur was surprised—he had thought the entry was grand—but she was right. The beech trees looked older today, as if they had weathered a century of stormy nights. The shadows that they cast over the road seemed dank instead of cool.

The dramatic turn that unveiled the house didn't surprise him anymore, but Katy had apparently never seen it before. "Wow," she said. "Splendor."

"Do you notice something strange?"

"What?"

"The front door appears to be open." Arthur accelerated, throwing up a shower of the carefully laid golden gravel. When they pulled up to the entrance, Arthur sprang out of the car, not waiting for Katy. "Wait here?" he said over his shoulder.

"Why? It's only an open door."

The gaping portals of Emrys Hall so distracted Arthur that at first he didn't notice the long grass growing up through the flagstones of the portico. Walking ahead, he felt his footing shift and slide.

"Careful," Katy said behind him. Arthur looked down. A loose paving stone had slipped under his feet. "A bit of a shambles when you get up close."

In surprise Arthur saw that she was right. Grimy streaks ran down the face of the house; the upstairs windows were dull and dirty. "It's changed," he said, disturbed.

"Since the eighteenth century? Not that much."

"No, I mean since just yesterday. They had put a lot into upkeep. It was nearly perfect. Something's very wrong."

Katy looked at him, her moodiness replaced with intrigue. "Well, it's not exactly overgrown like Sleeping Beauty's castle. I mean, what are a few weeds and a cracked step or two?"

But by this time Arthur had entered the foyer. "Pen?" he called. "It's Arthur. Are you here?"

The high domed ceiling with its floating Italian cherubs looked down blankly. "No one's home," Arthur said.

"You never can tell. Maybe she's in the garden. Are these relations distant enough to shoot us if we trespass?"

Arthur turned to her. "No, really, I'm worried. There were people here yesterday—my aunt and the butler at least, and a guest of sorts. I came away very late and didn't like leaving her here alone and unprotected."

"Three people isn't alone, and it is her home, after all. Most people don't need protecting from their servants. But I don't mind if you want to look around." Arthur gave her a grateful look.

In the empty drawing room, one French door was ajar. Arthur examined the curio cabinet, which showed signs of forcing. Katy saw the scratch marks around the lock and nodded. "Someone might have tried to pull off a job," she said. They made their way through the abandoned pantry and kitchen, where signs of rodents lingered around the flour and sugar bins. Ten minutes later, they were back in the foyer, contemplating the stairs.

"I think we should go up," Arthur said. "The bedrooms are on the second floor and the servants' quarters just above." They went up to the second-floor landing, which led to a long corridor branching off in two directions. But despite the foreboding atmosphere, which seemed to promise a body in the library at the very least, they found nothing, only faintly musty rooms, many half-empty.

"It's spooky. Whoever lived here simply walked away," Katy remarked. "I hate to sound dense, but you didn't notice any of this yesterday?"

"Like I said, it wasn't like this yesterday."

They were standing in the master bedroom, which was designed to look like a medieval cloister. The groined vaulted ceiling resembled the roof of a Cistercian refectory. Gargoyles adorned the huge cold fireplace at one end, and the windows were set in stained glass. One window at the far end had been broken, leaving blue and red splinters on the floor. By the looks of the outline left in the leaded panes, some kind of animal had been portrayed.

Arthur opened the two wardrobes filled with clothes, one for her, one for him. Nothing had been touched. There was not a single empty hanger.

"Look at this." He was holding up a glass container the size of a jelly jar. "Recognize it?"

Katy shook her head. "It looks like some kind of paint, egg tempera or some such."

"It's makeup, theatrical facepaint." Arthur pointed to the label. "The color is cobalt blue."

"Strange choice, if you ask me. She could have bought eyeliner."

"Except that this isn't her wardrobe. It's his, and the bottle wasn't out in the open. I found it under a pile of old shoes in the back." Arthur rummaged deeper in the wardrobe but came up empty-handed. "Did you find anything?"

Katy, standing in front of a lady's dresser, shook her head. She had pulled the drawers out to examine their contents; the scarves, hosiery, and sweaters were neatly stacked.

"I'm going upstairs," Arthur said.

They both scoured the third floor; this time Katy took one wing while he took the other. The doors to the maids' quarters were locked. Peeking through the keyhole, Arthur saw darkened rooms with neatly made beds and lace curtains over the windows. Most of the other rooms were for storage, stacked with furniture. He rejoined Katy at the other end of the corridor.

"Nothing here," she said. "Everything's locked." She was standing before the last door at the end of the hall. Arthur surprised himself by reaching around her for the doorknob. He turned it and it gave.

"Strange. It wouldn't budge when I tried," Katy said hesitantly.

Arthur opened the door and looked inside. "It's the biggest room, so I imagine it was the butler's." He started to step in when he heard a choked sound. "Katy?" He turned and saw that her face had crumpled and tears were rolling down her cheeks.

"Oh, what's wrong with me?" she mumbled. At a loss for words, Arthur watched the tears leaving gray tracks around each side of her nose. "I'm sorry," she sniffled. She reached inside her pockets and drew out a wad of tissues. Dabbing clumsily, she managed to smear her mascara even more than the tears had.

"Let me." Arthur took the tissues and carefully outlined her eyes. His touch was delicate and precise; as soon as she felt it, a new stream of tears started.

"I'm making such a fool of myself," she moaned.

"It's all right," Arthur said soothingly. Strangely, he didn't feel embarrassed, only sad for her, and curious. "Did something happen?" Katy shook her head miserably. "Look, you go on down. I'll just be a second." Katy bit her lip doubtfully, then retraced her steps down the corridor and descended the stairs. Arthur walked into the butler's quarters—a black tie thrown onto the floor and the bell on the wall told him his guess had been right.

Unlike the other rooms in the house, this one showed signs of a hasty departure. The wardrobe was thrown open, wire hangers littering its bottom. A spare sock lay beside the bed; he thought he saw the imprint of a large suitcase on the gray wool blanket neatly folded at its foot. Everything else had a military orderliness to it.

The bedstead was narrow, as with most Victorian beds, but at one end were two pillows side by side. There was no other sign that Jasper was married. Arthur lifted one pillow and sniffed—it smelled of rose perfume and sweat.

The only other notable thing was the pale square on the wall where a picture or mirror had once hung. Arthur ran his fingers over the space. There weren't really any clues in the room, so why did he have a sense, like a bloodhound baying over a footprint, that he had found the beginning of the trail?

Arthur sat down on the butler's empty bed. He felt caught between two worlds, unable to decide. The scabbard in the ashes had been pushed to the back of his mind, just as he had pushed back the events surrounding the crow in the drawing room. But he knew that these were clues left like bread crumbs in the forest to entice him away. Why couldn't he go where they led? He had once watched a trainer at the zoo outwit a thieving howler monkey that had snatched a woman's purse through the bars of his cage.

The monkey had perched itself too high to be reached as he rifled through the distressed woman's things. After ten minutes of coaxing he wouldn't come down, until the trainer walked in the cage and held out a lump of sugar. The animal reached for it, and the trainer pulled the sugar just a little out of his reach. The monkey leaned farther out, the sugar was withdrawn a bit more, until he was trapped—he either had to abandon the purse or give up the sugar.

With a howl of frustration that was almost deafening, the monkey complained bitterly, but eventually he jumped down for the sugar cube, and the purse was rescued. When he had witnessed this little drama, at age eight, Arthur had thought the trainer was a master of psychology. Now he identified much more with the monkey.

He stood looking out the window, which was high enough to command a splendid view of green Somerset farms and dales. He sighed. He wasn't going to come up with a theory to satisfy Westlake. Arthur stood up, feeling sober and alone. A movement below, green against green, caught his eye. Sunlight flickered over distant fields; clouds sent moving shadows up and down dale. But the movement he had spotted was different. Arthur strained his eyes and then was sure. He bolted from Jasper's room, running pell-mell down the corridor. The marble stairs were slippery, but he bounded down them two at a time. Bursting out the front door, he paused for a second to get his bearings.

"What's gotten into you?" Katy was leaning against the car, just like that morning, a cigarette in her hand.

"I saw somebody from the window upstairs," he said, panting. "A woman in a green coat with a green felt hat."

"I didn't see anybody."

"She was half-hidden in the trees. I barely caught a glimpse, but I'm sure it was her."

"Who is she? Your aunt?"

Arthur shook his head. It must have been among the alley of huge beech trees where he had seen the woman. The woods to the east were too far away. "Wait here." He ran down the graveled drive—the first of the beeches was only a hundred yards away. Pounding along, he felt afraid and excited. In the dim light of the alley all was stillness, but as his eyes adjusted, he saw her again. The lady in the felt hat was facing him from between two gnarled old trunks. She looked just as she had last night, at the fire, but something was different about her, too. Arthur saw her beckon; the look on her face was intent and serious.

"I found you." He was panting as he stopped in front of her. "You were right—I did find something in the ashes."

She didn't acknowledge this remark but said, "You're not quite right about finding me. We've been searching for you for a long time; the only question is what to do now that you are found. Can you come away?"

He was mystified. "Now? Where are we going?"

"Where you will be safe. It's time."

"How long would I be away?"

"Longer than I can say. The court of miracles will protect you while we form a plan. But you must give up your investigation. Otherwise you will long to come back here, and that will be your undoing." The lady in the felt hat spoke deliberately, gravely. Arthur pulled back. "You're afraid."

"I'm not sure." Arthur looked over his shoulder at Emrys Hall, and he saw Katy get into the car. She honked twice, then started to back down the drive toward them. "I need time to think." The lady in the felt hat grabbed his arm, but he continued to look at the oncoming patrol car.

"Don't think," the lady whispered. "You don't belong in this business. It's a matter for the police."

He felt foggy and confused—she seemed to assume that his old life was already over. "I don't know," he mumbled again. He saw an image of his mother, left utterly alone without explanation.

The lady in the felt hat let out a muffled groan. "Not good enough."

A burst of anger filled Arthur's chest. "It has to be good enough. I may be crazy to listen to you at all."

The lady shook her head. "They're the crazy ones, those out there. Come to the court, you'll see."

But he had turned to gaze at the patrol car, which was now just fifty feet away. One arm was waving outside the driver's window. "Katy's spotted us. We couldn't get away if we wanted to."

The lady in the felt hat was starting to look agitated. "You're wrong. We can get away. It's up to you. What you will, will be." Strangely, her voice came to him as a harsh buzzing. Fear spread foglike in his head.

Katy called out, "Callum, they've just radioed in. They've found Merlin. Come on." She sounded excited.

"It's a lie. Don't listen," the lady in the felt hat begged.

"I've got to go," Arthur said coldly, starting to move toward the car, which had stopped outside the alley of trees.

"Can't you see? She has to stop, she'd be found out if she came any closer." The lady's voice was almost totally garbled now, nearly a dull roar.

Suddenly Arthur's head cleared. He turned to her. "You *are* crazy. You need help."

Tears came into the lady's eyes. A piercing wail issued from her throat, making him jump. "Lost! Lost again and forever!" The cry came from a depth Arthur never knew existed, like the cry of an animal caught in a steel trap. Katy stepped out of the car.

Arthur made up his mind. "Listen, you really do need help. We'd better take you in." He reached out to seize the lady by the arm. She backed away.

"Come to your senses," she hissed desperately. "When Katy was crying, inside the house, you wiped her tears."

"How did you know?"

"Ask yourself—why didn't she look in a mirror? Why did you have to wipe the mascara away?"

Arthur stared at her. "What does that matter?"

"It matters a great deal, sire." The lady in the felt hat had backed into the trees, beyond his grasp. "It's your only hope. Be careful. Pray we meet again." And then she was gone.

Dazed, Arthur turned around. Katy hadn't come any closer. She stood on the edge of the trees like a child afraid to enter a haunted house.

"Come out, Arthur," she called. Her voice was sweet in a way he had never noticed before. He started toward her. How odd. He'd put her down as plain-looking, but actually, standing in the burnishing morning sun, Katy was altogether different. She smiled, and a rush of desire burned in Arthur's body. Beautiful—she was enticingly and suddenly beautiful. A silvery laugh reached his ears, and he began walking faster.

"Silly," she teased. "You shouldn't have gone away like that." Now her arms were open, such smooth, soft arms. Her hair gleamed like ripe wheat, and it flowed where it should, covering her shoulders in a mantle of loveliness. Arthur couldn't imagine why he'd never kissed her. He accepted her embrace, every dream of love fulfilled. "My darling," she whispered.

He was frantic with longing for her. "Where can we go?" he asked, his voice clotted and strange.

"I'll show you. Just get in the car." Katy held the front door opposite the driver's side open. Arthur got in, not noticing that only his reflection and not hers was cast in the car window. Katy got in the driver's seat, started the motor, and smiled. "I knew you'd come."

"You did? Why?"

"Because you like sugar too much." She laughed and put the car in gear, pulling down the drive with a spray of gravel. Arthur felt himself sucked into the tunnel of the overhanging trees as a shard of ice pierced his intestines.

PART TWO

ALCHEMY

16
DREAMING TIME

THEY NEVER DID FIND THE CAVE. SIS AND TOMMY KNEW THAT Merlin had intended to take them there. "You cannot live in the woods forever," he'd said. "Mordred is going to take over the land and make it submit to him, but the cave will always be mine."

"But we can't live in a cave, either," Tommy pointed out.

Sis looked disturbed. "We already have a home," he said, wishing very much that Merlin would take them back to it.

"I'm not taking you to the cave permanently," Merlin assured them. "But Mordred already found his way into the sacred grove; I want you to have some place safely outside the web of time." However, now that he couldn't remember how to be Merlin, Derek seemed as lost and confused as they were.

The Questing Wode became frightening at night. Feet crept, scurried, padded, and pattered over the forest floor, ever out of sight. Black trees loomed at terrifying angles, clutching at them. When Sis sank to the ground, unable to go another step, it was as much from fear as exhaustion.

Tommy crouched beside him. "It's getting too cold. We should try to start a fire and wait until dawn."

"I suppose you're right." Derek felt around in his trouser pockets, pulled them inside out, and produced a small packet of pipe tobacco, two shillings, and some lint. "I don't seem to have brought matches, which is peculiar, since I wouldn't leave the house without my pipe. It's gone, too."

"When you were murdered, they must have taken all that," Tommy speculated.

"Why?"

"To make you harder to identify. According to the papers, the police didn't find any ID on your body." Referring to Derek's death had become oddly commonplace.

"Or maybe the matches were inside your overcoat," Sis said. "I wish you hadn't thrown it away when we crossed the stream."

"Oh, yes, I threw it away," Derek repeated absently. His recollections still came and went.

The little boy said, "And Merlin got food from its pockets, all kinds of lovely things. Could you give that a try? I'm awfully hungry."

The man looked at him sympathetically. "We're all hungry, but if Merlin can materialize food from his pockets, I'd say he could pull it out of thin air, too. The pockets don't seem to be the vital ingredient."

"I'm not so sure." Tommy could be made out in the darkness holding up something. "Here's a bit of cheese and biscuits. They were in my jacket."

"You saved some," Sis exclaimed gratefully, and it was all he could do to wait for Tommy to split the food into portions and pass it out.

The older boy was perplexed. "But that's the point—I didn't save any. I'm quite sure I ate my share, and the rest went back into Merlin's coat."

Sis shook his head. "You must have saved some. Otherwise you'd be the wizard."

"Think what you like. I didn't put matches in my jacket, either, but look." Tommy struck a match, and his face shone in a small halo of amber light. They all felt a mixture of wonder and gratitude, although the boys couldn't help missing the one who had provided for them so well. Without further word Tommy lit a pile of dry leaves and twigs, and a few minutes later a confident blaze was going, which they fed with larger pieces of wood.

Negotiating their way in the dark, Tommy had mistrusted the forest. However, by the light of the fire he saw that they had halted in a clearing, a comfortable patch of meadow as even and groomed as a manor park. "Meadows are generally marshy at one end," Derek observed; Tommy agreed to go exploring to see if there might be water. He ventured out and soon found spongy turf criss-crossed with tiny rivulets.

When he came back into the warm circle of the fire, Sis had already fallen asleep leaning against Derek, who warmed him as best he could by putting an arm around his shoulder. "You can sit on the other side," Derek told Tommy softly. "If we hold on to one another, it'll conserve heat as the fire dies."

"No thanks. We should take turns feeding the fire. That way it won't die down." It was a rational suggestion, but Tommy uttered it stiffly.

Derek sensed that offering to hold the boy had not been greeted well. "I'll take the first shift. You sleep. For some reason I'm still wide-awake. Maybe being dead was restful. Doesn't Shakespeare say, 'And our little life is rounded with a sleep'?"

For reply, Tommy curled up in a pile of leaves with his jacket buttoned to his chin. Relying for survival on someone who sounded like a schoolmaster wasn't a pleasant thought.

Tommy never got to take his shift tending the fire. The next thing he knew, the morning sun was in his eyes and the dampness of the forest floor had seeped into his clothes. He sat up, brushing leaves from his face, and found that he was alone. "The fire's gone cold," he thought groggily, but it wasn't. The blaze was as high as ever; even a small stack of neatly piled kindling was next to it. A few moments later he heard steps as Sis and Derek appeared.

"We didn't want to wake you. We've had a drink and a wash at the wet end of the meadow," Derek said, "and we've found some food."

"In your pockets?" Tommy asked.

Sis shook his head. "No, wild mushrooms and berries from the woods. See?" The little boy triumphantly held up double handfuls of both. Derek demonstrated how to fix the mushrooms on wooden skewers. They propped these by the fire, and soon a delicious roasting smell filled the air. "How do we know these aren't poisonous?" Tommy asked.

"I'm hardly an expert, but I avoided anything shaped like a toadstool. We just took the upright ones that look like honeycombs—morels, I believe they're called," Derek said.

"We had to wash them to get the ants out," Sis added. "Derek's going to show us how to smoke bees out of their hives so we can get honey, and there's wild mint we can soak to make tea."

Tommy was less than enraptured by this news, despite the fact that he'd promised himself not to resent Derek for forgetting how to be Merlin. "I hope we're not taking our lives into our hands," he muttered. "I mean, even if these are usually safe to eat, Mordred could have poisoned them. Don't forget, he knows we're here." A look of fright crossed Sis's face.

"Let's talk more about him," Derek suggested. "It doesn't do any good being frightened and not talking about it." Sis looked down, ashamed, and Derek said, "I'm frightened, too, but do you actually know anything about *him*? I write books, and Mordred, otherwise known as Sir Mordred, cuts a sinister swath in the old legends. He's the bad hat who is credited with betraying Guinevere's secret love for Lancelot, sowing mistrust among the knights of the Round Table, and finally killing his own father in hand-to-hand combat. So the legend runs."

"It's not a legend. He's about to kill his father for real," Tommy said. "And if we're not careful, he'll finish us off in the bargain." The boy seemed to relish the astonished look on Derek's face. "Mordred's army is camped in these woods—we've chased part of it—and if he wants to, he can hear us talking right now."

Nodding in confirmation, Sis turned to Derek. "Can't you tell? Merlin taught us how."

"By listening, you mean?"

"More by just knowing," Tommy said. "I would have already made us all keep quiet, the way Merlin did, but Mordred isn't paying much attention to us just now. If my guess is right, he's on the attack against the king. We'll be part of the mopping-up operation."

"I don't want to be mopped up," Sis observed grimly.

"This may sound rather thick, but what you're saying is that we're in Camelot, aren't you?" Derek asked. "How can that be?"

Tommy felt like moaning. Derek stood up and began to pace. "It's taken a while to figure out, but I now realize something—I wasn't simply dead. Dead people stay that way—barring miracles of course."

"You were in some sort of halfway zone. Merlin said it wasn't easy to explain," Tommy said.

"I dare say. And you believe we're now in Camelot?" Derek paused. "How marvelous!"

"It isn't marvelous at all. We're not getting home without Merlin's help, and for all we know he's gone forever." Despite his promise to himself, Tommy had unleashed the full flood of his resentment against Derek.

"I'm sorry," Derek said soothingly. "But you have to see the other side—if Merlin returns, what happens to me? I'm not sure I fancy being half-dead again, or whatever I was." He caught the growing look of despair on Tommy's face. "You think I'm letting you down, don't you?"

Tommy sighed. "No, it's not your fault. You can't help it if you can't bring Merlin back."

"Maybe I can." Derek's words surprised the boys, who began to look hopeful. He held up his hand. "Wait, I don't mean I know how to become Merlin again. But look at this." He showed them a finger stained bright blue.

"I've seen that before," Tommy said excitedly. "Merlin showed me just before he left, and he said it was important."

Derek nodded. "It is important. Before I was waylaid, I came very close to finding the hiding place of the old wizard. You see, I don't think Merlin ever dies or leaves, but sometimes he is forced to remain out of sight from the rest of us. The reign of Camelot was not the only time he lived in the world; it was just his last sighting, so to speak. This blue paint was worn by the high priests known as druids. They lived many hundreds of years before Camelot, and legends say that Merlin taught them their secrets."

"How did you find all this out?" Tommy asked.

"That's a long story, which I cannot tell you all at once. But we have enough time to at least begin. When I first became intrigued by Merlin, I had only a pile of dusty, untrustworthy manuscripts to guide me. Awful murky things they were, full of superstition and lies, mostly. But even so, they led me to a belief that England was once a different land—as magical as these woods, and the focus for that magic was wizards. Wizards are a cheap commodity today, peddled in cartoons and the comic pages and so forth. We've totally forgotten their importance.

"Unfortunately, the druids can't tell us much—they lived long before anyone wrote reliable history. When the Romans conquered Britain, they encountered the last of the druids, who were probably a fairly weak lot by then. They couldn't defend themselves against the Roman invaders, who eventually drove them to the sea and burned them all out. Anyone who knew Merlin would have died.

"The more I read about all this, the more ignorant I grew. I found myself getting restless, looking out my window and seeing nothing remotely like the land of wizards. Without telling anyone, I started wandering alone through the countryside. My feet led me down abandoned lanes, and the familiar green farms suddenly looked very sad. A deep sorrow seemed to have seeped into the soil itself, after thousands of years of men taking from it. Do you understand? I think that's why Merlin led me here, back before all the sadness and waste began."

The two boys had listened closely. Most of Derek's words went over Sis's head; Tommy understood more of the man's passionate sorrow. "I don't think we're back before everything sad began," he said soberly.

"You're right, of course," Derek sighed. "There's always been trouble of one kind or another."

"No, that's not what I meant. We're *exactly* where things started to go wrong. We saw Mordred's men kill the king's stag, and I'm sure that's just the beginning. Mordred's come to crush Arthur, but his motives aren't just hatred—he wants to destroy Merlin, and if he does, nothing will ever be the same again." As soon as he said these words, Tommy wondered where they came from.

Derek regarded him deeply. "You're quite extraordinary. I've been thinking about how you produced food and matches from your pockets. One could look upon that as a kind of trick, probably arranged by Merlin so that we wouldn't get into trouble. What you just said, however, made me shiver."

"Me, too," Sis put in. "But I don't know why."

"Because it's true," Derek said. "We spend most of our life cooking up all kinds of untrue things. Why? So we won't be afraid. The mind likes to soothe itself with stories, and after they get made up, we run around under their spell. But if you look closer, there's one huge spell engulfing all of us."

"What is it?" Tommy asked.

"*Him.* Mordred has infiltrated everything. His spell makes life gray and joyless. It fools us into thinking that we exist for no purpose besides mere survival. It dooms us to age and get sick and die."

"So that's why he doesn't have to show himself. He's everywhere," Tommy said.

"Not quite. Every once in a while, like summer lightning in a night sky, there's a flash of wonder. That shiver going up your spine is the wizard's touch—that's what I call it. The spell hanging over us has done its work very, very well, but it's not strong enough to convince us that we are doomed."

"You must be a good writer," Sis said admiringly.

"I wonder. You see, for the longest time I wrote about fairies and giants and wizards in the spirit of fantasy. By ordinary standards, Camelot isn't real. We couldn't possibly be here; the beginning of all the bad things in this world couldn't be traced to Mordred. So why does it feel so true?"

Neither boy answered, but Sis opened his mouth wide, as if to scream. No sound followed, and for a second he was frozen like a statue. Tommy turned around just in time to see a solid muscular shadow cross the meadow. It was very close, yet his eye could hardly make it out, so skillfully did its stealth avoid any exposure to the light.

"It's some kind of beast," Sis was finally able to say.

"A beast that doesn't belong here," Derek added, "unless black panthers managed to roam much farther out of Africa than anyone ever imagined." They spoke low, but the shadow stopped and turned a pair of yellow eyes in their direction. The animal hesitated, and Tommy grabbed Sis's arm.

"Get down," he whispered urgently. "Merlin said that we mustn't be seen." Instinctively, the little boy ducked. The panther lifted its head, catching their scent. Even from fifty yards away, the three humans could see that the animal was pondering their presence and what it meant.

All at once Derek stood up and started walking out into the clearing. "No," Tommy warned, but it was too late—the panther bared its fangs and growled. Unintimidated, Derek stood his ground in the middle of the meadow, staring the beast down. Its black flanks heaved, a sign that the panther had traveled long and hard. Then its moment of doubt ended, it turned its yellow eyes away, and seconds later the animal loped back into the woods, intent on its journey.

Tommy and Sis ran up in great agitation. Derek was already starting off, following the panther. "Wait, you don't know what you just did," Tommy protested angrily. Derek paused and faced the boys. "You may be right," he agreed coolly, "but it had to be done."

"What do you mean? Merlin warned us not to get ourselves noticed."

"But Merlin isn't here, is he? And waiting around for Mordred seems rather pointless, I think you'll agree. We're on our own; besides, it's about time the other side realizes we're here, too. The panther has some sort of magical connection with Merlin."

"How do you know?" Tommy asked.

"I just do. Isn't that the method Merlin was teaching you?" Tommy grudgingly agreed, his anger and alarm beginning to subside.

When Derek set out over the meadow again, the two boys exchanged glances and followed. Unlike the crashing horsemen when they were chasing the stag, the panther left no visible trail. "How are you tracking him?" Tommy asked. "I don't see anything, not even trampled grass."

"Neither do I," Derek said, unperturbed. "I'm just going where I feel like it. That should be good enough." He threw these remarks casually over his shoulder, keeping up a long stride. The boys were having to scramble to keep up.

"That doesn't make any sense," Tommy argued. "You can't just go where you like."

"Why not?"

"Because you might be going the wrong way."

"Wrong way? I shouldn't worry about that too much. If you don't know where you're going, it doesn't matter where you begin."

These baffling words had to content the boys. The sun grew hotter and rose until they were almost stepping on their shadows. Derek only called a halt when they arrived at the brow of a large hill almost clear of trees. The ground was heavily trampled with hoofprints.

"I think they congregated here and then spread out down there." Derek pointed down the hill, where the tracks fanned out to the right and left in several columns. "They probably split up to take their battle positions on the other side, where we can't see them. Because the trees get thick again at the bottom of this rise, we won't actually see any troops until we get nearer the castle." He seemed to have a sure grasp of the terrain, and the boys had to admit that his peculiar method of tracking had led them in the right direction.

They moved cautiously downhill until the forest resumed again. Derek paused under an overhanging tree. "That's where the panther waited until they passed." He pointed to one lower limb whose branches were barely bent.

"Are we going to follow, too?" Sis asked.

"Yes, after we rest a bit." Derek found a damp depression in the ground where some brackish rain water stood. He crouched and took a sip. "Not too nasty. At least it's not green. We could drink this or take our chances that a stream will appear soon." Tommy and Sis felt uneasy, but they were too thirsty to resist. They knelt and took a drink from cupped palms.

Hesitantly Tommy said, "You're leading us right into the battle, aren't you?"

"That would be my guess."

"Well, Merlin told us that interfering changes things. We'll disturb the web of time—that was the phrase he used."

"In other words, we'll throw events out of kilter and history won't be the same afterwards, is that it? Well, if Mordred is going to spoil everything anyway, what's worse than that?"

"Getting ourselves killed. That would be a lot worse," Sis said.

Derek stood up and paced again, as he had back at camp. "Look, do you think our being here is accidental? In the Questing Wode, there's supposed to be a purpose for everything. So shouldn't we assume that we aren't lost and alone?" The boys looked doubtful. "I know we feel lost, but that's always how it feels when you come up against something unknown. In a way, we're quite fortunate, because we already know the battle's outcome—Mordred will win. We come from the world that proves it."

"But we're unarmed and helpless. What chance do we have?" Tommy asked.

"That's not for us to know yet. I remember a saying: 'The worst curse you can put on someone is the life he's already leading.' I'm tired of being cursed. I don't think I even want to go back." Derek had thrown off his hesitant timidity, and now his strength of purpose was so great that it made the boys feel strong, too. Instead of sickly yearning for home, they felt the wind of the future and wanted to follow it. Sis cleaned his face in the brackish pool and pulled up his socks; Tommy took off his jacket and tied it around his waist.

"I'm ready," he announced. As if to answer him, the ground

shuddered, and they felt a rumble approaching like a tidal wave. The sound of huge stone walls splitting open was upon them.

"Where's it coming from?" Tommy cried. Sis had grabbed a tree to keep from falling down. But before Derek could answer, the rumbling drowned out everything, and the world seemed swallowed up in the crack of doom.

Merlin stretched on his cot and slowly woke up. The harsh clangor of weapons in the courtyard below didn't hasten the process, which he found quite enjoyable. He had been to many places in his dreams; in fact, he had been everywhere past, present, and future, which meant that he had experienced all the events happening so far.

The enemy entered the west barbican of the castle; shouts of war and panic made a harsh din. Despite the peril befalling Arthur and his court, Merlin felt quite agreeable. He yawned and pulled on his crewelwork slippers with the pointed toes.

"Five, four, three, two, one, here he is," the wizard muttered.

At that instant a small field mouse scurried into the tower chamber and boldly ran to the edge of his right slipper. The tiny creature was exhausted. "Tsk, tsk," Merlin said. He stretched to take another enormous yawn. The gesture appeared very casual, but as his arms swung up, he hit the high perch where Archimedes the owl was just unfurling his wings. The owl screeched in alarm and drew its wings back so as not to fall, which gave Melchior the two seconds he needed to transform himself back into his proper shape.

"Master, it's a catastrophe!" the apprentice cried in distress. "Mordred has breached the walls, and—"

"And nothing," Merlin snapped impatiently. "You might at least thank me for saving your life." He pointed to the owl, who sat preening its feathers, trying not to show its extreme annoyance at missing the mouse.

"You don't understand," Melchior rushed on. "Everyone's life needs saving now." Ignoring him, Merlin sat down at the table in the middle of the room and began to write a note. Melchior ran to the slit window and looked down at the scene of warfare below.

"You've got to do something," he implored.

"I am." Merlin finished his note and read it over before joining Melchior by the window; he took in the murderous scene. "Good," he murmured.

"Good?" Melchior couldn't believe his master's heartlessness; his voice trembled with emotion. "What can be good about the killing of all these innocent people? What can be good about the kingdom being destroyed and Mordred gaining total victory, which is what will happen unless you stop it."

"Stop speechifying. What's good is that this is turning out to be an extremely satisfactory lesson. Don't you notice something different?"

"In what way?"

"To begin with, you're early. As I recall, the last time Camelot fell, you ran into the room when I was already writing my note at the table. You scurried up, and without turning around I said, 'Back so soon?' You replied, 'I've been to their camp. This is the army of Mordred.' The old wizard pronounced these words with deliberate care, like an actor anxious to get his lines right.

Melchior was baffled. "I never came in before. I came in now."

Merlin shook his head. "That's why this is such an excellent lesson—a lesson about time. Sit down, calm yourself, and recall." The apprentice found it difficult to tear himself away from the window; his heart yearned to prevent the carnage that was sweeping all before it. "Come away," Merlin said more sharply.

Reluctantly Melchior sat down in a chair that had walked over to accommodate him (wizards amuse themselves by making their furniture perform tricks). He did his best to obey his master's command to be calm.

"I have pledged myself to turn you into a wizard," Merlin began, "and that is not achieved through a collection of useless potions and spells. If anything, you're already under a spell that I must waken you from, the spell of time. True wizards are not bound by it; we live in the past, present, and future all at once.

"You and I are both in this room together, but our experience is very different. For example, I was aware that you returned a little early this time. So there are at least two versions of today going on."

"Will that save anybody?" Melchior asked, still worried about the raging battle.

"Oh, yes." Merlin suddenly handed his apprentice an oxeye daisy from a jug on the table. "Look at it." A small ladybug was crawling from the yellow center of the daisy up one petal. "Imagine the perspective of that creature. It sees a broad white petal ahead of it, and seeing only that, it travels in a straight line from one end to the other. It moves on a very narrow path, yet that's its vision of the whole flower.

"People live their lives in the same way, along a narrow path from past to present to future. When they come to the end of their little petal, they die. But as wizards, we see the whole flower. It has many petals that coexist at once, and we can choose which one to travel. How can we do so? Because we know the truth—that we are existing in all times at once. Do you understand?"

"I think so. I'm not just here in this room, even though I feel I am." Merlin nodded. "No one is just here. The straight, narrow lines of time are actually threads of a web that extends into eternity."

Another flash of insight hit the apprentice. "If any single version of time is a choice, then there can't be just one today. Camelot has fallen before."

"And it never quits falling. The web of time is very roomy. Camelot can fall as often as anyone could possibly wish."

"Or doesn't wish," Melchior said hopefully.

"Ah, so you do see," Merlin said, pleased. "The fall of Camelot is one petal of time's flower. Every other petal is a version of the same event, only very slightly modified. Do you know how many petals there are? Infinite. No possible outcome can be left out. If you use up all the versions of an event, there will be just as many left over to choose from."

"What's going to happen in this version today?"

"A merciful twist." Merlin pointed out the slit window to the courtyard below. "See that lad?" Amidst the clamor and chaos, a small boy was dashing toward a mounted knight.

"Ulwin." The apprentice watched the young page desperately brandish a pitchfork and plunge it into the flank of a mounted knight's horse, causing it to rear and scream. "Bloody brat!" the knight shouted in a rage.

Fixed by dread, Melchior heard Merlin whisper, "Concentrate. This isn't the first time you've seen this, is it?" The apprentice couldn't be sure. The courageous page had nimbly escaped the onrush of the furious knight and turned again to strike home into the horse's side with his pitchfork.

Melchior's heart pounded, but absorbed as he was, some part of his mind stood aside, uninvolved. "Yes," he agreed, "this has happened before." It was from his uninvolved mind that he spoke, the part that did not accept the illusion of time. Yet how strong the illusion was! In the courtyard below, the blood of men and horses flowed, filling the gutters; the air was filled with maddened screams. Suddenly alarmed, Melchior turned on Merlin. "I'm afraid. To die once is horrible enough, but if all this repeats itself a million times—"

The wizard held up his hand. "Keep watching."

Ulwin was now surrounded by three knights, who closed in upon him from all sides. They raised their battle-axes, but the page dropped to the ground as they converged on him. For a breathless second Melchior thought he had been trampled, but in a thrice the page was up and running. The tide of killing swept past him.

"Is he safe?" Melchior asked.

Before Merlin could reply, Mordred's captain rode into sight. He was galloping full tilt, but when he spied Ulwin, he reined his steed to a halt. The boy was backed against a wall, his only exit blocked by horse and rider. Melchior could see his eyes widen, his mouth move in prayer.

The captain drew his crossbow and reached back to fit it with an arrow. "Now observe," Merlin said. It seemed an amazing stroke of luck. Instead of finding an arrow, the knight's hand met with an empty quiver. He cursed, threw his bow at the cowering boy, and dashed on. Two seconds later, like a harried badger finding its hole, Ulwin had escaped through the wall and was gone.

"A merciful twist," Melchior echoed, feeling a flood of relief in his chest.

"Yes, but you don't know why. The reason is that the arrow destined to kill the boy—the arrow that should have been in the quiver—is buried in a shallow hole in the forest."

Melchior looked puzzled. "Who buried it?"

"Oh, you'll have time to find that out later," Merlin said nonchalantly. "Perhaps it's another version of Ulwin who has come back to save himself." The wizard chuckled at the complications that made Melchior's head swim.

"Is nothing really real, then?" the apprentice asked.

"Oh, every version of time is real, but none of them is complete—that is the point. A single arrow has changed the course of fate, do you see? And that is our hope, at least in this version. Mordred does not realize yet that his schemes have been disturbed, because the disturbance is so minute. But it takes only one loose thread to unravel, and the whole trap falls apart."

Merlin straightened up and dramatically inhaled until his lungs were full, then he leaned over and blew a cloud of dust from the table in the center of the room. The motes swirled up into a beam of sunlight coming through the slit window.

"Attention!" Merlin ordered.

Melchior turned his eyes, watching the dust dance in the light. His sight seemed unusually keen, for he imagined that he could actually focus on each mote. Hundreds, thousands, then tens of thousands of them were held in his mind as they formed and reformed into exquisite patterns, ghostly images that poised in air only to dissolve and be reborn again.

"What do you see?" Merlin whispered very close to Melchior's ear. Melchior opened his mouth to answer but couldn't. "Good. One should be dumbfounded to see reality for the first time—worlds coming and going like dust in a beam of sunlight. What is the wizard's knowledge but that? Oh, dear, my note."

Merlin suddenly pushed Melchior aside with a rude shove.

Before he could think, the apprentice heard a crash. A glass retort had been smashed, and when he looked closer, he saw that the cause was a stubby bolt from a crossbow.

"That arrow was meant for you," Merlin remarked calmly. "It wouldn't have killed you, but I wanted to spare you the pain." Melchior was able to mumble a brief thanks before his master clapped his hands. Without further ado the apprentice disappeared. In his place was a tiny falcon. Merlin hurriedly tied the note to the bird's foot and carried him to the window.

Squirming, the little merlin uttered a shriek and bit the wizard on the fleshy part of his thumb, drawing blood. "I know I haven't told you enough," Merlin apologized, "but this particular drama is one you'll just have to live through." With a toss he loosed the bird into the air. "Go to the king!" The merlin took a second to right itself, then quick as thought it aimed its bulletlike flight toward the open window where Arthur was seated.

17

SEEKERS

PENELOPE REES EXPECTED TO LOSE HER MIND BY TEN THAT MORNING, eleven at the latest. Strangely, it hadn't happened. She had been wandering the open road with Melchior since dawn, leaving Emrys Hall behind, and her shoes were blanketed with manure-scented country dust. Melchior had said almost nothing since they set out.

"Stupid of me to forget my watch," she thought to herself, "but judging by the sun, it's not yet noon. Why haven't I cracked?" She wasn't even terribly afraid, which would have been a natural enough reaction.

"I'm still sane, thank God, but this is a very strange turn of events," she admitted. At a moment's notice she had abandoned her home. No trace of her husband had surfaced, and the person she had put her trust in was a moody half-wizard. "Where are we going?" she asked aloud, hesitant to break Melchior's trance.

He looked at her calmly, undisturbed. "That depends."

"On what?"

"On everything."

Since he didn't volunteer further explanation, Pen had to be content with this obscure scrap. Melchior's lean body fit well into Derek's old shirt and trousers, but his face belonged, she thought, to another age—in a painting, it could have belonged to a medieval angel blowing a trumpet at the Last Judgment. *In the world but not of it* was the phrase that came to mind.

As they kept on walking, the layers of grime and fatigue continued to pile up. Yet Pen felt lovely in a way, as sudden unattachment can affect people who slip away from the "real" world. Every so often a clanking tractor passed by, and the farmer driving it would give them a rude, half-concealed stare. Otherwise there had been no traffic. The lanes themselves were beautiful, lined with untouched hedgerows dating back to Robin Hood. White May blossoms were coming out in profusion like snow falling up instead of down. Occasionally a stone bridge arched over a clear stream. Looking down, she could see the fleeting shadows of fish, elusive trout like opalescent ghosts.

Without warning, Melchior said, "You'll have to do better."

There wasn't any recrimination in his voice; Pen was caught off guard. "Better at what? I'm walking as fast as I can. Actually that's not true. We haven't been walking fast at all, have we?"

"It's not the speed holding us back. Your mind is shut tight, like this." Melchior held out his hand making a fist so tight that the knuckles were white. "You're keeping us from where we need to go."

"And where is that?"

"Wherever your mind will take us. At present, we're just walking the same dull road. We need to break out."

This felt unfair to Pen. "Maybe there just are these same dull roads."

Melchior shook his head. "It won't help to be offended. It's not you alone; it's how you have all been trained. See that man?" He pointed up ahead to a figure in the distance sitting under an old crab-apple tree. "Who is he?"

"He's just a tramp, I suppose," Pen replied, a bit uneasy. Tramps did not fit into her social agenda, which made her vaguely ashamed, but there you are.

"Are we tramps?" Melchior asked.

"Definitely not."

"What would make us tramps?"

"That's hard to say."

"We don't have money or a place to stay. Is that enough?"

Pen didn't like this reminder of their situation; she shook her head. "That's not enough. Some people can't turn into tramps, no matter how hard their luck, while others seem to become trampy very quickly—I guess it all depends on whether you feel hopeless, down-and-out."

"It's a state of mind, then? A predisposition?"

"Yes, you could say that." They were coming closer to the tramp, who could be seen lifting a jug to his lips and taking long swigs from it. In between these swigs he whittled a stick.

"What if that tramp is a tramp because of *your* state of mind, your predisposition?" Melchior demanded.

"Mine?"

"Everyone creates the world they perceive, and we all perceive according to impressions fixed in the past."

"That sounds very abstract."

"It's not. It's the way we create things, events, other people."

"Come now, I can't create other people. I'm not God, or if I am, I hope I'd create better people than that."

Melchior didn't smile. "You aren't responsible for creating the souls of other people, but how they relate to you is your creation. If you have an enemy, he is created in your own heart; the people who make you afraid make others happy, the ones you hate are loved by others. We've passed a dozen people already who could be our salvation, our guides. But you've shut them out. Can you see this one as a guide?"

They were close enough now that Pen made out the tramp's wiry black beard and matted hair. He looked like a bear and would likely smell worse. "A guide?" she repeated doubtfully. "To where?"

"Out of here," Melchior replied with a wide sweep of his arms. "You're used to living in this world, but if you could only see, it's like a net closing in on us. We need to find where the net is torn, otherwise we'll never escape. Since dawn I've been looking for someone who's already made it out and can show us the way—a guide."

The tramp spotted them as they drew almost abreast of his tree. "Come on," he called, "I ain't gonna put the twist on you." Pen shifted uncomfortably. He was fixing them with a crazy stare, one eye slightly askew. His gaze seemed to exert a magnetic effect, as if no amount of polite avoidance could prevent the encounter.

Pen sped up, pretending to be deaf. "I can't do it," she whispered fiercely to Melchior, who was trying to linger.

"I know you're afraid."

"You're right." She could feel her pulse pounding in her throat.

"Why are you afraid? Because he's different? Don't you see, that's our only hope—that he's different *enough.*"

Pen slowed down. She glanced over her shoulder at the tramp, who lifted his jug in merry salute. "I don't know. I'll admit one thing—he does look like some sort of escapee. He might be dangerous." She could see that the tramp was much larger than Melchior physically, but then the apprentice had managed to overpower Jasper. "Maybe you could test him out a bit, just to get acquainted with his level of psychosis."

"See, you're not so afraid anymore," Melchior said approvingly. He had her by the elbow and was easing her back toward the crab apple.

The tramp appeared delighted at this turn of events; he pounded his feet on the ground and hooted, "Didn't you bring your box with you? I don't have no box." As if to demonstrate what he meant, he held up the large bandanna that contained his worldly possessions. "See?"

"No, we left without boxes either," Melchior replied.

The tramp laughed. "No one leaves without boxes. It's too hard." Melchior nodded. Pen would have shied away if Melchior hadn't given her a nudge from behind. She almost stumbled into the tramp's lap, then found a place beside him on the dry, patchy grass that grew in the crab apple's shade. The tramp had been mumbling to himself, but now he became more coherent.

"Is you looking for the old queen?" he asked suddenly. Stymied,

Pen heard Melchior take in his breath sharply. "Have you found the cave yet? What's in your bag?"

"Nothing," Pen replied hastily. The black velveteen bag with the stone in it was tied around her waist, and she hadn't noticed it peeking out from under her windbreaker when she sat down. She pulled it closer to herself; Melchior seemed content to watch them both.

The tramp had apparently run out of questions. He rolled his eyes up at the birds flying in and out of the crab-apple tree. After a while one eye strayed from this amusement and fixed itself on Pen. Her discomfort grew, but she decided to sit tight. The tramp remembered his whittling stick, took it out of a back pocket, and idly shaved off a bit with his knife. He took a long swig on his jug, then passed it to Pen with a look that said, "I dare you."

Her stomach did a queasy flip, but she took the dare. The cider was sourly sweet and prickly on her tongue.

"Is the old queen waiting for us?" Melchior asked.

The question seemed to disturb the tramp. Evasively, he stared up again at fledglings unseen in the branches. "I was travelin' with the Rom for a pretty bit," he finally said (Pen knew that this meant Gypsies). "I asked them where she was, but they don't know. No one knows. Maybe she's died."

Melchior shook his head. "No, the old queen hasn't died," he remarked quietly. The tramp shot him a searching glance, not at all the stare one would expect from a wandering mind. "If you're seeking, we'd like to join your search."

Pen's interest quickened. Was Melchior testing to see if they had found their guide?

He stood up and declared in a strong voice, "We have the stone, and we're willing to share it. But the rest is unknown to us. Who is left? What is lost? We have to find answers before *he* finds us."

If the wizard's apprentice expected this speech to unlock a secret compartment in the tramp, he was disappointed. "You wants me to go, go with you? I don't know if I can," the tramp mumbled doubtfully. "There's dragon traps about, and the blood and bones of many are caught in them." His vagrant eyes had returned to watching some sparrows squabbling overhead. The air was still; Pen became aware of bees buzzing nearby, creating a drugged lull in her mind. The warm sun made her stiff, aching muscles relax. She must have dozed then, for the next thing she knew the sun had gone out. She sat up straight, feeling a chill come over her.

But it wasn't sunset. Someone was standing in front of her, casting a long shadow. "Can I see the stone, please?" a woman's voice asked.

Pen felt a rush of gratitude that it was a woman and not another tramp. "I don't know," she said, half-asleep. Getting adjusted to the light, she saw that the woman before her was short, solid, and oddly dressed for May in a green overcoat and felt hat. Her frank, open face looked like the face of a farmer's wife. "Are you from around here?" Pen asked.

"If you mean do I have a house like yours, no. I'm out in the open."

Pen's heart sank—a woman tramp. She felt with her hand to make sure that the velveteen bag hadn't been stolen. "Actually, I don't have a house either, not anymore," Pen said, standing up. Her bones creaked a little, but she felt surprisingly refreshed. Nothing had changed. Melchior and the tramp—the first tramp, that is—were still sitting under the tree, as if waiting. The sun had dipped a little west of the zenith.

"This is a beautiful old tree," the woman in the felt hat remarked, looking up admiringly. "I've heard it said that trees are the living creatures closest to humans. They know and endure; they are patient and wise. But of course trees aren't interested in doing evil. And their suffering must be different—not being able to run away and all." She looked keenly at Pen. "Being out in the open is too hard. You should go back."

"I don't want to."

"Why not?" When Pen didn't answer, the woman in the felt hat laughed. "Not knowing why is encouraging. This journey smashes expectations, ruins illusions. You still have a lot of illusions, but going back isn't one of them. I have been where you are and I know."

The woman's manner was suddenly so assured that Pen couldn't help but blurt out, "Are you the old queen?"

The woman shook her head. "No, she is part of our search."

"Who are you, then?"

"We don't have a name nowadays. We used to be called the court of miracles."

It was a strangely beguiling name, but Pen was sure she'd never heard it before. "Is he part of your court?" she asked, indicating the tramp.

"You could say so. All of us have to live by strange means; don't be too quick to judge." The woman in the felt hat looked around and a sense of urgency came over her. "I hope you're rested. We have to go." She immediately turned on her heels. Pen expected her to take to the road, but instead she headed for the copse of nettles and brambles that skirted the crab apple a few yards off. Pen looked to Melchior for a decision; he was already getting to his feet. Apparently their guide had come.

"Oh, and we should go quietly," the woman in the felt hat said over her shoulder. "It's better to leave explanations until we reach the cave." She smiled and waited up; when Pen caught up to her, she squeezed her hand reassuringly. "Don't worry. Bringing the stone is a great thing you've done. We all must thank you." The small party formed a single file and entered the underbrush.

After the first few yards it became tough going; choking vines had wrapped themselves around the dense thickety bushes, and it was all Pen could do just to make headway. Looking at her feet, she lost track of time or where they were going. Pen kept directly behind the woman in the felt hat, with the mumbling tramp on her heels and Melchior bringing up the rear. She assumed that the tramp was mumbling to himself, but she became aware that he was crooning a song:

O, what can ail thee, knight-at-arms!
Alone and palely loitering?
The sedge has withered from the lake,
And no birds sing!

The tune was doleful. Pen vaguely remembered the words. They were from a poem she knew in school—Keats, in a melancholy mood—but the way the tramp's voice had changed was what pierced her heart. She looked back at him. His eyes were clear now, as if he had dropped an inner disguise. His voice took on a beguiling lilt.

I met a lady in the meads
Full beautiful, a faery's child;
Her hair was long, her foot was light,
And her eyes were wild.

In its low throatiness, his voice sounded intimate. *Strange creature,* Pen thought, but just then a tendril of bindweed seemed to reach out and grab her ankle, requiring all her attention not to fall.

Suddenly the woman in the felt hat stopped. "We're not going to make it," she said to no one in particular. "The web isn't opening." Her expression was puzzled. "I was sure that the cave was here, but it's not. We've been wandering for the past ten minutes or so. I'm sorry, but I'm confused, and I shouldn't be."

"It's her," the tramp said, pointing at Pen.

She cringed, turning red. This was the second time in one day that the burden of being lost had been placed on her. "I really am trying."

"No, no, not to worry," the woman in the felt hat replied. "Everyone starts out this way. You see, it's just so difficult, this business of leaving the world. We're all tied in with invisible strands. Let's rest." Without bothering to look for a soft or clear space, she planted herself on the ground, letting her body push the weeds and brush aside. As the others followed suit, they found themselves squatting like red Indians, hidden as if waiting to ambush unseen game. Or to be ambushed.

Melchior and the woman in the felt hat found it easy to sit very still, but the tramp was fiddling and humming, obviously nervous. His eyes weren't clear anymore, and he didn't seem to like having Pen with them. "What's your name?" he asked her abruptly.

"Pen. What's yours?"

"Pen," he repeated, ignoring her question. "That means Pendragon."

"Exactly," the woman in the felt hat concurred.

"Why do you say that? It's actually Penelope."

The woman shook her head. "We're seekers, and the way we find what we're seeking is by clues. He thinks your name is a clue, and I do, too."

"I'm not sure I understand—a clue to what?"

"To whether we are on the right track. Things happen in patterns and spread out in lines, but you can't see them. Clues drop in all around, however. Sometimes they creep past like shy animals in the underbrush. Sometimes they fall on you from above like a bird of prey. Sometimes they penetrate your armor like weapons. We're just the ones who happen to notice."

"The court of miracles, you mean?" Pen said. "And those who don't notice remain trapped in the net."

The woman in the felt hat looked pleased. "A clue is how it begins. Certain of us don't fit into this world very well. We're labeled crazy or misfits. Clues more or less seek us out; otherwise the normal, sane people would crush us. The time comes when we have to choose whether to just remain misfits or to follow the threads dangling in front of our noses." She was on the verge of explaining more when a troubled look came into her eyes. "It's not safe to stay here much longer."

"Agreed," the tramp put in anxiously. Pen looked at them both, questioning.

The woman in the felt hat said, "You see, there's a kind of game or contest afoot. A terrible game, I might add, but that is neither here nor there. Being seekers, we are a prime target."

"Who plays this game?" Pen asked.

"Dragons," the tramp declared. "The white dragon is after us, and I'm afeared the red's never showing up."

"He'll come. I've met him," the woman in the felt hat said.

"If only you hadn't lost him again," the tramp moaned, his voice sunk in deep sadness. Pen considered him. She wasn't afraid of the bearish, smelly man anymore (although he fit remarkably well the image of a bogeyman taught her as a child). Her bewilderment came from the way he and the woman talked, in a private code she couldn't break.

Pen noticed that the others were all concentrating on her. Despite the announced danger, they weren't ready to move. "I'm afraid I misled you," Melchior said quietly. "There is no guide but you."

Pen opened her mouth but nothing came out.

"You cannot see it, my dear, but we have reached a crossroads," the woman said. "Unless you can come up with something, there are no more clues."

The words had a powerful effect on Pen's mind. Suddenly all her defenses went down, and there was nothing left but pure frustration. "I can't do it," she said, trying to suppress her turmoil.

But the turmoil grew. Exhausted, baffled, her mind wanted to scream in rebellion at the nonsense she had been hearing since Melchior mutated from a dying bird. Her temples pounded. She felt nauseated and dizzy. The only crossroads she had reached seemed to lead to madness, unless she turned back. "So I didn't crack until afternoon," she thought, grateful that a little irony still registered.

Pen lurched to her feet, but her stomach only became more rebellious. The sweet-sour taste of cider came back into her mouth. "Take me home," she mumbled, wondering if she would faint.

"I think we're losing her," Melchior said, his voice faint and distant.

Pen closed her eyes; a darkness inside her was growing dense and ever more dense. She saw herself walk to the edge of a chasm, a deeper blackness that was sheer void and destruction. She was glad to arrive there; if the leaping-off point were guarded by damned souls, she would have pushed them aside for her chance at escape. There were no guardians, though. The way was open; she was free to leap.

Gathering her resolve, for some reason she hesitated. Why? The void, sensing her hesitation, reached for her eagerly, cleaving to her feet like a pleading lover. "Merge with me. Forget. Be nothing," it cajoled.

It was what she wanted, but still she hesitated. There, a sound. The void slithered up to her calves, reaching for her loins. "Don't listen, just come to me," it begged, more loverlike than ever. But the sound, so faint, as if coming from the bottom of a bottomless pit, was still there. On the very edge of the chasm, Pen knew what it was. Laughter! The pit was not oblivion, it was not sweet forgetfulness.

"No!" she screamed, backing away from the edge. Roaring with anger, the void seized her body with an iron-fast grip, as if it could not dare to defy the master of death. "No!" she screamed again. Convulsed with icy pain, Pen made a supreme effort and opened her eyes.

A band had tightened across her chest. It could have been her heart squeezing with distress. No, it was the tramp's arm. She inhaled the beginning of a scream, then stopped. The tramp's arm was muscular and warm; its strength was not violating her but pulling her back into safety. "Don't leave us," the tramp said urgently.

"Where am I?" she asked weakly.

"You're still with us," the tramp said. "They want you back, but you're still here."

"They?"

"The old ones inside you. None of us is alone. We carry everyone inside us—mother, father, teachers, friends—who gave us a place in the world. They want you back, or their world will fall apart. So they think, and so must you. But they are the dying ones. All that will fall apart is their fear." Pen was staring now. It wasn't possible that a filthy tramp could make such a speech. His eyes were wide and clear again, speaking a depth of yearning she could feel in her marrow. "Stay with us. Please try, Pendragon," he pleaded.

Pendragon—why did he keep saying that? At least the word gave her mind something to do, something other than screaming and flying into a million pieces. Think, think. Of course—the last name of King Arthur. Her mind felt relieved by the thought that maybe she was cracking their code, and it wasn't mad after all. Pendragon. Her memory was like a honeycomb; its cells burst, letting forth stored sweetness.

Now she knew. Pendragon was important. It was one of those words of power she had told Arthur about when he saw the stone. On the surface this word meant something innocuous—"head dragon," the old Welsh way of referring to a rightful king. A faint thrill passed through her. "We don't want to fall into the white dragon's trap, do we?" she said aloud.

"It's got the blood and bones of many," the tramp said somberly.

"I know," Pen murmured. "Let me think."

Melchior was regarding her with a smile now. Pen began to feel how tight her mind had been, just as he had told her, but now, as she relaxed into accepting their weird situation and the coded way that was the only safe way to talk, the myth of the two dragons, red and white, came back.

The honey of memory flowed more easily. A vivid image came to mind of a cold night years ago when she and Derek were slumped in saggy leather chairs before a fire. Yes, it was Derek who had read to her about the two dragons. It was his voice she heard in her head unfolding a legend born out of a magical event: Centuries past, a weak, violent king named Vortigern had stolen the throne of Britain from its rightful heirs. It was a time of war and strife. Pushed back by his enemies, who gnawed at his kingdom like rats around the edge of a cheese, Vortigern was desperately trying to build a tower to defend his castle. But every time it was raised to a certain height, the tower sank into the ground and collapsed.

Vortigern summoned his soothsayers, who told him that they could not unravel this mystery, that it was only known to "one who was not born of a father." No one had any idea how such a person could be found until the sudden appearance out of the forest of a wild creature who called himself Merlin. Merlin's mother had told him that she had conceived him with a spirit instead of a man. To prove that it was he whom the soothsayers had foretold, Merlin approached the tower. "Dig there, where the tower has fallen, and you will know its secret," he instructed. Vortigern obeyed. Beneath the site an underground pool was discovered, and in it two dragons were fighting.

"One white, one red," Melchior said close to Pen's ear. Ah, so she was right. Pen looked up to see that the woman in the felt hat was visibly more confident. "We can't wait much longer," the woman warned. Pen held up her hand. What had Derek read about the dragons? Their combat held its own layer of secrecy. At first the white dragon succeeded in driving back the red, much to the king's delight, because Merlin had told Vortigern that his throne was linked to the fortunes of the white dragon. Just on the point of defeat, however, the red dragon gained new strength; it surged back, seized the white dragon by the neck, and triumphed.

"Arthur," the tramp muttered. Yes, that was it. Arthur, raised in secret by Merlin, was the red dragon. The combat in the pool was a prophecy, foretelling his return. The return of the king.

A firm hand was on Pen's shoulder, and she looked up to see that the others were already on their feet. "The trail has opened," the woman in the felt hat declared, starting off in the same direction they had already been heading. If there was a new trail, Pen couldn't see it. The thickets were just as impenetrable, the brambles as sharp. But things had changed; she was part of the game.

The sun had almost touched the horizon when the party came to a halt. It was mysterious that they could have gotten so far without running into a motorway or seeing habitation. Pen was too exhausted to think much about that.

"Congratulations," Melchior said. "You got us here." Pen looked at him in surprise, but before she could speak, something new caught her eye, a faint blue glow emanating from a shadowy spot ahead. "This is a very tricky moment," Melchior said, almost whispering. "The white dragon lays traps everywhere. I don't think he's laid one here, but . . ." Leaning down, he picked up a coin from the littered leaves at their feet. Puzzled, Pen didn't have time to examine it.

The others were ahead of her now, moving slowly. She had the feeling that they were acting as scouts or point men in a battalion entering a minefield. Whatever a dragon trap was, they would enter it before her. "Why am I so important?" Pen wondered. Perhaps it was the stone she had tied in the bag around her waist. After a second, the tramp gave the high sign, and she gingerly made her way to rejoin them. "Melchior?" she whispered, but just then his head disappeared as if he had been beheaded. Pen was dumbstruck. She turned, but in an instant the tramp's head also fell from sight, followed by the woman's. "What?" Pen stammered. She was completely alone.

Fighting panic, she walked around, examining her surroundings. The blue glow was stronger now, and she saw that it came from a large hole buried in vines. One had to look closely even to notice that any opening existed, but that must be where the others had dropped. Now a hand was extended from the hole, reaching for her. "Don't jump, but come in quickly," a muffled voice said; it sounded like Melchior's.

Pen was too apprehensive to step right in. She bent over the steep bank, trying to secure a footing amid tangled vines and slippery loose earth. She might have hesitated too long but for the apprentice's strong hand, which found her arm, gave a pull, and suddenly she was inside, half-squatting in a narrow, low tunnel. "The others are ahead. Come," he said.

Crouching over, Pen inched her way forward, making out Melchior's form ahead in the blue glow. The tunnel was oppressively cramped. Her breath became jerky, she wanted to cry out. Just then, however, the tunnel ended, and Melchior stood up. Everything was brighter now. They were in some kind of main chamber whose ceiling rose higher than her eyes could reach. The blue glow came from the lower walls of the chamber, which were lined with iridescent crystals.

The tramp and the lady in the felt hat were on their knees some yards away, drinking from a pool. Pen joined them, taking swift gulps from a cool, surprisingly fresh spring. "I'm sorry we slipped out of sight like that," Melchior apologized. "But there was danger." He handed her the coin he'd found at the entrance to the cave. Pen felt the thing being placed in her hand and realized it wasn't a coin, for the surface was ridged and horny. Holding it up, she could see a faint hint of the blue light through it. "A dragon scale," she said, wondering.

The tramp nodded. "But we'll be safe here."

"Where is here?"

"Between two worlds. Merlin's cave is his refuge, but long ago it disappeared from mortal sight."

The mention of Merlin startled Pen, but before she could ask any questions, the woman in the felt hat said, "We've found your husband." The words struck like electricity. Pen waited expectantly, not daring to speak. "He's not dead, but he is in a very delicate state, a state of suspension one might say." Pen didn't react. The woman in the felt hat seemed to sense her dismay. "I came as soon as I realized it was you. We've had so much to search for, for so long. I hope you understand."

"I want to see him," Pen managed to say, her voice strained.

The woman's face turned grave. "That's not possible for the moment. We had hoped he would come with us to this cave, but please don't be alarmed. You and he are still together. All of us are being drawn together in the web of time, yet for the moment he is needed where he is."

"Where is that?"

"To tell you is not so easy. Some would say he's slipped into the past, but that is not accurate. Past, present, and future are illusions, or to put it another way, to separate past, present, and future is an illusion. Better to say that he is testing an event line."

Pen reflected. "You mean he's changing events in some way?"

The woman nodded. "We all change events, but mostly unconsciously. It is not just the past that shapes the future; when your husband crossed over, he began to change the past from the present. The present is the opening in time that many have searched for." Pen glanced at Melchior—so he had found a hole in the net after all.

"I'm still very worried," Pen said. "Can't you take me to him? If you know where he went and how, you should be able to take me there."

A heavy silence fell over the others. "It was difficult to bring you this far; you are very new at the game," the tramp finally said. "If you can trust us, the web of time will wait." He placed a finger to the center of his chest, just over the breastbone. "Events stream from us along invisible lines, and no event is fixed. Instead, each person is constantly testing lines of possibility. That is why we see time as a web, a fragile collection of threads constantly woven minute by minute. When you consciously learn to weave events, you are ready to enter the web and alter it. But not before."

Listening, Pen knew now that she had slipped away. Since childhood she had suspected that certain people don't actually die or disappear, despite the stories in the newspapers or from distraught families. They utter a dissent against the world by leaving it, slipping away through a hole in the net. "I think I can trust you," she said quietly, "but can you at least tell me what Derek is doing?"

"Yes, we can tell you that," the woman in the felt hat said. "In fact, we've come here to lend our aid." She sat down on the floor of the cave and closed her eyes. Melchior and the tramp did the same, forming a loose circle. "Join us," bade the woman. "The place where your husband has gone is not far off. He is about to make a stroke that will decisively change the game."

Pen sat down, uncertain. The blue glow made them look like mystics in meditation. She closed her eyes. At first nothing happened. A rush of thought and emotion clouded everything. Her mind was still balking at this new way of being, but she would be patient. She needed no more reassurance that Merlin's cave was a safe place. No enemy could intrude here because no maps showed the territory lying over the edge of the world—she had found the entrance to the cave of the heart.

18

RIDER ON THE HILL

THUNDER FROM A CLEAR BLUE SKY—THAT WAS THE ONLY SENSIBLE explanation for the crack that almost tore the forest apart. Tommy hit the ground, knocked off his feet by the concussion. All around him the treetops swayed like tall masts in a gale. "They're going to fall," he thought in panic, searching around for Sis. Tumbling debris filled the air. The marrow in his bones seemed to quiver.

Then he saw that Derek had pulled Sis to the ground, shielding him with his body. "We're all right," Derek shouted over the cataract of sound. "Cover your head."

Tommy drew both arms over himself as boulders heaved out of the ground and the streams shook like rocking dishpans. The blast seemed to last forever, but in fact it took only a few seconds. When the ground quit shaking, Tommy stood up. He could still hear rumblings like the aftermath of an earthquake or a massive rock slide. A plume of black smoke could be seen rising somewhere in the distance. He found Sis and Derek half-buried under pine boughs, unhurt.

"It's *him,*" Sis said knowingly, shaken though he was. Tommy nodded and pointed into the distance where the forest ended like a green sea lapping in waves at the base of a high hill. On the crest a lone rider was sitting. "I think he's watching," said Sis.

"Yes, but not us," Tommy speculated. "He's too busy for that." In fact the rider was preoccupied with controlling his mount, still rearing and stamping in terror at the horrific thunder that had rolled over. Horse and rider were far away, and as the wind carried the plume of smoke over them, the pair vanished in the gray shroud. But the three of them in the forest knew who it was. They watched until a stiff breeze revealed that the hilltop was bare.

"Do you think he made that deafening noise?" Tommy asked Derek. They had brushed all the leaves and dirt from their clothes and hair. Large branches littered the forest floor in every direction; the piteous cry of fledglings could be heard from the nests that had been blown to earth.

"I certainly didn't see any lightning," Derek said, "and there's not a cloud in the sky. If that was really Mordred on the hilltop, it must have been his work."

"But why?" Sis asked.

No one answered. They all felt a foreboding sense of disaster, fearing what would lie just over the brow of that hill. Another rumble began to faintly shake the ground, and they tensed. But the air didn't crack with another blast—this time they heard the sound of horses' hooves. "There are a lot of them," Tommy remarked. "More than just the few we were following." On the other side of the hill the sortie of troops must have swelled into an army.

"I suppose we're too late," Derek said.

"Too late for what?" Tommy asked.

"Too late to keep things from falling apart, too late to stop *him.*" Derek's mild voice sounded morose. "I don't know what we could have done. But if we'd just been a little earlier or a little faster . . ." He left the thought to finish itself in each mind. Without discussion the three companions began trudging up the face of the hill. They came to the end of the forest, then climbed the crest in half an hour, to stand on the same spot where horse and rider had stood.

The hilltop was bare except for a lone pine standing sentinel, but the grassy slope was scorched, as if recently burned by a racing fire. Sis pointed to where hundreds of hooves had trampled a wide swath through the blackened sea of harebells and jonquils decking out the slope. The swath ran toward a large turreted castle, more perfect than any other they had ever seen, but marred by a huge rift in the outer walls wide enough to allow three horsemen to ride abreast into the inner courts.

"Why is it so quiet?" Sis asked. One would have expected to witness a violent clash of arms down below, but the silence was total, as if the castle had magically turned into a vast tomb. No human figures scurried back and forth; small motionless specks could be made out here and there, no doubt bodies left where they had fallen under the warm spring sun. Even the carrion birds hadn't had time to gather and fill the air with hungry calls.

Sis glanced at Derek, who was some distance off, stooping as if to gather flowers. When he stood up, however, he held something dark and shapeless in both hands. Strangely, it looked like a shadow, but when the boys came closer, Derek warned, "Stay back. I'm not sure it's safe." They saw what it was then—a patch of black smoke or fog. The plume of blackness that had enveloped the rider on the hill somehow had left a scrap of itself behind. Derek stared into his cupped hands as if into the bottom of a well.

"Don't!" Tommy cried.

But Derek had already drawn his hands to his face and with a deep breath inhaled the mysterious vapor. He coughed violently, his eyes closed tight, then he staggered, his face twisted like that of someone overpowered by a waking nightmare. The boys ran to him, but he held an arm out. "Wait," he gasped. They watched, silent and powerless. Derek closed his eyes again, giving himself over to the vision.

It works! It works!

Derek felt a wave of raging excitement so suddenly and so violently that it almost made him sick. This was not his own emotion assaulting him, and he knew immediately where it must have come from—the rider. Instead of being a distant image, the rider was right next to him, and with another breath of the foul black fog, he was in the rider's mind.

The hag didn't lie. It works!

Derek could see now as the rider swung his head from side to side, surveying the chaos of tumbled walls, shouts of terror, and roiling dust. Derek drew a deep breath, trying not to vomit. A surge of exultant hatred swept over him. Derek didn't have time to wonder how all this could happen, or why he was able to penetrate Mordred's defenses. He had to probe deeper.

He entered swiftly into a memory flashing through Mordred's mind: A dark, filthy room lit by suet candles. A bed, rumpled and sweaty in the guttering smoky light. "I have a present for you," a woman murmured, leaning close on the pillow. Derek shivered as Mordred recalled the stench of her breath, like marsh gas. Sycorax, the witch. She ever so softly whispered into his ear. Gentle as her voice was, the words burned his eardrum.

"Attend and do not forget," she hissed. "Marvelous thing, isn't it?" Her voice was full of smug satisfaction. "I gave up my beauty to acquire it, and now it's yours." Mordred nodded, and despite the revulsion in the pit of his stomach, he gave her a caress. "A bright toy, but use it once only," the witch warned. She was gathering her filthy rags from beside the bed to leave him, her withered flanks swaying in the yellow half-light. "You are not so charming a lover that I would grant you this boon twice. But power is what you crave, and I am here to please." She cackled, planting a last, blistering kiss on his cheek.

Derek struggled against despair. Now he knew how Camelot had fallen. Desire to possess the shout of doom had lured Mordred into Sycorax's bed—only she knew the secret, and driven by his need for vengeance against Arthur, Mordred had paid a high price for it. Derek felt his own body sicken with the toxins of the witch's lovemaking. It had taken weeks for Mordred to recover his senses after their tryst.

"You've gone too far. Come back," said a voice.

"What?" Derek thought, confused. The voice wasn't from a source he could see.

"Come back. You have to." The voice sounded worried but far

away. Tommy—it was Tommy's voice. Derek shook his head, pulling back from Mordred's mind.

"Derek?"

A patch of bright sunlight filtered through his eyelids, and then he was back. Two anxious faces were gazing up at him. Derek put his hands on the boys' shoulders. "I'm all right." He had no idea how he looked, but from their expressions, it must have been ghastly. He sat down, breathing regularly until the nausea began to fade.

"It *was* him," he said, pointing down at the ruined castle. "He used a monstrous shout to split the walls. I could see all of it; that black fog was some kind of residue he left behind when he vanished. If you think you're strong enough, I'll show you." He held out both hands for the boys to take.

Tommy shrank back. "If you were in his mind, wouldn't he know it?"

Derek shook his head. "He won't know until he checks back into his past, which is where this residue comes from. We'll have to take that chance, but so far he's been so preoccupied that he hasn't had time for us, or else his arrogance makes us insignificant. It's all right."

They sat down, forming a ring. "You've been aware of him before when I wasn't. So just close your eyes. If it gets too strong, let go and look at the sky." Tommy nodded, looking at Sis. They were surprised by Derek's new authority and confidence. He hadn't turned into Merlin, yet he was more than they had once supposed. They shut their eyes.

"My lord?" A raspy voice penetrated the boys' ears, and they felt the heavy menace of Mordred's presence as they slipped into his mind.

"My lord?" the raspy voice repeated, this time with a touch of fear.

"What is it? Speak, fool." Mordred turned his eyes toward a mounted soldier who had met him halfway down the hill. The boys knew that they were in the moment right after the rider vanished from the hilltop. Tommy jerked back, almost letting go of Derek's hand—the soldier was the same man who had killed the stag in the forest. The boys could tell who he was now—the captain of Mordred's knights.

"The first column is mounted and ready," the captain said. "And the second column is behind them, weapons drawn as you commanded. If we want to breach the walls, we must move now." He pointed at the castle down below. The impact of the shout of doom had killed the guards on the ramparts, and replacements were hastily scurrying around like ants whose hill had been smashed by a careless footstep.

"Good," said Mordred. He rose in his stirrups and gazed out over the double flank of banished knights. They were massed on the hillside, straining to launch their assault. Mordred had no illusions that any of these troops served him out of loyalty. They hated Arthur with the darkest hatred mortals can manage. "You men in the first rank," Mordred called out, "are my bravest, truest soldiers. I expect you to take the king and show no mercy to his vassals. Mark whom you hate and strike. But take heed: the men behind you are drawn and aiming at your backs. If you falter, they will kill you on the spot, and then *they* will be my bravest, truest soldiers. Advance!"

"And pray for your wormy souls," the captain muttered.

Mordred wheeled upon him angrily.

"We feel the need of your leadership, sire," the captain said hastily. "Will you come, too?"

"I am staying here for the moment." Mordred glared, defying the captain to contradict him.

The captain bowed his head in a show of meekness. "Safety first," he murmured before spurring his horse and galloping down the hill.

For this little stroke of insolence, Mordred could easily have killed him, but there was already much savor in the day—small pleasures could wait. In any event, it wasn't fear that kept Mordred posted on the hill but suspicion lest Merlin had set a trap for him.

Hearing the rumble of Mordred's troops as they advanced, the castle had broken out in frenzied alarms. A brass bell clanged in panic. A gentle breeze carried the sweet smell of war up the hill. Mordred's horse stamped the ground, yearning to follow the other mounts into battle.

"Back," Mordred muttered, tightening the rein so hard that the bit cut into the horse's lip. There was no use rushing—an easy prize smelled of a trap, and this prize was absurdly easy. One misstep and Merlin might still find a successful ruse. The wily old fool in the tower had stayed his hand so far. Mordred would hold back until his opponent stood revealed.

The next part was almost too intense for Tommy and Sis to watch.

The first column had reached the fatally weakened fortifications. The captain, who lived by a desperate recklessness, jumped his mount over the rubble and charged the few men inside who had managed to draw into a tiny band of defenders. They were quickly routed as the next dozen knights rushed through the breach. From his vantage point, Mordred could see inside the outer courtyard, which remained empty. Why? His captain must have been asking the same question. He circled impatiently, swinging his sword against a scattering of panicked servants, but of Arthur's knights there wasn't a trace.

Mordred's suspicion brewed. Somewhere in the innards of the redoubt there had to be murder holes where hidden knights lurked, waiting to pour burning pitch on whoever passed underneath. Every castle was outfitted with such secret contrivances. Now the first column of soldiers had all gained the courtyard, milling in confusion with the captain at the center. Mordred could sense their nervousness. He was glad he had put the second column at their backs with weapons drawn to stiffen their resolve. Hesitant, the first column formed a loose battle square before moving en masse through the inner walls. Mordred braced himself, expecting the swoop of a thousand arrows or a cascade of boiling oil to rain on their heads.

Nothing.

The inner courtyard was eerily empty, too. Amazed as they

were to meet no resistance, Mordred's soldiers didn't pause a second time. They let loose a roar of rage and charged at the last obstacle, the giant wooden gates leading to the castle's great hall. From the rear a battering ram was brought up, swinging impatiently on its wheeled cart. Before the weapon even could be brought into play, the maddened soldiers began hacking at the gate with their swords, and one impetuous knight, who had paid no attention to the order to withdraw, was crushed by the first hammer blow of the battering ram. His screams disappeared in the hollow thud. In a matter of seconds another assault ripped the iron bindings of the gate, which groaned as it splintered, the wood itself seeming to bemoan the catastrophe to come. Mordred watched all this with mounting satisfaction. There was no doubt, he thought—this was going to be a very good day.

"Enough. That's enough," Tommy said in disgust. Derek and Sis opened their eyes. Tommy had broken the circle and was pacing back and forth on the hillcrest. "You're right, we are too late, and now we haven't even got a way to get out ourselves." The boy's face was hard and set, trying to keep tears away.

"How *are* we getting out?" Sis asked, turning to Derek.

"We're not."

Tommy stopped his pacing, but before he could respond, Derek stood up. "We're not here to leave. We agreed on that, didn't we? That's why we crossed the stream."

"But we're too late anyway. You said so yourself," Sis put in.

"Then you think Merlin wants things to turn out this way?" Derek demanded, his arm sweeping toward the scene of silent destruction.

"What do you think?" Tommy said defiantly. Without answering, Derek held his hands out again. "No. I'm not going back to *him,*" Tommy said, shaking his head.

"You must. It's through him that we have a chance to win." Derek's words astonished the boys, who drew back. "Don't ask me to explain right now. Just come." Derek beckoned. Reluctantly the boys formed a circle, their eyes darkened, and the unholy glee of Mordred filled their heads. *Yes, this is going to be a very good day.*

Mordred watched his troops smashing through the great gate of the castle like a jagged blade ripping a wound. He felt a surge of triumph, and a laugh filled the air. It took several seconds before Mordred realized that the laugh wasn't his. His head swiveled from side to side. There was no one about.

"Who's there?" he called. The laughter came again, as if from the flowers themselves, exultant and joyous despite the hurt they had taken when the soldiers rode over them. "Who mocks me?" Mordred cried. Before his words could die away, the laughter redoubled, and now the skies seemed to send back a roar of pure delight.

Mordred was more infuriated than ever. He drew his sword and brandished it in the direction of the gleaming wizard's tower, which rose above the fray in calm repose. "Is that you, old man?" he shouted. "Then laugh at death, laugh to see everyone you love crushed to a mass of guts beneath my boot!" Mordred opened his mouth and shouted with all his might, directing malevolence at the tower with every fiber of his being. He did not care that Sycorax had warned him to use the shout only once. If his soul could be damned twice over, if his muscles tore into shreds with the effort—it would be a small price to pay.

His second shout was so intense that it scorched the earth as it passed over it. Sedges, grass, and flowers shriveled as in an instant the sound assaulted Merlin's tower. With pounding force the roar echoed off the walls, sending Mordred's horse to its knees. He cursed and jumped off as the animal rolled on its side in agony. In the bright sunlight Mordred had to squint to make out the tower, but even at a distance he could tell that the glassy coating of the walls was starting to crack.

Small fissures opened in a crazy-quilt pattern. The first chunk of obsidian fell from the topmost parapet, then a second and third. Mordred was beside himself. The fetid hag had lied after all; he could use this weapon at will. The sense of unlimited possibility was almost too much for his body to contain. "Die!" he screamed, his mouth agape to the heavens. The tower shook again as the eastern wall below the slit window buckled and heaved.

All at once everything gave way. Like a decapitated head the crown of the tower fell, briefly exposing Merlin's room to naked sunlight, and almost before it hit the ground, the rest of the tower exploded. Some of Mordred's own knights luckless enough to be nearby were crushed as massive blocks of stone shattered to the earth. In less than a minute all that remained was a chaos of tumbled masonry and black dust. The horizon stretched out, unbroken by the tower's profile.

For the first time in his life Mordred knew why men prayed. He raised his arms upward, but instead of giving thanks, he screamed in exultation. Fate, fate had told him he would win, whatever the cost. He had paid without stint, and now everything would be his. He staggered to his feet and strode to his fallen horse. The animal was still twitching from the pain of having its eardrums torn; its eye sockets were faintly bleeding.

"Get up," Mordred commanded, pressing his hands in a spell. The horse, healed instantly, rose to its feet. Before mounting, Mordred looked at the plume of black smoke that rose against the blue sky, higher and higher. No doubt Merlin was making his escape by riding the vortex as it disappeared into the distance. Let him. Mordred didn't care what hole the old conjurer found to crawl into, so long as his defeat was assured.

The wind shifted, blowing the black cloud over him. Tommy and Sis realized that this was the moment when they had first spied the rider on the hill, but there was no time to think about it. A mounted knight began to approach. In a moment, the captain was in front of Mordred again, panting so hard he was barely able to give his words utterance.

"The king!" he gasped. Without a word Mordred pushed him aside. He whipped his horse until it all but flew over the scorched ground. In no time he had galloped to the castle, across the drawbridge, which his victorious men had lowered, and was racing through the inner courtyard. He leapt to the earth and regarded the gaping maw of the shattered gates.

"Captain!" Mordred cried. The man appeared behind him, half-dead from trying to keep up with Mordred's pace down the hill.

"Go in there and clear the way," Mordred ordered. After a moment a subaltern appeared at the gate signaling the all clear. Mordred entered. The floor was slippery with blood, but despite the corpses littering the way, there were no groans from the injured. His men had taken him at his word to give full vent to their hatred.

In the hall itself there was still a tumult of hand-to-hand combat. One of his own sergeants blocked his path: "It may not be safe yet for you to enter, my lord." He bore a long gash over his left eye, from which his eyebrow was dangling grotesquely, like a caterpillar.

This sight and the pile of bodies inside the hall made Mordred feel nothing. He silently pressed on, looking for only one person. The hall was darkened by tapestries over the windows, a muffled red glow filtering through their rich threads. Shadows huddled in the groins of the high, vaulted ceiling like patient birds of prey.

"Where are you, Father?" Mordred said the words coaxingly, hoping the king had crawled away to hide behind an arras or under a fallen vassal. "Come on out now," Mordred said like a mother wheedling a shy child.

But Arthur wasn't hiding. He was still on his feet, and when he heard Mordred's voice, he turned a gaze of infinite sorrow upon him. "Here," he said in the gloom.

Mordred smiled, drawing his blade. From the vaulted ceiling the shadows shrieked in a piercing cry, as if a hawk lived there and wanted to warn the king of his doom.

The next events were darkened in Tommy's mind. Mordred slipped away like a wraith. Tommy felt warm streaks down his cheeks and then the touch of his fingers wiping them away. He opened his eyes. Sis was sniffling, wiping his face with a dirty sleeve. "It's all right, it's going to be all right," Derek was saying, consoling the little boy.

"How can it be all right?" Sis demanded.

"You'll have to trust me. I haven't figured it out, but Merlin wouldn't bring us here otherwise." Derek stood up. "I don't think much time has passed since what we saw. Mordred's army has disappeared, but that's not such a surprise. Somehow they appeared in a flash this morning. I'm going down there."

Tommy leapt to his feet. "Shouldn't we all go?"

"It wouldn't be good for you," Derek replied somberly.

"If it's the bodies," said Tommy, "we've already seen them, haven't we? There couldn't be worse."

"It's not just the bodies. *He* might still be there."

Sis stood up, shaking his head. "He's not, or we would feel him."

Derek hesitated. "You haven't thought about the possibility of a trap. Why did Mordred let us sense him in the first place? Maybe he's just luring us in." Neither boy answered. Derek reflected for a moment. "All right. We'll walk down there together, but if I tell you to stay back, you'll have to—no questions." The boys mutely agreed, and the band of three set off down the path the army had cut into the scorched hillside.

The going was easy, but as they neared the castle, the enormity of the destruction preyed on their minds. Stone blocks as large as wagon carts had been pitched from the walls, now stuck at crazy angles in the soft earth of the surrounding fields. The gash in the ramparts was black and jagged, and the boys turned their eyes from depressions in the new wheat where bodies had been hurled a hundred yards. When they were close enough to be within the shadow of the castle, a mantle of darkness settled on their shoulders, as if Mordred were announcing, "Mine!"

There weren't any signs of occupation, however. The invaders had departed, leaving no survivors. Derek led the way as they climbed over piles of rubble to enter the outer courtyard. He glanced over his shoulder when the first scattering of broken bodies could be seen. The boys set their jaws grimly and nodded for Derek to proceed. Their footsteps rang hollow on the gray cobblestones as they walked past pools of deep scarlet that were rapidly turning brown. From the nearby stables horses neighed in fright, which almost came as a relief against the appalling quiet. The castle was a tomb. They crossed the inner courtyard of the main redoubt and saw ahead of them the splintered remains of the door to the great hall.

"Perhaps you should wait here," Derek said.

Tommy shook his head. "If you'll let us, we want to go with

you. Whatever we're supposed to find is in there." The hairs on the back of their necks tingled, and they looked up. The shrill cry of a hawk came from above. It seemed like a signal. Derek saw no reason to refute it, and he continued with the boys in tow toward the great hall.

None of them would clearly remember what they saw there. If Arthur had a throne or a crown, it escaped notice. The sumptuous tapestries, the huge vaulted ceilings of white limestone, the huge round table that dominated the center of the room—all paled beside the piles of bodies. They had already walked past one scene of carnage after another, but somehow this was different. The knights sprawled on the floor with their swords in their hands had names—Percival, Lancelot, Galahad—deeply imprinted in their minds. They were walking into the place where legends die. None of the dead were in armor, and their wounds were vividly open to sight, like the expressions of desperate struggle on their faces. It was hard for Derek to believe that he was there to regain something; the hall seemed a testament to loss, total loss.

The sadness in the hall was so overpowering that they had to stop. "Do you want to leave?" Tommy asked Sis, who looked pale and drawn.

The little boy shook his head. "We're here to find something, aren't we?" He raised his eyes and looked for a sign of hope or purpose. He was the first to spot the severed hand nailed to the wall with an arrow.

"No, don't look," Derek said.

"So we have found something." Tommy's voice was low and serious. Derek held him back from approaching it. The hand seemed to be reaching for something. Despite all the other horrible expressions of violence around them, this one seemed the worst, and yet it was a sign, too—they all felt a charge of recognition.

"Why is it there?" Sis asked.

But Derek wanted to pull the boys away from the gruesomeness. "That's enough," he said, grateful that the light was dim, drawing a merciful cloak over some of the more shattering horrors around them. He opened his mouth to say something, but another voice spoke. "You boys, stand back. Some illusions are bad for the stomach."

Tommy's head whipped around. They had keenly longed for Merlin's return, but it still caught them off guard.

"What a strange folly, the way these mortals keep trying to die." Derek suddenly held his body more erect, and it was amplified with a surrounding glow, a pale outline of another person.

"You mean they aren't dead?" Tommy blurted out.

Derek turned toward him, and as he did, the glowing form followed his motions in light-filled arcs. It was a beautiful sight, and the boys found it impossible to keep their eyes on the carnage littering the hall.

"Of course they're not dead," Merlin's voice replied. "Everyone knows that."

"They do?" Sis exclaimed.

"Eventually, but that's the sticking point. People generally don't find out until it's too late."

"A lot of them must have found out today," Tommy remarked dryly.

"Exactly." Merlin strode over to the windows and threw back the heavy tapestries, allowing in the afternoon light. "I think we should let our guest out. She's over there, in case you didn't notice."

The boys whipped their heads around. At first they saw no one, then a faint presence, similar to the nimbus surrounding Derek's body but darker, emerged from a far corner. Almost as soon as they set eyes on it, it faded away.

"Who was it, a ghost?" Sis asked.

Merlin shook his head. "Mother." Their expressions made him burst out laughing. "Mordred's, I mean. Her name is Morgan le Fay, and she was most anxious to be here. She hoped to grab something out of the fray." He walked back to the center of the room and picked up a large overturned chair. As he sat down in it, the boys had no way of knowing that it was the king's chair, the one from the round table.

"Did she get what she came for?" Tommy asked.

Merlin lifted a hand and waved them to two other chairs nearby. "No. She didn't." The air seemed to tremble when he said these words; there was a faint shriek and a ruffle in the tapestries. "Gone," Merlin muttered.

"But we saw her, didn't we?" Sis said.

"Don't count yourself too lucky on that account." Derek's body had stretched itself out comfortably in the chair; the glowing form pulsated and brightened. Its features were indistinct, although the shape of a long flowing beard was unmistakable. "I must tell you that she will get what she's after, sooner or later. Or her son will. You've only gotten a reprieve."

"What do we have to find?" Tommy asked.

"That's the difficult part. If I tell you, they will find out, too."

Tommy's face screwed up in frustration. "But that doesn't make any sense. How can we find something if we don't know what it is? It's impossible."

"I used the word *difficult,* not *impossible.*"

Merlin ceased looking at them and let his eyes sweep the room. His gaze paused on a fallen body lying in the deepest shadows. He seemed to drift away, and they knew it must have been the body of the king. Merlin's eyes were not sad but deeply reflective. "A good boy," he murmured, before looking back at them. "Do you think you can succeed—along with him, I mean?" He thumped his chest, indicating Derek.

"Succeed at what?" Tommy asked. "You haven't told us yet."

"What good would it do for me to tell you if you aren't going to succeed?" Pleased with this odd logic, Merlin leaned back in his seat and waited.

At first the boys were stymied. A flicker of intuition guided Tommy. "Before we can answer you, we have to know why we came here."

"To talk to me. Why else?"

The boy nodded. "Right." He paused to think. "Also, we'd like to know how we're going to get back home."

"Where is home?"

"I don't know exactly. Across the stream."

Merlin shook his head. "No, you'll never get back across. There isn't anything on the other side. Not for you."

Tommy opened his mouth to protest, but a glint in Merlin's eye warned him to stop. He paused again to think, then nodded. "All right, I can see that. But if we're never to go back, where will we go?"

"Where you're led. That's what I'm going to help you with. I've decided to let Mordred have this place. He almost won today."

Tommy looked around. "Almost?"

"Within a hairsbreadth. It often turns out that way, although just as often it doesn't. Wizardry isn't a democracy. I had no choice when Mordred gained our knowledge, it is not for me to judge why." Merlin spoke more seriously, with a hint of resignation. "If it hadn't been for you, Mordred would have succeeded."

"What did we have to do with it?" Tommy demanded.

"You disturbed the web of time. I can't fill in all the blanks for you. Suffice it to say that a wizard's life differs from a mortal's in one very unique respect: he lives backwards in time. He is able to foretell the future because he has already lived it, and he is not crippled by memories of the past because it hasn't happened yet." Merlin raised a hand to fend off objections. "I don't expect you to understand, but what I'm telling you is true. And this is why it's important: A hundred years from now, Mordred will be less powerful and more vulnerable than he is today. Two hundred years from now he will be merely malevolent. In your own time, which is many centuries away, he is only a child."

"So he isn't Mordred in our time?" Tommy asked. "Maybe we've met him already."

"Yes and no. You haven't met *him,* the wizard. You've met someone with, let us say, possibilities."

"Who?"

"Oh, it's not so definite as that. Wizards don't move in straight lines. Mordred is shifting all the time. At first, very far in the future, he is a mortal, but then his talents develop, and shapes are not such a problem. In your time he is still a hatchling—still susceptible to danger yet not a mortal anymore. On the verge of flying but still in the nest, if you see what I mean."

The boys nodded. "Then we wouldn't necessarily recognize him, even if we did meet him," Tommy ventured.

"Exactly. He thought he could ignore you, because what you're going to do—if you succeed—hasn't happened yet. Tomorrow is a time he has already experienced, and he assumes his tomorrows are safe."

Tommy shook his head doubtfully. "I don't think I'm able to follow. If we're going to defeat him—I mean, if we have a chance to—why aren't you staying to help us?"

"Ah, that would violate my bargain." Merlin's voice was firm. "But I can tell you more about what's been happening. As wizards go, I am far older than Mordred, which means that I gained our knowledge much further in the future. Remember what I just said, that wizards live backwards in time. Being older, I understand him better than he does himself. He will realize that someday, but not until long, long ago. There's much destruction in the future that he has already wreaked, but we can try to amend that."

The boys found that their heads were swimming with this new way of keeping time, but they decided to remain quiet.

"For a long while in the future," Merlin went on, "I have been chasing Mordred, trying to counter his evils. But today I realized how futile that is going to be. He will carry out his malice to the full. I can see that the past is going to contain much darkness, just as the future has. An evil nature evil work must breed. So I have proposed to Mordred that either you or he must succeed once and for all."

"Us?" Tommy said.

"Yes, because you are mortal, and in your time so is he, almost."

"When are you going to make your proposition?" Tommy said.

"I already did it tomorrow. The notion that you could harm or defeat him would be ludicrous in the past, but his vanity has been piqued. He has no doubts that he has won in the future."

Tommy shook his head, trying to clear away his confusion. "Let's be simple. Are you proposing some kind of fight, a combat?"

"To what purpose? The two of us have already experienced a future of unending war. Neither of us, Mordred or me, can die. And since I know him better than he knows himself, I realize that he wants the whole world, to swallow it up like a greedy boy craving all the pudding. Well, I propose to let him have it, and the stomachache it will bring." A smile crossed Merlin's lips.

"How can you let him have what he's already won?" Tommy asked. "The kingdom is laid waste, and King Arthur's gone. Our future is lost to him already."

"But there will be another time for all of this. What Mordred wins today he may have already lost tomorrow. Why do you imagine that he was so desperate for victory? Because he hasn't yet controlled the past. So let it be decided permanently—that is my offer. I will cede the web of time to him; I will forfeit my rights to interfere in human affairs. I am tired of protecting mortals, who reject me anyway."

Despite his meek features, Derek's figure seemed to grow and swell; his voice was stern, full of serious intent. "I cannot afford to toy with him anymore. I truly am weary of fighting. In multitudes of worlds he wins, in multitudes he loses. I pursue him through an endless maze of dark and light. All he can hope for is eventually to become as weary as I am. But Mordred is too green, he hasn't realized this and never will until long ago."

"Then why did he take you up on your proposition?" Tommy asked.

"Vanity. I showed him a picture of us ages hence, looking like two crippled knights eternally hacking at each other with rusty swords." Merlin laughed and stretched out again in the king's chair. "I told him, 'You have seen your enemy, and it's not me. It's repetition. Who would have thought it? Your taste for evil has always seemed insatiable, like a bottomless well. But it isn't enough. What will you do about the sheer tedium? Some things are far worse than death.'"

"What did he say to that?" Sis asked.

"He thought it was a trap, naturally. 'Why are you offering this wager to me now?' he said. 'I'm young and far from fatigued, while you are old and weary. Why should I give up before my time?' I replied, 'You and I will always go on like this. Your youth will hang like a heavy cloak on you as ancient centuries creak past. If you like, I can show you the thousands of years you have already passed in this guise.'"

"And he believed you?" Sis asked.

"He believed this." With a movement faster than their eyes could follow, Merlin's forefinger touched them on the forehead. Tommy drew back, suddenly afraid that he was about to plunge into a vision such as the black fog had induced. But Mordred's menacing presence didn't return. Tommy's eyes remained wide open. After a moment he saw that Merlin was looking over his shoulder. Tommy turned, and there was Mordred, a dazzling youth with golden hair. He held a sword poised over the neck of a fallen noble.

Arthur. Tommy recognized the dark corner of the hall where Merlin's eyes had seen the body. Only now the king was alive, gazing up at his bastard son. His face was calm, despite the point of the blade aiming at his throat.

"Die!" Mordred hissed as he struck with full fury. The sword found its mark, and his father gurgled in his death agony, spurting blood. But before Mordred could feast on the sight, something new caught Tommy's attention. It was like a thread or filament. His mind followed it, and suddenly Mordred was standing over Arthur again, his sword raised exactly as before. Eagerly he struck, but this time he missed—Lancelot had risen from the floor and stabbed him in the back with Excalibur. Before Mordred could cry out, Tommy sensed another thread. He followed it and saw the poised sword once more. This time he didn't wait for another outcome.

"It's the web of time, isn't it?" He looked at Merlin, who was still sitting quietly in his chair. "Did you see that, Sis?" The little boy nodded. "It's like millions of threads all woven together, and I was able to follow any one I wanted to."

"Don't be so surprised," Merlin remarked. "Following the threads of time is what humans are already doing, but I gave you a moment of wizards' sight. Wizards see the whole web, and we are free to follow any strand, which means that we create any event as easily as you dream. Mordred has been intoxicated with this ability, and his power is such that he drags the rest of you into his evil fantasies of suffering and death. However, he hasn't taken into account one vital thing—he will have to live every version of time, follow every thread in the web. That is his curse."

"So are we still in the version that happened this morning?" Tommy asked.

"How should I know? Wizards haven't experienced the past yet. But as you can see, Mordred and his mother have vanished."

"So they won?" Sis said, then caught himself. "Or they lost. Which is it?"

"It is neither, yet it is both. As I explained before, they hoped to seize something from the fray, but they failed, despite the fall of the kingdom." Merlin pointed to the severed hand on the wall, and the boys had a glimmer of what the sign meant.

"What you're saying, then, is that we still have a chance," declared Tommy.

The old wizard looked at him approvingly. "Mordred has a gambling streak. And he hopes to find a way to defeat me once and for all. That's why he hasn't crushed you. He needs you."

"For what?"

"To lead him back into the future. He's overlooked something there, and if he doesn't retrace his steps, he will fail this morning. Camelot appears to have fallen, but it won't if this morning doesn't go as planned."

"So tell us what to do," Tommy pleaded.

Merlin shook his head. "I can't deprive you of your quest. Find what Mordred wants before he finds it himself."

"But if we're leading him to it, won't he grab it first and probably kill us in the process?" Tommy asked anxiously.

"Perhaps."

Merlin stood up and walked to the window. "It's getting late, and I have things to do yesterday. Let me tell you what Mordred has agreed to. I shall leave the world for a time. He will have all power without check or opposition. If, on his own, he is not able to hold his power, you mortals will win. There will be no dark rider on your hill, evermore."

"That's absurd," Tommy protested. "You give all power to him, and yet Mordred might lose?"

"Yes. It is all between him and you."

"Is that your scheme? To sneak some mortal all your spells and charms, whatever you call them?"

"No, I can't do that. It's the one thing you must forgive me. I am a soothsayer. I can foresee what ruination Mordred is about to inflict once I leave, and the millions who will sing his praises for corrupting them. I've lived the future, and its lifeblood is polluted with evil."

"Then it's hopeless," Tommy said mournfully.

"Oh, totally. Hope is a drug Mordred especially likes to inject." The old wizard's voice sounded cheerful; the boys could only stare. "Don't worry about that. Hopelessness is going to be one of your greatest allies." Imperceptibly he had been moving away from them and now stood at the far end of the hall.

"Don't leave," Sis begged. Merlin looked at him, as if entertaining a flicker of hesitation, before turning toward the door. The boys leapt out of their chairs and ran the length of the hall.

The old wizard had crossed the inner courtyard with amazing speed and stood by the smashed gate and fallen ramparts of the outer yard. Tommy was the first to reach him. "Tell us one thing we can look for," he pleaded, feeling lost and anxious.

"Look for? You'd better start with what you can't look for." Merlin pointed silently to the corner where the body of the king lay. The boys stared—they could have sworn that a weapon lay on the floor next to Arthur's outstretched hand, but now the floor was blank. Merlin leaned over, and Tommy felt the brush of his beard.

"Begin with the sword," the old wizard whispered, as if wanting no one else to overhear him. Tommy started. It wasn't Merlin's voice anymore but Derek's, and the beard didn't exist. In the long shafts of afternoon light Derek's body no longer glowed.

Derek stood up, his figure diminished back to its former size. "We'd better get out of here," Tommy said urgently to Sis. "I think he's back to being Derek again."

"Of course I'm Derek. Where are we?" The voice had completely resumed its normal mild confusion. "Do you think it's such a good idea to go into the castle?"

Sis and Tommy pulled him hastily through the outer courtyard. The ruptured walls of the castle laid open a space for the western sun to shine through; walking into the light, the three intruders seemed to be melting into the sun.

"Where are we going?" Derek asked.

"Away," Tommy replied. "I have a feeling we've seen the last of Merlin, so we're not safe here anymore."

"Merlin?" Derek mused. "Did I say anything helpful?" He regarded the boys in gentle bafflement, allowing them to lead.

Tommy decided not to take the risk of talking anymore. He left Derek's question unanswered. With luck, he reckoned, Mordred had departed the castle for good and missed their intrusion. Without luck, he knew, a deadly blade would be flying through the air into their retreating backs.

19

THE BETROTHAL

WHEN ARTHUR TOLD HIS MOTHER THAT HE WAS GOING TO MARRY Katy Kilbride, she bit her lip and looked away. "Will you be wanting invitations? Mine were on old parchment with purple ink. I was a very silly girl."

"I think we'd prefer not to, Mum. If that's all right." Arthur looked at Katy, who nodded slightly.

Peg Callum didn't catch this exchange; she began to wander a bit. "Chapel services never suited your father. He didn't exactly hate weddings, but he hated neckties and found any excuse not to wear one. He wanted us to get married in a meadow with cows, of all things. Imagine." She ventured a timid glance at the bride-to-be, who was radiant. That was customary for brides, but in this case Katy's glow made Arthur's mother think of a hot stove or a branding iron.

"Do you wish us happiness?" Arthur suddenly asked.

Peg couldn't tell the motive behind the question. Her son seemed totally smitten with Katy, but—was she imagining it?—there was a hint of trouble in his voice. Peg fiddled with her necklace. "Why do you think I wouldn't?"

"No offense."

If only they would go away. Peg was sorry to find that she wanted Arthur out of the house, but she needed time to figure it all out. He hadn't come home two nights straight, worrying her half to death. And when he did appear, embarrassed and evasive, he hardly spoke to her before announcing that he was getting married.

Katy broke the awkward silence. "I think you'll be pleased to hear that Master Ambrosius is performing the ceremony."

Peg stared, confounded. "Is he, then?"

Arthur nodded. "He's ordained after some fashion or other," he said tolerantly. "It's what Katy wants, and you know you and Dad never raised me in the church." His mother's distress was obvious, and he felt confused. What was the matter with her? Under the table Arthur felt the reassuring squeeze of Katy's hand. Just this touch made him ache with desire. They were so in love that it was impossible to be apart physically, and almost as difficult to share company with other people.

The pair stood up. "I'll be in the car," Katy announced. "You'll want to talk to your mother alone."

Left by himself with Peg, who remained sitting on the sofa, Arthur looked blank and detached. "Well, I guess this must seem like a pretty rash decision." Peg didn't nod or reply. He pulled a note from his pocket and handed it to her. "I, um, plan to stay at Katy's from now on. That's the number. If you don't mind, I'll just leave my things here a bit longer. I mean, I'm not abandoning you or anything. I hope you know that."

"Yes," she replied, but her tone was ambiguous.

The car started outside, coughing a few times before idling impatiently. "I should run it in for a tune-up." The pointlessness of Arthur's remark was so obvious it made him just want to go. He leaned over the coffee table. Peg shrank back into the sofa cushions, but not before he had kissed her on the cheek. "I know it's hard," he said stiffly, "but I love you."

When he was gone, Peg got up and opened the liquor cabinet. "Oh," she murmured—there hadn't been any alcohol in it since she cleaned out the malt whiskey after Frederick's death. She rearranged some Dresden figurines on the mantel, rewound the clock, stared around blankly, then stepped outside. She focused on the spot in the street where Arthur's car had been parked, like a safari scout expecting to find lion tracks. She couldn't shake the sense that Arthur was in terrible trouble. "What am I doing? What can I do?" she thought. She was alone now. Not much family had come to visit her husband in the cancer ward before he passed on, none really. If it hadn't been for Arthur by her side . . .

She looked again at the place where his car had been. This time she found herself wishing that the black Ford was still there, never having left. A sense of abandonment descended over her, worse even than when she had been widowed. "Am I going into shock?" she thought. Her mind had been protecting itself with numbness, but now it raced with names she could call: Ambrosius, Pen and Derek, Westlake. Someone had to know what was going on. She went back inside and picked up the phone. She dialed Pen's number, still scrawled in a tattered address book. Three rings, then she hung up.

"What would I say anyway?" she told herself. People always thought weddings were beautiful. If Arthur's decision had been a touch too sudden, there might be sniggers about a bun in the oven. Otherwise, what was amiss? Even a lonely, rather panicky mother seemed an appropriate part of the picture. And if Peg pushed it too hard, trying to gather allies on her side against the wedding couple, suspicions of mental imbalance would fall upon her, not her son. Peg picked up the phone again and dialed. "Chief Inspector Westlake," she said. The switchboard girl put her on hold. Five seconds, ten seconds, half a minute. She became so nervous that she was about to hang up when a man's deep voice growled, "Westlake here."

"Is this Chief Inspector Westlake?" *Oh God, he'll think I'm a gibbering fool.*

"Yes, I'm pretty sure I have my name right." He fit the picture Arthur had given her.

"I don't believe we've met before," Peg said haltingly. "I'm Arthur's mother."

"Constable Callum?"

"Yes, that's right."

There was silence at the other end. Either Westlake was waiting for her to state her business or he was reacting to who she was. Peg took a chance on the second possibility and let the silence dangle for a few seconds. "Can you come down to the station?" Westlake finally said. "I'm here till five, but it would be best if you could come immediately. Alone, if possible, and without telling your son."

She felt a strange mixture of relief and alarm. "I'll have to walk, but it won't be five minutes." The line clicked dead.

The bells in the old Norman church tower chimed three as she rounded the corner off the High Street into King's Road. Squat and ugly, the King's Road police station was unfamiliar territory to her. She'd found it difficult to accept when Arthur became a policeman, and she had never asked him to take her there on a visit.

The reception area was empty except for the station sergeant's high desk. "Inspector Westlake," Peg stated nervously.

The station sergeant cocked an ear. "Who?"

When she spoke up louder, he directed her with a nod of his head down a long corridor to the right. He must have used the intercom, because Westlake was preparing for her at his door, pulling on a lumpy gray jacket and tightening his necktie.

After motioning her inside, Westlake pushed forward a sagging old leather chair. "Thanks for coming over. As you can imagine, suspensions of this type are embarrassing to the department, and of course we are sensitive to what it does to a young officer's career."

"Suspension?"

"It's only temporary, just until we can get some kind of explanation. I'm sure that's what you want as well."

"I don't know. I mean, yes, explanations would be helpful. Can we start again? Are you saying that Arthur has been let go from the force?"

Westlake sat back in his desk chair, registering surprise. "Apologies are in order. It seems I've sprung a nasty surprise on you. My fault, but given that you called, I assumed it was about your son."

"It is, but—"

"This is getting stupidly awkward. You can tell me the purpose of your visit as you see fit. My concern is that Constable Callum did not appear for duty two days in a row. He took leave without notice or permission. In addition to this dereliction of duty, there were, uh, embarrassing circumstances." Westlake fidgeted with a pencil, caught himself, and set it down decisively on his blotter.

"Being with Katy, you mean?"

Westlake cleared his throat. "I'm an old hand, Mrs. Callum, mustered into police work straight out of army service, and I suppose I'm rather old-fashioned. Frankly, having women on the force has given me nervous moments. In this case the liaison between your son and Constable Kilbride caught us very much off guard." Like many men in authority, Westlake had turned hopelessly stiff at the prospect of discussing anyone's personal life. Peg wasn't surprised when he used that very phrase.

"Callum's—I mean your son's—unofficial business shouldn't be a concern of the department. But—and again I must speak frankly—his obsession with one particular case has added to our worries."

"You mean Merlin?"

Westlake nodded. "The papers will lead us a devil of a dance. To claim that a dead man was stolen from an ambulance, well—" Westlake sighed. "Of course to call it an oversight would sound preposterous."

Peg found it difficult to keep still in her chair. "You're confusing me, Inspector Westlake. When Arthur told me about the missing body, I got the distinct impression that you had given him permission to investigate. Of course I don't know about such matters."

"Nor should you. In police work discretion is of the utmost importance. But to be absolutely frank, Mrs. Callum, I'm concerned about Arthur's emotional state at present."

"Because he's marrying Katy Kilbride?" Peg exclaimed, almost laughing despite herself.

Westlake looked disconcerted. "No, no, dear lady, of course not. I have no right to an opinion in personal affairs, though some might say that he seems to have mistaken mashed potatoes for caviar. No, my fears are centered on the simple fact that your son's dead man has been found—alive."

"I see." It was obvious to both of them that she couldn't possibly see.

Westlake reached across his desk and pushed a button on a console. "Send in McPhee, will you, Sergeant?"

A moment later there was a tap at the door and a beefy constable entered, removing his hat when he saw Peg. "You wanted me, Chief?"

Westlake waved McPhee to another sagging leather chair. "This is Constable Callum's mother. I felt it would help if you filled her in on our missing man."

"We picked him up just after dawn. He was wandering the road in a shabby state. Seemed disoriented and put up a bit of a struggle before we persuaded him to come along." McPhee paused, wondering whether to continue. "In my opinion he's loony, but then that's for the doctors to say, isn't it?"

Peg was uncomfortably aware of the two policemen keeping their eyes on her. "Who was he?"

"We don't know yet," replied Westlake. "The man in question is, as DC McPhee indicated, not coherent at present, and he may be ajudged mentally incompetent, once they check him out at the geriatrics infirmary. Since he appears to have spent considerable time out of doors, it's routine to check for pneumonia."

"Then he wasn't dead after all," Peg half-muttered.

"Probably he was unconscious, and when he found himself in the back of an ambulance, he panicked and jumped out," McPhee said. "There's quite a few places where the ambulance had to stop, intersections and such."

Peg looked anxiously from one man to the other. "You're wrong about Arthur. He's always had his head on," she said, hearing how feeble the protest sounded. It was probably better to keep quiet; she gathered her purse and stood up. "I'm very grateful you were willing to see me. It was very decent. You could have kept this entirely under wraps."

Westlake nodded. "Officially it is under wraps. I'm sure you understand." He led her to the door.

A recollection struck her. "I'm hopelessly vague about these things, Inspector, but didn't Arthur tell me that you were at the scene of the crime?"

"We're not so sure that there was a crime," Westlake pointed out.

"But were you there?"

McPhee and Westlake exhanged glances. "As a matter of fact, no," the detective inspector replied. "Callum and Kilbride are intimating as much in their statements—or what we have of statements. So far it's just been one telephone conversation after we tracked them down. This is all very preliminary, and either one or both of the officers in question may choose to resign rather than submit to an investigation."

"Where were you that night?" Peg blurted out. She was amazed that she had the nerve; the two policemen became noticeably uncomfortable.

"It's not me that's to be interrogated," Westlake said sternly. His voice softened. "I'm sorry to have been the bearer of bad tidings, Mrs. Callum. Go home now. If we need your help any further, we'll call." With a last gentle touch on the shoulder he ushered her into the hallway, paid his respects, and closed the door.

Peg took a few halting steps before realizing that she didn't really know what she wanted to do or where she should go. She was still rooted to the spot when Hamish McPhee came out. He looked grave and sympathetic. "Ma'am, won't you let me take you up front?" He wrapped an enormous hand around her elbow and with old-school courtesy accompanied her down the hall. If she hadn't been so rattled, Peg would have found it funny.

"I can make it home on my own," she assured him when they reached the reception area.

"Are you sure? I can call you a cab."

"No. I mean yes. That would be lovely."

He walked to the sidewalk and with two fingers to his mouth gave a whistle like a doorman. A taxi approached from a nearby hack stand.

"Is Katy Kilbride living around here?"

McPhee shuffled uneasily. "Yes, ma'am, about three blocks down. It's a big shambling place, owned by a fellow named Ambleside."

She was startled. "Amberside, you mean?"

"That's it. Family goes back a long time hereabouts, so I'm told. My dad came to Gramercy after the war, but that makes us newcomers to hear the townies tell it." McPhee held the cab door open for her. "Do you want me to give the driver a destination?" he offered. But she was already inside with the window rolled up.

"Where to, mum?" the cabbie asked.

Peg looked nervously at McPhee, who continued to hover about. "Just drive."

The cabbie shrugged and pulled out. When they had rounded the corner and King's Road station was out of sight, she tapped on the glass. "The geriatrics infirmary," she ordered, and settled back for the ride.

Katy stood next to the bed, pulling her jeans and top on. Arthur had been asleep for a few minutes while she lay on the pillow and watched his face. She smiled. Watching Arthur while he wasn't looking had been a habit, growing into a fixation. Lightly she touched his hair and nose and mouth without waking him up. It was all as incredible to her as if a statue had come to life or a dream had materialized out of thin air.

She stopped to close the blinds against the afternoon sun and went downstairs. The kitchen was gigantic and antiquated, with a pull cord to turn on the light. Even in the afternoon the gloom was deep. "Oh, it's you," she said. Under the swinging bulb, Amberside sat at the kitchen table, the tarot splayed out in front of him, in the twelve-card array of the horoscope.

"How can you see that in the dark?" she asked, opening the fridge. "Is there any milk? I'm dying for some cornflakes."

"Exhausted?"

She shot him a look and got out the milk bottle, which had been hiding in the back. The cereal was stored in the highest cupboard to foil the mice. It made her self-conscious to eat in front of Amberside, though he had always said the kitchen was communal; anyway, anything had been better than having to make do with a hot plate in her room. Katy pulled up a chair at the yellow laminated table, its top torn and greasy. "For a dealer in antiques, you don't much care how you live."

He ignored her, concentrating on the circle of twelve cards before him. "The major arcana make all the difference, you know. Look at this. Fool and High Priestess." The two cards were displayed at the lower right of the circle. "That's you and Arthur, and the placement signifies May or June in the horoscope."

"Fate's on schedule," she joked idly, chewing her cereal before it got soggy. "What do those cards mean exactly? I don't much fancy him as the Fool."

"Don't you? It's all a matter of context. Look at the card closely—the Fool's smiling, careless. His foot is poised on the edge of a cliff, yet he heeds no danger. Yes, for better or worse, he's fortune's fool."

"I think I like that, actually. We'll both step off the cliff together," Katy said, laughing.

Amberside eyed her closely. "But there's more to it, my dear. The Fool is capable of sudden change, just when it's least expected. He is identified with old gods of passion and destruction. He is also the first of the trumps, leading the whole deck. Enter with him, and you enter all the possibilities that the tarot offers. Some are darker than you may suppose."

Katy yawned. She had lived in the house long enough to be slightly bored by Amberside's stage-magician manner. "Look, you don't mind, do you?" She got up from the table and took her bowl to the sink.

"You didn't ask about the High Priestess."

She turned, smiling. "That one at least sounds nice."

"*Nice* is such an inadequate word. This is one of the most mystic cards in the deck. What does it show? A woman standing on the stairs, lilies in one hand, a crystal sphere in the other. Doesn't she remind you of a bride? But of course she'll never marry."

"Why not?" Katy asked, holding on to the edge of the sink.

"Too many secrets. The High Priestess lives in dreams, fantasies, intuitions. Do you want to know who she really is? Persephone, captured by the dark god to become queen of the nether regions."

"I once saw a lingerie shop called King of the Undie World. Quite funny, that." Neither of them smiled. As she left the kitchen, Katy half-expected him to follow. She found herself pausing at the bottom of the stairs. Amberside had hung an elaborate French gilt mirror there. She looked in it, curious. Why do people fall in love? She had the same face Arthur had ignored all along. She put her hand to her crinkly hair and fluffed it discontentedly.

"I'd like to perform the wedding here, if that pleases you." Amberside had appeared at the door of the kitchen, which was darkened behind him. "There aren't many other boarders this time of year, just before the summer rush. Did you know there was a chapel in this house?"

"No. These old places are amazing."

"Quite. I believe the original family prided itself on breeding missionaries. I can show you the chapel now, if you like—it's restored."

"No, that's all right. I trust your judgment." She started up the stairs and then turned. "I don't mean to ignore you, it's just—"

"You're in love. A common sickness. I understand the best remedy is a week in bed," he said ironically. Katy didn't react. She was staring past him, and her face looked stricken. "What's the matter?"

She pointed at a tall ground-floor window. "There was a man there," she said, her manner agitated.

Strangely, Amberside continued to face her, not turning to see where she was pointing. "Really?" he said quietly. "What kind of man? Someone from your dark past, judging by how white you look—you're chalk." His voice carried a level, unsympathetic tone. "Don't joke, I'm quite shaken. One second he was there, the next he was gone. He stared directly at me, and he looked positively—"

"Hateful. I know. I'm thinking of hiring him to work on the grounds for a week. He was in service for a long time, but his temper got the best of him. Made quite a row before leaving. His name's Jasper." Amberside revealed all this in a casual voice, but he kept his eyes fixed on Katy. For some reason that name made her tremble; she felt a surge of fear.

"Why would you keep such a man around? He might be dangerous," she said nervously.

"How would you know that if you've never met him before? Anyway, I like dangerous people. I have a theory that the dangerous people in this world are just projections of the rest of us. We go around like milksops, thinking we leave the evil to others when in fact there are no others. 'Stare at a monster long enough and you become a monster.' Who said that? Never mind. It should be, 'Stare at a monster long enough and you'll realize it's yourself.' I think that's much more honest."

"All right, if you say so." Suddenly she felt desperate to wake up Arthur. They could just hold each other for a while.

"I see you want to go," Amberside said blandly. "We can discuss my little theories later. But you do think everyone has a darker side, don't you? Then it's entirely possible that the darker side has been projected out into the world as a class of criminals or misfits or deluded dreamers."

"You may be right, it just sounds strange. I do think we bottle up our dark side, most of us."

"Unless we find the opportunity to release it. But then such opportunities are rare and frightening. No one would venture into them unless they could be sure of absolute secrecy. A little cowardly, I suppose, but all of us have a profound wish to repress our shameful instincts. Imagine what you would be, for example, if you let all your rage out, or all your lust."

"That's offensive," Katy replied sharply. She felt confused, and an irrational fear possessed her. It wasn't Amberside she wanted to run away from but, of all things, the gilded mirror at the bottom of the stairs.

Unheeding, Amberside pressed on. "As I say, secrecy is a profound need. For all we know, you and I have done things we won't even admit to ourselves. That's the ultimate secrecy, isn't it?"

Katy shook her head. "You're quite a talker. I could have been upstairs five minutes ago."

"Well, I wish you joy of your bed, madam," Amberside said with a flourish. "A maiden who has not lost her head is not using it well."

The color drained from Katy's face. She felt sick. A smell like rotted mushrooms filled her nose. Then the front door opened and the man she had seen in the window stood before her. He stared into her eyes meaningfully, his face flushed deep scarlet.

"Fay," he mumbled.

She was trembling harder now. "I don't understand. That's not my name. Leave me alone," she cried, afraid somewhere deep in her soul that if she stayed, she would understand. She turned quickly and headed upstairs so that Jasper wouldn't catch her undisguisable fear and revulsion.

20
DUST ON THE ROAD

THE HUT EDGERTON FOUND IN THE WOODS DIDN'T HAVE MANY rats in it. He was glad of that, very glad. Some bygone gamekeeper must have abandoned the hut—a rusty fox trap hung on one wall and bits of rabbit fur littered the floor. In the back room the roof was caved in, but the front room, where the glass was intact in the windows, proved livable. The boy spent most of his time there, waiting until dusk to make forays into town to find food. When he got back, he'd roll himself up inside some old carpet padding he had dragged up from the dump. It kept him warm, barely, while he slept.

One night Edgerton was shocked to see his father trundling up the path to the hut in his wheelchair. "Jerry, it's me," he called. "Help me up." Edgerton didn't move. "Jerry, have you got it? It's you or me 'as got the sword, and I know it ain't me." Amazingly, his dad negotiated the rocks and scree in his wheelchair, cursing softly under his breath.

The boy was trapped, and the hut had no door to lock. He heard the wheelchair come to a stop, then his dad hauled himself up in the doorway, sweating from the climb. "We all miss you," Paddy said. "You wanted us dead, but you're forgiven."

With a knowing smile he blew a tongue of flame from his mouth, filling the room. Shrieking, rats leaped from the woodwork. Flame caught the boy's hair. He screamed, beating it out with his bare hands. Then he woke up, trembling, from the nightmare.

Day broke without a sunrise. It was the third morning since he had run away, and he couldn't stop shivering and sneezing. Black, whispery rain had fallen during the night, soaking him. In disgust he heaved the carpet padding out the door. His energy was ebbing by the hour, and bad dreams didn't help.

"You've got to eat," he told himself. His stomach was sore from the scraps of sausage rolls and chips he'd managed to scrounge from behind a pub. Did he dare risk the school? Someone there, one of his mates, could sneak bread and milk out to him. The boy's stomach growled at the prospect, but he was sure the school authorities would turn him over to the police if they got their hands on him.

"It's not worth getting nicked," he thought. Hiding out in the woods had been an act of calculated desperation. The police never searched there except as a last resort, and no one from St. Justin's knew his private haunts.

The morning was getting on, the sky quilted with low, gray clouds. The boy scrambled down the ravine leading from the hut into a narrow defile, notched like a rifle sight and heavily overgrown. From ten yards away, you couldn't see the ramshackle dwelling at all. He trudged toward town, thinking about food and money. Neither would be easy. He didn't really have any tight mates. The altar boys were his crowd, but what did they amount to? A loose gaggle of mean, marginal boys, not to be trusted. He wouldn't trust himself, and he was the best of the lot.

Heavy droplets spattered the leaf canopy overhead. He looked up, and one smacked him in the eye. Edgerton cursed. It was strange to think of his own home as only a pile of raked-over ashes and charred lumps. He'd taken a chance and sneaked by to see it the night before. The cold embers clinked when Edgerton kicked them. They weren't telling any secrets.

"Why did he do it?" he thought. His dad had been moody and

mostly drunk for a long time. After the accident at the print shop laid him off, there had been no living with him—you had to walk around on eggshells. The week before, he'd caught Edgerton sneaking out with a beer bottle under his jacket.

"Where do you think you're goin' with that, exactly?" his dad had asked, blocking the kitchen door with his wheelchair.

"I hadn't thought it out, exactly," Edgerton replied sarcastically.

"Don't you lip me. I can still twist your head off with one arm. I was contributin' by the time I was your age, have you ever thought of that? That useless school of yours costs us dear enough."

"I don't notice as you've got anything to be dear about," Edgerton remarked with cold spite.

The moment was getting ugly when his mum came in. "You've got to be allowing with your dad, Jerr," his mum told him, tears in her eyes. "Since the accident his leg's pained him really bad. Can't you do it for my sake?" The boy didn't say anything, but for the next few days he kept out of his dad's way as best he could.

The night of the fire he hadn't seen his father for hours. Edgerton was shut up in his room, listening to tapes and smoking cigarettes out the window so his mum wouldn't catch the smell in the morning. Winnie had gone out. His dad had done a bit of yelling downstairs, nothing radical. About eleven Edgerton performed the nightly ritual of carrying the wheelchair upstairs while his dad watched sullenly from the couch. He always waited until the boy was in his room before clumping upstairs supported by his cane on one side and his wife on the other.

After his parents closed their bedroom door, the house went quiet. The place was such a thin little cheesebox that he hadn't felt safe taking out the sword. *I'll lay here for a bit till I'm sure they're asleep.* Edgerton pulled the chain on the overhead bulb so the crack under the door wouldn't give him away. Ten minutes passed, then fifteen, and he started feeling drowsy. The door must have opened and closed without his hearing it, because the next thing the boy knew there was someone in the dark beside him. Edgerton almost jumped out of bed.

"Easy now. It's just me." It was his dad. Edgerton could smell the whiskey breath on him.

"What's goin' on?" Edgerton asked. His dad was a low bulk in the darkness, rolling from side to side in his wheelchair. "Go back to sleep, Dad," he said sharply, the adrenaline in his body pounding like a drum corps. Edgerton reached for his bedside lamp, but with a sweep his dad knocked it to the floor.

"Give it me. Where is it?"

"Where's what? You're actin' crazy."

His dad approached the bed and started rocking the mattress violently. "Get up, you stupid sod. It's not yours. Don't you think I want to walk again? Give it me." Edgerton could see his dad's head waggling in the dark and was so frightened it made him sick.

"C'mon, Dad, just get out," he whispered fiercely. But his dad was strong as a bull from years of lifting rolls of newsprint at the shop. He tipped the boy out of bed onto the floor and reached frantically underneath his mattress. Without seeing, Edgerton knew his dad had found the sword.

"Bloody right," his father exclaimed, holding up the long, thin shape. "Bloody right."

"That's mine! You can't steal it, you're crazy," Edgerton protested, climbing out from under the tangled bedclothes. And his dad must have been crazy, too, because he unsheathed the blade and pointed it at his son's throat.

"Get back." He'd never given off such black menace before, and the instinct for self-preservation made Edgerton step back. The chair wheeled around to the door. His dad kicked it open and left the room.

Maybe I should have run after him. The thought kept going through Edgerton's mind. He didn't know if he loved his family, but they didn't deserve to die. Ten minutes later, Edgerton smelled smoke as it started seeping up from below. He was out of bed, pulling on his jumper and sneakers, getting ready to hit the streets. He wasn't going to stay around that sick bastard. Smelling the smoke, he raced down the hall and roused his mum, who was a dead-sound sleeper.

"Where's Paddy? Where's your dad?" she mumbled groggily.

"Don't mind that, we've got to get out."

"Don't mind? You must be off your head. Paddy, Paddy!" Edie had started shouting, and when the first lick of flame came out of the heating duct, she began screaming. "Oh my God, Paddy, where is he?"

It took all the boy's strength to pull her downstairs. The blaze was spreading incredibly fast. Looking back, the last thing they saw was his dad's wheelchair in the sitting room, empty, engulfed by sheets of fire. His mum broke down and became hysterical.

"So your throne's in flames. Serves you right," was all the boy could think.

Looking back, Edgerton didn't know why that particular phrase had come to mind. Maybe because of all the times his dad would mumble, while drunk, "I'm still king in my own house." Let him be king of that pile of ashes. It wasn't worth digging a hole for him now. Then it hit the boy that he was stuck on something: How did his dad get the wheelchair downstairs that night?

When he reached the edge of the woods bounded by the stream, Edgerton turned right. He'd decided to head for St. Justin's, less than half a mile away. There was one hiding place he knew about where he could hole up and no other boys would find him. It would be warm at least. Now the gray, quilted clouds were spitting rain again. Edgerton's shivering grew worse, and he quickened his pace.

"Merlin abandoned us long ago, and all he left behind was the stone," the woman in the felt hat said. "You cannot imagine the trials that have been endured to keep it within the court of miracles. It has been our hope, our only hope. We were stunned when it suddenly disappeared."

"How did it disappear?" Pen asked.

"We supposed that it had been stolen from the cave we just left," the lady in the felt hat said. "But first it might be better to ask how you came into possession of it." It was late morning. They had made their way back from the crystal cave to the road. The tramp led the way this time. The woman in the felt hat stayed by Pen's side while Melchior, as before, brought up the rear. The weather was bright, but up ahead they could see lowering, gray clouds. The storm was rapidly moving toward them.

"I got the stone quite by accident. I found it," Pen explained.

The tramp shook his head. "There are no accidents in this affair; there is only some purpose we haven't yet understood."

"Where did you find the stone?" the woman in the felt hat asked.

"At Emrys Hall, where I lived before meeting you." A realization struck Pen. "You let me lead the way to the cave. Did you wonder if I'd been there before, when the stone was stolen?" The lady in the felt hat nodded and began to say something. Pen cut her short. "You don't have to explain. I understand. You can't afford to trust anybody from the outside." She stopped and reached under her jacket for the black velveteen bag. "Here, take it. I don't have any claim on it."

Surprisingly, the lady in the felt hat didn't seem eager to receive the stone. Instead she gazed at the bag, thinking to herself. "It doesn't make sense," she finally remarked, "to lose the stone after so much travail and then to get it back so casually. We are very grateful to you, to be sure. The stone has been guarded for centuries, but it has never fully revealed itself. What have you read in it?"

"'Clas Myrddin.' I saw that much."

"Then that's what it wanted you to know, but those two words are just the key to deeper meanings. Could you read on?"

Pen shook her head. The little group was silent, walking slowly toward the storm clouds.

"A road is good for telling tales," the tramp said. "Could you tell us how you found the stone? It may give us a clue."

"It was left in the maze. And I believe it was left by my husband. He was on the run, evading capture or something of the sort. Since it wasn't safe to contact me, he must have left the stone as a sign."

The lady in the felt hat absorbed this information for a moment. "You never saw your husband in the maze, then?"

"No, I can only guess who it was. The night after Derek vanished, I couldn't sleep at all. I was in terrible distress, my mind racing. From our bedroom window you can see out onto the gardens, including the maze. The moon was full, and as I was too restless to stay in bed, I happened to go to the window. There was somebody down below moving about, a man on foot, and he was heading into the maze.

"My intuition told me it was Derek. I threw on my robe and ran downstairs. I didn't think to take a flashlight; I was too agitated. No one else was about, yet I couldn't shake the feeling that I was being watched. It took all my courage to enter the maze. The yew walls are very tall, you see, forming dark, narrow passages—quite an intimidating place at night. But Derek and I always considered it special, and I know the passages blindfolded.

"As soon as I entered, I felt for the right-hand wall. The maze is devious—it begins with a false turn to the left, then another to the right, before the real opening into the maze appears. I had gotten that far when I realized I'd put myself in jeopardy. There were muffled voices coming behind me, and I could hear footsteps ahead. In a maze you can only go in or out, the other paths being dead ends. In a panic I saw that I was trapped. I suppose I could have taken one of the dead ends and hidden there as best I could, but I'm not the kind of person who can just cower and wait. If Derek was already inside, that's where I would go.

"I'll never know how he got out, but as I hurried toward the center, the footsteps ahead died away. One turning after another was empty, and so was the center itself. As you can imagine, I was very confused. And then a sound, a low growling sound, made me almost drop from fright. A large animal was in there with me. I couldn't hear people anymore. Irrationally, I imagined wolves, which would be impossible in this day and age, or a large mastiff."

"Only it wasn't," the lady in the felt hat said.

"No. It's taken me a while to figure that out. It wanted something else. What transpired next happened very quickly. I was frantically pacing the center of the maze when my shoe hit something. I bent down and found a flat, round river stone. I picked it up to throw if I had to defend myself, although of course I couldn't have stopped a large hunting animal by throwing a rock at it."

"You didn't need to," the tramp said.

"How did you know? The animal, whatever it was, came very close—I could sense its presence in the shadows. Its form was indescribable. It was like a boar with long tusks curling to its eyes but far more horrible. I was terrified. The thing crouched, but it daren't actually jump me. I stood there with the rock in my hand, and the beast paced back and forth just out of arm's reach. It never walked into the moonlight, which shone over the top of the high yew walls. Even without seeing it well, however, I knew that the beast was frustrated as it kept pacing. For the longest time I didn't move. I resisted the impulse to fling the stone at it, which would have been a hysterical act."

"And a fatal mistake," the tramp said. "The animal was some sort of transformation. The stone kept it at bay."

"I suppose you're right. The beast stopped pacing, and after a moment I realized that it had vanished. Whether it ran off or melted into thin air is anybody's guess. Once I had regained my nerve, I walked out of the maze and back into the house."

"And you didn't see anyone at all?" the tramp asked.

Pen shook her head. "The scene was quite deserted. I could have been walking in my sleep and dreaming the whole thing. I only recall my surprise at seeing a light in an upstairs window where my butler lived. He keeps very regular hours, yet it must have been two in the morning when I came out of the maze, and his light was still on."

Silence greeted the end of Pen's account. The progress of the walking party had slowed to a crawl. The storm on the horizon now filled half the sky, and the air felt oppressive, like a heavy blanket.

Melchior spoke up. "Do you know where we're going?"

The lady in the felt hat replied, "To town, since the road appears to lead that way. But we are not much tied to the ordinary world. We have no particular destination, and yet every new moment is our destination."

"I believe you must have met my master somewhere, because he often talked like that," Melchior remarked. "I can tell you something more about the stone." The lady in the felt hat nodded, not breaking her stride. "The stone is not simply Merlin's sign," Melchior began. "He kept it in his room atop the tower that overlooked Arthur's court. The name of the stone is Alkahest, or 'metamorphosis.' Where it comes from I don't know. The legend existed that the stone could turn base metal into gold, but Merlin mocked such notions. 'Greedy parlor tricks. I don't need a few more coppers in my pocket or a bucket of ducats, either,' he'd say. He scorned the motley crew of alchemists who wasted their lives over fuming beakers. 'Most of them are charlatans, which is bad enough,' was his opinion. 'The ones I pity are the dreamers who will die pursuing their delusions. Their children will be lucky to inherit a lump of lead, much less gold.'"

"The stone holds the secret of true alchemy, then?" the tramp asked.

"Yes. When Mordred destroyed the wizard's tower, the stone must have gotten lost in the ruins, or perhaps my master transported it. In any case, we know that his enemy never found it. Merlin has kept his promise to absent himself from the world, but I'll tell you a secret: I believe that the Alkahest may be him in another form. Metamorphosis."

The tramp gave the lady in the felt hat a significant look. The storm clouds were overhead now; as they trudged and talked, the little band set up a hypnotic rhythm. After a while the lady said, "I also know a bit more of the tale we are piecing together. The stone wasn't transported away. It was picked up from the rubble by a small boy escaping the destruction of Camelot. He became the founder of our court—Ulwin was his name."

"Ah," Melchior said. "And what did he know of the stone?"

"Very little at first. Ulwin's most urgent priority was to escape and hide. That was difficult enough, given Mordred's cunning. When he realized what he had, Ulwin knew that the stone must be protecting him, and in return it had to be protected at all costs. The court of miracles grew up around the stone, as its guardians. But we have never stopped escaping and hiding. The stone seems to bring that fate. As Ulwin told us, 'Others may live in houses and sleep in beds. You will be the dust on the road, the wind in the wind.' And so we have endured, despite everything."

"I'm sorry, but what do you get out of it?" Pen asked suddenly. "You said you can't read the stone. Wasn't it pointless just to keep guarding it."

"Perhaps," the lady agreed. "But we were given a choice, either to take up the sorrowful task of waiting, or to live in a world whose sorrows may never end. In his old age Ulwin was gifted with prophecy—the tongue of fire. He declared on his deathbed that the stone would be read one day, and that would mark the defeat of the white dragon."

"Meaning Mordred?" Melchior asked.

"Safety lies in not speaking too plainly," the tramp cautioned. Abruptly he stopped speaking; Melchior felt that some intense feeling was being suppressed. The tramp's face grew resigned and sad. "Let me rest," he said, sitting down by the side of the road. The others gathered around him. It was several minutes before he could speak again. He addressed Melchior. "You said you witnessed the destruction of Camelot. Did you see my king die?"

"No," Melchior replied. The poignancy in the tramp's voice was unlike anything he'd ever heard. "I saw Mordred put the sword to him, but he didn't die. Merlin worked a wonder behind the veil of death."

The tramp put his face in his hands. "Merlin, Merlin. He could have saved my king and all of us with one finger, but—ah!" He turned away, his shoulders quivering.

Tears stood in Melchior's eyes. He was trying to think. "I believe I understand. You thought you saw the king die, didn't you? But what you saw was only an illusion. I can't explain Merlin's motives. He only told me that it was not rightful to interfere anymore."

"And so Merlin condemned us to this world of pain," the tramp burst out. "This test of faith has gone on a long time. Does it ever end?"

"I wish I could tell you." Melchior stopped, afraid that his words had caused more turmoil and hurt than they had eased.

The tramp began to look calmer. "My mind's too wild to hear you well. Be patient. You saw me there that day, too, but you don't know it."

"Who are you?"

"I was called Lancelot of the Lake—but I hardly know myself as that anymore. The chase has led me into too many hiding places, too many masks. What I am now no man can say. Dust on the road." He spoke thickly, as if his burden were too great to express. "For a long time I was alone, but the court of miracles drew me in. I had turned into a monk living in a cave far north of here." He looked reproachfully at the lady in the felt hat. "I should curse you for finding me, lady. I thought I had reached a corner of the world so dirty and small that no one would torment me again."

"I didn't mean to find you. It just happened. That's the only way we can escape Mordred's notice, since any plan we make is open to his discovery. The birds fly here and there without a plan, and God takes care of them. Take heart, friend. Your place is here, in the court of miracles, not in a dirty corner." The lady in the felt hat said these words with infinite kindness, and despite himself, the tramp smiled.

"I once had more faith than any man alive," he said. "I thought I would die next to my king, yet I only wake up again and again and again. At least I've learned that death is no easy escape."

"Which should give you hope that Arthur is not dead, either," Pen said. The others looked at her, surprised. "I don't see how the servant can be reborn and not his master," she said, feeling more than a little self-conscious. "Pardon me, but from what you've told me, every life is a story that must unfold. People have grown used to confining their lives to a brief sliver of time, but it may be that we just go on and on. I didn't know that before meeting you three, but I do now. I can't blame you for losing faith at times, but the story isn't ended yet."

"I don't expect an ending," the lady in the felt hat replied.

"Long ago I found a home, just living in the moment. The road we walk is the only story we'll ever know."

"But if your whole life is spent seeking and never finding, then Mordred has won," Pen said.

"You may be right," the lady responded wistfully. "But this storm troubles me more right now. Let's get to town if we can. In my bones I feel something coming: the reading of the stone is upon us, and it may bring an ending none of us could have predicted."

21
THE FURNACE

"One, two—you likes that, huh? Well, don' rush me, just chew on that awhile and I give you more."

Joey Jenkins, the school furnaceman, was talking to himself as he plied his shovel in long, broad swings. His arms and shoulders were rumpled with muscle. The furnace he fed was a massive hulk, like something stripped from a locomotive, or like Moloch, the insatiable demon of the time of Moses. It gobbled up heaps of coal, especially the soft, smoky grade the school board allotted. "That's right, eat it up," Joey encouraged, as if talking to a baby. If he was paying any attention to Edgerton, who watched glumly from a corner, he didn't let on.

"I have to stay here, just for a night," the boy said nervously. He was shivering all over, his wet hair dripping onto clothes soaked to the skin.

"Huh," Joey grunted noncommittally. He produced a grimy bandanna from his seat pocket and wiped the sweat and coal dust from his brow; then he sat down on an overturned apple crate. He seemed to be contemplating. "Why should Joey take you in? You never been nice to him."

Edgerton fumbled in his pockets. "I've got a little money, and I could get more, maybe." He held out the coins.

Joey started to laugh, showing his teeth. "How you get more—steal it? You stole what you got probably, yeah?"

The boy flushed with anger. "Look, I don't need your permission, you don't own this place. For all I know, you're not supposed to spend nights down here, either. Maybe I should tell somebody."

"Tell who?" Joey said, his eyes narrowing. "I bet you done run away, that's what Joey thinks. Maybe it's me could make trouble for you, eh?" Edgerton got to his feet, eyeing the door. "Sit down, sit down," Joey said calmly. "We both make no threats, okay?" The boy reluctantly complied. "Joey wants to be regular with you, see? He mean no harm, but he want the truth."

A cold rain was beating against the soot-smudged windows of the furnace room. Edgerton nodded. "Good," Joey said. He stood up to feed his baby again, thrusting in a double shovelful of fuel. The fire roared and spit yellow flame. Over the din the black man shouted, "You and me, we got us somethin' in common, d'you know that?" He didn't wait for the boy's reply. "Someone come in here and steal a thing from Joey. You know what I mean?"

"No."

"You sure? A few nights ago I was gone, just for a bit, but when I come back, this thing was stolen. It's best you tell me."

"I already told you, I don't know what you're talking about," Edgerton said irritably.

"Well, it's funny, you know? Joey never met a boy what talks to him or a master what can look him in the eye. Then you show up, sneakin' down here to cozy up. Why's that?"

"Because it's warm. It's my business if I want to get away from school."

"Maybe, maybe not. Joey's not interested in turnin' you in if you return what's his." With a clang, the furnaceman threw his shovel down, making Edgerton jump. "The thing you took is no good stolen; it'll only make trouble, for sure."

"If it's trouble, why do you want it back so bad?"

"Don' play round with Joey, all right? His eyes, they see guilt when they see it."

"Listen, I didn't know you were going to get this weird. I'm leaving." But before Edgerton could move, Joey reached a huge paw out, grabbing him by the arm. Edgerton yelled, "Hey, let go. What do you think you're—" Unheeding, Joey dragged him up the stairs, out into the storm. The darkening clouds were made deeper by the twilight that was fast falling. By the door stood a rain barrel under a gushing downspout.

"I'm not foolin'."

"I'm clean, man, why don't you believe me?"

Joey grabbed Edgerton by the neck and thrust his head into the barrel. The boy tried to scream underwater and inhaled half a lungful. Joey pulled him up gasping. "Water cold, yeah? You wanna tell me now?"

"Go to hell," Edgerton cursed, choking and spewing.

Joey shook his head. "That's a mistake. Maybe you like, I can try the furnace on you."

Edgerton's eyes widened in genuine fear. "No! You're crazy!"

What Joey might have done next remains moot, because out of nowhere a missile, a large chunk of old brick, flew through the air and hit him on the side of the head. He reeled, seeing stars. Reflexively his paw clamped tighter on Edgerton's arm to prevent him from squirming loose. Another chunk of brick sailed in, narrowly missing Joey's temple and grazing his hair. His sight cleared a little; sheets of rain made it impossible to see more than a few yards, but he dimly made out that his assailants were two boys, about twenty feet away.

"I sees you," Joey shouted, pointing at the taller one—Tommy, he thought he was called.

"I'll hit you again, I'm warning you," the taller boy called out, hefting a large cobblestone. The smaller boy was picking up his own rock, while Edgerton twisted and writhed like an eel.

"C'mon," Joey growled. He pulled the kicking boy back downstairs, slamming the door behind them. The two assailants were left alone in the rain.

"What do we do now?" Sis asked, dropping his rock. "I knew this was a bad idea."

Tommy was panting from anger and excitement. "Do you have

a better idea? The police picked up Derek; we were lucky to get away." He looked at the closed door. "We've got to go in there." Above the furnace room were two small windows. One was covered over with cardboard, the other was opaque with soot. He ran to the sooty window and started to rub it with his sleeve. "I can't see a thing." Using the edges of his hands like windshield wipers, he managed to clear a blurry view of the scene down below.

"Is he killing him?" Sis asked, peering over Tommy's shoulder.

"I can't tell, not for sure." The blazing furnace cast a patchy yellow glow into an otherwise black room; on the fringe of the light two figures embraced and swayed like demons dancing at the mouth of an inferno.

"We've got to go in there," Tommy said again. "Remember the morning we left school, and you didn't want to come back in here? Well, I wound up right at this spot, and I saw some kind of light. It was coming from down there, in the furnace room. Before I could investigate, Joey caught me. He thought I was Edgerton. For some reason he wanted to nab him."

"He's got him now," Sis said grimly.

"Yeah, but there was another thing: Joey started asking me if I knew where Arthur was. He sounded mental, but who else can we turn to?"

"We're mental if we try to take him on. I say we go back for help," Sis insisted, shaking his head.

"You can if you want to. We'll just get busted. I'm going in." Tommy backed off a few steps and ran at the door, shouldering it hard. It flew open with a bang, sending him stumbling downstairs into the room.

"Wait!" Sis cried anxiously. "Where are you?" When there was no reply, he had no other choice, either. "I'm coming in." He plunged into the dark stairwell, groped for a handrail that didn't exist, and nearly ran up Tommy's back.

"Hold on."

"What's happening?" Sis whispered. His eyes adjusted to the gloom, and he saw Joey standing over a dark heap—the fallen body of Edgerton, who lay on the floor limp and floppy.

"Is he dead?" Tommy exclaimed.

Joey glanced up; his face was crumpled with emotion. "No, he fell, that's all. He was fightin' against me, and when I let go, he lost his balance and slipped." Sis started to back up the stairs, prepared to scream or flee. "No, don't," Joey pleaded. "We can take care of this." After an uncertain moment, the two boys approached closer. "I seen you before. You come back," Joey said; he didn't sound dangerous. Tommy nodded grimly. "That's good. Joey be good to you if you trust him."

There was a faint groan, and they all saw Edgerton move, first a hand, then his whole upper body. He was trying to sit up. "C'mon," Joey coaxed, lifting the boy to his feet. "You be all right. Mostly knock the wind outta you."

"Get the hell away!" Edgerton cried, but he was so wobbly that he almost fell into the furnaceman's arms.

"Give us a hand, boys, over there." Joey pointed his chin at the far corner of the room. Tommy went over and found a box of rags; he pulled out a tattered blanket. Sis dragged the overturned apple crate closer as Joey eased Edgerton onto it.

Edgerton pushed away the blanket being held out by Tommy. "I don't want nursing," he protested angrily. He put his head in his hands while the three others waited for his next reaction. "You're not going to take me in, you know."

"No one's gonna bother you, if'n you give me back what's mine," Joey said.

"I had as much right to it as you. What'd you do—nick it from the trash?" Seeing the menace that came into the man's face, Edgerton added hastily, "Keep your cool, man. I don't have it anymore."

A stricken look came over Joey; he gave a deep sigh, almost a moan. "No, I was afraid of that. I was just hopin'," he said mournfully. He got up and idly began pitching scraps of coal into the furnace. "It's never comin' back to Joey," he murmured.

"What's he talking about?" Tommy asked.

Edgerton glared, pushing strands of wet hair from his face. "Shove off. No one asked you to muck into this."

"It's the sword, isn't it? We're after it, too," Sis put in. When

Edgerton's jaw fell, the little boy visibly swelled. "See? I was right. And we're gonna get it first."

"What do you know about it, anyway?" Edgerton said suspiciously.

Tommy put his hand on Sis's shoulder before he could answer. "We know enough. And if Joey's right about you stealing the sword, we probably know a lot more than you do."

Edgerton's hands were doubled into fists. "I didn't steal it," he said angrily. "I told you I found it." He stood up, staggering slightly, then righted himself. "You can't keep me here against my will."

Joey shrugged. "You're the one what wanted to stay," he observed calmly. He turned back to stare into the fire. Edgerton eased himself backward a few steps, still afraid that the man might jump him again. He was beyond the fringe of yellow light cast by the furnace when his steps could be heard hurriedly clumping upstairs and out the door.

"Are you sure we should have let him go?" Tommy asked.

"What good was he doin' here? Fightin' won't get it back." Joey sounded weary. "You can go, too. Joey don' imagine you're here for his company."

"We're not going to steal from you, if that's what you mean," Tommy replied. "We need your help."

The man leaned on his shovel, reflecting. "Very strange. Joey work here long time. No one come round. He be like invisible ghost. Now three boys wash in outta the rain, and we start talkin' about some kinda mystery, except who's gonna tell the truth? You?" Tommy's jaw tightened. "Well, we all here for a reason, that's what Joey think."

"If the truth will make a difference, why don't you start?" Tommy asked.

The man shrugged. "Fair enough. I got nothin' to lose. I been workin' here long time, like I say, and no boys talk to Joey. So I just work and pay no mind. One day I hear an awful ruckus. You remember when doggie got burned?"

"Chips," Tommy said. "Everybody knows Edgerton did it."

Joey shook his head. "Then everybody is wrong. It wasn't him, it was some man. He come around, sneakin' like. Poured kerosene on poor Chips and light him."

"How do you know?" Sis asked.

"I be right there, 'cause I was trackin' the man once I seen him. I ran up and grab him. 'Why you do such a thing?' I yelled. He just smiled and pulled me off. 'To catch your attention,' he say."

"You—why?" Tommy asked.

"Dunno. I goes to help doggie, but the man, he just stand around and watch, not tryin' to run or anything. 'Don't worry, there's enough racket to attract the others. You come with me,' he says, and starts to walk away. I don' know what to do. I very angry, but after a bit I follow. He was a strange man."

"What did he look like? Have you seen him in town?" Tommy asked.

"Maybe. Him tall, skinny, got black hair very slick. Joey keeps to himself, don' know many people in town. Anyway, the man knows his way round; he come straight down here. 'Now we can talk,' he says; he had a real dangerous feelin' to him. 'Did you see how easy it was for me to get to that dog?' he said. 'That's how easy I can get to you or any of the boys here.' When he say that, I become very, very mad. 'It do no good to threaten me,' I shout. 'Get out.'

"But he sat down, calm as anything, and considers me. 'Don't go off half-cocked,' he says. 'I'm not going to hurt you. In fact, I want you to work for me.' And what do you think? He holds out a fat roll of quid.

"I says, 'I don' like you. I don' need that money.' He just look at me. 'That's what I thought you might say. But perhaps my little demonstration has made you reconsider. St. Justin's has been here for such a long, long time.' "

Joey paused, lost in recollection. "The man, he have some kinda power in him, because when he say that, I can see, clear as a picture, everything goin' up in fire. I hear boys screamin' and walls crashin'. I wanted him outta here bad, so I says, 'What kinda work you want from me, anyway?'

"He likes that, very much. He pushes that fat roll at me and says, 'It's yours.'"

"Where is the money?" Tommy asked.

Joey pointed his thumb over his shoulder, gesturing toward the furnace. "You think I take money so's boys not burn alive? I just want him to go. But the man is in no hurry. He looks me over nice and slow, smilin'. I was doin' everything I could not to angry him. Then he says, 'I want you to find something for me.' I nod my head. 'Okay, what?' He says, 'A sword.' Well, I coulda bust out laughin'. 'You're surprised?' he says. 'O'course I am,' I say. 'I ain't got no sword.'"

Sis interrupted, "But you had the sword down here. Didn't Edgerton steal it?"

Joey shook his head. "No, I didn', not yet. I told him so, but the man gets up and says, 'You just look, and tell me what you find.' I ain't got no phone, I tells him, but he say, 'I'm around. I'll find out.' That make me shiver. I'm a brave man, but he had somethin' dangerous in him."

"And did you find the sword?" Sis asked.

Joey nodded gravely. "Oh, yeah, Joey found. And you know where? Out there." He pointed in the direction of the school's dump. The boys couldn't see it through the walls, but they knew it, a waste tract down the back of St. Justin's Hill. It was far older than the school itself, starting out as a marshy hollow where a prehistoric lake had retreated. Sometime in the Middle Ages, when the village was a mile away, cartloads of refuse were dumped in the hollow. As time passed and the village grew into a town, nobody ventured to guess how many layers deep the dump was—one history master at St. Justin's jocularly threatened to lead an archaeological dig on it, which someone might have done except for the smell.

"That's where Joey takes his ashes," the furnaceman went on. "They won' let me drive the truck, so I haul by hand, with a barrow." The wheelbarrow in question was propped up in a dim corner. "When it's wet, the ashes pack down, but if it's dry, I likes to dig 'em in a bit. One day I was workin' with my spade, plannin' on goin' down maybe six, seven inches, when I hits somethin'. That's pretty common on such kinda ground, old ground. And here's what I found." He got up and walked to a battered cardboard box near one wall. The boys couldn't see what he pulled out, but when he returned into the light, he was holding a broken arrow. "It was real shallow and buried on purpose like, one piece crossed over the other." Intent on his story, Joey didn't notice the agitation on their faces.

"Was the hole fresh?" Tommy managed to ask.

Joey shook his head. "Not so fresh, I think. See how wormy this here wood is." He held out the arrow for inspection; the shaft was decayed to the point of crumbling, but the feathers were intact and bore the stippled black-and-white markings of falcon plumage.

"Amazing," Tommy whispered.

"Things rot fast around here. Maybe magic stops the rot." Joey didn't pause to explain. "I pick up the arrow and turn it 'round, wonderin'. But it was startin' to rain heavy, like today, and I wants to get back inside. I dug my spade in one last time, and that's when I found it. The sword was just under, by a few inches."

"That's fantastic!" Sis suddenly exclaimed, unable to contain himself. "That arrow means us. We buried it—I mean, Tommy did. If the sword was underneath, then we're the ones who were meant to find it. We must've just shown up here late, but now you can help us get it back. I mean, will you help us?"

"How could you bury that arrow? Look at it. No one have any arrow like that now."

Tommy heaved a reluctant sigh. "You said you wanted the truth. Well, we were there when King Arthur lost the sword. Actually, Merlin made it disappear. I think Sis is right—Merlin must have put it under the arrow, knowing we'd recognize it. And we're not crazy."

Joey's expression wasn't one of disbelief but of a deeper disturbance. "Do you know what you're askin'? . . . No, you don't." Slowly he stood up and pulled off his dirty gray jersey; underneath he wore a white T-shirt. He pulled the neck to one side, exposing his shoulder. The boys flinched. Even in the dim light of the furnace room they made out the shape of a handprint burned into the man's flesh. It was dark against dark, like a black stain, and it looked new.

"How did that happen?" Tommy asked, his throat tightening.

"The man. He came back. It was nighttime, and I was frantic, lookin' everywhere. The sword was gone; Joey couldn't believe it. I was knockin' lumber every which way. I never heard him comin' in, but there he was. 'You found it,' he says. 'No, I didn't. Get outta here,' I yelled. 'Oh, yes, it's here,' he declare.

"Then I laugh in his face, loud and harsh like. 'What makes you think I give it to you, anyway, mister?' I was just crazy over losin' the thing, only I can't tell you why. There was somethin' about it. Then I says, 'Besides, it's gone. See for yourself.' If you think Joey was goin' crazy, the man starts tearin' the place apart. He push lumber and boxes until his hands are bleedin'. And then all at once he stop and look at me, a cold and dangerous look. 'I want it back now,' he warns.

" 'What you gonna do, give me some more money?' I says, and I laugh again. He shakes his head, and before I know, my hair is standin' up like a porcupine. What does he go an' do but walk to that furnace and stick his hand in. His hand! I musta start screamin', but he pulls it out, glowin' red, not burnt, and before Joey can move, he puts that hand on me. I passed out, 'cause the next thing I see is the ceilin', with me lyin' in all that tore-up lumber, and he was gone." Joey let the neck of his shirt fall back into place.

"So you're afraid to help us?" Tommy asked.

Joey glared. "Don' talk what you don' know nothin' about." Tommy could read the man's face now, and what he read was anguish.

"We're not frightened," Tommy said. "Merlin told us that Mordred can lose. Do you know who Mordred is? He's the man who did this to you."

"Then it's my business whether I kill him or be afraid of him."

"You can't kill him. You're in this with us. Remember? You were the one who told me to come back if I needed to find Arthur. Why did you say that?"

"Arthur? That's the name on the sword. I find it one day when I sat polishin' it. My fingertip run across some letters, and lookin' real close, I see *Arthur.* It was only there a moment, you know. The next time I looked it was gone. That's all I know, excep' for some reason it fascinate Joey to have that thing. It make him hopeful. Can you tell me why?" An unexpected look came into his weathered face, both inward and innocent, like someone remembering in a flash some sweet dream of childhood.

"I can't tell you, but there's a man who can. Do you want to meet him?" Tommy asked.

"What man?"

"His name's Derek."

Joey seemed to reflect, then shook his head. "No, it won't do no good. I lost it; I had my chance." Whether a long-buried memory surfaced or a last disguise fell away, Joey suddenly cried out, "Hah!" He threw his shovel down and began pacing the room. "Why you come back? So Joey can be tortured more? Let me be."

"We're not torturing you," Sis exclaimed. "We're your friends."

"Hah!" This time the cry merged into a wail. "You my friend, you say? Then what you gonna do if Joey help you? You gonna give him the sword back?" Sis shrank and bit his lip. "I thought so," Joey said bitterly.

"We can't give it to you," Tommy protested. "It's not because we don't want to. There's a lot else at stake." But Joey had already picked up his shovel again and was throwing coal into the furnace with renewed ferocity; his refusal to discuss things any further was plain enough.

"We wouldn't ask if we had anyone else to turn to," Sis said pleadingly. Somehow the words sounded wrong, although he didn't mean them wrong. The muscles at the base of Joey's neck bunched up.

"C'mon, let's go," Tommy said. "This wasn't a good idea, and we've still got to find Derek." The two boys went upstairs into the rain, closing the door behind them.

Covered by the roar of the fire, Joey muttered, "Don' talk what you don' know nothin' about." He was hurling the coal now like a demented slave or a soul despairing of ever being unchained from hell's furnace. "I guess Joey not gonna be popular no more."

22
GYPSY CAMP

"SIR, WON'T YOU HELP A POOR MAN OUT?" THE VOICE FROM THE shadows implored. "Just a bite of food and a pint."

"Wha—what did you say?"

"I'm in need, sir. Please. I can show you something."

It was dark and rainy outside the pub, and Arthur was drunk. "Show me something? Why should I care?" he said sourly.

"You would if you knew me, sir," the man coaxed, coming closer. "I'm a good'un through and through." He leaned over confidentially to impart this information, and Arthur drew back. The man gave off none too sweet a perfume. Wiry black stubble covered his jowls, and he shifted nervously, staring down at his shoes as if self-respect were a long-lost illusion. Unmistakably he was a tramp.

Arthur tilted his head back, blearily taking in the swinging wooden sign on its creaky chains. "What is this place anyway?"

"This here? The Orb, sir. Everyone from around these parts knows the Orb."

The lettering came into focus and slipped out again. "The Orb and Merlin. I've been here, haven't I? Forgot." Arthur felt in his pockets, fingering the last two pounds he had to his name. "I'm feeling flush tonight. Why don't we go inside and top it off?"

To his surprise, the tramp held back. "You're the soul of kindness, sir, but if you don't mind, I'll ask you to bring me pint to the door."

"Bring it out? Ridiculous."

"You don't have to give me the evil eye like that. I remember when you was kinder."

"Remember me?" Tight as he was, the reproach stirred a ripple inside Arthur, too deep to acknowledge. The tramp eyed him peculiarly. *This one's a few sandwiches shy of a picnic,* Arthur thought. Suddenly he felt thirsty and had a strong desire to brush the tramp off. "I'm going in," he announced a shade too loudly. "You can follow if you like, but it's on your own tick." He pushed open the thick oaken door, its glass panes fogged by the smoke and warmth inside. The Orb and Merlin was packed. The early crowd, the late crowd, and the occasionals had all decided that it was too dismal a night to stay home.

He started pushing his way to the bar. "Ow!" He'd barked his shin against a table with four men around it. One of them sprang up, his shirt soaked with beer. "Hey, watch it," the man warned. "Easy there, mate," another said.

Arthur gave a civil nod, wanting to avoid a fight, and kept going. "Old Peculier," he said to the barman. "A half." It wasn't the commonest drink, but since tourists favored the Orb and Merlin, it stocked a variety, and a glass was soon put in front of him.

Before draining it, Arthur surveyed the room. *Funny, everyone must think I'm like them.* Bored, unhappy at work, unhappy in bed, mismatched with a shrew, worn-out—there were a dozen common or garden reasons why the others were getting drunk. They had no idea how special he was. He put his fingertips gently to his chest. *Still there.* He tilted the glass and let the beer slide down his throat in one cold draw. The thing in the middle of his chest didn't even notice. Heavy, burning, tight, it ignored this latest infusion of anesthesia as it had ignored all the rest.

"Another?" the barman inquired as he set Arthur's change down.

Arthur considered the offer. He could try to black out. That might be effective. "No, I'll wait a bit."

The barman nodded tolerantly. He recognized Arthur from the night before and the night before that, as did the barmen at the Mortal Man, the Known World, and the Pestle. But Arthur didn't tell them his name or anything about himself. If somebody chanced to recognize him from his days on the force, he turned away.

Only two things made tonight's visit any different, the tramp being the first. The second was that Arthur bothered to look up over the bar where a picture hung. It depicted a wizard with a pointed hat, a long flowing white beard, and an orbed scepter. The expression on the wizard's face was indescribable. Whoever painted it must have been trying for a mystical effect, but what he achieved was a cross between peevishness and heartburn. Merlin cast a dyspeptic eye on the crowd below, who in turn ignored him completely. All but one.

Arthur smirked. "You forgot the witch."

"What's that, sir?" the barman asked.

"He needs a witch." Arthur pointed to the picture. "Or maybe he's bonked her with that stick. Maybe she's still around but he's out of commission."

"Have it any way you like." The barman shrugged. He had long ago ceased even seeing the painting. Arthur lost interest and turned to look over the room.

She was there. He blinked owlishly, not quite sure. But it was her all right. The thing in his chest noticed, too, making him wince with pain. She was sitting alone at a table for two, as though waiting for him. Her face was half-turned away, but even without looking into her eyes, Arthur felt sick with desire.

God, how can they just stand there? Her beauty was like a miracle, and yet the other men in the room were chatting as if there was nothing unusual. Her blond hair cascaded over one shoulder like a carelessly tossed cloth of gold, and her breasts looked bare beneath a cream-colored jumper. Her skin was glowing, as if lighted from within. If he didn't know what he knew—that she was the most dangerous thing alive—Arthur would never have been able to control his desire.

His hands were sweating as he realized that he had started to cross the room. So he wasn't going to control himself after all.

She looked up as he came near. "Sit down?" she said politely.

He stopped, the thing in his chest tearing like an iron claw. "You came here. What do you want?"

She didn't reply, and he could tell that she didn't quite know how to handle him.

"Excuse me," he blurted. "I'm going now."

"Don't. You frighten me, the way you're taking all this." Katy's face suddenly brightened, and a smile came out like the sun, almost staggering him with hope. Then Arthur saw it wasn't him she was smiling at. She waved to a man who had just come in the door, but he didn't see her yet.

"Over here," she cried, waving a bit more frantically. It was Amberside, who spotted her and waved back. "Could you possibly sit down, at least? Before there's a scene."

A scene? Arthur felt the urge to laugh; if he had, it would have emerged as hysteria.

But Amberside was there quickly, standing between him and her. "Sorry, Katy darling, I was trying to get another appointment with Westlake. It looks very good for reinstating you." Amberside kissed her and began to sit down.

"What's happened to Katy?"

Amberside must not have heard Arthur, but the look in Katy's eyes made him glance over his shoulder. "Sorry, I didn't see you standing there. Won't you join us?"

Arthur shook his head slowly. "What's happened to Katy?" he repeated drunkenly. He felt as if he were going to be sick.

Katy looked anxious. "This is embarrassing," she said in a small voice. "I don't want a row. Not here."

"Oh, there's not going to be any row," replied Amberside. "I say, Callum, whatever happened to all's fair in love and war?"

"You don't love her, and there's nothing fair about your kind of war."

Arthur saw Katy reach her hand across the table, clutching at

Amberside's. He smiled and patted her. "I'm a very lucky man. In a way, this show of jealousy is flattering. I know I'm not as young and not as good-looking as—"

Arthur felt like screaming. Making a supreme effort, he said, "You two did this to me, didn't you? I was the dupe, and now the trap's shut. Just tell me who you are. You owe me that much."

Amberside regarded him with utter blandness. "It's remarkable when real people talk like the soaps, isn't it, darling?" Katy nodded weakly, looking more nervous.

She can't quite carry it off, Arthur thought. *He's got the real steel.*

Amberside squeezed her hand harder. "Steady on, I'll get rid of him," he whispered. He stood up and took a step toward Arthur. Now his bearing conveyed a hint of menace. "This is really quite a bad show, my friend. We're getting married in a couple of days, and if you were any kind of gentleman—"

"He ain't no gentleman. D'you need any help?" It was one of the same men whose table Arthur had bumped into earlier.

"Quite all right, thanks. I can handle it." Disappointed, the man backed off, muttering. "You see?" Amberside said, smiling confidently.

Arthur knew that if he stayed, he would scream. The evil behind the bland façade was unbearable. Arthur turned to see the picture of Merlin over the bar; it stared at him, offering no comfort.

A week earlier, Arthur had become jealous after noticing that Katy and Amberside took opportunities to be alone together. He heard whispered conversations that died as soon as he entered the room. "Don't confront me like this," Katy had flared when he mentioned it to her. "Either you trust me or—" She didn't finish the sentence. But his jealousy stung like a venomous snake, and one day, when he thought he heard the two of them behind the bedroom door, he began pounding, all control lost. "I'll knock it down, I swear, if you don't open it." And Amberside had opened it to reveal the horrid image seared into Arthur's brain. He had seen what he had seen, but it was impossible to accept.

Remembered images of horror swam up through the drunken haze in his brain like sea monsters: a shattered mirror, Katy crouching on the floor growling like a beast, Amberside holding the door ajar for Arthur to see. In pain and panic he saw himself reaching, pleading, "I love you, I love you so much." Her growling became guttural speech like that of a human dog—"Get out!"

He couldn't recover from that, and for days his brain reeled. What was the real her? How did she make herself beautiful to him when other men saw the same dull girl he'd known before? Nauseated by the memory, Arthur turned on his heels, moving the dead weight of his body across the floor.

One, two, one, two—he found himself counting his steps to make sure that he kept going. Once he made it outside, he felt better, the nausea receding in the cold, dark rain. It didn't seem possible to ever get her back. He realized that he had been enchanted and despaired.

"You look terrible, mate. Tossed out by the missus?" It was the tramp again. He must have been waiting in the shadows by the door. "I think I'd better show you that something I promised."

Arthur felt like smashing his face in. He doubled his fist and took a wild swing, but somehow the man's face wasn't where it was supposed to be. The swing threw Arthur off-balance, sending him facedown into the mud.

"Give you a hand, governor?"

"Bastard. Don't you mock me." Arthur staggered to his feet and instantly slipped again. The tramp was softly laughing. "Christ," Arthur muttered. He spat mud, unable to rid himself of the grit between his teeth.

"C'mon, let's go. They're waitin' for you."

What kind of nonsense was this? "Lemme go," Arthur protested, too drained to try violence again. Beyond caring, he let his face settle softly into the mud. He felt a strong hand lift him, and in a moment he was leaning over the hood of a car.

"He looks bloody awful," a strange voice remarked.

"He's not himself," the tramp said. The back door opened and Arthur felt himself being heaved into the car like a sack of potatoes. He slumped to one side. The upholstery against his cheek was slick, cold plastic.

Cheap car, he registered, then saw streetlights passing overhead before things blurred into a grateful nothingness.

He woke up with the sword cradled in his arms.

"Where am I?" he mumbled.

"Here."

"Where's that?"

"Just lie still and try to hold on. It's sharp, and a bit cold, sorry to say." It was the tramp, but Arthur barely noticed that. The sword was inescapable, pressing down on his chest with incredible weight. He had no idea it was so heavy. He tried moving his right hand, but somebody seized it. "No," the tramp said. "I told you to lie still, remember?" Yes, of course he remembered. Arthur felt his chest heaving the blade up and down. It was balanced perfectly the entire length of his body, extending from feet to throat.

"Do you think you can sit up now?" the tramp asked after a moment.

"I don't want to," Arthur protested, his voice distant and feeble.

"No, you must." The tramp's strong hands were lifting him. It was agony to sit up, and as the sword was removed, he felt like a child losing the most precious thing in the world. "Cry if you like." Arthur shook his head, but hot tears were streaming down his cheeks. A mug was put into his hands. "Go ahead, drink it." The tea was so bitter he almost choked. "Just sip." The kindness in the tramp's voice penetrated another veil of grief, and Arthur heard himself sobbing.

"You found me, didn't you?" Arthur's voice was weak, but it was beginning to sound as if he belonged to it. His eyes were open now. He could see two men, the tramp and the one who must have driven the car. They were sitting by his bed inside some kind of small room cramped like a ship's cabin, lit by an overhead kerosene lamp. "I might be sick," Arthur announced, nauseated by the smell of kerosene.

"Right, we'll just step out. The rain's over," the tramp said. When they helped him to his feet and out the door, he saw that it wasn't a cabin they were in but some kind of wooden caravan or wagon. "Mind the steps," the other man said. A blast of cool night air hit him in the face, and then he was out under the stars, which were bright and silvery, as if washed by the rain.

"Amazing," he murmured, looking around. They had emerged into a circle of six wagons painted bright red and green, all illuminated by a huge bonfire in the center. Gypsy wagons—he remembered his mother talking about them. "I thought you people were all gone."

"So they say," the stranger responded. The two men were walking him in a slow circle, as if cooling off a racehorse, helping him get his legs back.

Arthur's head felt fuzzy, but a storybook name came to mind. *Lancelot.* He looked at the tramp quizzically. "Lancelot?"

"Don't speak too much, my lord," the tramp whispered. Arthur could hear tears in the man's voice—no, an emotion too profound for tears. Silently they circled a little more. "Can we go back inside?" the tramp suggested. "I don't wish the others to see you until everything has been made clear." Arthur nodded, and they went back up the wooden steps. His stomach had settled, and the kerosene fumes no longer made him queasy. He noticed that the two men didn't sit down until after he did. That was how it used to be, he thought to himself.

"I want you to meet a friend," the tramp began.

"Paddy Edgerton," the other man introduced himself, holding out his hand. Arthur shook it and got the distinct feeling that this friend was uneasy, unsure of himself. "I'm new here, too. So bear with me."

"Where's here? I don't recognize it."

"We move around, but this is the court of miracles," the tramp said.

The words jolted Arthur's mind. All at once he was a boy in the crystal cave, and Merlin was teaching him—what? The image faded. "Court of miracles," he repeated tonelessly.

"Yes, my lord. We've been waiting for you, but don't expect to remember us," the tramp said. "Not a one of us." A mournful note was in his voice.

Arthur was puzzled. "I do remember you, though, don't I?"

A wave of emotion crossed the tramp's face as he struggled to reply. "We're all changed," he finally said.

"You must be." The words sounded so inane that Arthur wanted to laugh.

"This is the only court remaining from the old time." The tramp's voice was as quiet as the night. "You know that, don't you? Merlin has vanished, ages have passed. We are, I'm afraid, clinging by a thread." Arthur stared at him, confused, then a surge of grief hit him again.

The stranger, Paddy Edgerton, stood up, looking more nervous. "Some of this talk is hard for me to handle. Maybe I should leave."

The tramp shook his head. "It would be helpful if you'd stay. Just to tell the story." Arthur wasn't listening, and this exchange came to him as if from far away. Paddy Edgerton sat back down, and the tramp leaned closer. "Put your hand on the sword. Hold it there."

When his fingers rested on the cold steel, Arthur drifted back from far away. "A story?"

"Yes. We've accomplished something incredibly important by getting the sword back, and this man, our friend, is the one we have to thank for it." Arthur must have looked blank, because the tramp added, "You know this is Excalibur, don't you?"

This time, the jolt that the name sent through him was too strong. Arthur groaned and doubled over as pain seared his throat, the cruel steel of the enemy slashing the soft tissue. The choking thickness of blood filled his mouth. "Let me die," he tried to say, but the mercy of dying wouldn't come. The pain ebbed, slowly, until he found himself in the cabin again.

The tramp was on his knees, holding Arthur in a strong embrace. "No, no, stay here," he was begging, his voice desperate. Arthur moaned, weakly pushed the tramp's arms away, and sat up.

Visibly upset, Paddy Edgerton was wrestling with himself. "This could just be madness. The whole thing could be."

"No," Arthur said. "The madness would be to leave again. None of us are getting out unless we can get through together."

The clarity in his speech caught Paddy and the tramp off guard. "I suppose you're right," Paddy admitted reluctantly. "Well, if it's my story you want to hear, I don't mind. Where do you want me to begin?"

"Begin where you first found out about the sword," the tramp suggested.

"All right, then, that's as good a place as any. My boy, Jerry, found it first, I don't exactly know how or whereabouts—we're not speaking much, him and me, these days. Must have been last week. He was hiding and skulking about a bit more than usual." Paddy stopped, unhappy. "Beg pardon, I'm bein' mean to him." He wiped his face and looked away. "You see, you're not the only one what has run into some strange things. But I'll get to that.

"My boy must of found the sword without telling anyone. The first thing I really knowed was when a gentleman came by to the house one day. I was crippled then, confined to my chair. Permanent, they said." These words made him halt again, trying to hold back tears. "Jesus and Mary," he muttered, wiping his eyes roughly. "I'm sorry. This is turning into a regular crying match."

"We're not in a hurry," the tramp said.

Paddy nodded and went on. "This gentleman called himself Amberside and said he lived in the neighborhood. Big house at the bottom of our street, mansion really. I was reluctant to let him in, but I needed a spot of company. You don't know what it's like being cooped up for a man like me, active all my life. This bloke informs me that he goes by the professional name of Ambrosius. 'What kind of a name is that?' I ask him. 'And what kind of profession are you in?' Sounded like some kind of stage act to me.

"He says, 'Where I got the name doesn't matter. I'm here to offer you my help.' Of course I imagine he's gonna put the twist on me some way, but before I can open my mouth, he stretches his hand over my bad leg. Not touching it but just waving his hand in circles, very slow. It made me nervous, but in a second I could feel my leg getting warm, and then it twitched. You see, it hadn't budged for over a year, not a hair. 'You can move it now, can't you?' he asked me. I nodded, too scared to speak. 'Try getting up,' he says.

"I can tell you, my heart was jumping. I held back and suddenly he barks, 'Now!'

"I almost shot out of that chair; before I knows where I am, he's holding me up from one side. 'That's right, come on,' he says. I took a step or two, and then it all gave out. I toppled, and he barely got me back into my chair or I would've flopped in a heap on the floor. 'What are you doing to me?' I said, shaking with rage. 'You can't just come in and mess with me.' I felt cheated, the way he lifted me up and then took it all away.

"He sat there looking at me for the longest time, then he says, 'My powers are limited.' Now what the hell does that mean? 'I can heal you, but not by myself alone. It takes more, you can see that, can't you?' I just let him talk. 'You have a boy, I believe?' he asks. I tell him I do. 'He has stolen something from me, and I need it to heal you,' he says. Of course it was the damnedest thing, don't you know? I've no doubt my Jerry might've nicked a thing or two—I'm not simple—but I couldn't grasp the other. 'My boy can heal me?' I asks. 'No, no,' he says, getting irritated. 'He's a thief.'

"It's one thing for me to bad-mouth my own boy, but this rankled me. 'Don't call him out a thief unless you can prove it,' I says. 'I'll just go and call him.' Ambrosius got upset then. 'You're a fool,' he says. Then he stood up and started out of the room.

"'Wait,' I called when he was almost to the door. 'I'll try and get it back.' He looks at me. 'You won't get it just by asking, you know.' I says, 'Okay, I'll do what it takes.' The last thing he told me was, 'See that you do,' and then he slammed the door. I was stunned. I can tell you, I drank so much that night, the missus wouldn't talk to me. But I had my mind made up."

"And how did you get the sword back?" Arthur asked.

"I'm not proud of what I did. I grabbed it from under my boy's mattress, him screaming and yelling. It was a scene. I got out of his room, holding the sword in my lap, and when I rolled to the landing at the top of the stairs, there's Ambrosius at the bottom. 'How'd you get in?' I asked. 'Never mind. Give it to me,' he says. I backed away. 'Give it to you? Not till you do what you promised,' I told him. His eyes were all dark and excited, you'd think we were arguing over a woman.

"But before he could say anything else, it hit me. *I don't need him.* I'll never know how I knew that, but I took a deep breath and stood up, right out of the chair. 'Give it to me!' he cried, only he was hissing more like a snake.

"Suddenly I knew that if he got his hands on that thing, I wouldn't live to tell the tale. 'Get out of my house. I'm calling the police,' I warned him. I started walking toward the phone in the hall by my bedroom, and this time I'm not unsteady like when he conjured me; I'm really healed. When I picked up the phone, the line was dead, and a few seconds later there's the smell of smoke. Maybe I should have waked everybody up, but my first instinct was to run downstairs, to get him."

"And you were able to run?" the tramp asked.

Paddy sighed deeply, trying to handle his feelings. "I didn't have time to think about miracles, you see. In five bounds I was downstairs, running for the cellar door. Billows of smoke were coming up now. Then I realized something. This was a trick. In my excitement I'd forgotten the sword. I could hear him clumping about upstairs. What could I do? I had to risk hiding down there, hoping that he wouldn't kill Edie or the boy. I knew he'd kill me if he had half a chance.

"It couldn't have been two minutes, but in that two minutes I died for Edie and Jerry, I can tell you, praying to keep them out of harm's way. I was right, though—that demon Ambrosius came racing down the stairs. I could hear Jerry banging on our bedroom door, trying to raise his mum. But I didn't have no time to think of them anymore. When Ambrosius came running toward the front door, I tackled him. He fell, and my luck held. The sword slashed him across the face. He screamed, and I made a grab for it."

"I didn't see any scar on his face tonight," Arthur said.

"You wouldn't. I'm sure he can do things we'd call, like, unnatural. I'm a strong man, even after a year in a chair, but his arms could've crushed me like a soft apple. That's what I mean by bein' lucky—I could never have bested him in a fair fight. In two shakes

I had the sword and was on my feet. I dashed into the street, hearing a wail—the sirens was coming. Then the house went up like matches. I caught one last glimpse of it over my shoulder and said a prayer for Edie and the boy. After that, God help me, the only thing on my mind was getting away."

As it trailed off, Edgerton's tale left behind a wake of silence. The wind had come up, and the swinging kerosene lamp made the room seem to sway. "We were lucky to find you," the tramp said. "One of us saw you run away that night, and we tracked you through the back streets to the fields. It wasn't so hard after that."

Edgerton nodded. "I wound up in a farmer's toolshed that night and would've stayed there, except I was afeared of being found out. But I wasn't far from here, right?"

"Not far," the tramp agreed. The two men left off speaking.

Gravely Arthur said, "I am troubled by this story. How much can we believe?"

"I swear it's true. How else would I be able to walk?" Paddy asked, his tone truculent.

"No one witnessed that," the tramp reminded him. "We watched you on the road for several hours, wondering what to do. Amberside is a hunter, and he knows that the bigger the game, the bigger the bait to catch it."

Paddy considered this. "I kept running and dodging the best I could."

"He could have used you unwittingly. You left a trail he may be able to follow, if he didn't deliberately set you on the trail." All at once a note of authority had entered Arthur's voice, causing the other two to turn to him. "I can't help thinking to myself—he already had gotten to you twice, then suddenly you are conveniently lost." The words were almost an accusation, and Paddy Edgerton gave Arthur a sullen glare in return.

"It's not for me to suspect you," Arthur said softly. "Here." He held the blade out with steady hands, as if it weighed next to nothing. Paddy Edgerton took it without joy, then sat in pensive silence. The tramp wanted to protest, but a look from Arthur stopped him.

"We can't fool ourselves into assuming we've taken Amberside's measure," Arthur said. "It's not in my power yet to protect you; I can barely protect myself."

Paddy spoke without looking up. "Do you think I don't belong here?"

The tramp answered, "That's for you to decide. Belonging here is a choice."

"What I mean is, if I take the sword, it will protect me, but what about the rest of you? I've had time to think. When Ambrosius, or Amberside as you call him, made a show of healing me, I fell for his game. When he asked for the sword, I almost gave it to him. That frightens me."

"So it should," said the tramp. "The face of evil can wear a mask of kindness or mercy or even love when need be. We have been at the game a long time, but its deceptions are more twisted than even we can imagine."

"How would you protect yourselves if I went away, then?"

"As we did before. The court has survived like a leaf, letting the wind blow us where it will. We are masters of evasion."

"And is that any kind of life?"

"It's the one we know," the tramp said simply.

After a pause, Paddy said, "Then, if you'll let me, I want to stay." The tramp smiled with gratitude, but Paddy shook his head and turned to Arthur. "I'm not holding the sword, though. I've had its benefit, if you can call it that. You want me to be safe? I don't see how I can be now. He'll be after me again."

"Yes," Arthur agreed quietly.

With the slow solemnity of ritual, Paddy held up the sword. "I'll do my best to be faithful to you. No promises, and I may tell you eventually that I can't stand it, that I have to go back. Any sensible man might."

Arthur nodded as exhaustion overcame him. The tramp drew a blanket around Arthur's shoulders and laid him gently back onto the bed.

"I'm going to go now, just for a while," Paddy said quietly, standing up. "If I left a trail for Amberside to follow, it's better that

I lead him away from you. I hope to be back soon." He turned to go, but he felt his hand being taken by Arthur, who bowed his head and kissed it, as a vassal would to a king.

Uncontrollably, Paddy started laughing and crying at the same time. "It's really funny. I was a pretty worthless character, you know? Always have been, only I couldn't face it. I never told anyone, but I fixed that accident at the shop what laid me off, and you know why? So I could fail on my own terms. That's a sick kind of dignity, ain't it? The sword put me back on my feet, and my secret is that I never wanted that. Maybe you've made a mistake."

Arthur shook his head, his eyes closing into a dreaming, fathomless half-sleep.

Paddy departed abruptly, leaving the door open for a moment before the wind slammed it shut. It was impossible to see him fleeing in the dark or to hear his footsteps, wherever they led. The silence was broken only once, when Arthur thought he heard a scream. It was probably an owl hunting small night creatures, or perhaps its prey. The kerosene lamp swung crazily, and the swaying room seemed to be lost at sea. Then the wind blew out the lamp. If there was still a world outside, it couldn't be seen anymore. The two men left in the wagon had no choice but sleep, letting the night flow faster and faster from one unknown to the next.

23

THE DARK EARTH

MELCHIOR PREFERRED TO SLEEP ALONE BENEATH A WAGON RATHER than inside the stuffy cabins. Peering through the green-and-red-painted spokes, he saw Arthur arrive after midnight. The return of the king deeply excited him, but the tramp and the lady in the felt hat had agreed that Arthur needed a period of adjustment, until morning at least.

Sleeping under the wagon afforded little protection from the elements. The ground chill seeped into Melchior's bedclothes, which were swaddled tightly around him. Only a slit was left for his dark, exotic eyes. He had slept this way countless times across the foot of Merlin's cot, like a palace guard from the *Arabian Nights.*

When the apprentice awoke in the cold of dawn, the Gypsy camp was still. No birds sang. The surrounding woods dared to breathe only in light rustlings, as though something important was expected.

"You're up."

He turned to see Pen standing above him on the steps, clutching herself in the door of the wagon.

"Yes. I'm waiting."

"Me, too," she said. "I thought I might as well get dressed." Melchior got up, unfurled his bedding, and stretched like a cat. Arthur's wagon stood directly opposite them, across the small clearing. The bonfire in its center had subsided to a gray hummock of ashes and lumps. "Is this a real Gypsy camp?" Pen suddenly asked. "I don't see how the townspeople could miss us."

"But they do. This place is like the crystal cave. Merlin left it to be found by those who know how to find it, and nobody else. Someone walking down that road"—he pointed to the dusty lane lined with wagon tracks that curved into the camp—"could pass us by and see only an empty field."

"Is this a place Merlin might come to, then?"

A surprised but pleased look came into Melchior's eyes. "I hope so. He is dreaming this place, and we are sheltering in his dream. But the existence of the camp is fragile. It will dissolve or be smashed—one or the other."

"Mordred has destroyed every place like this, once he has found it, hasn't he? But it's lovely for now, safe and lovely." Pen was holding her arms up toward the sun, which had just broken over the circle of green-black firs on the edge of the camp. A first feeble warmth of sunlight promised a fair day.

"I wasn't going to tell anyone, but I have to leave soon."

Pen's face clouded. "Why?"

"Because my master bids me. One thing I can do is step in and out of his dreams, which is how I'm able to protect you. If there is to be a reading of the stone, Mordred's attention will be aroused. That will be the most precarious moment of all. If we succeed in reading it, he will be brought to the edge of defeat, and his reaction will be wrathful fury against all of us. And if we fail—no good can come of saying what he will do then."

"Does Merlin want you to lead him away?"

"Possibly. I only sense that I must go."

Under other circumstances, Pen might have felt afraid, but losing Melchior brought only sadness. "Then I'm on my own, alone?"

Without answering, Melchior mounted the steps and stood next to her. He took a ladle hanging on a nail by the side of the wagon and dipped it in the rain barrel nearby. The fresh water that had gathered overnight tasted dusty and sharp, as if it carried the scent of the storm.

"No," he said, his voice soft but firm in its assurance. "The camp may vanish, but you won't be alone. You've started out; you're walking on the road. The people who haven't started out yet are the ones who are alone."

"Is that really true? I never used to feel lonely, but over the past few days there have been moments when it's been like—"

"Like dying," he finished for her. "Dying to your old self. That's different. What was your life before? Every moment you lived brought something to see or feel or think about, but every moment brought death in it, because experience fades, turns from a living spark to a dead memory. Bit by bit this load of memories has built up into a huge coral reef that you must shoulder. No one can take the burden away or carry it for you, and to carry that mass of death is the loneliest task in the world."

"You make it sound horrible, but if life is so unbearable, why don't we change?"

"Habit. Mordred counts upon the numbing effect of habit."

She remembered, with a pang, that Derek had once spoken to her in exactly the same way. "My husband thought that wizards existed to give people hope that they weren't powerless."

"Yes. To renounce power is to let *him* have it. Mordred is like a dark cloud over the earth. He feeds off fear. War and crime, famine and poverty, all make him grow. But there's a secret he doesn't know. The earth is more than the sum of its suffering. Despite habit and numbness, a person can find the beginning of the road, and if one has courage, the whole enormous load of fear—the dead weight of the past—can be shed."

Melchior regarded her with his deep, liquid eyes. "That's what you did. You abandoned the known world, all at once, and struck out for the one territory Mordred has no power over: the unknown."

"Isn't that the loneliest way of all, though? To walk and walk, facing the unknown with nothing to show for it? Derek used to say that waking up to a new morning was the most terrifying prospect each person must face."

Melchior nodded. "The terror is there, certainly—Mordred has made sure of that—and even after you break free, fear casts shadows for a long time. Mordred counts on that, too. He's put grinning demons at the gate of freedom so that no one—or very few—will see what lies beyond."

"And what does?"

"Just what you described—a road where every step brings the unknown. Have you found out what that road is called?"

She shook her head.

"Love. The free road, the dust on it, the steps that leave no footprints, they are the way of love." Melchior's voice rose again. "Love can't be captured. Everything you mortals call love turns poisonous as soon as it is snared. But my master taught me that behind the door to freedom, past the demons of fear, there is nothing but love."

"I was wrong, then. I'm not to be lonely ever again, am I?"

"No. In the name of love loneliness is impossible." Melchior put an arm around Pen. The sun had risen higher behind them, warming their shoulders. The wagon door opened across the clearing; Arthur stepped out, bearing a sword in his hands that gleamed like liquid sunlight. The tramp emerged with him, but when Arthur started toward them, the tramp let him go by himself.

"I'm extremely glad to see you, Pen. It seems like ages." Arthur's voice was neither shy nor uncertain but newly strong.

"Yes, ages. I'm sorry I left without telling you, but things happened." She stopped, hardly knowing what to say. Melchior took her hand and had her sit down on the steps.

"The web of time is almost closed," he said, addressing Arthur. "You have found the sword, or more accurately the sword has found you." He looked toward Pen. "And the same has happened with the stone. This is remarkable and probably unique. In Arthur's time these two things could be summoned only at Merlin's behest. I want to tell you what Master told me about them.

"Excalibur has had many lives, and only Merlin knows them

all. When the sword first appeared, the ancient Welsh called it Caledfwlch, which signified 'hard lightning.' For them its power was violent but righteous. Whoever wielded it had justice on his side. When he regained his throne, Arthur needed it for the same reason, to prove that he was the rightful king.

"Merlin searched the depths of the earth and sea to fetch the sword back from oblivion. When the wizards grew disgusted with mortals, they refused to leave Excalibur in their hands, where it had always been wielded for blood. Merlin had other designs for it, a mystical plan that mortals were hardly aware of. He contrived that the sword of violence should become the means to end violence. I believe that Mordred has no suspicion of this and only wants the weapon for the sake of power and fear."

"Will the sword end violence by killing Mordred?" Arthur asked.

"That has been a temptation, but it is impossible to kill evil. The sword can only come into the hands of one who is ready for the great work—alchemy."

The word wasn't what Arthur or Pen expected. "I told you that the stone was called Alkahest, or metamorphosis. When you saw me transform from a bird into this shape, I knew that you two were the ones chosen to learn this knowledge. The fact that you found the sword confirmed this. The true name of the sword, you see, is *destiny.*"

The apprentice grew pensive. "Not everyone, even among the wisest, believes that mortals can renounce violence, but Merlin had faith. 'They are as vicious as wild apes,' he would say. 'But apes would be ashamed of their morals. I have been on the verge of abandoning them countless times. In the end, this is the only hope.' And he would hold up the Alkahest."

Pen had been looking at Melchior, hoping to preserve an image of him in her memory for comfort after he left. Now, as his voice grew softer, she focused on it completely. "Will I be able to remember all this?"

"Don't try. This is not the kind of knowledge you learn; it is the kind you become." Melchior went on, "The alchemist combines four elements in his cauldron, and from these he produces a precious substance—gold. The four elements are earth, air, fire, and water. Each is a mystery, not an ordinary thing.

"The alchemist knows that earth, air, fire, and water are the stuff of earthly existence. Rocks are earth, the wind is air, the sun is fire, the sea is water. When these were put together, life resulted, but here is the mystery. Earth, air, fire, and water aren't living, so how could life be made from them? When the alchemist says 'gold,' he means 'life,' that is the secret end of his research. Mordred rules a world of death, but if we read the stone aright, we will steal the secret of eternal life from under his nose."

Melchior smiled at the thought, but Pen shivered, fearing to listen anymore. Her fear warned that they were treading on forbidden ground. "Why are you telling us this?"

"*Why* isn't a question you can ask about fate. Fate *is.* It is the tip of the knife, the sticking point that pins you down without escape."

"You're frightening me."

"There's nothing to fear in what *is,* only in what we imagine or remember." But a worried look had come into Melchior's eyes.

"Remember? I just remembered something about last night. I was dreaming about dragons . . ." Pen stopped. Impossibly, a patch of ground fog was creeping through the forest, despite the clear sky overhead. Pen wanted to point at it, but she knew that the others didn't see it. It wasn't fog but the mist from her dream. She had seen it creep under her door then, seeping into her room until mist filled it. *Wizards have powers to raise a mist.* She somehow knew that, and her heart raced. Lapping over her bed, the mist had quickened and pulsed. Perhaps it was Merlin. She had reached out, and the mist boiled. A scaly snout and leathery wings began to emerge, and she screamed.

Now when Pen came back to her waking senses, she saw that Arthur was badly shaken, as if somehow he had been in the dream with her. He was staring at the ground fog now, which was creeping through the trees with deliberate stealth. Melchior didn't seem to notice, but his demeanor had also changed. He was looking at her dispassionately, like a doctor probing a patient for a suspicious growth.

"If I could prepare you better for this, I would, with all my heart," he said gravely. "You still have fears inside you, and *he* will know that. You'll have to trust in me as I am trusting you."

"All right." The taste of iron was in Pen's mouth, and she found herself trembling as the mist reached the clearing.

She looked around. The others had come out of their wagons now. The tramp was still posted across the clearing. The woman in the green felt hat stood at the bottom of the steps, studying Pen and Arthur and Melchior. The other faces, five or six of them, Pen didn't recognize, except for one man nearly hidden in the shadow of the trees, who reminded her of Paddy Edgerton.

The mist was gathering around them all, enveloping them up to their knees, then their waists. No one noticed or reacted. "Is it time?" the woman in the felt hat asked. Pen knew that they expected her to produce the stone, to begin the reading of it that was their longed-for miracle. She felt an overpowering urge to bolt, to rush down the steps and fling the woman in the felt hat aside before running home as fast as she could. She heard herself heave a deep, penetrating sigh. The swelling mist boiled, just as in her dream. Her muscles were trembling uncontrollably, and through dimmed eyes she could see the worried faces of Arthur and the apprentice.

Melchior squeezed her hand. "What's happening?" Pen gasped, but before anyone could reply, a deafening roar shook the wagons. Instinctively she felt around her waist, but the velveteen bag wasn't tied there. She had left the stone inside, and suddenly she knew it was a mistake.

"I've got to—"

Her words were drowned out by a blasting cataract of sound. Melchior was tense and poised. "I feared this," he said grimly. A third roar came, followed by a shadow that darkened the mist, which had already blotted out the sun. "Save the others," the apprentice shouted. The air had suddenly filled with acrid smoke, and she couldn't see anyone but Melchior. He shook his head.

"We've come too far. There are no others. The court is being smashed." Somehow, beyond her ken, he had the velveteen bag in his hand; he thrust it at her. She had just enough presence of mind to tie it around her waist.

Now the mist had vanished, and the looming shadow overhead took shape. Something vast and scaly hovered in midair. Its acid breath stung Pen's cheek, and she saw the beast's eyes, as large as serving plates. In her fear and the mad urge to run away, she couldn't tell if the beast was white or red. The first lick of flame made the wagons explode in hellish heat, but Melchior had already pulled her fifty feet away.

"Keep running!" he shouted.

He pushed her violently toward the tall firs. Instead of knocking her over, she was sent flying on her feet, leaping in bounds over rocks and logs.

Dragon.

The hideous thing screamed, and she felt scorching heat at her back. Terror left no room in her mind to think, but she knew that Melchior had stayed behind. She looked back over her shoulder. All the wagons were on fire. The people had scattered, if they hadn't been burned alive. Only a black panther stood in the ghastly light of the flames. It had the dragon around the neck, biting deeply. Red blood spurted over its jaws as the serpent-monster writhed in agony. But it wasn't hurt enough. It raised a razor-clawed foot and pierced deep into the panther's side. The animal fell limply to the ground, not even quivering.

There was no time to look back anymore. The trees rushed past Pen's face, as if they were running, not her. Hot knives tore her lungs as she gasped, hardly able to draw breath. Time disappeared, becoming an endless corridor to flee along, but as she gained distance from the camp, the sense of being alone grew stronger and stronger.

She reached the edge of the woods and would have kept running if she hadn't stumbled over a sight she hoped never to see again in her life: the motorway. Two lanes of asphalt lay in her path, separated by a concrete divider from the two opposite lanes.

The sheer ordinariness of a paved road stunned her. In the next moment she recognized it as the road that ran a few miles from Emrys Hall. She felt confused.

Her heart was beating like a rabbit's, but it was getting hard to remember why. It was hard to recall anything before she found herself by the roadside. She had passed from one world back to another. By the sun it must have been nearly noon, Pen reckoned, and a steady flow of traffic zoomed past. A horn honked impatiently. She must have drifted too close to the cars. *Be careful.* She turned right and walked at a steady pace toward home.

Another vehicle, a heavy lorry, thundered by, making the air shudder. For a moment, Pen imagined that it must be a Gypsy wagon. She quickened her pace, breaking into a dog trot; she had to get home. Whether the dragon pursued her or not, she craved getting back to where it was safe. She was still terrified and reluctant to think about what had happened. Only in the very deepest well of her heart was she glad beyond gladness that the great work had begun.

Dust is more than dirt; it is the calling card of the past. Dust stirs memories of what has been lost or forgotten when nothing else remains. Dust had never frightened Derek before, but he stood in the doorway of his house, shaken and speechless. It was the dust that told him his wife wouldn't be there. With absurd inadequacy he found himself saying, "She's usually such a neat housekeeper."

"I'm sure," Peg Callum said politely.

Through the open portals of Emrys Hall dust had settled like a thick shroud. It covered everything. The marble floors wore a gray, furry carpet of it. The handrails of the stairs dripped in musty swags, and even the chandelier's crystals had lost their luster and looked like dirty rock candy.

"Pen?" Derek shouted. He stepped into the deserted foyer, leaving the first footprints, apparently, in ages. There was the scurrying of tiny clawed feet, then silence. "Pen?"

"Maybe we should be careful. It looks haunted," Tommy said uneasily.

Peg replied, "I think ghosts take a generation or two to settle in." The shock of the dilapidation seemed to make everyone utter absurd remarks. Only Sis, coming inside after the others, kept quiet. It was the biggest house he had ever seen, and therefore it was intimidating, but as for the dust, small boys ignored that. He hid things under his bed at school—Spiderman comics, cricket balls, a bird's nest—that gathered a fair amount of it.

"How long have you been gone?" Peg asked. "Do you have any way of reckoning?"

Derek shook his head. "I don't think it's how long I've been gone that did this," he said grimly. "Someone is trying to wipe out the fact that I ever lived here." The peeling wallpaper and the green mold staining the radiators mutely underlined his point. It felt like a place, Derek thought, where one could be buried alive.

The thought made him feel another stab of fear for his wife. "I'd like to look around by myself, if you don't mind."

"Yes, of course. But after that, perhaps we should leave." Peg vaguely felt, since springing Derek from the geriatrics clinic, that the police would catch up with them. Not that he had committed a crime. "I'm resurrected from the dead," he had said when Peg found him in his hospital room, "but as far as I know, you can't be convicted for that."

The charge nurse who had shown Peg to the room looked suspicious and relieved at the same time. "This is good news, isn't it? Someone in this world knows you after all."

"I'm his sister-in-law," Peg offered in a hesitant voice.

"And who may he be? We have to know before we can release him under your care."

"Derek Rees. Sir Derek Rees." Peg glanced uneasily at Derek, who was sitting in an armchair, his head turned away.

"Really?" the charge nurse exclaimed. "You know, I think I've even heard of him."

Derek looked up. "I'd like to be alone with my visitor, if you don't mind, Sister." The nurse exited, and Derek shook his head. He stood up and walked to the window. His expression was very far away, but then he turned back to her. "I'm sorry, I didn't even say that I'm glad to see you. But I am, fearfully glad."

Peg crossed over and embraced him. "I don't know why I came here. You can't imagine how surprised I was when I saw it was really you. You're Merlin—I mean, the man the police have been looking for."

"Yes. I should have known I couldn't just reappear. I was walking home by the motorway when they spotted me."

"Did you get those clothes at a jumble sale?"

Derek looked over at his shirt and trousers, which were hanging over the back of a chair. Dust, blood, sweat, grass stains, leaves, bread crumbs, cheese, and road tar spackled every inch that wasn't torn or stretched out of shape. "A record of my journey," he said, grimacing. He held out his arms and embraced her again; Peg began crying softly into his hospital robe.

"Things are so frightening," she said in a choked voice.

He held her gently. "I know."

When she had come to herself, they checked him out of the infirmary; despite her curiosity and suspicion, the charge nurse allowed Peg to sign the forms. "Doctor says you're all right," the nurse admitted, "and the police don't have authority over you—I checked."

"Good of you," Derek mumbled.

They had only come to Emrys Hall as a last resort. Tommy and Sis had met Derek outside the gates of St. Justin's. When they'd picked Derek up, the police hadn't spotted the boys. In case of trouble, the three had already agreed to meet behind the school. "We thought you'd be in jail," Tommy said. Relieved as they were to see Derek, it was a sad reunion. The boys sketched in their encounter with Joey and Edgerton. "We've lost the sword," Sis mourned. "I wish we hadn't left the other side." The boys wanted to run away again. Derek proposed instead that they hold a strategy session, if they could find a safe place to confer. It had taken two hours to walk through the sodden fields to Emrys Hall. Traveling on the roads was too conspicuous. Now they were weary and their nerves on edge.

"It's not safe here," said Tommy, surveying the wreckage of what had been a home. "*He* did this."

"We won't stay long," Derek said. "Chances are that the place is as deserted as it looks. But I want to see if I can find a clue about where Pen might be. Wait here." His shoes gathered clumps of dust as he crossed the foyer into the drawing room. It was musty and dank. No one had disturbed the layers of dust on the upholstery. Derek didn't pause to examine the room. "You can come in here if you like," he called. The others trooped in and began pulling cobwebs off the chairs.

"All it lacks is Miss Havisham's cake," Peg remarked. "And a rotted wedding dress."

"Don't fret, I'll be back soon," Derek promised. The others sat down gingerly as his footsteps retreated upstairs.

"Do you think we'll have to stay here tonight? What if we don't find anywhere else to go?" Tommy asked.

Peg looked around doubtfully. "I don't see how we could."

Sis walked over to the curio cabinet, its doors ajar. He idly closed them. The French doors to the garden were also open, exposing the silk curtains to the driving rain, which had stained them in long brown streaks. Blown leaves from outside blended into the floral pattern of the Aubusson carpet.

"Are you a friend of Derek's?" Sis asked.

"We're kin. He's married to my sister."

"She should be here, shouldn't she? If she's not, something might have happened to her. Is she your older sister?" Peg nodded. Sis's eyes were wistfully fixed upon her. "Me and Tommy don't want to be in school anymore. It wasn't so nice before—"

"It was beastly," Tommy put in.

"That's right, it was beastly." Sis nodded. "I wasn't brave then, so that made it extrabeastly."

"Are you braver now?" Peg remembered that her own boy, Arthur, had been as sensitive and small as this one at that age.

"You had to be brave where we went." Sis's face was serious. "The woods were cold and we mostly didn't have any food. People were killed in front of our eyes. It's very dull being back."

"I imagine."

"When we first got back, I thought about going around and

telling everyone about our adventures, but Tommy told me it wouldn't do any good. Everyone still sees us the way they did before. They don't realize that we've had—what are they, Tommy?"

"Exploits."

"Isn't that a brilliant word? Exploits. On the other side, exploits were incredibly scary. Sometimes I almost cried." Tommy snorted. "Don't be mean," Sis chided. "A girl would have cried the whole time, but there weren't any around."

"Fortunate indeed," Peg commented. "Girls tend to take the shine off an exploit."

With considerable feeling Tommy said, "I don't think so. A shine is exactly what a girl would have added."

"And now what's to become of you?" Peg asked. "No exploits, sick of school, and not yet up to girls."

Sis shook his head disconsolately. "I don't know. That's why Derek says we need a strategy, so we won't forget and become ordinary again." Neither boy seemed to have anything to say after that.

When Derek came back downstairs, he carried a jar in his hand. "As far as I can tell, the house has been abandoned, but someone has been rifling through my things in the bedroom. I found this on the floor."

Tommy recognized the jar as theatrical makeup. "We've seen that before," he said excitedly. "Merlin told us to look for blue paint. It's a clue, he said. And Joey Jenkins told me the same thing."

Derek nodded. "It's quite astonishing what this blue paint got me into, and this." He held up a single brown kidskin glove. "This was in a drawer beside the wardrobe. I must have left the house with just one in my pocket, the one *he* might find if he searches hard enough. It's worrisome. Don't ask me why, but I don't like leaving that behind."

"We can return it to you if you like."

The voice made them all jump. "Who are you? How did you get in here?" Derek demanded angrily, turning to face the bulky figure in a gray suit all but filling the doorway.

The intruder's demeanor was cool. "My name is Westlake; I'm a police inspector, and I came in the same way you did, through the open front door. I didn't realize anyone was here." He held out a worn black ID holder with a badge and photo card. "I presume that you are Sir Derek Rees?"

"That's right."

"Well, sir, my apologies for intruding, but it would be helpful to have you satisfy a few inquiries. I recognize Mrs. Callum"—Peg nodded, frowning—"and I should probably know who these two boys are."

"I'm not at all sure you should," Derek replied guardedly. "Your business is with me."

"This business, as you call it, has had a strange way of drawing in the oddest characters. Quite unique in my experience. Do you mind?" Westlake took out a large white handkerchief and dusted one end of a Second Empire divan; he sat down like a weary potentate. "Are you two from St. Justin's?"

Tommy and Sis looked nervously at Derek, but before he could respond, Westlake laughed. He didn't sound amused. "Come, come, you haven't stolen the crown jewels, you know, and this isn't an interrogation. So far as I know, the facts surrounding the disappearance were suspicious but not criminal." He turned to Derek. "You did disappear—I mean, you weren't kidnapped or anything?"

Having Westlake come to the point so quickly unsettled Derek. "I can't confirm or deny that," he stammered.

Without warning, Westlake pounded the cushion next to him, sending up a puff of dust. "Let's not play games, shall we? You, Sir Derek, have led the police a merry chase. Apparently you walked out of this house a week ago without telling anyone where you were going. I say 'apparently' because your wife and servants did not report a missing person, which would lead me to assume that you had your own motives. Perhaps they had theirs as well.

"Somewhere in your roamings that evening you ran afoul of some nasty business—of what sort I am still unaware—because the next thing we know, several constables are reporting by radio that your body has been tossed into a ditch beside the motorway. They say you are deceased, which is doubly odd. Firstly, you are most definitely not deceased, as we can all attest. Secondly, policemen are trained to be precise in their observations. So what were you, drugged?"

Westlake paused, raising his eyebrows like an actor playing the part of a displeased Chinese mandarin. When Derek failed to reply, the inspector heaved a sigh. "Right, then. I'll just go on filling in the details. It was getting dark when your body was found, the weather rainy, which made it difficult to observe your condition. Let us give everyone the benefit of the doubt on that score. An ambulance arrives, you are dispatched to hospital, only somewhere en route, you regain consciousness.

"And then you do something remarkable. Somehow you manage to open the ambulance doors and slip out while the vehicle is still moving at high speed. No one saw you, including motorists on the road. The ambulance drivers had no idea what was going on." The inspector stopped.

"Is that all?" Derek asked. Westlake glared.

"As you've already stated, in your opinion no crime has been committed," Derek went on.

Westlake smiled scornfully. "Do you know what the press is dead keen on, far keener than a crime? A mystery. I haven't had a moment's peace since the Merlin case—that's what they call it—got hung around my neck. Two of my best junior detectives have been put on probation and are suspected of incompetency, at best, for thinking you were dead. One of them still stands by his story. Do you really expect me to willingly accept no explanation?"

"Won't all that trouble simmer down now that I'm back?" Derek asked quietly.

"In time. For the moment I haven't disclosed that you are back. The papers will hound you until you drop, you can be sure of that. There will be no escaping, particularly if we tell them that you were found wandering in confusion like some vagrant or lunatic. Not quite what's expected of the peerage, even in this day and age."

"If you don't mind," Derek said after a moment, "I'd prefer to handle this myself. I regret that the papers got after you; I'm sure it was a dreadful nuisance. But my wish is to keep this a private matter, unless, of course, you have a specific crime worth your investigation."

Westlake shook his head in exasperation. "Did you tell him that it's your son who's under suspension?" he asked, turning to Peg.

"Yes."

"If you were a real policeman, you'd know what was going on." They all turned to Sis, who had made this unexpected outburst. "Can't you feel *him*? We can."

"Him?" Westlake said. The little boy had shut up, but Westlake could sense the unspoken tremor that had passed through the group. His frustration boiled over.

"What is the matter with you people? Don't you live in the real world?" Westlake stood up, brushing dust from the seat of his pants. His nose crinkled with disgust. "And this house." He seemed at a loss for words. On the point of leaving, he picked up the makeup jar, which Derek had set on a side table. "I never fancied Sherlock Holmes much. Redheaded leagues, shrunken monkey paws, ghastly hounds—it's never like that. The mysteries that I've solved involved dogged persistence and the ability to sit for long hours in a desk chair with characters you'd just as soon never meet.

"Crime is very hard on the backside, in my experience. But eventually you wear the blighters down. Somebody with the usual dreary motive went off and did the deed. Unless they're just the criminal type, which is drearier still. But you, Sir Derek, are turning out to be another kettle of fish." Derek imperceptibly shrugged his shoulders. "All right," Westlake said, turning away. "I can show myself out."

He began to move his heavy body out of the room, which seemed almost empty without him. The others heard his clumping tread in the foyer, then the creak of the rusty hinges as the front door was pulled behind him.

"He won't give up," Tommy said, breaking the ominous silence that Westlake had left behind him. "We had better devise some very good strategy, or else—" He stopped in midsentence.

Derek looked at him quizzically. "Or else what, Tommy? The

worst that will happen is that the police will run around in circles until they get worn out."

The boy shook his head. "Mordred hasn't shown any sign of noticing us since we came back, but he's not going to let us just slip through the cracks, not this time."

"Perhaps," Derek agreed somberly. "But how do the police fit in?"

"I don't know." Tommy looked confused. "I could just be overreacting."

"I don't think you are."

Surprised, they looked toward Peg, who had remained silent throughout the inspector's visit. "Something's not right about that policeman."

"Not right?" said Derek.

"I went to him the day you reappeared. He told me two lies—that he hadn't approved Arthur's investigation into the Merlin case, and that he himself didn't see the body in the ditch. But Arthur told me he did."

"Couldn't it just be police politics?" Derek asked. "Our Westlake didn't seem keen on negative press coverage—it fair humiliated him. He had every reason to want to distance himself from the Merlin case."

This reasonable explanation was met without reply. Peg and the boys looked troubled, nursing their vague suspicions. The possibility that Mordred was influencing the police was not out of the question.

Westlake by now was about to get into his car. As he marched over the golden gravel, spottily cluttered with debris from the trees after the recent rains, the inspector couldn't help but respond to the amber light of late afternoon. It had always been the glory hours of Emrys Hall, and it bothered him that so little care was devoted to the magnificent hulk. Panes of glass were broken here and there; the flagstone under the portico was heaved up and weed-grown.

"Upkeep," he said to himself, making a mental note to find some former staff members and ask them what had happened. Cooks, butlers, and maids had to have been kept, at least in the past. This case more than baffled or irked him—it had gotten to him like poison ivy, toxically, he thought. His sense of rationality was affronted. An insidious air surrounded these events such as he had never experienced, despite the fact that no crime had been done.

"Get a grip, Reg," he told himself. He opened the car door and began to ease himself behind the wheel, then saw a woman walking toward him across the expanse of lawns beside the drive. She was tall, over fifty, and was looking in his direction with a look of—what?—dismay. He couldn't be sure. Westlake stood up again and waved. She stopped, as if considering whether to approach or not. A quick turn of the head told her that she couldn't very easily escape, so she waved back and walked toward the car.

"How do you do?" the woman said once she got close enough. "Are you here to see my husband?"

He tried not to look surprised. "Actually, yes. I'm Chief Inspector Westlake, and you're Lady Penelope, I take it. You look like your pictures in the paper."

She nodded. "Has there been some trouble hereabouts?" Her voice sounded only marginally worried.

"Trouble? No."

"Ah, well, that's a relief." She smiled, and it looked genuine, if tired. "Sorry not to have been here when you arrived. I was out for a spot of exercise. Overtaxed my limits, I'm afraid."

"I won't keep you."

She had passed him and was almost at the door when Westlake remarked, as an afterthought, "Pardon me, but you don't seem at all surprised that I was talking to your husband."

"Surprised? Well, no, although we don't have many visits from the police, of course. We live quietly."

"What I mean is, you don't seem surprised that Sir Derek is at home."

She smiled more politely, like someone indulging a tiresome but innocuous stranger. "He's usually home at this time of day. Writer's hours, you know. Will there be anything else?"

There was a lot else, Westlake thought. He had taken in that her shoes—elegant, open-toed, of Italian basket-weave design—were ludicrous for someone who'd been out for a spot of exercise. She also seemed flushed and worn-out. And as for her lack of surprise, he suspected it was calculated. After all, this was the woman who had refused to report her husband missing to the authorities.

"No, nothing else," he said, tipping his hat. Penelope Rees gave him another vague smile, opened the door, and disappeared into the dust-covered mysteries of her house.

24
WHITE WINGS

WHEN THE DRAGON ATTACKED THE GYPSY CAMP, MELCHIOR desperately wanted to run like everyone else, but he found himself walking instead with deliberate steps straight into the fire of the monster's breath.

"Why are you making me do this?" he pleaded. "I'm frightened." He knew that Merlin, for whatever reason, was guiding him. As he dropped into a crouch on the ground, the apprentice didn't will his transformation into the black panther, either, yet as his hands curled into paws and his flanks lengthened and swelled with coiled muscle, he was grateful. The ferocity of the panther's nature muted the pain when the dragon tore into his side, lifting him off the ground with the blow. Melchior twisted on the beast's impaling claw—it would be only an instant before the venomed point pierced his heart.

That split second before death, however, was time enough to feel an agony of loss and failure. In the nick of time Mordred had found them and prevented the reading of the stone. In the panicked confusion, Arthur was shouting something—Melchior could see his mouth move, but the words were drowned out by the dragon's roar. The others scattered, stumbling through the smoke and fire. Through blood-dimmed eyes they seemed to dissolve away.

The dragon's jaw worked savagely, snapping at the panther to vent its wrath. It had no desire to feed, however, and when its prey lay completely still, the dragon tossed the body aside. It held itself hovering above the ground on leathery wings. The rush of wind blew ashes from the dead bonfire across the panther's body. Nearby the burning wagons tottered and collapsed in a heap, scattering sparks.

No one remained to see if the dragon lingered or departed swiftly. The sky was clear, and the noonday sun made the flames of destruction eerily invisible, like waves of heat rippling from a mirage. Around the clearing, the black-green firs shivered as the tips of their branches were singed. A passing cloud dimmed the sun momentarily, making the flames more visible, and the forest waited, wondering if the conflagration would spread. In its depths the forest did not sorrow—it was nothing to it if a fire wasted the land. The secret of seeds had been learned eons ago; the old firs would bow before the fire, giving way to the next cycle of life sleeping in the soil.

Only the panther lying on a carpet of needles aroused interest. Timid animals, mice and squirrels, shrank from the pungent smell of its blood. Some nearby foxes wanted to approach, their mouths salivating, only they hadn't worked up their courage yet. The vixens paced the forest floor while their kits barked impatiently. If a stoat or civet was sneaking about, it remained wary, too.

But all the sharp teeth were to be disappointed. Storm clouds gathered and rain began to fall torrentially, in great gray sheets. The scavengers crept back into their dens to escape the downpour, which doused the dragon fire. The firs were out of danger now. The silent breath of the forest merged with the hissing of the rain. The only undaunted creatures were a flock of crows that had smelled death from miles away and come to investigate.

"Nasty. Just the sort of weather I loathe," the old crow muttered to itself in annoyance. Cold droplets splashed into its eyes. With wings soaked and heavy, the bird flapped down through the trees. It longed for its snug burrow in the nearby fields, but the crow mind, pulling with a single will, denied him.

We are called. It is meet.

Called? Meet? The old crow shook its wet feathers and looked around crossly. Below him, in the shadow of the firs, lay the outstretched body of some kind of animal, large and dark in the rain. The whole flock noticed it at the same time. There was a quickening of wings and a sharpening of sight.

The smell of death didn't revolt the old crow, but it didn't excite him, either, not like the others. If he'd had the nerve, he would have asked for permission to sit in the treetops and simply observe. The flock, however, would have been distressed. There was talk already. Behind his back they were calling him things, vague mutterings such as he pretended not to hear.

The flock tightened its formation now and began to settle around the dead animal. Because of their numbers, they had a boldness that the foxes lacked, and one large male, a leader, began to peck rapidly at the soft tissue around the panther's mouth, while another, as large and experienced, took an eye.

In a moment, this tentative probing would end and feeding would begin in earnest. The old crow felt bored. It was extraordinary not to share the flock's hunger, but he had to face facts. He had changed. He had been drifting in and out of the crow mind, but there was no one to share his wanderings with, except for Melchior, and he had disappeared.

As the flock moved in around the panther, the old crow was the last to settle. The panther's cheek had been ripped open, and three young females were greedily pulling at the flesh. "Don't fret, he's beyond feeling anything," the old crow told himself. He looked around nervously to see if anyone had noticed this sudden spark of compassion.

"Mustn't go off your head," he thought. "Not safe." Pretending to be hungry, the old crow pushed his way to the fallen animal's side, near the opening made by the dragon's impaling claw. Out of respect for his age, some junior members made a place for the old male, but slower than they would have in the past. A faint revulsion for carrion began to form in the pit of his stomach.

"It's just a matter of time before they turn on you." The old crow pushed the thought from his mind and focused on the trickle of blood oozing from the animal's side. He put his beak to the blood and rubbed it around, wanting to give a good appearance of relish at the feast. The blood remained warm as it flowed into the rain. This surprised the old crow. The blood should quickly have turned cold. He dipped his beak again, and this time the trickle of blood wriggled, as if alive. With a caw of alarm the bird jumped back. The younger members began to press in behind him, muttering something scornful.

With a twist of the head, the old crow put his eye very close to the stream of blood. Then he saw. It wasn't just wriggling, it was escaping. And before his eyes, the thin stream of blood transformed itself into an elegant scarlet snake, as if a Chinese court painter had drawn it with one stroke of the brush.

The old crow was so astonished that he cawed again, loudly. A ripple of disturbance passed through the crow mind, and a hundred black eyes turned to stare. With a snap, one of the nearby youngsters made a stab for the scarlet snake, which had crawled completely clear of the panther's body. But the greedy youngster was too slow. The old crow snatched the scarlet snake up and instantly flew away.

He rose toward the tips of the firs, knowing with a fair certainty that the others wouldn't follow, not while the feeding was good. But though their bodies stayed behind, their displeasure did not. Like toxic vapors it incensed the air around him. The old crow rose higher, gripping fast the snake, which had now gone limp in his claws.

What are you doing? Come back. The crow mind pulled with all its might, and although the little snake wasn't at all heavy, lifting it felt like an immense task to the old crow. He could sense the snake's terror, and he badly wanted to console it, to tell it that it wouldn't be devoured, but it took all the old bird's strength to resist the others.

Save yourself. Come back.

It was incredible how much fear was generated by the defection of a single bird. When he finally landed in the top branch of the tallest evergreen, the old crow was trembling, and he almost lost his resolve. He had poised his beak, ready to peck out the serpent's eyes, when the snake said, "You're back."

The old crow drew back. "That is an extremely inadequate remark, given that I have just saved your life." He gave an extra tight squeeze of his claws before releasing the snake. "Besides, I'm not the one who's back. You are. Don't you remember flying away to join those ridiculous people?"

"I didn't find them ridiculous." The snake had coiled itself around the branch like a braided red silk cord. "But it was wrong of me not to thank you properly. Please accept my apology and my gratitude." The snake raised its head to look the old crow in the eye, which also helped to avoid looking down. Melchior found that he was deathly afraid of heights.

The old bird shuffled nervously from foot to foot, barely listening. "Where do you want me to take you?" he asked abruptly. "I don't think it's safe here. And I don't mean because it's high. Heights are exhilarating. Really, you must not have learned much as a crow, if I do say so."

"No," Melchior said meekly, "I suppose I didn't, because I am getting terribly dizzy." The branch he was coiled around was very cold. Combined with the rain, it made Melchior feel sluggish and weak, and he wondered if he had the strength to hold on much longer. He could hear a chorus of angry, disgruntled cawing from beneath the tree.

"Come on," the old crow said. He picked up the scarlet snake in his claws again, being careful to grasp it gently, and rose into the air. The frigid wind was excruciating to Melchior, but he was too enervated to protest. The miracle of having escaped death filled him with joy, despite his numbness.

His awareness had begun to fade in and out when he felt a sensation of agreeable warmth starting to suffuse his slim body. He realized that the crow had deposited him on a large rock, which being under an overhang hadn't gotten chilled by the rain. But also the old crow was nestling over him, imparting the warmth of his feathery body.

It was such a motherly gesture, and Melchior couldn't understand what had put such tenderness into his old friend. He waited, reviving slowly, until the crow spoke. "Are you better? We haven't much time."

Melchior wriggled out onto the exposed surface of the rock. "Not much time? Why not?"

"I'm already missed, and soon they'll be after me. Since you left, things have been brewing. The sword is back, and the stone."

"You know about that?"

"Not just me. The others know as well." The crow spoke grimly, which baffled Melchior.

"I need to rest here a bit; I don't think I have another transformation left in me. The dragon's attack was unexpected, and I fear some mortals are lost."

"No, not lost. But let's not speak of mortals for a moment." The old crow looked pensive, as if searching for the right way to begin. "I have to ask you something. Did you mind dying?"

The oddity of the question, and the tension in the old bird's voice, made Melchior wonder. "That's hard to say. Haven't you died before?"

"*We* have not died. But that's different, isn't it? The crow clan isn't diminished by the death of one of us. One bird is like one leaf falling off a tree."

"But now you find that it does matter?"

"I can't quite tell. Ever since I began to have my own thoughts, I've felt afraid. What if I die alone, away from the flock? I don't think anyone of my race has ever worried about that. But mortals do, don't they?"

"Very much."

"Then I'm becoming like them. That's appalling." The old crow's voice sank in deep gloom. "Do you know what the others have started calling me? *White wings.*"

"Is that bad?"

"Bad? I can't remember a treachery so deeply cursed. We would only call someone that—well, I don't know what it would take." Melchior wanted to console his old friend, but before he could speak, the crow's mood changed abruptly, turning almost ceremonially stiff. "Please forgive me, I've been unforgivably rude to babble about myself. The truth is that much graver matters are unfolding."

"Mordred. You've seen him?" Melchior asked, sensing what the old crow meant.

"*You've* seen him and felt his claw through your heart. It took a great deal for him to assume the dragon shape. Our race has watched and waited, and we know him well. This is the first time in our memory that Mordred suffered pain to shift shape."

Melchior was surprised. It had never occurred to him, nor had Merlin imparted it, that wizards could decline in power or fade with time. "I'm glad you told me this."

"It's my neck that I did. You see, *he's* recruited us, my clan, I mean."

"You're against Arthur and the others?" Melchior was astonished. "But you've never taken sides before. You've always just watched and waited."

"This time is different," intoned the old crow in a baleful voice. "Mordred has us spying for him. That's why we were around your camp—we told him where you were." The old bird sounded deeply ashamed. "The others don't seem to notice. He's stolen into our mind like a thief in the night, and they act as if everything is normal." The old crow gave an agitated croak. "It's a terrible thing. You see, we have never felt hatred before. It was not given to us; it is not in our nature. When Mordred taught us to hate, it crept up so gradually that no one felt any different."

"Except you." The import of the old crow's situation was just dawning on Melchior.

His friend shuffled nervously from one foot to the other. "I'm miserable. I told you that you had infected me, and you have. I don't belong with the flock. I'm ruined."

"You'd be ruined if you did belong," Melchior said quietly. The rain had stopped and a fair wind rose from the south. "You're not in the party of hatred. I don't know what will happen to the others, but you at least have escaped."

"Escaped?" the old crow cawed angrily. "What good does that do me? I want you to fix it. I've watched and waited for you ever since you abandoned me. Rid me of this disease."

"I can't," said Melchior, shaking his head mournfully.

The old crow was beside himself with distress, clacking his beak and fluffing himself wildly like a feathered porcupine. It is impossible to say what he might have done next, except that a presence passed overhead. The old crow did not have to look up to see what it was. He'd never set eyes upon an eagle in his life, yet his ancestral blood curdled, knowing certainly what was about to befall.

"His Lordship," the old bird croaked. He spread his wings and flattened himself on the ground, as much in awed reverence as in surrender—the king of the birds was there to mete out his death. Melchior shivered, fearing that the great talons, which were now fearfully near, might be for him. Without a cry the eagle swooped, and in an instant the old crow was gone.

Unless they are attacked by eagles, crows have no enemies powerful enough to seize them from the air. The sensation made the old crow nauseated and dizzy. His heart pounded wildly, but a voice said, "Calm yourself. I am not here to deal your death." The crow was too stupefied to speak as the eagle started a vertiginous spiral into heights of air above the clouds.

The crow was sick with fear, but he looked down and saw that the familiar green fields of Somerset had vanished. The eagle was flying over a desert, its desolation stretching out in all directions. "What land is this?"

The eagle didn't reply but climbed higher. The landscape could have been scoured by the angel of death. "Look!" the eagle's voice commanded. Then it dawned on the old crow that he had been snatched from the earth to be given a vision. He remembered that eagles were the sovereign messengers of wizards, repositories of their deepest wisdom since druid times. Could this be the way wizards saw the earth? Looking down as the voice had commanded, the crow quailed at the scorched wasteland.

"This is your reward for abandoning your flock. Seize it."

Seize what? The old crow was bewildered. All he felt beholding this bleak desert of suffering was his own fear, and yet there was a twinge of the pain that mortals called compassion. He saw no reward in that. Suddenly there was a tearing sensation under the feathers of his breast. His heart flashed out as the eagle screamed in fierce joy. A bolt of tender lightning shot through the pain, and from the old crow's throat an equal shriek of joy sounded.

"What's happening to me?" he gasped. And what had happened below? They were flying so high now that the desert had dwindled away, and only the spangled earth, green and blue and white, reflected the splendor of the sun.

The voice of the eagle intoned, "Know thyself. You have lost your flock. We have known few or none who have done such a thing."

"What does it mean?" the crow said, shaking.

"It means you are a solitary bird, unique in all creation."

The crow marveled, but it no longer felt the agony of isolation. An urgent question formed in his breast. "Teach me of the solitary bird."

"Feel what you are at this moment, above the wind that carries your flock. This is the view above pain, because you have escaped the web of time. From now on you will dwell in the highest branch of the tree. You will want for no company, even of your own kind. You will aim your beak to the skies. You will sing, but softly and only to yourself."

The eagle's wings enfolded him for a second, then His Lordship opened his talons and the crow plummeted toward earth like a rock. The eagle, with a last piercing shriek, vanished above the clouds. For an eternity the crow fell, unable to catch wind in its wings. It cried out, and although none of his clan had ever sung before, when the old crow opened his beak, a liquid melody issued forth. It filled the air with joy and floated like a benediction over the earth.

Free!

The crow's wings caught the wind now, and his plummet became a soaring arc. He sang again and again, and each new note brought the same tender lightning he had felt before. He was a solitary bird alone in the endless sky, and yet he would never be alone again.

As quickly as it began, the vision ended. The old crow found himself breathing heavily, sitting on the ground next to the scarlet snake. It took a moment before he could catch his breath. The two of them sat, letting the warm south wind blow over their backs.

"You must tell me what you know of Mordred," Melchior asked anxiously.

"Mordred? What?" The old bird was disoriented. Did the snake know where he'd been? He stared into the serpent's eyes, which were also scarlet, and sensed that he'd seen everything but wanted nothing said, as if to seal a silent communion.

The old crow wanted to burst out with his vision, but he thought a moment, then said in a serious tone, "Yes. You need to know that Mordred is finished toying with these mortals. This morning's attack was only the beginning. The old queen will not be in hiding much longer. The gathering of the court will happen in her presence, and a new kingdom, blessed and free, will have its slender chance to be born."

Melchior stared, astonished at the prophetic tone of his friend. "You're sure of this?"

The old crow nodded. "Mordred will do anything to prevent such a birth. He must have made an unholy bargain to get the power to turn into a dragon, and if that isn't enough . . ." He let the thought linger unfinished.

Melchior felt a flash of intuition. "The old queen is under Mordred's control. When did that happen?"

"My kind doesn't count in years. We have watched for a thousand hatchings and many more. But one day we flew near the crystal cave, and we saw her. She was standing outside, gazing at the sky. She is very beautiful, but for all that, I felt sorry for her."

"Why?"

"Because she looked so vulnerable, and she couldn't hide any longer. Guinevere has been protected by Merlin through the ages. She has been secreted in convents and castles and caves, yet that is over now. She risked exposure, and although Merlin had devised disguising identities for her, *he* found her, despite all these precautions." The old crow said these words rapidly, in a state of considerable anxiety, and Melchior realized that a betrayal of confidence was taking place. That's how the others would see it.

"Take care, we can't be found here together. I've opened the future to you, which our race is sworn never to do, because I didn't want Arthur to be destroyed, and the chance of a new kingdom with him." The old crow cawed in astonishment at his own feelings. "Don't pity me. Farewell." The grizzled bird gave a flourish of his wings, for all the world like an old thespian relinquishing the stage with a sweep of his cape.

Melchior was at a loss. His heart surged at his friend's courage, knowing that a betrayal of hatred is no betrayal at all, but the essence of love. A chill came into the air. Melchior shuddered, imagining that the dragon's shadow was passing overhead. No, it was just a small, faraway cloud.

"The others are right. You do have white wings."

The old crow was no longer within earshot, however. He must have taken flight the instant the cloud appeared. Melchior realized that he was weary beyond weariness. He crawled toward a warm crevice between the rocks where he could rest and ruminate. The cloud grew darker, and when he looked up, Melchior saw that it wasn't actually a cloud but a flock of black birds.

The flock circled in one spot, waiting. A single speck approached it, flying resolutely. Melchior wanted to cry out a warning, but it was useless. The speck was the tiniest particle of black rushing to join the larger blackness. It merged into the center of the flock, which tightened around it. There was a menacing cry, a clattering of metallic wings, and then nothing more, nothing at all.

25
REUNION

Pen didn't think for a minute that Chief Inspector Westlake believed her little charade in front of Emrys Hall. She had put on a good face, but they both knew that she was shocked to hear that Derek was inside. Instinct told her not to reveal anything to the police, though she had nothing to hide, not really. If fleeing from dragons had torn her clothes and streaked her face with sweat, that was her business. One heel broke as her shoe caught a loose paving square by the door, but she kept her composure, feeling Westlake's eyes on the back of her head. Once inside, however, her reserve broke down.

"Derek, are you here?" she shouted. The vaulted ceiling only gave back a dead echo. The wind blew through the open door, raising swirls of dust. Pen coughed, all but choking, and called again. "Derek, where are you?"

She strode through the foyer into the drawing room. It was deserted, but to her relief she could tell that someone had recently been there. The thick dust on the furniture was smeared with handprints. A tea tray stood littered with crumbs and used cups. She made her way hastily into the pantry, which smelled of sour milk and rotted fruit. A bowl of lemons and oranges had turned green with mold. Pen opened the bread cupboard and saw a rat staring back at her. She jerked away, but the rat kept staring boldly, as if she were the intruder.

Suddenly she heard a sound behind her, although its exact location was impossible to fix. She retraced her steps, looking eagerly into doorways but finding no one. When she got to the foyer again, the air was still so murky she could hardly breathe. There was a loud bang, and her heart sank. The noise had just been the front door hitting its jamb in the wind. Pen crossed the entry and shut it. She suddenly felt drained. A sense of defeat overcame her. If only they'd managed to read the stone . . .

"Ah, my dearest."

She held her breath as a man emerged from the dusty dimness. A hand touched her shoulder, drawing her into an embrace. "My dear, dear Pen." It was Derek after all, his voice muffled against her shoulder. Pen hadn't cried since he left, but now the tears came in a torrent, hot and salty at the corners of her mouth. "There, there, darling," he murmured. His touch eased the grief, but not all at once.

"What happened to you?" she asked, her voice ragged.

"Don't talk," he said soothingly, and he was right. It was better that they simply make contact again, reassuring each other with their bodies. After a few minutes Pen said, "You weren't here when I came in."

He looked at her, his eyes all tenderness. "We were in the garden. It's just sheer luck I came back for one last look before we left."

"We?"

"Three of us besides me. Two are boys whom you haven't met. The other's Peg."

Pen drew back, wiping her cheeks. "My sister? Is she involved in this now?" she asked in surprise.

Derek nodded. "A huge amount has happened, and a lot of it revolves around her son. You remember Arthur, the policeman? That is, he's become a policeman. It must have been years since we saw him."

"I've seen him in this house only a few days ago. He came here looking for you after you disappeared. In fact he's the one who found your body." It was Derek's turn to be astonished, but before he could question her, Pen said, "We're not really home again, though, are we? The house is so awful; it seems to have decayed overnight."

"I know. I expect blocks of stone to start falling on our heads any minute, or rambling vines to bury the place. Do you think you're up to going into the garden?"

She let him lead the way, leaning on his arm. When they got to the drawing room, long shafts of afternoon light were seeping through the dank, stained curtains. The room seemed to be entering a melancholy season of its own.

"Can we stop for a minute?" Pen asked. "I need to hear what happened to you first." They sat down on the dusty settee. "That policeman at the door must have been very curious."

"Yes. He's cobbled together a plausible story, but I'm afraid I've been where the police mind can't possibly follow. Where shall I start?"

"With the night you left."

"I can tell you what I've pieced together, but I haven't discovered everything myself. You remember that I'd fallen into the habit of walking in the country by myself, just to think. One day I came across some unusual stones by the side of the road. They were gray and pointed, almost like teeth; they stood in a circle some thirty feet across, each about waist high. I was very surprised, you know. There are detailed maps of these kinds of ancient rings, and yet this one wasn't on any map I'd ever seen.

"I went home, and I don't know why I didn't mention it to you. For some reason I kept thinking about those stones. How could they just be sitting there by the side of the road? I decided to return, and that's where I headed the night I left. It was only a short detour from the village, but I didn't calculate the time well, and when I arrived back at the stone circle, it was getting on sunset. Not that there was any sun; a drizzle had started to fall and was turning into rain.

"You'd think I would've just taken one glance and kept on my way, but without thinking, I approached the circle. It was well kept up. Whatever farmer owns the field had plowed around the ring, taking a scythe to cut down the weeds inside it. I went into the very center, which was traditionally considered the most powerful sacred spot. It was empty. I was rapidly getting soaked, and I didn't feel anything particularly sacred, but when I looked down at my feet, a round stone caught my eye."

"Clas Myrddin."

Derek paused in his narrative and sat back. "So you got it?"

"Yes." Pen patted her jacket, feeling the weight of the black velveteen bag underneath.

"When I picked the stone up, I read those words on it; they made me very excited. It was a thousand-to-one chance that the stone was actually connected with Merlin, but why else was it there? That's when I saw *him.* He had taken the shape of an old man with a long white beard, dressed in white robes. Seeing him there at the edge of the circle caught me off guard, and I didn't reflect at the time why he didn't just walk inside."

"He couldn't. That was Merlin's ring."

Derek nodded. "He didn't say anything, either, but just slowly beckoned as if he wanted me to come over to him. I picked up the stone and put it in my coat pocket. The rain was falling harder now, and I couldn't see him well. I went over, and that's really all I remember."

"Did he attack you? How did you wind up in the ditch?"

"He must have hit me on the head with something hard—they say it's common to lose memory when you've been knocked unconscious. Then he must have driven me away and dumped my body for dead by the motorway."

"Did he really think you were dead? Maybe he wanted you found."

"To begin the game, you mean? I don't know."

"When the police found you, you were wearing a white beard."

Derek grimaced. "*He* put it on me, with cosmetic gum, no less. It was no doubt his way of thumbing his nose at Merlin."

Pen glanced toward the ravaged curtains, wind blowing in

through their holes. "He has a sense of humor, I suppose. How ghastly."

Derek had turned grave. "Mordred is someone to be greatly feared. About that I have no doubts. Yet he is every bit as important to this mystery as Merlin is. They've been at their wizards' game or combat for a very long time, and we just happened to stumble into it."

"Stumbled? I don't think so. Why didn't Mordred kill you while he had the chance and simply take the stone?"

"He gave it a good try, but Merlin took over my body. When I came to, he was talking through me, which is doubly strange, because he promised not to interfere in human affairs, and then he jumps in like that."

Pen stood up. "Maybe they both thumb their noses at each other." While Derek was telling his story, she had been tempted to show him the stone, but some instinct told her not to. It was getting late. The last long light of day had almost crept from the room. They went into the garden to join the others.

"I don't believe it," Peg exclaimed, rushing to embrace her sister. "I prayed that you'd come back, only it's all so strange."

"Very strange," Pen agreed. They had a huge amount to talk about, but very little time in which to do it. Despite the separation of years, the sisters fell into much the same rapport that had joined them years ago, and it was not difficult, even in their excitement, to await the quiet hours that would fill in all that needed to be said. Tommy and Sis came forward shyly, and when Derek introduced them as the bravest boys he'd ever met, they turned color. Everyone wanted Pen to tell her story. She began, but when she reached the part about the Gypsy camp, Peg grew agitated. "You saw Arthur there? When?"

"Just this morning, and only for a moment." Pen's voice was subdued. "The sword made its way into Arthur's hands only last night. He has experienced some terrible shock—of what kind I'm not sure. But he was all right, Peg, on the apostle's monkey," she said, lapsing into a family expression they had shared as girls.

"Whatever Arthur has gone through, it must have been necessary. I know you're worried sick about him, just as I was about Derek." Her husband took her hand and squeezed it. "Yet in some peculiar way, all the strange events of the past week have formed a pattern. Only we didn't see it at first. How could we?"

The boys were greatly excited by the news that the sword was back and wanted to know everything about where she'd seen it. "There's a place out there"—Pen pointed to the gardens and beyond—"called the court of miracles. Its members have been searching for Arthur a long time, and when they found him, he became a different person. He became their king."

A startled look crossed Peg's face. "The court of miracles? I've heard of that."

"Tell us," Derek urged. "It could be another part of the puzzle."

"Let me think. . . . Yes, the tarot. In the tarot deck there are four suits of cards—wands, coins, swords, and cups. These were created a long time ago, before the Middle Ages, to symbolize where everyone belonged in society. Wands were the rough staffs carried by farmers and humble workers. Coins represented the merchants, swords stood for the soldiers, and cups for the church. Everyone was supposed to fall into one of these four categories, ordained by God, but some didn't. There has always been a motley crew of beggars, simpletons, geniuses, and mad people who refused to fit in. In the tarot they're known as the court of miracles."

Pen nodded. "They call themselves the ones who walked away."

"I would also include another class of misfits," Derek said.

"Wizards?" Peg said.

"If you like, but I was going to say saints."

"Yes," Peg agreed, then fell silent.

Pen said, "I've gotten to know these people. They've lived for ages on the fringe of society, being hunted by Mordred, surviving by stealth and evasion. It's tragic, but in some way their plight must fit the pattern, too." She paused, as if considering whether to say something more. "The reason I came back was that a terrible catastrophe occurred. We were attacked by a dragon. Everyone ran away, and their camp was destroyed." Pen turned to her sister. "I don't expect you to believe all that, but Arthur was there, he saw it, too. I only hope he got away."

Peg looked dazed. "It seems too absurd. Dragons? It makes my head swim."

"I dreamed about it before it happened," Pen added. "A dragon materialized out of some kind of fog or mist. For all I know, my dream made the real thing happen."

"It's not your fault," Derek corrected. "I'm sure it was Mordred. Wizards have powers to raise a mist."

"The same words came to me in my dream," Pen said, wondering. "How did you know?"

"It's part of the lore. In fact, if you look into Arthurian legend, it's how everything began."

Before Derek could explain, Tommy interrupted, "I'm not surprised a dragon attacked you. Wizards don't only raise mists; they change shape whenever they want to. The fact that we haven't seen dragons only means that Mordred felt safe before. He must have felt safe for a long, long time."

"But now Mordred is being forced to defend himself. He'd have to, wouldn't he, if Arthur and the sword are back." Derek turned to Pen. "You said you were at the camp. Could you take us there?"

"It's gone, I'm afraid, and even if it weren't, I'm too confused about directions to find it again. There's no way Arthur would have remained there, either."

"Then he's got to come home eventually. I don't want to disturb your plans, but I'm going back. If something's wrong with my son—" Peg's voice broke, she covered her face with her hands, and her body shook with sobs. It was difficult to imagine anyone whose heart was breaking more quietly or modestly. She leaned on Pen, who murmured, "No one's going to keep you from going home, but it's better if we stick together."

Her sister nodded, beginning to compose herself. "Yes, I see that. But you all seem obsessed by this Mordred you keep going on about. I don't know what to think. The court of miracles hasn't produced any miracle that I can see. Do you believe they ever will?" The bitterness in her voice silenced the group.

Without thinking, Pen reached inside her jacket and pulled out the black velveteen bag. "Look." She drew forth the Alkahest. "If there's going to be a miracle, this will be its source." She was going to ask her sister if she could read the words engraved on the stone when Peg stood up, greatly agitated. "No," she protested, and bolted from the room. The others followed her with dismayed eyes.

"Let her go," Pen murmured, putting her hand out to restrain Derek. "She's the only one of us who didn't make a choice." Unless the choice had been made long ago in secret, she thought to herself.

Peg ran into the foyer. The dust in the air hadn't settled but only grew darker as the sun waned. She was perplexed and frightened, her mind panicked at the thought of being pulled into a world the others shared, or had been hypnotized into imagining. She only knew she desperately wanted Arthur back, wanted to look in his eyes again and be reassured by his presence. The possibility of that ever happening seemed to be drawing further and further away.

"Where are you?" she called softly.

Standing alone in the clouded atmosphere of the foyer, Peg felt a cool sensation against her cheek. She touched it, and her fingers came away moist. The swirling dust no longer looked dirty but was turning a clean, luminous white, like pearly fog.

The wizard has power to raise a mist. The thought made her afraid. She took a step backward, intending to turn and retreat, but the mist followed. Peg felt herself frozen in place. A wizard's mist was alive—somehow she knew that, too, with utter certainty. The white shroud could conceal a dragon or a man. She shivered, but this mist did not feel dragonish. No, a man was inside it, one who wanted her desperately, beyond anything else he'd ever wanted.

Igraine.

The mist was calling, not to be denied. She felt sweat break out on her body. The same mist had been her ruin once. She saw herself in the past as a beautiful, unsuspecting lady, lying in her tower alone. Her pillow was rumpled in anguish. Peg's chest ached with the awareness that she was back in that time and yet here also.

Igraine.

The panic that might have sent her running out of the house ebbed. Her mind delivered up the casket of memory and opened it.

Bells rang out over snow, and her lady-in-waiting's hands shivered holding out her gown. London had been cold that Easter. In the morning hoar frost sparkled from the new sprouts of hellebores and jonquils. "The service, my lady. We mustn't be late." Igraine ran through the halls, catching the strains of a Gloria in the distance.

Even with the royal chapel thronged by nobles, fingers of frost reached in, coating the iron grill over the choir stall. She rushed to her pew, followed by censoring eyes. Her husband, Duke Gorlois, was in a foul temper, hardly fit to take Communion. When they returned to their apartments, he cursed the king. "We have to leave. Did you see how he shamed you? The priest noticed him ogling, everybody did. I won't stand for it." She gazed modestly at the cold stone floor, feeling the impotence of his fury, for he was only Duke of Cornwall, and King Uther could do as he wished. His desire for Igraine wouldn't be checked, not by a priest or a mere husband.

Gorlois was rash, however. They walked obediently behind the king in the progress through the palace, but as soon as the paschal feast was concluded, Gorlois spirited her away in a carriage whose windows were shrouded in sackcloth. It was a grave insult to the king, leaving without his permission, and as Gorlois's temper cooled, he grew morose. He saw Uther's face again in church and understood with dread that events wouldn't turn out well. So much passion for a woman could only lead to disaster.

"Did you say something?" Gorlois growled at Igraine. She sat in silence on the other side of the carriage. If Uther's inflamed heart had touched her or merely revolted her, she didn't let on. "I said, did you speak, my lady?"

Igraine turned pitying eyes on Gorlois. The king had placed two footmen on either side of her chair at the Easter banquet table, each holding out wine in a golden goblet. But she had not drunk, preferring to keep her Lenten vows.

At first the lightning was held in check. She and her husband had been back in Cornwall a month and the daffodils had faded before disaster struck. The outraged king was marching an army against Gorlois, who by the most optimistic estimate was outnumbered ten to one. "I have only one place where he can't get at you," he told his wife. "Tintagel."

It was the highest, farthest, most forlorn place. Although Igraine had heard many legends about Tintagel, Gorlois had never taken her there before. The castle seemed to stride over the sea, mounted on high rocks of the wild Cornish coast. Fairies could have built it, or people so ancient that even the druids couldn't remember their names. Massive breakers pounded the promontory from all sides, and entry was vouchsafed only by a narrow rock defile wide enough for one person at a time.

"You'll be safe here," Gorlois told Igraine the hour he departed. "Three men with swords can hold off the whole accursed English army until I return." She wondered if he believed his own bluster, for it was unlikely her husband would live to see her again. She waited alone in the tower over the sea. In the near distance she could see a large cave carved by the ocean at the base of a cliff. Merlin was supposed to live there, but if he did, she never saw him.

That was the night the mist came. Igraine had gotten out of bed, troubled and sore at heart. She wanted to pray, but she was distracted by the creeping mist, which blanketed the ocean and reached eagerly up to her window. Her candle guttered as the door opened.

"My lord!" She was overjoyed to see Gorlois back, but when she ran to embrace him, he shook his head and put two fingers to her lips. "No questions," he said.

They lay in the dark, and he loved her with a passion strong enough to erase her fear. It was as if they had just wed, and they luxuriated as in the first tender days of romance. She was lost in love's embrace, yet not so lost that she could banish her curiosity. Why didn't her husband speak? What of the battle that had threatened all of their lives? He was as secretive as Eros visiting Psyche. They fell asleep in each other's arms, and when cries and lamentations came to her ears, she woke up to find him gone.

"Woe, woe, the duke is slain!" Her lady-in-waiting was pounding on the door, wailing. "You have no husband, lady. What shall we do?"

"What do you mean?" Igraine cried, not daring to unbolt the latch.

"The duke was killed yesterday in battle a hundred miles from here. The messenger is half-dead from bringing the news." And then Igraine knew that her lover had not been Gorlois, albeit that she had conceived a son that night. Three months later Uther Pendragon came to claim her as his bride and queen. She did not protest or speak. The mist never returned, and she never asked about it. But when her newborn son was only a few hours old, Merlin walked into the midwife's chamber and looked into the cradle, as sly as he was silent.

"Give me that babe," he ordered. The midwife set up a howl, until she saw, trembling with fear, that the king himself was wrapped in the shadows behind the wizard. "Do as he commands," Uther muttered bitterly. No one ever told the queen why her child was given away. Merlin never returned, melting back into his forest. Igraine lingered, a living ghost, until she died in the spring knowing two things. She hated Merlin and his mist, and she longed full sore to see that baby again, whose eyes and name she never forgot—Arthur.

As Peg gradually came back to herself, she felt tears streaming down her cheeks. So the mist knew. Her longing had not been ignored, and in the fullness of time she had come back for Arthur. It would crush her to lose him again.

"Peg?"

Her sister was standing beside her, a perplexed look in her eyes. "I don't trust him," Peg murmured distractedly.

"Who?"

"Merlin. I can't help feeling that he's pulling my son away from me. How can I fight back?" She stopped, embarrassed. Her need for her son went deeper than society would understand, not because there was anything wrong about it, but because society isn't prepared to imagine a soul wandering through time to heal its grief.

"You can't fight back," Pen said. The two sisters were silent for a while. "I don't know if I trust Merlin either," Pen went on quietly. "Or if he even exists. He seems to draw us on without revealing much. But we're enmeshed, each of us, and we don't have a choice now. Here, we'd better go." She took Peg's hand and led her out the kitchen door into the service area. Derek and the boys were waiting in the car, an old Rolls that Derek had brought around from the garage.

Peg got in the backseat between Sis and Tommy. "I don't know where else to go," she murmured. The car's interior smelled of stale Moroccan leather. "Have you formed some kind of plan?"

"The best we can do now," Derek replied, "is to go to your house. The boys have been sensing Mordred's presence here, and so have I. Look around. This place couldn't possibly have disintegrated so fast on its own. This isn't natural; it's malevolent." He released the clutch, letting the powerful engine dig in and rush them forward.

"Do you think this is the last we'll see of the place?" Pen asked somberly as they pulled around the front and headed down the long drive, its flanking trees nearly black against the violet sky.

"Perhaps," Derek said. "I still have the feeling that I've walked away. This wasn't really a homecoming."

"No," his wife admitted.

"I'm not sure I want to be back," Tommy volunteered. "We don't fit in anymore, anyway. Finding a place is just something we'll keep on doing, until it happens."

Derek looked at the boy in the rearview mirror. *It?* He had no way of knowing if the others were pondering the same inexplicable fate Tommy had alluded to, had framed in one troubling pronoun, but by their silence they each must have retreated into worlds of private reflection, and that told him enough.

26
THE WEDDING GAME

As the blessed day approached, the bride-to-be found it harder and harder to sleep. Katy felt as happy and excited as she should be, but there was something else, too. Sometimes, in the middle of the night, she would find herself sitting up in bed, her ears ringing with a woman's shrieks. The outcry sounded terrible, high and keening, so full of anguish that Katy wanted to run out of her room to comfort the tragic victim. Images of a mother watching her child drown or a lover being stabbed filled her heart and set it pounding.

What stopped her from jumping out of bed was the suspicion that Katy herself was the source of these shrieks. So she lay quietly in bed, even though her hands would be cold and sweat stood on her brow. If she had shrieked, why didn't someone come? No one ever did. Her room had been moved next to Amberside's. Neither of them believed in old-fashioned prudishness, and they shared a bed until one day, just before the ceremony, Amberside suggested separate rooms. "Just for now. It preserves a touch of decorum."

"Are you joking?" Katy had asked, more than a little offended. Amberside—she still found it hard to think of her former landlord as Terry—smiled and asked to be humored. She gave in, but when her dreams turned into nightmares filled with shrieks, she longed to be back in Amberside's bed. She didn't bring it up, however. She had finally decided that the shrieks must only be dreamed, or her cries would have woken the two live-in maids Amberside had taken on to prepare for the wedding.

Exhausted by lack of sleep, Katy walked through her days in a queer, half-dazed state. "The new girls are too much for you to worry about, darling," Amberside said. "I'll manage them. Don't give it another thought."

So Katy became a wraith in the house where she should have been its future mistress. She saw the two young black girls—from Kenya, she thought—polishing the silver, dusting the mantel, sweeping the stairs, and in general putting a gleam on everything. Not that Amberside had neglected his dwelling. He was a spotless housekeeper himself. "It's only the garden I've let go," he declared one morning over breakfast. "But that's where Jasper comes in so handy. You'd think he was born to trim hedges and thin rose trees."

"I wish you'd let him go. I hate that man!" Katy's voice was filled with passion, but Amberside looked more amused than alarmed by her outburst.

"Hate him? Tosh, what grounds could you possibly have? Jasper pulls his weight around here, not to mention that he's down on his luck. Lost his last position and came away without references. Well, if I have a soft spot, I can only hope you won't hold it against me, darling."

Katy had learned that her intended's mildest statements counted as law, and there was no chance he would reverse himself. The discussion of Jasper was closed, despite the queasiness she felt whenever she laid eyes on the new gardener.

Gramercy High Street didn't afford much in the way of wedding paraphernalia, other than a card shop for the invitations and a second-rate bakery for the cake. Amberside wouldn't have these, however. He insisted on taking Katy down to London to buy everything. In every shop he turned out to be a fanatic for detail, and settling the smallest point took hours. If some pasteboard stock wasn't the right weight or hue, if the italic engraving leaned a bit too far to the right or left, he would throw the sample down in disgust. He marched out of half a dozen bridal shops that seemed perfectly all right to Katy.

"Let's just go," he said at the last one. "I'm only getting married once, and I'm not having it ruined. I detest shoddiness."

"But, Terry, I'm exhausted. Isn't this gown pretty enough? I don't see what bothers you about it." She didn't have the nerve to add, "I'm the one who's going to wear it, after all." Amberside was paying for everything. Her parents were keeping their distance, embarrassed because they eked out their existence in Hull on a tiny policeman's pension (Katy had followed her father into the force when her mother produced no sons).

It was late in the day when Amberside finally approved of a gown, much to Katy's relief. God knows there wasn't much joy left in her shopping by then, only nerves and anxiety. The salesgirl was packing the pile of ivory lace and satin into a box when Amberside spotted a small bunch of flowers embroidered at the shoulder.

"What's that?" he asked, his voice dripping with disgust.

"Lily of the valley, sir," the salesgirl said.

"It won't do." He pushed the box away. Clutching at it, Katy cried, "Darling, I think the flowers are sweet, and besides, they're very small. Why the fuss?"

"No fuss. I just won't have you looking like a tart." Katy's face flushed deep scarlet in front of the young salesgirl, who stared openmouthed. Amberside raised his voice for everyone else to hear. "It's trash."

"Don't say that," Katy whispered, feeling dizzy.

"Why shouldn't I? You're not used goods. You're a beautiful young girl. They can strew nasty gewgaws over frocks if they like, it's none of my concern, but I won't slap something like that on your back." Without further ado he stomped out of the shop and hailed a cab.

The incident would have been ludicrous if it hadn't been so humiliating. Katy barely kept her head up trailing behind him out of the shop, but she wasn't one to cry. She was quiet on the train home. Doubts filled her head. She began to wonder if Amberside cared for her feelings at all, which was bad enough. But in truth her mind was struggling with a deeper, more insidious possibility. Was their engagement a charade, even a form of subtle torture? The elaborate shopping expeditions, his refusal to find anything that was good enough for her—was it just a devious way of ridiculing her?

"A penny for your thoughts, darling," said Amberside, pressing her arm gently.

Katy woke from her reverie. "Nothing worth a penny." Suddenly their first-class carriage seemed unbearably small and stuffy, reeking of stale cigarettes. She was on the verge of bolting, but his touch soothed her. Looking in his face, she didn't see a trace of mockery or deceit.

"I was just being silly," she said, leaning against his warm body for reassurance.

It was absurd to doubt him. He loved her, had loved her the longest time. That's why she had left Arthur, whose jealousy had gotten to be intolerable. One night it blew up into a terrible row. Arthur had jumped out of bed and was standing across the room in his pajama bottoms. He was shouting, and he'd never even raised his voice before. "You're leading him on. Don't tell me you're not. Do you think I'm a fool?"

"Calm down, you're imagining things."

"Look at yourself," he said, disgusted.

"What's wrong with the way I look?"

"You might as well wrap the goods up and put them in a window. Aren't you ashamed?"

"No. No one's ever talked to me that way. Stop it, Arthur. Someone might hear you."

"Someone? You mean him." Arthur's face was contorted and purplish. "Who gives a great goddamn what he hears? Why are we staying in this house anyway? So you can shack up with him next?"

"Stop this, I mean it."

"You stop it, you stop it! Don't play the innocent with me. You're the one who chased me, remember? I could've gone out with anybody, but I pitied you." She drew back, shocked. "I'm sorry, I shouldn't have said that." But when she looked in his eyes, it was true—the passion that had seemed like an answer to her prayers was gone. When she began to cry, Arthur paced the floor and didn't touch her. His apology sounded tossed off, careless. "It's either me or him. Bedhopping's not a sport I'm willing to engage in or watch."

"Get out! Get out!" Her humiliation and hurt erupted into a scream of rage. And then Arthur had grabbed a few clothes, stuffed them angrily in a bag, and stalked out, not saying a word.

Whenever Katy thought of Arthur now, that final scene returned to mind, blotting out the love that had come before. The black hatefulness of the things he'd said had poisoned it. Distraught, she had flung herself on the bed that night. She didn't hear anyone come in, then a soft touch roused her. "Darling, you're back," she thought. Only it wasn't Arthur. It was Amberside, standing there in his robe and pajamas looking embarrassed and concerned. His eyes were soft with kindness.

"I couldn't bear to hear you crying."

Katy was in such pain that she couldn't help herself. She opened her arms, holding them out to him like a frightened child.

"Are you sure?" he whispered. "I've adored you for so long."

She wasn't listening. All she heard was her deep, wounded need. The pain was unbearable. Amberside stayed with her until she calmed down. He stroked her shoulders and breasts, making her feel desirable again. "You're beautiful," he whispered. "No one should call you ugly." She trembled. Somehow he knew her worst fear, that love would be denied her because she wasn't pretty enough, desirable enough, good enough.

Her despair gradually gave way to a strange ecstasy of forgetfulness. His lovemaking drew her down into not just pleasure or release but oblivion—kind, kind oblivion. Amberside was the only one who could make her forget Arthur, not by replacing him but by making her forget blame and remorse. Under other circumstances this would have disturbed her, for she had pined for Arthur the way Amberside said he'd pined for her. Almost overnight Arthur dissolved in her memory like wispy fog, and the next morning she could hardly even remember the terrible row. "Don't you know why he's gone?" Amberside asked. And he pieced together for her what had happened. He'd heard it all from down the hall, so of course he must be right. Arthur really did say all those terrible things.

After the incident in the bridal shop, Katy insisted on being taken home. Over the next few days, things got smoother. Amberside mellowed, his fanaticism lost its edge. Even the nightmares seemed to subside, and Katy had the vague sense that something had entered her dreams, a soft presence that soothed her shattered nerves. If only she could remember who or what it was, but she'd never been good at remembering her dreams.

The only other unsettling event occurred the day before the ceremony when the police showed up at the house asking questions. Katy was in high spirits. She had been practicing wearing her veil and rushed into the sitting room to show Amberside. "Darling, darling, what do you think?"

"Darling isn't here at the moment. He's gone for tea." She lifted the white lace, recognizing Westlake's voice. "How are you, Katy? Isn't it bad luck to let the groom see you that way before the wedding?"

"I—what are you doing here?" she stammered.

"I'm here to see your Mr. Amberside. He was a witness to the fire down the street. It was arson, you know, according to the report, and possibly attempted murder to boot. There's still someone from the family unaccounted for. Know anything about it yourself?"

Before Katy could reply, Amberside walked into the room carrying a tea tray. "Sorry, can't find those bloody girls. I suppose they're on a break." He set the tray down, acknowledging Katy with a small nod; he didn't seem to notice the veil.

"Excuse me, I'd better go upstairs."

"No need to. You're a policewoman, after all," Westlake remarked coolly. "Two lumps, no milk, thanks." Taking a cup, he raised it to his lips and eyed Katy over the rim. After years of practice, Westlake's thoughts didn't give themselves away. He could have been the model for a jowly Buddha or the cat that ate the cream. Katy wavered in the doorway.

"Do stay, darling," Amberside echoed. "I just happened to bring an extra." She sank nervously onto the settee next to him and took a cup. "Well, commence the interrogation, Inspector," Amberside said genially. "I'm getting married tomorrow and nothing quickens the blood like being suspected of murder."

"It's not an interrogation, and you're not suspected of anything. Certainly not murder." Westlake's voice was dry but indulgent. "In point of fact, our initial report on the Edgerton fire was filed by an officer who said that he ran into you several times at the scene that night. It appears that you were instrumental in aiding the family."

"Glad to be of help. Neighbors, you know," Amberside said modestly.

"Um. You didn't fraternize with neighbors like the Edgertons, though, did you? I assume that a great gulf between you was fixed." Amberside chose to stay silent, holding the teacup to his lips. "Did you, for instance, know the boy, what's his name?"

"I haven't the slightest," Amberside said without pause.

"Jerry. The boy says he knows you." Katy saw Westlake hold his breath slightly. She knew him well enough to suspect that he was bluffing.

"Knows me? Did he say that? I'd like to meet the boy and hear him say it again, because unless he came around to break windows, I don't recall the lad at all." Amberside sounded slightly contemptuous. Had he seen the trap? Katy wondered.

"I see. In that case, why did you collar Jerry Edgerton near the scene of the fire? PC Callum reports that you were angry with the boy, and there was a struggle." Although addressing Amberside, Westlake was now looking directly at Katy, like a nearsighted snake that has lost its prey but has found another. She knew that he would notice her slightest reaction to the mention of Arthur's name. She kept a blank face and sat as still as possible.

"Collar the Edgerton boy? If you'll pardon me, do you consider

PC Callum the most reliable source, Inspector?" Amberside turned to Katy. "Didn't you tell me, darling, that he'd been imagining things?"

Katy hesitated. "As you know, we were partners on the force," she began haltingly.

Amberside broke in. "I'm sure we all want to be frank. He had a soft spot for Katy, you know, and unfortunately I let him under my roof for a while. Perhaps he started the fire himself."

Westlake ignored this barb and waited. Katy said nervously, "I, that is my husband and I, haven't seen Arthur for a while. He took our engagement—Terry's and mine—badly."

"Unspeakably, I should have said," Amberside declared, and rose to his feet. "Well. Is there anything else I can help you with? This business of the Edgerton fire seems to have fallen a bit flat."

Westlake pursed his lips. "Yes, I suppose it has. Unless we find the missing sword, of course."

Katy didn't know if this remark was dumb luck or a brilliant stroke, but it hit the mark, for Amberside couldn't disguise his perturbed emotions.

Westlake's eyes were canny now. "Do you have something to tell me about that?"

"A sword?" Amberside repeated, regaining some of his composure. "I had given up hope of ever recovering it. I told you the Edgerton boy might have been prowling around here. He must have stolen it."

"I'm confused. You see, my knowledge of this sword is a bit sketchy. All we found was a scabbard in the ashes of the Edgerton house. What sort of sword was it?"

"Medieval, very early medieval. It came into my father's possession many years ago."

"It's very valuable, then, I suppose?"

"Very."

Westlake appeared to ponder. "How do you think it got clear of the fire? Was it before or after? Did the boy take it? Is that why you accosted him on the street?"

Amberside's face colored slightly, but he replied without hesitation, "No, of course not. I already told you that was a fiction."

"Yes, you did tell me that."

Katy observed this game of cat and mouse with mounting concern. She frankly had no inkling what the stakes were. The sword seemed pointless, since Westlake hadn't even seen it. Why had he brought it up? All she could tell was that his real motive for visiting the house had not been revealed. The revelation, if it was on the brink of exposure, never came, because Jasper chose that moment to walk into the room.

"Mr. Amberside, sir? Begging your pardon, but I was looking for the leaf rake."

"Not now. I'm being interviewed by the police," replied Amberside curtly. The way Jasper suddenly stiffened would have been comical if it weren't for the genuine fear he betrayed.

Westlake turned to him. "And who might you be?"

Jasper looked imploringly at his master, who explained, "This is Jasper. He works in the garden, and he boards here. He came into my employ after the fire. The day after, actually." Westlake made a low noise in his throat that signified grudging acceptance of these useless facts. Jasper turned to go.

"Did Lady Penelope fire you for cause?" Westlake shot his question at Jasper's retreating back.

Jasper's head whipped around. "Beg your pardon, sir?"

"Your former employer, Lady Penelope Rees. I'm in charge of the Merlin case. I'm sure you're not totally ignorant of the affair, since as a matter of record you were let go at Emrys Hall three days after Sir Derek vanished. I merely wondered why you were sacked." The inspector's voice was languid and calm. "Weren't you the butler there for several years? Got on well, didn't you? It seems very odd, your leaving abruptly just then." The snake had hooded its eyes, Katy thought, and was at its most dangerous.

"I don't know what you mean." Jasper had turned around, his face a mask of fright.

"Is the question that hard to understand? I asked why you were sacked."

"I wasn't sacked. I left on my own, sir." Westlake waited silently, and the tactic worked. Jasper added in a rattled voice, "I didn't hurt anybody, I didn't steal anything, either."

"I wasn't aware that something was missing, other than Sir Derek."

Jasper looked nervously from the inspector to Amberside. He licked his lips with a pale, pointed tongue and said, "I only meant I was honest. There was no cause for being let go, none at all."

Amberside smiled. "That'll do, Jasper. No doubt your splendid composure has convinced the good inspector that you've committed every murder in the surrounding five counties."

Westlake rewarded that one with a grudging smile, but when Katy laughed, Jasper shot her a hard look. She stiffened in her chair seeing the hatred in his eyes. "It was a funny remark," she wanted to say, but Jasper had turned wooden-faced and left the room.

Katy stood up. "I think I'll go as well. I feel a bit of a fool sitting here in this veil."

"Nonsense, you look a picture," Westlake offered with quite insincere gallantry.

"Adorable," Amberside murmured.

When she turned to leave, Westlake muttered something under his breath. She couldn't resist asking, "What was that?"

"Felicitations. I was wishing you well on your upcoming marriage."

"Thank you."

Walking upstairs was a minor torment. She had the feeling that both men were laughing at her behind her back. She got to her room and sat down on the bed, undid the pins holding the veil, and held it thoughtlessly in her hands. Westlake's questions about the arson troubled her. She'd never known that Amberside was under suspicion. Why had he assaulted the boy? He must have been lying when he denied that. She realized that he kept a great deal from her—his whole life as Master Ambrosius was something he never spoke of, for example. Westlake hadn't shown his hand, but she felt he must have come to send her a message. The Westlake Katy knew wasn't accustomed to acting in a blatant fashion, yet he'd been playing the clumsy copper, indulging Amberside in his farcical theatrics.

You're in danger.

She felt she knew exactly what the message was. But whom was she in danger from? Jasper perhaps, if there had been violence connected with Derek Rees's disappearance. Katy had been on suspension for barely three weeks, yet her life on the police force seemed far away and shadowy, dim.

A car started up outside and pulled into the narrow turnaround in front of the house. Katy walked to the window. Westlake's police sedan was slowly negotiating the cramped drive. What was he thinking at that moment? She had no idea, but when she glanced down at her hands, she found she had been wringing the veil so hard that it was nearly ruined.

Just as she was preparing for bed that night, a knock came at the door. "Come in."

It was Amberside. His polite tap must have been one of those points of decorum he was fond of. "You look tired, darling. I was worried. I'm glad you're going to bed early."

She nodded absently, feeling surprisingly little joy at tomorrow's prospect. She was sitting at her vanity taking off face cream with a wadded tissue.

Amberside walked up behind her and started stroking her hair. "We've come a long way. Do you know how I think of us? As master and disciple, not just husband and wife." His voice sounded musing, almost dreamy.

She stopped dabbing at her cheeks. "Disciple? What a queer thing to say."

"Ah, don't be too literal. There are things one person can teach without the other even being aware of it. That's how marriages are. Do you know what I've taught you?"

"No."

"To let yourself go. I detected a raging love in you, waiting to be released. That's what you've longed for, isn't it?"

She flushed slightly. "I wouldn't call our relationship wild, Terry."

"You wouldn't? You just don't see what I do." He lifted her long ginger-colored hair in both hands as one might lift a wedding train to keep it from being sullied by contact with the earth. The gesture, which should have seemed tender, reminded her of a puppeteer picking up his strings. She sat very still, waiting for him to let go. Instead Amberside immersed his face in her hair and inhaled deeply.

"I—please don't."

Katy was sorry the instant the words escaped her. Amberside lifted his face and looked at her. He wasn't hurt. No, thank God, he was just surprised and concerned.

"You're right, I am tired." Katy raised her face and he kissed it before leaving.

When she got under the covers, Katy expected to have difficulty falling asleep, but she didn't. A heavy drowsiness fell over her almost immediately. The last thought she had was one of gratitude as she felt herself slide down the soft slope to unconsciousness.

Hours ticked by, unknown to her. There were no nightmares, but she did have a visitation from the soothing presence that had hovered over her dreams recently. Only this time the visit was more vivid, almost as if the presence wanted her to remember. A dream began in which Katy saw herself as a beast in a dark, fairy-tale land. The beast was hideous, a troll with a boar's head. It lived under a bridge, rutting in the river mud with yellow, curved tusks.

The beast was lonely. The neighboring villagers were in such fear of it that they crossed the bridge only at night, moving quickly and keeping their lanterns covered. As much as it ached to be with people, the beast couldn't desert its hiding place, because it had once greatly offended a powerful witch. She had placed a spell on the beast's tusks, which grew so fast that every morning they curved up and reached its eyes, threatening to blind it. The beast was wild with terror seeing how close the points came, but somehow, just when the horrible pain seemed inevitable, a beautiful maiden appeared on the bridge, carrying some apples in a basket of gold. She threw the apples down to the beast, and the instant it ate them, the tusks shrank back down, so that the danger was removed. Katy felt removed hearing this tale, but at the same time she was in it, was both beast and maiden.

The same ritual was repeated over and over again, until the day came when instead of eating the apples, the beast simply looked at them, tears rolling down its cheeks.

"What are you doing?" the maiden cried. "Eat them quickly or you will be blinded."

"I can't anymore," the beast replied, shaking its head.

"Why not?" the maiden asked sadly. "Haven't I come every day, a thousand times over, to save you?"

"Yes, that is true, but that does me no good, for I don't trust you to come again tomorrow." The maiden went away in tears. Watching her depart, the beast knew it had lied. In truth it had fallen in love with the maiden, but ashamed of its ugliness, it lacked the courage to tell her. The beast lay down in the river mud, thinking, "Better to die like this than to have her break my heart."

At that moment, however, the maiden ran back onto the bridge. "I love you," she cried, and she threw the last apple from her basket down to him. The beast's heart should have swelled with joy, but he groaned, unable to see where the apple had fallen. The tusks had grown swiftly, and with a terrible flash of pain, the beast was blind.

It must have been nearly dawn when a man's voice emerged from the dark. Katy stirred, feeling the weight of the quilted comforter being lifted from her. A rush of cool air greeted her body. Groggy, she felt her legs getting colder—her nightgown was being pushed up. "I didn't hear you," she mumbled. His arms were around her now, his mouth pressed through the cloth to her breasts.

"Let me, oh, let me."

The urgency of his body was heavy and strong. A flush of desire was spreading through her, too, and she didn't want to wake up. She wanted everything to happen in this half-slumber, where she knew she was beautiful. She didn't want the wedding now, didn't want to be wrapped in glaring white. If only her lover would always come to her in the dark and let her be beautiful.

Something was happening, though. The man's urgency began to turn rough. Her hands pushed at her eager groom, resisting the roughness of his touch. "Don't. Wait," she protested sleepily. Katy opened her eyes, and a hand went over her mouth to stop her from screaming.

"Don't scream. I have to." Jasper sounded afraid of her, yet desire fought with his fear. The predawn grayness shining through the window lit his face, revealing his sick, unquenchable need. Katy violently wrenched her head from side to side, trying to bite him, trying to release her muffled scream. She was fully awake now; her head was pounding.

"Jasper," she rasped. He pulled away, and his face betrayed unbearable fear. She reached out a hand and clawed him across the face. "You forget yourself," she said in a strange voice both seductive and metallic. "You know what I can do if I want to."

By now Jasper had jumped from the bed and was hastily pulling on his clothes. "You can't hurt me. He said you wouldn't." Jasper had backed toward the door, which flew open.

"Fool. I told you never to stay to sunrise."

Amberside stood in the doorway, shadowy in the half-light of dawn. He wore the faded brocade dressing gown he put on whenever he got up to make her breakfast. Katy fell back, suddenly weak and depleted.

"You?" she said almost inaudibly.

Amberside ignored her. "I don't think she'll give you any more trouble," he said in a dead tone.

Jasper shuffled nervously, then came back to the bed. Katy shrank back, opening her mouth to scream. "She's never made such a fuss before," he said, pinning her arms to the bed easily this time.

"No?" replied Amberside. Katy couldn't tear her eyes from the door where he stood, hands in his pockets. Amberside's eyes glowed, and she knew then the pure malevolence of someone who had planned, step by step, the insidious game of killing her soul. "I think she did shriek the other times," he said, turning to go. "But it's a big house and nobody heard her."

27
HEROICS

AS HE RAN PELL-MELL THROUGH THE FOREST, PANICKED AND AFRAID for his life, Arthur's mind kept screaming one word: "Coward!" It repeated itself relentlessly. "Coward, coward." Why hadn't he stayed to fight the dragon? He possessed a magical sword, or so they had told him, and he had been welcomed as the court's long-lost hero. There was no excuse for the rush of terror that had sent him flat on his belly in the dirt, covering his head to avoid the monster's fire-breath as it devastated the camp.

The dragon's first blast had blown a cloud of ashes and smoke furiously across the clearing. The lady in the felt hat had been directly under the beast's huge shadow. So had Pen and Melchior. They had all disappeared behind a gray veil as Arthur's eyes teared furiously. The tramp had taken his hand, shouting, "Wait here!" Then he, too, disappeared. A few seconds later Arthur felt the hilt of Excalibur being thrust into his hands. "I fetched it from the wagon," the tramp shouted. "Do you think you can—"

Another roar drowned out the tramp's words. *Do you think you can what?* Arthur thought now as he fled. Can stand and fight? Can save us? Whatever the court of miracles expected of him, Arthur had failed. In an instant, the wagon he had spent the night in exploded in a ball of fire. Despite not being able to see the monster, Arthur had jumped to his feet, grasping the sword in both hands. When the smoke cleared briefly, he could see the tramp's face, as stark and hard as granite.

"Get on my back, I'll carry you," the tramp shouted.

Arthur shook his head. "I'm strong enough, just run with me."

The tramp nodded. They set off at a trot, or something more like a frenzied drunken lurch, but it was the best Arthur could manage dragging the weight of the sword. Both men had seen Paddy Edgerton standing on the edge of the camp that morning in damp, bedraggled clothes. Now the tramp shouted his name, to no avail. He was unaccounted for, and a cloud of suspicion hung over him. There was little time to think about where he'd spent the night or whether he'd brought the attack upon them.

Arthur took the lead, clumsily bushwhacking with wide sweeps of the sword, occasionally looking over his shoulder to check on the tramp behind him. Soon the ground began to slope steeply, and it took all Arthur's concentration to stay on his feet. He didn't look over his shoulder for perhaps a hundred yards, and when he did, the tramp was gone.

"Lancelot," he shouted, using the tramp's name for the first time. Or did the man have a new name in this time and place? The answering echo was hollow and forlorn. The tramp seemed to have merged back into the tapestry of legend, like the rest of the court and the dragon itself.

The woods weren't deep, and Arthur had run to the edge of them in less than half an hour. From where he now sat, on a half-rotted stump, he could see a small farmhouse in the near distance. Should he go there and ask for help? It was unlikely anyone would put much stock in his absurd story.

"Lancelot," he shouted, cupping his hands over his mouth. "Lancelot." It seemed ridiculous. There was no Lancelot, there was nobody at all to verify that he wasn't loony. Arthur painfully raised himself from the rotting stump. His shins ached from barking against a sharp boulder in his flight, and his muscles felt weak and fluttery.

He could see a John Deere tractor combing straight furrows in a field of new rye. Brindled cows lowed in their pasture atop the rise as Arthur began to make his way slowly toward the farm. A thousand years ago, he thought with grim amusement, no one would have doubted his tale. The back of his shirt was charred and his hair matted with enough gritty ash to prove that he had survived a dragon attack. But he wasn't bloodied. With the exception of a few bramble snags and his banged-up shins, he hadn't a scratch on him.

With shameful certainty the tormenting thought returned. He had failed the court. And for that matter, he had probably failed Katy, too. Amberside would be marrying her in two days. No, one day was gone already, so it would be tomorrow. The threat he'd seen in Katy's eyes at the pub made Arthur's chest tighten. Amberside had won her unfairly, not in love or war.

The fringe of the woods where Arthur sat thinned out into stands of slender young birches. Their acid-green leaves shivered in the breeze, as if the dragon had frightened them, too. Arthur tasted a bitter woolliness in his mouth. The sword had become heavier and heavier as he dragged it along. Without a belt and scabbard, it wasn't possible to keep carrying the thing forever. Arthur dropped the blade onto the thin, patchy grass under the trees and gazed at it.

What do you want of me, anyway?

The sword was more than a cumbersome, useless weight. It had risen from the rubble of a lost kingdom he was once sworn to protect. But what did that mean now? Arthur didn't know. He regarded the tidy little farm in front of him and the clear blue sky overhead, amazed that such mundane things still existed. No, they didn't exist, not for him. He was with the dragons now. That's what set him apart, and the few others whose faces he now knew. The danger he stood in made no sense unless you were with the dragons.

Arthur stood up, his knees aching and stiff, the reluctant blade back in his hands. The only way to cope was to go on, so first things first. He couldn't very well go up to the tractor and say,

"Hullo, can you spare us a lift? Don't mind this. It's Caledfwlch—'hard lightning'—better known as Excalibur." That much seemed clear. But the dirt road leading to the farm probably joined up with a paved road somewhere up ahead. Arthur set out for it, skirting the new rye field, heading for the far edge of the property.

Under the warm May sun, he felt better—incredibly hungry but better. It hardly seemed possible that he'd been standing in a pub just the night before, and he was sorry now that he'd wasted his last few coins drinking. Arthur's shoes grew lighter, sloughing off their load of wet mud as the sun dried them. In a few minutes he crested a small rise and spied the motorway a quarter mile off. Suddenly a red Escort sedan approached him from behind, probably from the farm, and passed him. The driver was a middle-aged woman, who stared straight ahead. Tactful, he thought. Anyone who could ignore the sight of a man dragging a forty-pound battle sword down the road possessed remarkable tact. When he got to the motorway, the tarmac glistened in waves of heat. Arthur stood on the verge, considering.

Home. Westlake. Emrys Hall. Those were his three options, when all was said and done. Home was the safest, but it put his mother in danger. Westlake had the power to start up some kind of investigation, but what was there to investigate, so far as the police were concerned? Besides, he'd already burned his bridges there. Amberside, he remembered, had talked in the pub about getting an appointment with Westlake to get Katy reinstated. Surely Westlake was maintaining his position that Amberside was a respectable citizen, not someone who consorted with witches and conjured up mythical beasts.

Emrys Hall was the last and most logical choice. He could hide out there and perhaps scrounge a meal if he could get inside. He could also wait to see if Pen chanced to come home herself. Perhaps she'd made it back already, if she had escaped the camp alive.

Standing by the side of the road, Arthur craned his neck looking for signs of where he was. The tarmac stretched blankly in both directions. A few cars passed by, then a heavy lorry. A kid in one of the cars grinned and pointed at him. Arthur kept to the verge, head down. All at once a faint recollection stirred. He looked around. The road was still featureless, but he felt with sudden certainty that this was the same stretch of motorway where they'd found the body. Arthur waited for another van to pass, then dashed across the road.

Here.

The grass lining the slope of the ditch had grown higher since he'd last been there, obliterating any traces of a crime. The swath of short growth clipped back by the road crews was only a few yards wide. "There could be someone down there," Arthur thought. He had no idea why such a notion had entered his head, but he decided to go and have a look. The ditch was about twenty feet across and very deep. A rivulet ran through the bottom, he recalled, or it may have been accumulated rain that made the ground wet and spongy.

When he got there, Arthur found that he'd been right. Even in dry weather the soggy ground at the bottom of the ditch made sucking sounds under his shoes. Here the reeds stood nearly waist high. Merlin—the body they'd found—hadn't been thrown quite this far down the slope. A patch of shrubs bordered the opposite side, with a thin stand of alders and willows just beyond.

Arthur started spreading apart the rank growth with his hands, casting about the marshy ground. He didn't know exactly what he expected to find. Nothing, most likely. The reeds were raspy against Arthur's hands, and the saw grass inflicted invisible gashes like paper cuts. Arthur grimaced, then noticed a depression in the vegetation ten yards ahead. Anything could have made it—old tires tossed from a passing car, a fallen log. But he knew what it was even before he got close enough to see.

Paddy Edgerton lay faceup in his bed of damp weeds. His face had gone a claylike gray, and his mouth was open, as were his horrified eyes. Arthur bent down to touch him. The corpse was cold, and none of the clothing was torn. It looked rumpled and damp, just as it had when Arthur had last seen Paddy that morning on the edge of camp. Arthur looked up at the sky—the sun stood just after noon, he judged. Gently he closed the staring eyes and stood up again.

So now he knew something more about Mordred: he had a sense of humor. It amused him to leave another corpse to baffle the police. Or was it Arthur who had been meant to find it? He looked down again. There was no blood anywhere, but the impossible angle of the head told him that Paddy's neck had been broken—just like Merlin's. Arthur lifted the hands, looking carefully. Yes. Faint traces of blue paint were visible under the fingernails.

"See what you've done? I hope you're satisfied."

"I didn't do anything." Arthur swung his head around slowly. As surely as he had known about the body, he now knew that his accuser would be the boy. It took a moment to spot him, half-hidden in the tall grass. Jerry Edgerton had been sitting there for an indeterminate time.

"You stole the sword," he said bitterly. "Do you call that not doing anything?" Edgerton pointed silently to Excalibur, which Arthur had stuck into the soft earth, where it stood beside the corpse like a cross.

Arthur got up and waded through the thick reeds toward the boy. "Did you follow your dad here?" he asked, looking down at Edgerton, who didn't move.

"I didn't follow him, I followed you. I've been hanging about this stretch of road. I had a hunch someone would come along. It's where they found the old man's body, isn't it?"

"Did you know your dad was down here?" Arthur asked soberly. He reached out to touch Edgerton's shoulder, but the boy recoiled.

"Save your pity. He wasn't any use to us, not for a long time."

Arthur tried not to be shocked by the boy's callousness. He knew that in the families where things are worst there are few tears. Keeping an objective tone he said, "If you didn't know he was down here, then I suppose you didn't see who killed him?" He couldn't help interrogating the boy, although he tried to take the edge off his copper's voice.

When there was no answer, the two of them simply stayed where they were, Arthur standing over Edgerton, the boy staring at the body. They seemed to be keeping some strange vigil. By the swish of tires from the motorway, they knew that cars were constantly passing by, but none stopped. The ditch was deep enough to keep them out of sight.

Arthur broke the hostile silence. "What do you think we should do?"

"I don't care. Leave him here. It would probably be easier on my mum."

Arthur shook his head. "No, it wouldn't. Always having to worry, not knowing what had happened to him—that would be much worse than finding out." He stopped, realizing that despite his good intentions, he couldn't actually notify Edie Edgerton, because that entailed calling the police, and he couldn't risk surfacing in public, not yet.

The boy sensed something. "Are you on the run, too?"

Arthur was startled. "You could say that, although I haven't done anything wrong. It's not the police I'm running away from, but . . ." The sentence drifted off.

"Keep your bloody secrets, I don't care. I'm going." The boy abruptly took off, climbing up the steep grassy slope.

"Wait, we should stick together." Edgerton turned back, uncertain for a moment. "What I mean is, I could help you and you could help me. My mother has a house in town. You could stay there. Once we're safe, I could call the police. There's someone there I trust."

"And what do you want from me?" Edgerton asked suspiciously. Arthur decided to take a chance. "I need you to show me where you got the sword. I didn't steal it. It came to me rightfully."

"You lie," Edgerton spat out.

"Do you think it's yours, then?"

"It was me as found it. It came to me, nobody else." The boy bit his lip, sorry to have divulged even this scrap of information.

"Then show me where you found it. Someone's after me, and I need to gather people who can help me. Right now they're scattered and lost, but if I can go back over the trail, I have a chance of locating them."

"Who's after you?" Edgerton asked warily.

Arthur drew a deep breath, deciding to take a bigger risk.

"Amberside. You know him. He was the man who collared you when your house was burning down. You and I both suspect he started the fire, don't we?"

Edgerton couldn't disguise his surprise. "I thought it was my dad."

Arthur shook his head and said gently, "No, son, your dad was on the right side, whatever you may think. He prayed that you wouldn't be hurt in the fire." The boy looked away. "Amberside wants the sword. He's likely to have looked for it everywhere, trying to get to whoever might know about it."

Edgerton looked back. "You're right. You do need my help." He pushed his lanky black hair back from his eyes.

"The thing is, we have to work quickly. I'm no match for Amberside alone. If there are others who know about the sword, we need to contact them. There *is* someone else, isn't there?" Edgerton hesitated, then nodded curtly. The boy wouldn't relinquish control, Arthur realized, but his unwillingness to cooperate seemed to be softening.

"Okay, I'll show you," Edgerton finally said. "But I don't need to stay in your mother's house." He edged these words with faint contempt.

"You don't know how important this is," Arthur said gratefully. "Someone I love is in grave danger, the way your dad was. Amberside isn't just bad, he has a terrible power over people. He has power over her—my friend, I mean."

"What can you do about it?"

Arthur fought against a wave of hopelessness. "I don't know. I just can't stand by, do you understand? I would've saved your dad, too, if I could."

The boy stiffened and his gaze traveled up the slope. He was anxious to climb out of there.

"Before we go, I have to do one thing," Arthur said, touching Edgerton's arm. The boy shrugged, not communicating anymore. Arthur pulled the upright sword out of the ground and allowed the blade to rest lightly across Paddy Edgerton's chest. He lifted it again to touch each gray, stiffened hand, then the pale forehead. "I couldn't protect you, and for that I ask forgiveness," he thought, "but let this death be a beginning, not an end."

Aloud he said only, "I commend you to God," remembering the words vaguely from funeral services. Arthur had the feeling that Paddy Edgerton had not simply been a murder victim—he had chosen death, had walked into it willingly. The circumstances were clouded, but Arthur was sure it had happened that way nonetheless. For some, healing is too much to bear, and they hand it back, exchanging it for the fear they are accustomed to.

"Did you notice? His legs are straight. I hated him for walking out, but at least he had that much." There was an unexpected softness in Edgerton's voice, as if he had been pulled from being beyond reach.

"Do you want to?" Arthur asked gently, passing the sword to the boy. Wordlessly Edgerton lifted it, touching the blade to his father's forehead. The moment evoked in Arthur's mind a scene forgotten since boyhood, a faded color picture from a book of Arthurian tales. It was a sad scene, King Arthur dying in defeat on the battlefield. He was lying on the ground, mortally wounded by his bastard son, Mordred, whom Arthur had slain in return. The blade Excalibur still held in hand, he regarded his son's corpse with tragic mien.

The facing page told the story of Arthur's last moments. A single knight, Sir Bedivere, survived to remain by the king's side when the battle ended. Arthur had turned to him and said, "I am dying. Take Excalibur and throw it into that lake you see in the distance. Then return and tell me what you saw."

Bedivere trudged through the fallen and maimed bodies, ignoring the groans of the dying. He was gone an hour, and when he returned, he came empty-handed.

"Have you done as I bade?" Arthur asked. Bedivere nodded. "And what did you see?"

Sir Bedivere shook his head. "Nothing, sire, only the sword sinking into the water."

Arthur's face turned dark, and even while dying his displeasure was strong. "You haven't done as I commanded. Go again."

Bedivere went back to the lake where he had hidden Excalibur among the rocks, unable to bear throwing the sword into the water. The knight had only one arm, but now he raised the sword, circled it around his head, and flung it out over the lake. It tumbled end over end, then a woman's arm reached out of the water and caught the sword by the jeweled hilt. Astonished, Sir Bedivere watched the hand hold Excalibur high for a poised instant before pulling it back into the depths of the lake. He did not have to be told that the king had drawn his last breath.

Coming back to himself, Arthur saw that Edgerton was still resting the sword's tip softly against his father's forehead. Arthur looked at Edgerton's bleak face and realized what he was seeing. In legend, Bedivere, the last knight to see Arthur alive, had wandered the earth until he died broken, a recluse, but the web of time had drawn him back.

Uncannily they had all come back in place, enacting the roles from which fate would not release them. The boy in the roadside ditch was compelled to launch his father's soul as Bedivere had launched the soul of one who had been like a father to him. Arthur had no way of knowing if the two were the same person. He didn't even know what truth to place in the story of Sir Bedivere, one of a thousand versions in the endless recounting of Arthurian lore.

Yet what did that lore express, at its heart, if not the sorrowful glory of being human? Generation after generation, sons saw their fathers die and wept for not loving them well enough or long enough or truly enough. The glory was woven with the sorrow, and the lessons of myth and mortality, each blending into the other, would hold true until time's net opened and let its captives go.

Suddenly the boy murmured, "I will see you through the fire." He seemed to say it from his depths, as if in prayer. Whatever the phrase meant to him, nothing more was revealed. Words weren't needed now. Edgerton handed Excalibur back. The gesture was slow, measured, in the tempo of ritual, beyond anything Arthur could remember yet more fitting than anything memory could supply.

Edgerton looked up. "Can we go? Someone's coming." He looked tense, his eyes haunted by thoughts Arthur couldn't read. The boy was right—a gray sedan had pulled to the edge of the ditch, and the driver's side window started to roll down.

Arthur held back, wanting to understand the sacred moment that had just passed. He knew there was a clue in it, and then he grasped it. *You have tried the power of the sword. Now try throwing it away.* The Edgerton boy was there to show him that. For one moment, Arthur and the boy had risen to a privileged place where everyday acts took on mythical meaning. When humanity cannot ascend to that place, it is exalted in legend with the name Camelot.

Arthur could see the boy in a new light now, not as a dubious character randomly crossing his path but as a perfect piece in a perfect game. In seeing that, and only then, was it possible to feel love. Love is the tapestry woven of perfection, and each thread in it is as precious as all the others.

"Aren't you coming?"

Edgerton's anxious question drew Arthur back. "Listen, don't worry about the car for now. I want you to have this back." Arthur grabbed Edgerton's hand and wrapped it around the hilt of the sword.

"What?"

"I gave it to your dad, but he wouldn't keep it. It was meant for you."

The boy looked down, stupefied. "But why?"

"To start a new legend, I guess." Arthur laughed, and the weight of shame he had felt since running away from the dragon lifted. He realized that he had followed Merlin's lead in bestowing the sword out of love. It was the first step, small but crucial, in building the new Camelot.

"Let's go," Edgerton whispered urgently, his face glowing with excitement. Arthur nodded and stooped down to be better hidden in the tall reeds. With the boy following, he headed along the ditch. Fifty feet ahead they could creep out into a thicket unnoticed. They didn't wait to see the gray sedan's door open and thus never saw the curious spectator descend to search the bottom of the ditch and make his alarming discovery.

28

THE OLD QUEEN

THE MAGICIAN.

"You are beloved of the old gods, who will help you prevail in every situation," Amberside muttered to himself. He was alone in the kitchen, seated at the rough-hewn oak table he had known since childhood.

Ace of Wands.

"The final conflict is at hand."

The next card slipped easily into the pattern. Nine of Pentacles.

"A card of supreme satisfaction. Your efforts have led to victory." Amberside smiled, marveling anew at the tarot's power, which infallibly mirrored his own. He had almost completed the pattern known as the star. Six cards, radiating like spokes from a hub, surrounded a central gap where the last card would go. A child might have seen it as a snowflake. Amberside saw it that way when he was a child.

Outside, night was falling under leaden skies. The gloom in the kitchen was profound, but Amberside didn't need to see what he was doing. He rubbed his shoes over the worn patch in the linoleum, a patch he had made many years ago swinging his feet at the dinner table.

A dark shape seemed to materialize out of the shadows near the stove. "Go away," Amberside said irritably. Morgan le Fay had been pestering him for days. It was nearly impossible for her to hold a shape in this world unless he helped will it. She even needed him in order to enter Katy. Like the other wizards, she was losing her power as the future rolled on.

"Listen to me."

Amberside shook his head, trying to concentrate on the cards.

"You must."

He glared in the direction of the stove. With painful exertion Fay projected a form into the room, glowing dully. Her face wore a look of warning. "The last thing I need is a second mother," he thought. The kitchen had always been his mother's domain. She had fretted over his asthma and kept him from contact with other children. Most of all his mother liked to have him read the cards at this very table. "Terry, you're going to be something special," she would say as she rolled out marzipan rounds to cover the black fruitcake she made every holiday.

"Listen."

Fay's voice was desperate now, muffled and quavery like someone trying to speak underwater. Amberside noted her struggle with satisfaction. It irked him to think that there were powers greater than his. No, it infuriated him, which was why he had played this elaborate game with Merlin. He would be the first of the wizards who didn't grow puny with time.

"Get away, won't you?" he said petulantly. "It's all going perfectly. I only have to wait." The wraith of Morgan le Fay trembled but persisted. Amberside fingered the card that would go into the center of the star, the one called "the heart of the matter."

Death.

Amberside frowned, sitting back in his chair. *Death?* He stared at the depiction of a visored knight in black cloak looming like a giant over the landscape. Three people kneeled in supplication, holding out offerings. In the corner of the room, Morgan's form glowed brighter, as if encouraged by the card.

"If you don't need me, I'm going to bed early."

Amberside's head jerked around to see who had interrupted him. Standing in the doorway, Katy backed away nervously. "I hope I'm not intruding."

"Of course you're intruding," Amberside said, scowling. "I would remember if I had called you, wouldn't I?"

"I was just getting a bag from the closet to pack. I'd like to see my people, just for a few days."

"Do as you like, just don't expect to find a place for you here when you get back."

Katy looked even more nervous. "It's not much to ask."

"That depends. I'm not fond of disloyalty. What would you do out there anyway, try to prove that you can go back? You're such a fool."

Katy bowed her head. "It's only for a few days," she repeated weakly. Amberside didn't bother to reply. Unable to think of anything new, she began all over again, "So if you don't need me—"

"Idiot!" Angrily Amberside swept the cards onto the floor. "Damn it, the pattern's spoiled. Pick those up."

Katy turned on the light and stepped into the kitchen. The shadowy glow near the stove fluttered and faded away; Katy didn't notice. She was kneeling down and silently gathering the scattered pack. She and Amberside both knew this was purely a gesture of humiliation, a reminder. "There," she said, putting the stack on the table.

"You missed one."

Katy got back down on her hands and knees, fumbling for the stray card that had slid under the counter. Without a word she put it in front of Amberside, who turned it over.

Death.

Amberside stared in mute rage, as if she had done it on purpose. Before he could break out in a fury, however, Katy vanished, which suited him well enough. Amberside carefully reshaped the star, then riffled through the deck until he found the Magician again. He placed it in the center where it belonged.

After leaving the kitchen, Katy slowly walked down the long corridor leading to the chapel. She had started going there a lot lately, mostly because Amberside avoided that part of the house. She stopped in front of a large bay window overlooking the street. In the dusk she saw a shabby woman—one of the homeless, probably—standing on the curb outside the gates. Katy waved and the woman waved back before moving off down the street.

This was their ritual. Every day the same woman waited, staying as long as it took before Katy appeared at one window or another. Today, when the heat of the May sun began to linger into evening, her habitual outfit of green felt hat and coat looked particularly inappropriate. After she waved, the woman always left, making no movement toward the house. Nothing else ever happened between them, but in some way Katy knew that this was one of the only things in her life that Amberside didn't know about.

As Katy entered the chapel, she thought of locking it and jamming a heavy chair against the door. What good would it do? Her heart didn't seem to be beating; her chest felt constricted and cold. She had tried rebelling. Just that morning she had worked up the courage to phone the police, hoping to reach Westlake. Dully she had picked up the receiver.

"Ma'am?" a voice said. It was Jasper.

"I—I—" Katy stammered.

"I'm phoning in the grocery order. Would you be needing the line?"

She had hung up without answering, and her head fell backward. She was spent. Of all the dark fairy-tale spaces she had ever dreamed of, this was the final one, from which no reprieve was possible. The enchantment of her own fears had proved the most inescapable, and *he* knew it.

Katy walked to the front of the chapel and knelt behind a pew. *Father, forgive me, who have sinned against Thee.*

It was a dry, pointless prayer. Katy sighed. Her lungs ached from crying. Her hands were cut and clumsily bandaged since she had smashed the mirrors in the house. Amberside laughed at that, even when she tore down the antique gilt mirror at the bottom of the stairs. He let her wander his house like a ghost—no, a banshee. Weren't they the ones that wailed?

"You're not a prisoner, you know," he said. "Here's a key, the door's wide open. I'll even have Jasper bring the car around."

But her shame was like chains shackled to her legs, preventing her from walking out. Her last hope was that someone would rescue her on the appointed day. She didn't expect a wedding, of course, but in some desperate way the invitations she had written by hand and posted might send a message to the outside world. The day had come, however, and the chapel had been empty. Jasper must have filched the envelopes from the box before they were picked up.

Katy looked up at the high Gothic windows over the pulpit. A Victorian merchant prince had built the house, and in his dotage he had added a chapel to insure his connection to God. That was long ago. Now there were holes in many of the leaded panes. Several saints and martyrs had lost an eye or a nose to the weather, leaving gaps for the wind to blow through.

Salve me, Jesu Christe. Jesu Domine, salve me.

The choked-out prayer came against her will, and she wondered why it was coming in the old language. Like a thread the Latin pulled her back to another time. She still felt the cold stone floor against her knees, but she wasn't sure where she was anymore. Through the windows the town clock chimed six, which seemed odd. Convents didn't have clocks, not back then. Time was kept by rounds of praying, beginning before dawn.

Now she heard steps outside her cell, and somehow Katy knew it was the other sisters. There would be no more clocks as she felt herself carried back to the old time. "Matins, Reverend Mother," a timid voice called through the door.

"Coming."

Katy felt herself rising from knees stiffened from years of ritual. After all this time she still didn't feel safe. *He* knew where she was, even if she had fled the castle with the battered cup in her saddlebags. Arthur had brought it to her the night before Camelot fell, carrying it in a burlap sack. "Merlin isn't coming down from his tower, so all I can do for you is to give you this." He touched her cheek and tenderly said her name: Guinevere.

Now Katy was crying like a child. She saw the queen draw back, confused. "Why are you giving me this, sire? Is something about to happen?"

Arthur avoided her question. "Just keep it. No one knows that I have taken it and substituted another in its place. If we are separated, bear this with you wherever you go, and wait for me. By this sign we will be reunited."

Guinevere had arrived in the convent at Glastonbury under cover of night, but it was impossible to hide her identity. She had been patroness to many of the sisters. The abbess, at first overjoyed by the visit, grew somber when she heard of the catastrophe. "The world is very far away from us. No one will reach you behind these walls," she vowed.

"No one you can imagine," Guinevere thought to herself. The sisters kept calling her "Your Majesty" until she stopped them. "From now on call me Sister Ginevra," she said. "That's close enough to my real name." She would have preferred to have no name at all, to better protect the convent from *him.* She set the battered cup on her window ledge, and it did keep her safe, but although *he* was never able to penetrate into her cell, bitterness and grief did. One night she slipped out to the stables and let loose her horse, the one she had ridden from the castle, hitting its flanks with a switch until it ran off across the fields. No ladies-in-waiting or pages had fled with her, because none had survived.

Every evening at vespers Sister Ginevra blessed the memory of her husband and remembered his promise to come for her. Only it never happened. She died before anyone came, and with her the memory of the old queen died in the land.

Lifetime after lifetime she came back, fulfilling her pledge to wait. Katy saw herself sometimes as a child among the nuns, sometimes as a war refugee or an orphan whose parents had died in a famine. Her pursuer was relentless, however. She never saw his face, but she felt that the wars and plagues that dogged her through history were his means of intimidating her, wearing down her resolve.

Ages rose and fell, and the one constant was the battered cup, which somehow never left her care. Sometimes she found it by accident buried in a convent garden. Sometimes it was given to her for safekeeping by a dying abbot or wandering friar. Most marvelously, she once found it in the crystal cave—that was a beautiful time, when she felt fully herself and even lived for a while in Merlin's sanctuary. But other lives carried no remembrance, and eventually the perpetual vigil grew dry and pointless, like her prayers. The day came when she no longer recognized the Grail at all. She threw it away in a careless moment, hardly thinking about it.

Mordred saw his chance.

Katy stood up, aware that she'd thought *his* name for the first time. *To think I even loved him.* She raised her head and looked out the chapel windows at the gathering dusk. She understood her position fully now. *He* was going to put her through the final torture. That's what he'd had in mind all along. It wasn't going to be torture by fire or the rack (although she knew now that he'd never been reluctant to try these on her). He was going to torture her by pretending they were married, just that. It would be very ordinary and yet, at the most unexpected moments, it would be terrible beyond hell.

A banging noise came from the back of the chapel. Katy felt no impulse to turn around. It didn't matter if Amberside had come to mock her.

"Katy?"

Arthur's voice. She let out a small, bitter laugh. Amberside had taught her all about illusions. He could make it appear that Arthur was standing under her window at night, or he could project Arthur's face at the end of a dark corridor, anxiously searching for her. These conjurings always melted away, taking a piece of her with them.

"Don't you know me, Katy?"

Arthur walked the length of the chill stone nave and touched her shoulder. He wore a gentle expression on his face. She shuddered, remembering the fangs he had once bared at night when he had appeared at her bedside, leaning over to kiss her.

"Listen to me. Get up, we're going." His hands were lifting her up off her knees. She couldn't cry out, but she had enough strength to pull away, writhing like a cat.

O divine Redeemer, have mercy upon me who am unworthy.

Arthur backed off. He seemed tense, as if expecting an intruder. Katy lifted a fist and smashed it into his chest. Amberside had done a good job. Her bandaged knuckles seemed to hit solid flesh, and the groan from Arthur's lips was heart-wrenchingly realistic. She fell back on her knees and spied a black beetle creeping under a nearby pew. For some reason it seemed like a good idea to crawl under there and eat it.

"No."

Arthur—or was it his illusion?—held her back, and when she looked up, his face was creased with pain. "I've given him the sword," he said in a low voice. "He's letting you go. But I can't be sure he'll keep his end of the bargain."

"You don't have to conspire, you know. I'm well rid of her."

Amberside had come in by the back of the chapel. Arthur looked around. The man was twenty yards away, but he had had no difficulty hearing what had been whispered.

"You promised to keep off."

Amberside shrugged. "I'm as interested as you are in getting her off the premises," he replied carelessly. "She's crazy, and she'd have to be dumped anyway." Arthur was trying again to coax Katy up off the floor, but when she saw Amberside, she crouched lower, covering her head with her hands.

"I told her once that you were the Fool," Amberside said, advancing down the aisle. "No offense. It's just my hobby, the tarot. And she was the High Priestess. Do you know what those cards have in common?"

"Leave us alone."

Amberside ignored him. "A refusal to face life. That's the best way to put it. Both cards signify an addiction to fantasy. Don't blame me if she crashes into reality. It had to happen. In her case, I don't think she can take it."

"That's for me to worry about," Arthur said grimly. But sensing how deeply agitated she had become, Katy wondered if she really had gone mad.

Amberside was holding the sword in his hands, examining it

under the waning rosy blue light of the stained-glass windows. "This is a most valuable object. I've exercised great pains to find it. And now it's mine." Suddenly he whipped the blade in front of Arthur's face, missing it by a millimeter. "You see? I am leaving you alone, compared to what I could do."

Amberside threw the blade into the air as light as a toy and caught it by the haft. He was in fine fettle. "May I address you as Fool?" Not looking at him, Arthur had managed to gather Katy up and was holding her against his chest. "What I'm curious about, Fool, is what you know about this sword. Has it gained power over the ages or has it lost it? We really should find out."

"I know you killed people to try and get it. And I suppose whatever you've done to Katy is part of that, too."

"In a way. I didn't have a scheme, but I had some help. Did you know that my mother's name was Fay? She's very fond of me, and it's comforting to bring her around every once in a while. Katy served nicely. It was only a matter of bringing out a certain side of her, as you know." Amberside's words made Katy shudder, the memory of possession flooding back. Amberside paused to reflect. "But you still haven't answered my question. What do you know about the sword?"

"Get out of our way," Arthur said curtly. "That's not part of the bargain."

Whatever Amberside might have said was cut off by Katy, who whispered, "Are you real?" She was looking up wide-eyed into Arthur's face. The question amused Amberside, who burst out laughing. "If you're real, you'll let me die, won't you?"

"A very sensible request," remarked Amberside.

The clang of shod hooves sounded thunderous in the small enclosed space. The harsh ring of iron on stone almost drowned out Katy's scream. "What is it?" Arthur demanded.

A split second later he had his answer as an enormous gray stallion burst through the door behind the pulpit, smashing it to bits. It reared, thrusting its hoofs through a side window, hurling colored splinters in all directions. As if in a slow-motion nightmare, Katy saw blood spurting from around the horse's fetlocks. The animal loomed enormous in the small chapel. Katy wrenched herself free from Arthur's arms and reached out for Amberside. "Stop it," she pleaded.

"She still seems to need me," Amberside remarked calmly.

Arthur ignored him. "Come here, Katy, you'll be safe with me."

Katy shook her head violently. "Get out. He's making all this happen. It's the only way."

She saw Arthur hesitate, then he tore the sword from Amberside's grasp. "Halt!" Arthur shouted, attracting the horse's attention. Katy watched the animal wheel at right angles, fix a bulging black eye on Arthur, and charge. It wasn't a mad, motiveless charge but one full of grim purpose. The slow-motion nightmare made everything as clear as crystal. Katy saw the flecked sweat on the horse's flanks and the pink flesh inside its nose. Strangely, these details registered in her mind before she noticed the most obvious and dangerous thing: the horse had a rider.

"You can stop this," she begged Amberside. "Let him go."

Amberside shook his head. "I want to see if the sword is still with him."

Arthur had dropped to one knee now, holding the weapon up to strike at the horse's underbelly when it rode over him. An ironic smile crossed his lips, as if he had expected Amberside to pull something as theatrical as this—a mounted knight in full armor charging at him. The knight wore his visor closed, and the lance he carried by his side was lowered, aimed directly at Arthur's head.

Katy looked at Amberside's impassive face and closed her eyes.

"Halt!" Arthur shouted again.

Against her will, Katy opened her eyes and saw the mounted horse close with Arthur. The mailed knight swung his lance down as Arthur dodged to the left. Too late. The lance tip smashed into Arthur's skull, the power of the blow lifting Arthur bodily into the air. His torso slumped limply as the horse's rear hoof swiped sideways, crushing one outstretched leg.

"Very satisfactory," Amberside remarked. "I had my suspicions it was never his." Arthur was long past caring. A bloody smear trailed behind him as he slid down the side of a pew. Lifting the sword from Arthur's outstretched hands, Amberside said to Katy, "You're right. I could have stopped it."

There was no adrenaline left in her body, no scream in her throat. She felt an immense tiredness. A black veil falling over her eyes delivered the release she longed for.

When Katy woke up, she was alone and it was morning. A whole night must have passed, although Katy remembered nothing about it. She sat up, groggy and confused. Every time Amberside inflicted one of these waking dreams, she felt herself pulled deeper into the morass, finding it harder to reorient herself. At first she had been desperate to keep a grip on reality. Now a part of her was increasingly grateful for blurred edges, because if these tormenting scenes were actually real, how could she survive?

Katy looked down, half-expecting to see the dress she had been wearing in the chapel, but instead she was in her nightgown.

There was a rap on the door. "Arthur?" she whispered faintly.

The door opened. "Here's your breakfast, ma'am." Jasper set the tray down in front of her, ignoring the way she cringed. He walked over and pulled the curtains. "It's rather chilly this morning. Would you prefer the window open or closed?"

She looked at him, frightened and repelled. He had never returned to her room in the night, as far as she knew, but she loathed him and his show of familiarity. Was Jasper wandering between dream and reality as she was?

"Open a little," he said to himself, cranking the window. "Will that be all, ma'am?"

Katy slowly nodded. He left, stopping at the door to give a quick, respectful nod. Katy pushed the tray off the bed, and it clattered onto the Turkish carpet. A delicate sugar bowl spilled its contents. She picked up the bowl and hurled it against the wall, smashing the thin, translucent china the way Arthur's head had been smashed in her dream.

Another tap at the door, and Amberside stuck his head in. "There's an antiques fair on the other side of Wells. Do you want to come, darling?" She turned her head away. "Ah, you're a little tired. Stay in bed, then, and rest. I'll be back noonish." Ignoring the shattered china and spilt sugar on the floor, he shut the door, and she heard his quiet, decisive steps going down the hall.

Katy got up and walked to the window. Her pursuer had caught her after all, and she hadn't a scrap of power to defend herself. The ways of wizards were lost on her, but she knew enough to realize that *he* was manipulating moments in time, fashioning a prison of events that had spun out of her control. Soon no one would remember her, or if they did, it would just be as Mr. Amberside's invalid wife, who never left the house.

Tears came now, hot and bitter, and they might have blinded her to everything else had she not glanced out toward the street to see the homeless woman in the green felt hat and coat. She had never come this early before, and instead of searching each window to find where Katy might be, she was staring directly into Katy's eyes.

In a rush Katy's soul flew out to her like a bird dashing itself against the bars of its cage. The woman down below smiled and waved, as she did every day. Katy closed her eyes in despair. Her soul couldn't escape. She was where she was. Down on the street the woman waved again, puzzled that there had been no response, but Katy stood still. It seemed pointless to wave back.

29
INTO THE MAZE

PEG CALLUM PUT THE KEY INTO THE LOCK AND TURNED IT. OR rather she tried to turn it, but the lock was jammed. Dusk was drawing on, and the porch was unlit. "It sometimes sticks," she said. Then the light went on, and a stranger's face, bewildered but calm, appeared.

The door opened. "Yes, can I help you?"

It was a middle-aged woman, about Peg's age and height. She was wiping her flour-dusted hands on her apron and trying hard not to appear put out.

"Who are you?" Peg stammered. She felt Derek's hand on her shoulder.

"Pardon me? I was about to ask you the same thing. I saw someone standing out here on the steps, so I assumed you wanted me. Or was it my husband?" The woman acted polite but wary.

Over her shoulder, a man could be seen slumped in a lounge chair watching TV. "Is it from the ads, Alice?" he called, reluctant to get up.

"No." The woman turned back to Peg. "We found a stray cat and put it in the papers. That's not what you're about, is it?"

"I need to come in," Peg said abruptly, realizing how strange she must sound. Derek drew her back slightly from the door. "We thought we had the right house, Mrs. . . . ?"

The woman didn't answer. She was beginning to stare. Derek gave a warning glance behind him, where Sis and Tommy were about to pile out of the car. "Wait," he signaled. "Something's wrong."

Peg kept fumbling with the key in her hand. "This is my house, you see," she said in a careful, reasonable tone.

"Your house? Archie!" The woman in the doorway needed reinforcement now.

Her husband lumbered up, a cross look on his face. "What is it, anyway, if it's not the ad? This is Sunday, you know. A man would like some peace in his own castle."

Derek took the key from Peg's trembling hand. "We were told that this was a rental, by the agency. They gave us the key."

"Rental? That's daft. You've got the wrong place, mate." The husband took the key and tried it in the lock. "See? No good—does that satisfy you?"

"Absolutely. Sorry to bother." Derek took Peg's arm and walked her quickly back to the car. Behind him the man was keeping watch, waiting for them to leave.

"It takes all kinds," the woman said. And the door slammed shut.

Peg looked pale and shaken. "What's wrong?" Sis asked when she got back to the car.

Derek opened the rear door and eased her in beside the boys. "We're being erased, I think," Derek replied. "Or perhaps the word is *expunged.*"

"But it's my house," Peg repeated numbly, as if saying so might make things as they were before. Derek got into the driver's seat and started the engine.

"Just try and think," Pen urged her sister. "You were able to get a look over that woman's shoulder. Were your things in there?"

Peg shook her head in disbelief. "I shouldn't have left. I should have stayed put."

"I don't think it would have made any difference," Derek ventured. "I've been wondering how *he* would handle our return. He could have chosen violence. God knows he's not averse to that. But he's being subtle this way, I suppose, or amusing." The car turned out of Fellgate Lane. Peg couldn't resist looking wistfully over her shoulder.

"Are you all right?" Pen asked, reaching from the front seat to take her sister's hand.

"I don't know. It's such a shock."

"Derek, we need to find someplace to go," Pen said anxiously.

"I can't promise anything at this point," he said. "What this means is that we've all been forgotten. I assume that's his tactic. You described the court of miracles as those who walked away. That must be fine with him, because we're being driven into enforced oblivion."

"Does that mean that we won't be missed at school?" Tommy asked. "Or by our families?"

"I'm sorry, but I think that's exactly what it means."

They all sat mutely as the sullen gray streets passed by. The afternoon was turning cloudy, and the diffused light flattened the shadows, blending everything into uniform drabness. The car felt closed-in and oppressive. A few minutes later they were back in the country, but it did nothing to lift their spirits.

"It's all happening very fast, isn't it?" Pen said, breaking the silence. "Emrys Hall could be in ruins by now, I suppose."

"Do you want to see?" Derek asked.

Pen shook her head and stared out the window again. "I feel invisible. I have this fantasy that we could stroll down the High Street and no one would notice us. Funny, considering how hard some people have been searching for you." Derek stopped at a filling station, where Pen's premonition seemed to come true. The attendant barely looked at them while he pumped the fuel, taking the bills from Derek's hand and handing his change back silently.

"It's quite a trick, isn't it?" Tommy said when they were on the road again. "He's turned us into ghosts without killing us first."

"Let's find Merlin," Sis suggested. "He won't let this happen to us."

"Why not?" Tommy said bitterly. "He's let everything else

happen. It's the way the game was set up. He's not here, and there's no guarantee he ever will be."

"I'd call it a very cruel tease," Peg remarked. The two sisters met with their eyes, and Pen thought, "She's just realizing that there's no turning back." She remembered Peg as an infant nursing in their mother's arms. Because Pen was so much older, she wasn't jealous. She enjoyed observing the baby, who looked like an angel fallen to earth by mistake. Over the years as Peg grew up, she became more detached, more out of place.

She was one of those people, Pen thought, who have a hard time making friends with this world. It took a lot of work to accept that life brought pain, to make a workable peace with sickness and death and all the lesser horrors of everyday existence. Such people, if they fashion a rock of faith, never doubt God or rail against fate, but they never quite accept things either. After years of trying, Peg was being crushed. She looked bewildered and lost, staring out the window at the empty gray places. The fields and hedgerows looked foreign under leaden skies. This was no more their homeland than the anonymous houses were their home.

Suddenly Sis cried out from the backseat. "Stop, stop."

Derek looked in the rearview mirror. "What is it?"

"I saw someone. Didn't you see him, Tommy?" Tommy shook his head. "It was Joey, right back there." The little boy had rolled down the side window and was leaning out. "You have to stop or we'll miss him."

A stream of cars blocked the road in both directions, and it took a moment before Derek could pull off, negotiate a turn, and go back.

"There *is* someone. I can see him," Tommy said, getting excited. A lone figure was walking down the side of the road, his back to them, so it wasn't possible to make out anything about him except that he wore disheveled clothes and had his head tucked low between his shoulders.

"Who is Joey?" Derek asked.

"Joey Jenkins, the furnaceman at school," Tommy said. "He found the sword first but was afraid to help us."

The group felt a quickening of hope. The figure beside the road must have sensed them because he turned his head and they caught a glimpse of his face.

"Oh," Sis said, obviously disappointed.

Tommy shook his head. "It's just a tramp," he said sorrowfully.

Derek started to accelerate, but Pen put a hand on his arm. "Stop. I've got to see him."

They pulled over beside the tramp, who, far from shying away, walked right up to the windshield and pressed his face against it. When she saw the scraggly red beard, Pen shook her head. "It's not him."

The tramp kept his face close to the glass, peering in curiously. He grinned, revealing gaps in his yellowed teeth. "Lift?" he asked in a loud voice, but Derek had already thrown the car into reverse. The tires spun in the mud, and the tramp backed away in alarm. In a few seconds Derek had the Rolls back on the road. The encounter had left everyone shaken.

"I thought it was him," Pen said weakly. No one responded. The pale face pressed to the windshield had looked ghostly and lost. For all of them a troubling image came to mind of being homeless themselves.

Suddenly Tommy said, "Take us back to school."

Derek lifted his eyes to the rearview mirror. "To St. Justin's?"

"Yes. I've been thinking. We haven't found a safe place to go, and maybe we'll find Joey there. This could have been a clue."

"What makes you think the school is safe?" Pen asked.

"I don't know. It might not be. But even if everyone has forgotten us, I don't believe Joey would. He's the only person we know so far who has resisted Mordred."

"Is he your friend?" Derek asked.

"We tried to make friends with him. But Joey's frightened. He found the sword under that broken arrow we buried in the forest. Isn't that significant?"

Derek shook his head doubtfully. "His fear has had a while to work on him. But one thing's certain, a furnace room would be warm, and we need a place." The possibility of finding an ally removed some of the gloom in the car. A few minutes later St. Justin's loomed in the haze. The hulking edifice had never before looked inviting to the boys, but now it was almost a beacon of hope.

"Turn here, there's a back way," Tommy instructed when they reached the wrought-iron entrance gate. Derek skirted the main buildings, heading toward the service area in the rear. No one was about, except for some boys practicing soccer in a distant field. "The delivery trucks come in there," Tommy said, pointing toward the kitchen and laundry. "It's too risky to stop. Pull into the shadows as far as you can." He indicated the maze of alleyways, which had grown dark once the noon sun dipped from absolute vertical. Derek steered down the nearest cobbled alley. The car engine rumbled alarmingly within the enclosed space, and some roosting pigeons flew up in a panicked burst.

"Do you want to wait here?" Tommy asked. "I can run ahead and find him."

Derek climbed out into the claustrophobic, gloomy passage. "No, let's stay together."

Tommy nodded, waiting for the others. "It looks spooky, but I know this place pretty well."

He and Sis walked ahead, pausing only to get their bearings whenever one crumbling alleyway joined another. The two sisters and Derek lost their bearings quickly, and one time the boys got too far ahead.

"Where are you?" Derek called as loudly as he dared. The blank, staring walls echoed like a canyon.

After a second Tommy's voice answered, "We're just to the right. Come on." A large pile of refuse hid the corner, which was no more than ten feet in front of them. Derek and the two women rounded it to find Tommy and Sis standing motionless at the top of some stone steps leading down to a basement.

"What's down there?" Derek asked. "Are we here?"

The two boys looked up, their faces ashen. They made no attempt to speak. Derek and the women came closer and saw what it was: a bloody hand printed on the wall, clearly, with no smudges.

"How dreadful," Pen exclaimed in a low voice. From its sticky shine, they knew it must be fresh.

"Joey had one just like that," Tommy said. "Only it was burnt onto his back. Mordred left it."

Suddenly Sis cried out, "Joey didn't do anything wrong. He was afraid to help us, but he didn't do anything wrong."

"He didn't have to," Derek said darkly. They were peering into the stairwell. At the bottom the door was open, but beyond it lay only blackness. Tommy began to go down, but Derek held him back. "It's too dangerous."

"Then you stay here," Tommy replied sharply, wrenching himself away. Before anyone could stop him, he darted down the stairs and out of sight. In a few seconds his muffled voice called out, "He's here. Don't let Sis come down, just you."

Derek nodded, and Pen folded the little boy in her arms. "All of you wait here," Derek said.

Down in the blackness, it was nearly impossible to see. The furnace was turned off, and the room was cavelike and cold. When Derek's eyes adjusted, he saw Tommy crouching in the feeble light of a small overhead window. Derek walked forward until he saw that Tommy was crouched over a body. "Is it Joey?"

Tommy nodded. "His neck's broken. We almost got here in time."

"No, I don't think so. This was timed for us to see," Derek said gravely. He lifted the boy up, pulling him away. The black man's head was turned to one side at a queer angle, his legs folded under him. For a second Derek imagined himself, flung like a broken doll by the side of the motorway. "We couldn't have stopped this. It's *his* way, staying just ahead of us like this. He's reeling us in."

Tommy looked up. "I thought you said he was erasing us."

Derek shrugged. He glanced around, spotting a tarp thrown over some old machine parts. He took it and laid it over the body, but the tarp wasn't quite big enough, and a clenched fist stuck out to one side. "I did think erasing us was all Mordred had in mind. But perhaps he just hasn't gotten around to us yet."

They heard sounds from above, voices and feet shuffling. Tommy straightened up, on the alert. "Sis?" he called. There was no reply, but the sounds increased, and suddenly the small overhead window was blocked by a head. They squinted, trying to make it out, but whoever it was disappeared, and almost immediately a rush of footsteps came clumping down the stairs.

"Don't come in here," Derek warned, but the familiar shapes of Pen, Peg, and Sis were already descending into the dark room. Two others were with them.

"It's Arthur," Peg exclaimed, her voice trembling with excitement. "Can you see? Everything's all right, he's back."

Arthur Callum let go of his mother's hand. "What is it? What did you find?"

Before Derek could answer, he felt Tommy stiffen by his side. "Don't let him down here," Tommy's voice rasped. He pointed to the other figure, a boy about his own age who stood on the steps directly behind Arthur.

"You should all go back," Derek said, trying to block their view. But they had stopped of their own accord, shocked into silence.

"His neck's broken, isn't it?" Edgerton said.

Arthur gestured for the others to remain where they were and approached. "Let me see." He lifted the tarp at one corner, reached under to move the head a little, and stood up. "It's hard to believe I've found you, but you must be our man. Our Merlin."

Derek nodded somberly. "Are you speaking for the police?"

Arthur shook his head. "I think we'd all agree that we're far beyond the police now."

A yellow glare exploded over his head—Edgerton had found a light switch, which turned on one naked, dangling bulb. Peg gasped and then cried out. The walls were covered with more of the crimson handprints, but this time some were smeared, as if whoever made them had tried desperately to get away.

Edgerton walked toward the body. For the first time Tommy saw that he had the sword in his hand. "What are you doing?" Tommy challenged.

Edgerton kept advancing. "I'm going to bring him back."

Everyone felt too shaken to stop him. The handprints, gory and fresh, seemed to bear witness.

Edgerton was standing over Joey's body now, raising the blade to chest level. "I've felt the power of the sword. It was here, in this room." His voice was slow and ceremonial. "This death wasn't meant to be. The sword won't let it."

Tommy had the fleeting thought that Edgerton had gone crazy or was putting something over on them. The boy's eyes glowed, and his face was fixed with concentration as he knelt and laid the sword across Joey's chest. Closing his eyes, Edgerton's lips moved in silent prayer.

All at once Peg screamed. Joey's clenched fist, which had been sticking out from under the tarp, opened. They all saw it, but before anyone could react, the hand jerked up and slammed into Edgerton's head. He took the blow blindside, his eyes rolling up, then he fell backward in a heap.

"Get away!" Arthur shouted. Edgerton had rolled over to one side, so by sheer luck he avoided the stroke of steel aimed at his neck. Joey's hand had grabbed the sword and brought it down with a clang onto the cement floor, inches from where Edgerton's head had been. The tarp heaved as the body struggled to raise itself.

"Upstairs, all of you," Derek commanded.

Arthur had already pulled a dazed Edgerton to his feet and was pushing him stumbling toward the stairs. Pen and Peg gathered Sis, guiding him back toward the fading light. Only Derek and Tommy stood for a moment at the bottom of the stairs, transfixed. Joey let out a strangled roar and flung the last of the tarp away. His face was wild with rage, but there was glee in his eyes.

"Back! You're back!" he screamed as he planted a frenzied kiss on the edge of the blade, which cut deeply into his lips. Ignoring the flow of blood, he swung the sword around his head, smashing the bare glaring bulb. He lunged toward the steps as razor fragments of glass from the lightbulb showered the air.

If Derek hadn't anticipated the move, the blade in Joey's hands would have impaled Tommy, but instinct made him jerk the boy back. They retreated up the stairs, and for some reason the furnace-man didn't pursue them. His roar had turned to laughter now, drunk with triumph.

"You all was fools. You believed me," he cried. "*He* told me you would. 'Catch 'em out, Joey,' he say, and that's what Joey did." His words tumbled out in a delirious stream, but no one heard them.

Fleeing back through the maze, the group was strung out in a ragged line. The two sisters hadn't waited when they got Sis upstairs but plunged immediately down the alley with the boy in tow. "Wait, we'll get lost," he pleaded, but they didn't listen. Arthur and Edgerton could be heard a few yards back, their shoes pounding on the broken cobblestones. Tommy and Derek must have been bringing up the rear, although they were too far back to be seen. The maze swallowed them all, but by some wonder, after five minutes of running into dead ends, yawning holes, and mounds of rubbish, they found themselves running down the last alley, where the maze opened out into clear air.

"Tommy," Sis called when he could catch his breath.

"Here."

The little boy turned back, almost hysterical with relief. Tommy rushed up and grabbed him. "Don't worry, we made it, all of us."

It was true. Sis's eyes looked around, accounting for every face. "What happened?" he gasped, unable to piece together the explosion of events back in the furnace room.

"Mordred's not overlooking us anymore," Tommy replied grimly. "He's starting to turn things his way, using his powers." Tommy's hand, which had been gripping Sis reassuringly, came away moist with blood, which was staining Sis's shirt around the collar. "Don't be scared. You've got a small cut. I think some flying glass must have hit you."

Pen handed Tommy a handkerchief, and he pressed it to stanch the flow. Sis held still, panting but calm. As the others began to regain their composure, they saw that fragments from the lightbulb had also wounded Arthur's forehead and the back of Derek's right hand. Edgerton was untouched, but he had sunk to the ground, barely heeding what the others did, seemingly in shock.

Tommy turned his own hands over, examining them for cuts. "Look! Where did you get that?" Sis exclaimed, pointing to a blue stain that covered both of his friend's palms. It was the same blue they had all seen often by now.

Tommy stared dumbly, then said, "I felt Joey's broken neck, before Derek came down." He looked over at Arthur, who held out his own hands, as blue as the boy's. "You felt him, too."

"Blue paint," murmured Derek. "I once thought I understood, but now I'm not so sure. I thought that it must be part of the game to leave traces of blue everywhere."

Arthur nodded. "It's the same paint I found in your house. You had gone out planning to dress up as a druid, wasn't that it?"

Derek shook his head. "That's what I mean. It doesn't make sense. I owned a jar of that paint, it's true. But it's still at home. You remember, don't you, my dear?" Pen nodded. "Years ago we were invited to a party, Pen and I, and I did dress up as a druid then. I thought it would be amusing, because of the kind of books I wrote. I felt a fool, however, and stuck the paint away the next morning. It's never been out since."

Tommy regarded his hands in puzzlement. "So what does it mean?"

"It doesn't mean anything," replied Derek. "It's just a red herring, or rather a blue herring."

His feeble attempt at humor sounded jarring in the midst of their fright. No one spoke for a moment.

"I don't believe it," Tommy said. "It can't be meaningless. You won't remember, but when you were Merlin, back in the forest, you said this was a clue. What if it's Merlin's sign? What if he wanted us to know that we were on the right track? Didn't the blue paint always show up just when there didn't seem to be any use going on? That's how it worked in the Wode."

"We certainly feel lost now," Pen said. They all shared the

sentiment. Did Merlin know their predicament? The possibility that he might heed their plight, even from his invisible station, was heartening.

Arthur said, "There's no way, no normal way, that Joey could have applied that paint. We need to go back." He regarded Edgerton, who was the most shaken. "You originally found the sword in that room. Mordred knew you were coming back, he knew about all of us. So he tried to scare us away."

"Why bother?" Edgerton mumbled. "He could just kill us."

Arthur shook his head. "That's the thing—we all assume that he can kill us whenever he likes. What if he can't? What if his only choice is to frighten us out of our wits, so that we don't catch on?" These words sent a wave through the group, touching a deep chord of truth. Even as he was speaking, Arthur felt himself being drawn deep into a pool of half-remembered understanding. It was about dragons, something Merlin had told him, long ago in the crystal cave.

"Dragons are always possible."

He remembered that the two of them had been sitting by the fire when Merlin had spoken out of the blue, without preliminaries.

"What do you mean?" the boy had asked, raising his head. Arthur had been on the verge of falling asleep.

"This is a lesson about dragons, that's all. As I said, they are possible, always possible. Of course no dragons have been seen within living memory, not since they were banished by the wizards."

Arthur knew that the villages huddled at the edge of the Questing Wode no longer feared depredations to their crops. Earth once scorched by the old marauding beasts had grown green with time, covering the graves of their murdered victims. The horror that once flew in the night had been forgotten. "How can dragons return if you've killed them?" Arthur asked.

"Killed them? I didn't say anything about killing them. Dragons remain possible as long as mortals refuse to learn where they come from. I could lead an expedition to their foul nests and smash all their eggs, of course. Foxes and wildcats could eat the yolks, even if the brood had already grown embryo scales and hides. But mortals would never allow that. The secret of dragons is that *they are what people want,* as every form of evil is."

Arthur was silent and puzzled. "How can evil be what people want? Do you mean the bad people?"

Merlin shook his head. "No, evil is a necessity felt by everyone, good or bad."

"Why?"

"I once told you that this world is pure illusion. It looks real, but the first step of knowledge that the wizard must learn is not to trust his senses. Look around the world and what do you see? Light followed by darkness, joy by sorrow, life by death. If that is the truth, then the wizard's quest for eternal life cannot succeed, ever."

"Perhaps this world isn't the place for eternal life."

"So it would appear. The cycle of life and death continues forever, but only to the senses. What if it's all illusion? What if death only exists because people believe they were born, because they were told so by someone else. In fact, nobody can truly remember a time when they were not alive. Can you remember yourself before you were born?"

Arthur shook his head, wondering what this all had to do with dragons.

"Then perhaps you were always alive, and birth was simply a moment of forgetting." Merlin was warming to his subject, and when he did this, an edge of sorrow would often tinge his voice. "Why do the villagers fear us? Why am I reviled by stupid, zealous priests in the name of the Almighty? Because men fear nothing as much as the shattering of illusion. They will go to any lengths not to believe the truth. And what is the truth?"

The wizard held out his palm and tongues of blue flame sprang up from it. *"Light! It is all light."* The boy was amazed. Merlin's face was a mask of total concentration. "The light is all, and in the light there is only one thing—eternal life. It cannot be created or destroyed. The wizard is not afraid to walk in the darkness—indeed he must—because that is where illusion dies."

"The priests claim you dabble in darkness."

"We dabble in eternity. The wizard looks around him and finds the eternal in all directions. His only choice is what to do with it. Light is to be played with and shaped, which is the joy of our existence. It is also joy to pierce the illusion and find the wellspring of creative power."

"How can mortals learn to do that?"

"They are already doing so, but they don't know it. The illusion was created by them, and now they believe in it too strongly. They use their power to create a drama of birth and death, joy and pain. Don't blame them, it is their dance. In truth, the darkness has no power other than what they give it." Merlin placed his face close to the boy's. "I am going to tell you the secret of conquering evil. *You are the evil.* When you can face that, all monsters dissolve into the mist."

"Including dragons?"

"Yes. I told you that mortals refuse to see where dragons come from. All monsters live in a dark place where mortals stuff their fears and shame and guilt. It's a pitifully small closet, but black enough for all that, and out of it, as needed, things leap out to spread terror."

"But dragons kill people. Isn't that real?"

Merlin shrugged. "No one would believe in cheap illusions. If you ever encounter a dragon, you will be astonished by how credible it seems." His voice was amused and appreciative now. "I could scarcely do better myself." He held out his hand, letting the boy watch the blue flame dancing over his palm for a moment before it flickered and died.

Coming back to his senses in the entry to the maze, Arthur looked down at the blue stain on his palm, which seemed to glow. "We can't be fooled forever," he said aloud. The others looked at him, puzzled, but without another word, he headed off back into the maze. After a moment's hesitation, the others formed a ragged line and followed. Soon they were back at the top of the stairs.

Menace shrouded them like fog. "Do you feel *him*?" Tommy asked. Sis nodded. Arthur tensed, not knowing what to do next. He felt that the maze had somehow led them back in time. They were standing there exactly as they had before. Then he noticed a small detail: the crimson handprint was gone.

"Look," he said, pointing. Someone had washed the evil sign away. The door down below was still open, and as before it opened onto blackness, but this time there was a faint glow inside.

"You might as well come down here, boy," a voice called. "We both know you'll come back sooner or later."

It was Joey's voice, faintly mocking, and he seemed to be calling Edgerton. The group felt a rush of apprehension. Was this madness?

"Here, I'll help you down."

The furnaceman's hand appeared at the door, gesturing for them to descend. "Go ahead," Arthur said. The group slowly filed down the stairs, Edgerton first. When he entered the room, the furnace was on, casting a warm glow. Joey stood close to it, idly throwing in coals. He reached down and held something out. "You left this," he said casually. Edgerton took the sword silently, while the others gathered around.

"Your Majesty," Joey murmured when he set eyes on Arthur. "You're to go and get what is there for you."

Joey's voice had changed, its tone grave and respectful. All traces of demonic rage had disappeared, but so had the lilting Jamaican accent, and it was this that sent a chill down Arthur's spine. "There's something here for me?" He glanced nervously to one corner where the tarp covered a pile of machine parts. It hadn't been touched, and he could feel his chest tingle beneath his shirt.

"Ah, they never told me you'd be so timid, but then you're young," Joey said thoughtfully. His voice was still grave but not quite so respectful. A strong hand gripped Arthur's forearm, and with irresistible force he found himself being led to the center of the room.

"Calm yourself," Joey advised. "There's no harm here." Somehow the reassurance worked. Arthur felt himself relax. "Tell me what you see," Joey whispered.

Arthur looked around. "Nothing. What am I supposed to see?" A low growl came from Joey's throat. Arthur jumped. "It's too dark to see anything."

Joey's eyes shone, and he shook his head. "I told you there's no harm here. Don't look at me. Look into the room."

Arthur mechanically did as he was told. He saw nothing, but he felt faint waves of nausea, as if his body couldn't stand the strain of this test. He had no choice, however—they were all beset by dragons. As if sensing this thought, the others gathered around him in the glow cast by the hissing furnace.

"If you leave, we are lost," Joey said. "This is the moment." Arthur felt calmer, but he saw himself as a tightrope walker, walking the thinnest filament of grace to some immense promise, unless he fell, and then it would be a fall into catastrophe.

"I shouldn't be here," he whispered.

The words broke the trance, and the others seemed to sag, disappointed. Arthur wanted to bolt, but before he could, Joey grabbed his neck with a fierce grip. The rage was on him again. "You!" he spat out, and suddenly Mordred was staining the scene with his malice.

"Let me go," Arthur gasped. Joey didn't hear him, and the others didn't move to help.

"He's right," Derek suddenly said. "This is the moment." He was pointing to the wall, where the handprints in blood were starting to reappear, like invisible ink coming out over a candle flame. Arthur squirmed, fighting Joey's grip.

"Don't," Pen warned. Arthur held out his arms, begging them to help. Tommy started to move, then drew back. All at once they all realized that inside the circle a battle of wills was being fought, but not human wills. Wizards had chosen that moment as the pivot of time. No one would witness their combat because these warriors were unseen, outside mortal boundaries.

Joey had Arthur on his knees now, and the pain in his neck was like searing electric voltage.

Show me the sword, Arthur thought in desperation.

Heeding him, Edgerton stepped forward and held up Excalibur. Arthur waited for a sign. None came. The hand at his throat grew twice as powerful, stronger than Joey himself could ever be, and Arthur realized that Mordred was the master of the game. Merlin was holding back, would always hold back. Hadn't he despised the game as an illusion all along?

Arthur's body struggled against death, frantically fighting against surrender. He looked at his beloved Excalibur. *Slay my dragons,* he prayed. *Or if I am the dragon, slay me.* He knew he was taking a terrible risk, for there was enough dragon in everyone to keep the world suffering another ten thousand years. Yet somehow he also knew that this was the only way out.

Without warning came surrender. Arthur felt a new impulse, and it was—laughter. Joey's thumb dug into his throat, searching for his windpipe, but Arthur felt no pain. It had been a joke, all of it. There was no dying, there was no Mordred. There was only a dance that played itself out against the fabric of a smiling, patient eternity, and its spirit was Merlin.

The great secret dawned. Merlin would not fight Mordred again because he knew that *Mordred was himself.* The face of evil was just one facet of an infinite self existing beyond light and darkness, beyond life and death. Merlin had always known that, had accepted it, and Arthur had become his pupil to discover the same thing. A second ticked by, then Joey's grip loosened.

"Forgive me, forgive me," the furnaceman murmured. His voice was humble and contrite.

As Arthur's throat cleared, he was able to speak. "I want to do you service. What do you want of me?"

Joey peered at him with unmistakable anxiety. "Just look, my lord. I want you to look." Arthur felt calm. If reality was a dream, it was his dream now. His feet took him a few steps into the light of the furnace. And he heard an anguished cry from the black man, a cry that seemed to tear against a tremendous effort to smother it. Ages of desperation were in the cry, like millions wailing for redemption. It was beyond Arthur's ability to understand this, yet he knew. His foot knocked something over, and his arm swung out to keep himself from tripping.

He reached down in the half-light and picked up an object. It was filthy, but his fingers detected cold, smooth metal. The object had a grip like a candlestick—no, it was a tall cup. That was it, an old dirty cup filled Arthur's hand.

Lifting it up, he saw its simple, curved outline and faint burnished gleam. He saw through the dirtiness, and the cup was like half the sun dropped into the palm of his hand. Joy overcame him, then almost instantly it was replaced by sorrow. He thought of gold being polished by countless tears as the yeasty smell of new wine filled his nostrils.

Joey was standing a few feet away, his back turned. A tremendous surge of serenity and confidence flowed through Arthur. It emanated from his right hand, which gripped the cup, flowing in warm waves up his arm and directly into his heart.

"Behold."

The word held suspended in air. Joey turned. He couldn't speak, but his eyes melted with gratitude. He lifted his hand to touch the cup, then paused. "Do you know what you have there?" he asked quietly. Arthur didn't reply. He barely saw the faces of the others, hardly felt their various reactions. Edgerton and Tommy were kneeling. Sis's mouth hung slightly open, his eyes wide with amazement. Pen and Derek grasped each other's hands, until Pen remembered and reached out for Peg's also.

Then the veil of awe fell, and Joey shook himself. "Come into the light. It's creepy down here."

The group followed him upstairs. In Arthur's hand the cup glowed in the last orange rays of sunset. "Can I touch it, too?" Sis asked. "It's filthy, but it's lovely, isn't it?" They all wanted to touch it now.

"Do you think it's gold?" Tommy asked.

"To us it is," Derek said, and then nobody spoke. They all felt safe, all beyond Mordred's grasp whatever the final test that lay ahead might be.

"Shall I keep it?" Arthur asked, looking at Joey. "It was your quest, after all." He gazed into Joey's eyes, expecting to see a look he remembered—Galahad's perhaps, or Percival's or Gawain's. No single soul gazed back at him, however, but the souls of thousands. It was impossible to name all those who had sought the Grail.

"Sure, you keep it," Joey said, grinning broadly. "And whatever you do, don't pawn it." Arthur would have laughed but the spell was still too strong upon him. Joey was already walking away, melting into the maze of alleys. "If you need to find Joey again, you whistle for him. He always got an ear to the wind, if you know what I mean."

Their eyes followed him as he left. "Perhaps we have a chance," Pen said.

"Yes."

Arthur couldn't tell who in the group had agreed. They must have all agreed, in the name of the court of miracles. "Let's go before it gets dark," he said. Their fulfillment, like all miracles, had come in a form never to be predicted. Who would have looked for the Grail in the dingy alleys of St. Justin's, who would expect revelation to swoop upon them as quickly and elusively as swallows at dusk?

Arthur looked up at the narrow crack of darkening sapphire sky overhead. In fact there were swallows now, dipping for insects above their heads. The birds were singing in faint, ethereal chirps, and they looked as if they were made of light, pure light that could abide in the air forever.

The end of their wanderings did not come that night, not yet. It took the court of miracles a long time to figure out how to do battle with Mordred. Meeting in the crystal cave, they argued over a course of action, and finally it was the woman in the green felt hat who prevailed. "There's only one person who can teach us what we need to know," she said, and it was she who led the search across the land to find Melchior. For months they traversed the countryside, until winter arrived and hope began to fade.

"He could have been killed by the dragon," Arthur speculated.

"That's possible, but we have to trust his wizard's training," the lady said.

"I think he's trying to make his way back to where Merlin might be," the tramp reflected, "only he doesn't have enough power to turn back into his own form." A sense of discouragement settled over them, thinking of the thousand forms the apprentice might have taken.

When the first winter storms broke, the search party was camped on a hillside in Wales, debating where to go next. Sis, feeling restless, had wandered off, idly exploring a frozen meadow. Deep snow was a remarkable sight to a boy raised in warmer reaches. He lay down and made an angel in the billowing drifts. Then his eye caught something in the rocky landscape—a single low outcropping of stone. Sis drew closer, curious. The snow hadn't blown off it or melted. Here the rugged limestone was clean and dry, as if no snow had ever fallen on it to begin with.

The little boy bent down and peered into a crevice. Deep in the shadows a small scarlet snake was coiled. He gently reached in and pulled it out. The snake was warm, which surprised him, and it didn't object to being handled. Resting against Sis's fingers, the snake's breathing went softly in and out. When he brought it back to the others, Derek was delighted. "I didn't quite know where to head for," he said, "but if you'll let me have that, I know where it belongs." Derek nestled the snake inside his coat pocket, coiled around the Alkahest to keep it warm.

Sis frequently asked where they were going. "Tintagel," Tommy reminded him. Sis had never been to Cornwall, but there was a cave by the sea that Derek knew. It was mid-December before they arrived there, and the bitterly cold spray made it difficult to crawl down the face of the cliffs and enter the sea-washed cavern. Its floor was of black Cornish rock, polished by centuries of wear.

Derek reached into his pocket and pulled out the snake, still coiled around the stone. The roar of wind and sea reverberated all around them. When it was placed on the floor, the scarlet band didn't move. A surge of seawater rushed between Derek's feet and almost snatched the snake away, but Tommy dashed forward and made a quick save. "What should we do?" he shouted over the ocean's din.

"I don't know. Perhaps this wasn't right," Derek replied.

But the snake was wriggling violently in Tommy's hands now, and he set it down again. Raising its tiny, diamond-shaped head, the serpent flicked its tongue, testing the air. The group watched the head wavering back and forth, and if they expected Merlin to stride out of the sea or spring from the snake's body, their hopes were dashed. Sis had the idea of placing the Alkahest down beside the animal to help it change shape, but this produced nothing.

The group kept vigil in the sea-washed cave as night fell. The tide would drive them away soon, but they didn't want to give up hope. Only when the waves began to flood the last dry space did Derek say, "There's no use staying. I thought he'd come."

Pen said, "I suppose Merlin must honor his promise not to interfere, even for one of his own." The scarlet snake, chilled into a stupor, had been returned to the velveteen bag along with the stone.

Derek shook his head. "I still don't understand. If the promise is binding, why did Merlin occupy my body? Why did he leave the Alkahest in the maze and traces of blue paint as clues?"

"Maybe he didn't." Arthur's voice pierced the darkness.

"What do you mean?" Derek asked.

"Ever since we found a body in the ditch," replied Arthur, "we've assumed that you didn't have the power to do all the things that happened. But what if *you* are Merlin?" Derek looked shocked, but before he could protest, Arthur went on, "We're all part of Merlin in a sense, part of his dream. This cave is, too, I'm sure."

Tommy stood up, suddenly excited. "When we were on the other side," he reminded Derek, "you told Sis and me that wizards live backwards in time, including Merlin. Perhaps you're a younger version of him, just as Amberside is a younger version of Mordred. Maybe you both have nearly the same powers. That could even be part of the game."

Arthur nodded. "That would explain why Mordred didn't have enough power to seize the stone from you—it's yours by rights. He couldn't even go into the circle after you. You said so yourself." Unable to respond, Derek pulled forth the Alkahest, which still bore the etched letters *Clas Myrddin.*

"If I were Merlin," he finally said in a troubled voice, "why would I lead myself on this wild chase, not to mention all the rest of you? Why would I permit so much murder and violence to occur?"

"You will not know that until the reading of the stone."

The whole group turned as one to confront the speaker, and to their astonishment, Melchior walked out of the shadows into the mist of the pounding sea that filled the mouth of the cave. "You've brought me back," he said, bowing his head. "You are my Merlin." A wave of joy spread through the group, and one by one they came forward to embrace the apprentice or shyly touch his hand.

"Master is here with us," Melchior told them. "My search couldn't end until each of you claimed your part of Master's spirit." Then they knew that the fate of the court of miracles was to transform itself into Merlin, that his long absence from the earth had not been an abandonment but a necessary step in their destiny.

"You are not quite right to say that Master is weaker in this age, dark as it is," Melchior said. "He simply hasn't been recognized. Mordred has been gathering as much power as possible so that time would not make him waste away. Master knew that the future could not be saved unless his power was in everyone. Alone you would remain Mordred's victims, together you can take the world from his hands."

"How?" Derek asked.

"Every event is like a new thread spun in the web of time, and these threads issue from you." The apprentice placed a finger on Derek's chest. "There is nothing out there that you did not dream in here first. Mordred has dictated the event lines that you call reality, but there are infinite possibilities left. Reclaim your power; no one can dream forth a world of love and peace except you."

"I think," Derek said slowly, "that the time has come to return what we've been given, or rather, what has been placed in our safekeeping." He placed the Alkahest at Melchior's feet, followed by the Grail and the sword, which Arthur and Edgerton brought forth. "These came from a wizard. And if a wizard must claim them again, let it be you."

The sacred objects formed a circle, each catching a glint of sea-reflected moonlight. Melchior touched each one, then rose and handed back the stone to Pen. "For the future," he said, and beckoned them toward higher ground. In a silent line they followed him up the cliff face. There was no beach outside Merlin's cave, only slanting shelves of gray rocks that they had been perching on. The high tide left the rocks dry, but as soon as the sword, the stone, and the Grail had been positioned, the sea started rumbling to its depths.

Looking down, they beheld the sea swell in waves that reached higher and higher, sweeping over the rock ledge, not greedily but in an engulfing embrace. One moment the gleaming objects, sword and cup, were there, the next a swish of foam was hissing across an empty ledge.

"Don't despair," Melchior said. "Those were never your inheritance. They were tokens of an inheritance you must claim for yourself." Seated on the cliffs, Melchior continued to talk long into the night.

When he was finished, Arthur stood up as the rays of dawn touched the rocks. "This truth is the fulfillment of my heart, but there's someone missing. Until I find her, we are incomplete." Within the hour he had set off, and without discussion the others prepared to follow him, all but Melchior, who stood quietly by.

"Where will you go?" Derek asked as they were about to part.

"Over the sea and beyond, into the wind and out again."

No one fully understood Melchior, but they wished him well, knowing that his journey couldn't be shared. The last glimpse they had was of a young man standing on the sea cliffs wrapped in long blue robes, much as he had stood on the ramparts of Camelot.

30

CIRCLE OF PEACE

WINTER PROMISED TO BE HARSH EVERYWHERE THAT YEAR. BY early November all the trees on Mogg Street had dropped their leaves, except for the gnarled oak in front of Amberside's house. Like withered hope its crumpled brown foliage clung to the branches weeks after the first hard frost. One evening in late December, Amberside was surprised to see whirling blue light flickering through the oak's crown. Why had a police car pulled up into his drive?

The knocker on the front door rapped loudly. "What is it?" he demanded, opening the door no more than a crack to the burly constable who stood bundled up against the cold.

Hamish McPhee backed away, letting drop the heavy iron ring. "Police. May we come in?"

Amberside peered into the darkness. A light snow had begun to fall, sparkling like crushed diamonds under the streetlights. Behind the constable he saw two other forms, shadowy beneath the oak's outspread branches. "Come in?" he repeated querulously. "Not until you state your business."

One of the other figures stepped forward. It was Westlake. "We've had an emergency call from this address."

"Emergency? That's preposterous."

"I'm afraid not. We'd like to take a look around," Westlake replied coolly. He moved toward the door, and his companion joined him. When Amberside saw the face of Arthur Callum illuminated under the porch light, he stiffened. The three policemen stamped snow off their shoes and crossed the threshold. "The call came in at approximately seven-fifteen," Westlake said. "What was the name?"

"Jasper," Hamish McPhee put in. "We don't know his first name."

"He was a part-time gardener and handyman when I last saw him here," Arthur said.

"Well, he must be on the inside now," Westlake remarked. "He had access to the phone."

"That's not true," Amberside finally spoke up. "I've been beside the telephone the whole evening."

The Dresden clock on the landing struck the half hour. Amberside cocked his head, bemused, but before he could add anything, Westlake pointed toward the staircase. "I'd like to see your Mr. Jasper now, if you please. Does he live up there?"

"Yes, at the very top," admitted Amberside grudgingly, his attention fixed on Arthur, who didn't return his gaze. Westlake gave a nod, and McPhee trudged upstairs, disappearing around the corner of the landing.

"I take it you've been reinstated," Amberside said dryly.

Arthur nodded curtly. "This morning."

Amberside adopted his most insolent manner. "It surprises me that they'd take you back. You made such an embarrassing mess of a case that fizzled into thin air, and you were dragging Katy down with you until she married me."

"If you don't mind," Westlake interrupted, "I'd prefer that we not mix business with personal affairs." They all stopped talking. Amberside didn't invite his visitors to sit but left them standing at the entrance to the living room. McPhee's voice was barely audible when he called over the balustrade.

"Right then, up we go," Westlake ordered.

The two policemen climbed the stairs to the top landing with Amberside in tow. A door stood ajar at the end of the hallway.

"Here, Chief, have a look," McPhee said in a strained voice, stepping aside to let the inspector enter Jasper's room. A large iron bedstead took up most of the cramped space, and a butler's uniform was draped over a side chair, which had been overturned. A curtain rope was lashed to a heavy rod across the top of the window, from which a body hung, unmoving.

Arthur came up behind Westlake and, catching a glimpse of what was inside, gave a sharp intake of breath. "What is it?" Amberside demanded, not yet close enough to see.

It was the body of a woman.

"Get her down," Westlake barked. Although badly shaken, Arthur crossed the room and tried to reach up to take some weight off the rope, but Katy Kilbride swayed sickeningly out of reach.

"Help him," Westlake ordered. McPhee shoved the heavy bed closer and stood on top of it while Arthur embraced the body, doing his best to lift it. Amberside had entered now but made no sound.

McPhee began working at the noose, which was drawn tight, but beneath the rope he could feel cold flesh. "Christ, poor Katy, it's not coming off."

"Isn't there a knife or something about?" Arthur demanded, desperation in his voice. Amberside didn't respond. He seemed to be pondering the scene in front of him, neither shocked nor dismayed.

"Wait, I've got it now," McPhee exclaimed. The curtain cord loosened, and he slipped the noose off Katy, her whole weight sagging into Arthur's arms. The young constable staggered, and Westlake rushed up to support him.

Gingerly they lowered the slack weight to the floor. Then, as if some inner wire had snapped, Arthur collapsed on the bed, his face in his hands.

"Should we phone it in or search the premises first?" McPhee asked, barely able to control his emotions.

"Don't touch anything in this room. Scene-of-crime will want it all as it is, but take a look around." Westlake turned to Amberside. "You can identify this woman as your wife?"

"Yes, obviously," Amberside snapped. "You've seen her here yourself." The question obviously rankled, but otherwise he still showed no emotion.

"Can you explain this wretched business?" Westlake asked.

Amberside paused a second. "No."

Westlake went over to Arthur and asked in a low voice if he wanted to leave and wait downstairs. The young constable, obviously overcome, shook his head.

"Well, then." Westlake bent over the corpse, feeling the neck where it was discolored, then stood up again. "There's bruised flesh under the rope but no broken neck, as indeed there couldn't be, not when a person drops less than two feet. In such cases, hanging always inflicts death by strangulation."

"But that takes much more time," McPhee interjected.

"Yes," Westlake agreed. "Mr. Jasper, whose whereabouts we still don't know, called us less than twenty minutes ago to report an emergency. We will have to determine if enough time elapsed for this unfortunate young woman to rig up a rather elaborate apparatus, perform the deed, and strangle to death. I have my doubts."

Amberside hovered by the door. "Right," Westlake said, snapping his notepad shut. "McPhee, you find the telephone and call for an ambulance. Also notify a scene-of-crime officer to get down here on the double. Callum, you take this floor. I'll take the ground floor. If you find this Jasper character, bring him quietly. If you don't, send out an all-points bulletin. We need to check every room and then seal the premises."

Amberside opened his mouth to protest, but Westlake cut him short and ordered McPhee, "Get moving. We'll meet by the front door in ten minutes." The inspector turned rapidly to go, but not before he gave Arthur a sympathetic glance.

When he and Arthur were alone in the room, Amberside leaned against the foot of the iron bedstead. "I didn't know you had such a flair for drama."

"There's a lot about me you don't know," Arthur said, standing up. His face was calm, utterly devoid of the anguish he had been displaying moments before. It was a remarkable transformation. "It's taken me a while to figure out what kind of nastiness you were about." He spoke coolly, a note of defiance in his voice.

"And now you know?" said Amberside, raising his eyebrows.

"I think so. You don't want the sword, you never did. You want us." Arthur walked over to the window and pulled aside the curtains. Under the nearest streetlight a group of Christmas carolers had gathered in the snow, which was rapidly dropping a rumpled blanket over Gramercy town. Only they weren't singing. The small band of men and women, accompanied by two boys, were standing silently, looking at the house.

"Ah, reinforcements. Were you afraid that your policeman's charade wouldn't give you enough protection?"

Arthur shrugged. "If it was just me you wanted, you could have resorted to violence as you have against others. I've thought a lot about it. The people you found dispensable—Derek Rees, Paddy Edgerton, and Joey Jenkins—had something in common. They weren't part of the court of miracles. So it must be the court that you're afraid of."

"Afraid?" Amberside was smiling.

"By the way, you failed to eliminate two of your victims. Derek and Joey are still alive."

"That's a lie!" Amberside's anger flashed into the room, but only for an instant before he resumed his mask of imperturbability. "You really should stay in police work. Detection suits you. Not that I haven't done a little myself. Do you mind?" He got up and drew the curtains, hiding the group outside from sight. "I'll grant you one thing: you people are capable of surprises. I didn't expect this bit of sideplay." Amberside pointed to Katy's body on the floor.

"Don't worry, it's only temporary."

Amberside's neck muscles twitched before he regained his composure. "Fascinating."

"The court of miracles has been running from you all this time, and that was their mistake. You directed the chase, and as long as they ran, they missed the point. This game hasn't been about a sword or a stone or even the cup, has it?"

Amberside burst out laughing. "Very good."

"Glad you think so. Now you can tell me what it is you want from us."

"I'm not sure you'll understand. Few can understand me, you know." Amberside's voice grew plummy, like an actor warming up for a soliloquy. "This whole affair doesn't involve mortals—it never has. You're like mice in the wainscoting, scurrying about and never noticing that the house belongs to someone else."

"To wizards?"

"What's in a name? We'll say that there are beings who lift the curtain of appearances and find that reality is not what it seems. Have you considered what this world really is? I have. Wherever I look, I see reflections of myself."

"Merlin taught me much the same thing in the crystal cave. 'Look into the mirror of the world, and you will see only yourself.' But that opens a great temptation, doesn't it, to manipulate things selfishly, for your own ends."

"Temptation? I would call it a ripe opportunity. What good would it do for the world to be me if it wasn't also *mine*?"

"So you sought power, and you needed the court of miracles to test the limits of your power."

"So to speak. You were my foils."

"Yet the game hasn't been going all your way. Time has started to catch up with you, and the world you've been controlling so successfully is slipping out of your grasp, slowly but surely."

Amberside frowned. "Nothing is slipping out of my grasp."

Ignoring him, Arthur continued, "All at once you began to fear the future. The day would come, you realized, when you would be confined to a mortal body, and then you would be no better than other mortals, except for your pretensions to evil. Only you wouldn't be able to carry them out anymore, not in the same way."

Arthur put his face closer to Amberside's. "What was it like to feel yourself fading away? It must have been devilishly hard to figure out what to do. Time was going to snuff you out. And then you realized it couldn't happen. You were heading for death, but because wizards live backwards in time, death would also be your rebirth. Instead of coming to an end, time would curve back, carrying you with it. Bravo, it was a brilliant deduction, and all you had to do was wait and keep mortals distracted so that we wouldn't find out how weak you'd really become."

Amberside was staring with hate-filled eyes, but he said nothing. Arthur stood up and headed for the door. "Where do you think you're going?" demanded Amberside, startled.

"To carry out my duties. I'm a constable, and I have my orders." Arthur left the room, and Amberside hesitated. He glanced at the worn scatter rug where Katy's body had been placed. It was empty. For a second the tide of panic started to rise, but Amberside bolted to his feet and out into the hall, forcing himself into action. He grabbed Arthur, whirled him around, and lifted his hand.

"What's going on here?" It was Westlake, ponderously ascending the stairs. "I told you I didn't want anything personal interfering with our work." Amberside backed off. "What did you find on this floor?"

Arthur faced Westlake calmly. "Nothing, sir. The room at that end is locked. I asked Mr. Amberside to get the key, but he refused."

"You're lying," Amberside burst out, raising his fist again. Westlake reached for his arm. "Don't touch me," Amberside hissed. He suddenly crouched down, his eyes glinting, and folded his arms over his chest. By the dim light of the hallway, Westlake saw them turn into webbed wings. Scales appeared on the face that was no longer human, but extending into something massive, reptilian—a snout. Westlake looked at Arthur, who seemed unperturbed, then blinked. Amberside was still there, trembling with suppressed rage.

Westlake heaved a sigh. "Come on, then," he told Amberside, as if he had seen nothing unusual. "We need the key to that lumber room. Let's go down and get it together, shall we?" Mutely Amberside led the way.

Arthur listened for their tread descending to the ground floor before he ran downstairs himself. It was a short flight to the next landing, but his heart pounded. An invisible struggle for power—the last test—had begun.

Arthur felt almost sick with excitement. "She's got to be there," he thought. Mordred had shaped the future according to his will. Arthur had already forced a crack in it, but when an egg cracks, it is not the same as a birth. What he had to do next had never been done before. A mortal had to outdream a wizard.

When he reached the second floor, Arthur walked to the end of the hallway and opened the door. "Katy?" he said softly into the darkened bedroom. For a moment his eyes took in only a faint glimmer of light, then he saw a slim figure standing at the window, very still. Snow was silently collecting on the sill outside. What would she look like? Arthur had to push old images from his mind, banishing the terror and hurt that came with them. He waited for Katy to respond, but the crystal pivot of time didn't want to move. He felt the urge to push, but then an intuition told him, *Let go, allow, and it will be yours.*

He closed his eyes and let himself sink into the core of peace inside him, which he had named the Grail. Then Katy turned to face him. She looked pale, but not with the paleness of death. Her face was luminous, shining like a snowflake against the velvet darkness of the sky outside.

"I've been waiting," she said, and it looked as if small jewels had appeared at the corners of her eyes.

Beloved.

The word came to Arthur's mind as the faintest whisper before his thoughts surrendered once more to silence. He stepped forward, washed by a wave of peace against the tides of time. A bridge of gentleness had been thrown across a chasm, and they stood on either side.

"You don't have to wait any longer," he said. "I'm back."

Katy held out her arms. The jewels in her eyes were coursing down her cheeks now, clearing a path of purity. And then they were in each other's arms as if for the first time, innocence enfolded by innocence. "I didn't understand," Arthur mumbled, his voice breaking. "I didn't know what you were going through." He wanted to beg her forgiveness, but they were beyond asking anything of each other. He saw it in her eyes. She was with him in the little room but far beyond at the same time, exalted.

She's made it through. Guinevere was first. He went down on his knees and bowed his head against her pale, small hands. Her gaze bent gently, but she didn't move, only standing there, a queen in redemption, before the spell broke.

"I hate it here," she said, and the voice was Katy's. "Can we go?"

Arthur was up and kissing her now. "Yes, I'm sure we can."

Movements could be heard downstairs, and muffled voices seemed to be arguing. Katy looked around, considering whether to take anything. "I'm ready."

At the landing of the stairs Arthur looked down and saw Westlake and Amberside squared off against each other. "Get out!" Amberside shouted.

"You're insane, there's been a death here, and possibly a murder." Westlake was cold but furious.

"No, there hasn't," Amberside retorted, his voice shaking. He closed his eyes, as if willing the inspector to vanish.

"Careful, you're dealing with one of the most malevolent magicians in human history," Arthur said from the top of the stairs.

Westlake glared at him. "Have you all gone daft?" he growled.

The front door opened, blown by the wind, bringing in a flurry of white flakes. Amberside trembled in the gust of freezing air. "Get out!" he shouted again, but this time his rage was directed at a group of carolers at the door.

They walked in, much to Westlake's amazement. He pulled out his ID. "I'm sorry, this is police business. I'm in charge here, and you people will have to leave."

As if he hadn't spoken, a stocky woman in a green felt hat and coat stepped forward, eyeing Amberside. "You almost carried it off," she said calmly. She pulled a smooth, round stone from under her coat.

Amberside gathered himself. "You'll see whether I've carried it off."

"Carried what off?" Westlake asked. "Will somebody start

making sense around here?" He hardly registered that DC McPhee had run into the room highly excited.

"He's just outside. Look." McPhee pointed out the tall windows flanking the front door where a pale face was looking in from the other side.

Recognizing Jasper, Westlake shouted, "Get him!" But the face vanished like an apparition, or a slave suddenly freed from his chains. McPhee ran out to the sidewalk, only to see Jasper rounding the corner, his flight muffled by the thick snowfall blanketing the street.

"Do you want me to pursue?" McPhee asked as he came back into the room, but his question hung in the air with absurd irrelevance. Amberside had been surrounded by the carolers, who formed a circle around him. The woman in the felt hat was holding up some kind of lamp. McPhee looked again—it wasn't a lamp but a round stone that seemed to be illuminated from within. Amberside cringed as if the light were causing him pain. McPhee shot a glance at Westlake, who seemed rooted in place, then jumped as a voice behind him said, "You're a fortunate man to be here for this."

A bedraggled tramp with wiry black hair entered the room. He left the door open, allowing winter to follow him in. After that, McPhee couldn't speak or move but could only bear mute witness to what happened.

The tramp walked over to the circle, and a way was parted for him. Arthur had led Katy Kilbride to the opposite side. "Mordred," the tramp declared in a loud voice. "We are here to read the stone."

At the sound of his name, Mordred's form, the golden youth who was a king's shame, began to emerge from Amberside's shape. The haughty aquiline features melted like putty, revealing the fair young noble. "Who are you?" Mordred asked, his voice proud and unafraid. "Who dares speak to me in this wise?"

"We are Merlin," replied the tramp.

"Impossible. Merlin can't come here."

"He doesn't need to. That was your mistake."

Suddenly the lady in the green felt hat raised the stone higher.

It turned transparent and began emitting a beam of blue-white light. An opalescent sheen melted into the light, which began to move in waves over the walls.

"If you are Merlin," Mordred demanded, "then show yourself."

"We *are* showing ourselves," the tramp replied. Almost unnoticed, other people had been filing into the house through the open door. Silently they formed a second circle around the first. The light of the stone gleamed brighter as more entered, opening the circle of peace wider and wider.

Mordred began pacing back and forth. He was shaking with rage as Tommy stepped forward and placed something at his feet. The wizard stared. A broken arrow lay on the floor. Mordred shrieked in horrified realization: he had dropped one stitch in the fabric of time, yet that had spelled his ruin. Here was the arrow that should have killed Ulwin, who then would have never found the sword or banded together the court of miracles.

Mordred tilted back his head, but instead of another shriek, he let forth a single word: "Mother!" Half a wail, half a command, the word at first caused no response, then a shadowy form appeared in the corner of the room. It glowed dully, trembling on the edge of vanishing. "Please," Mordred whispered.

The dull glow flickered brighter, and Morgan le Fay approached the circle. "I am summoned. Typical of you to wait until you were desperate." She glared sharply at the lady in the felt hat. "Don't suppose you fool me. You've overstepped your power." The witch lifted her hand, and a low rumble shook the floor. "Release him," she intoned, her words covered by a deafening explosion. The circle of peace split apart as a massive portion of the ceiling fell in. At the same time the ornate brickwork around the mantel buckled, and the chimney collapsed. Before anyone could react, the walls crumbled all around.

"Gather, gather!" the lady in the felt hat cried. Blood was running down her forehead where a brick had struck her. She reached out her hands, trying to mend the rupture in the circle, but no one was there to take them.

Morgan le Fay rushed into the center. "Come!" she ordered.

Mordred smiled and allowed himself to be led out. As he passed the lady in the felt hat, he struck her with his open hand. Without a sound she fell dead onto the floor.

"No!" the tramp shouted. Caught by the fall of the chimney, he had been knocked momentarily unconscious. He staggered to his feet, but Mordred blocked his way.

"You were too late to save your king, Lancelot, and now this. I pity you." But the youth's mocking voice betrayed no pity. The house was in ruins, open to the street. The remains of the circle of peace wandered here and there. Many were wounded; all seemed to be in a daze.

"It would be pleasant to kill you, ladies and gentlemen," Mordred said, "but I think your future will be amusing enough." He began to stride over the fallen rubble when Morgan called, "Wait, attend me." Mordred turned. His mother was bent over, her face pale. "Too much," she gasped. "It took too much to save you." And in fact her fleshly form was starting to waver, disintegrating before his eyes.

"Are you coming or not?" Mordred asked impatiently.

Morgan turned pleading eyes upon him. "My child," she whispered with great effort, then in utter weakness her lips silently formed the word *help.*

"Say that again. I didn't quite catch it." Mordred smiled as his mother trembled, beckoning feebly. "You want me to approach? I don't know. Your final moments could be rather disgusting. Well, a child's duty." He went over to her and looked down. Morgan le Fay had collapsed in a heap, lifting one bony hand to caress his face. Her gaze was not accusatory but admiring, loving. Mordred allowed the hand to touch his cheek. A stream of burning vitriol shot from her fingers, searing his flesh.

"No, no!" he shrieked, lurching back as the acid etched red, burning scars into his gilded features. It must have been unholy acid, for the scars spread in a filigree of mutilation. "How could you?" he moaned.

"How could I? How could you? That is the question." The collapsed heap had risen up, not in Morgan's shape but a most unexpected one: Albrig, king of the elementals. All traces of womanhood had been replaced by the hunched figure of a hideous dwarf. "Magic for magic, a spell for a spell. But you never paid me."

The dwarf walked over to Mordred, who was crouched on the ground, hiding his face in his hands. "Or did you call it repayment when you cut off my captain's head and threw him into that well, eh?" With steely fingers Albrig pried Mordred's hands apart. "Not so bad. You'd be considered rather pretty if you went home with me." Mordred shrank back in pain and grief, hiding his scars again. "The trouble with wizards," Albrig said, "is that you have to wait a long time to get back at them. But I'm patient." He drew himself up and cast a regal eye over the others—everyone had stood aghast watching the scene of retribution. "Merlin!" he shouted.

At first there was no answer, then with slow gravity, the lady in the green felt hat stirred and sat up. She shook herself like someone roused from sleep, then lightly touched her forehead. The wound disappeared and all traces of blood with it.

"You!" the tramp said, all but speechless.

"Well, not for a while. I did keep away as I promised. Only now he's lost, hasn't he, and that ends the game." The lady smiled and raised her hand, and the circle of peace began to reform. Those who had been hurt stood up, their wounds healed, and one by one, the gathering took their places. Katy, Arthur, Pen, Peg, Edgerton, Sis, Tommy, and Derek were in the inner circle, and around them all the newcomers.

"Fitting. Most fitting." The lady's eyes gleamed magically, conveying the satisfaction of a master dramatist at the finale of his best comedy, but with a note of compassion that only the rarest comedy contains. Around the lady a nimbus of light formed, and for a few seconds the unmistakable outline of a tall wizard in cap and gown flashed out.

If Merlin lingered long, no one noticed, however. Their attention was drawn elsewhere. The walls and ceiling of the house having collapsed, the gathered people could see to the sky. Snow was still falling, and yet the stars were out. Mordred shrieked again, cursing all their souls. He crouched on the floor, his body contracted into a lump. The snow silently began to cover it while the circle widened and widened.

Hours passed, and yet the circle endured and widened as more people kept coming to add to it. It was as if a light had gone out into the world and everyone who dreamed of a new Camelot woke up. Each understood the message from the reading of the stone: *This is the world you have dreamed from the purity of your heart.* The birth of the new kingdom didn't depend upon everyone waking up. Millions slumbered on, but enough could hear. Merlin's stone had set up music in the air, bells whose liquid notes were ringing over all the earth.

When dawn came, there was no rubble anymore and no street, but only an open field with a small hummock under the snow to mark where Mordred had been. He wasn't gone forever, but his sleep would be long. A fresh reality had precipitated to earth, like snow falling from the stars. In the wintry dawn the sun felt unseasonably warm. McPhee shook himself, able to stir for the first time. He looked around for Westlake, who was still standing a few feet away, shaking himself awake. Only the two of them remained on the scene.

"They're walking away," McPhee said, pointing to Arthur and the others, now just a moving line in the distance. The line undulated over the fields, heading for the open horizon.

When they had disappeared, Westlake said, "We need to get back." McPhee nodded. They heard the sound of cars from the motorway, which gave them a sense of direction.

It took a while to clamber through the hindering snow, but eventually they made it back to a place they recognized, a traffic roundabout that headed off to town. Westlake stopped at a phone box to call for a ride.

"What are we going to say?" McPhee asked, offering his chief a cigarette.

"No thanks," Westlake said quietly. The constable pulled out a pack of matches, faintly astonished that his hands weren't shaking. Westlake looked at the passing cars. "I don't think we should say anything. Life has to go on."

McPhee watched the stream of people driving to work. A bus rumbled past, spattering mud from the dirty slush that the snow was rapidly becoming. A police car soon arrived, and McPhee stamped out his cigarette butt before getting in. The driver made no comment, and after a few minutes, the roofs of Gramercy could be seen up ahead.

Absently McPhee glanced at the rearview mirror. In the small rectangle was reflected the image of a castle, white banners flying from the ramparts. He wanted to cry out but instead looked over his shoulder. The castle loomed huge over the treetops, perfect and gleaming. At one extreme stood an impressive tower, dark yet polished to catch the eastern rays of the sun. High up in the tower was a slit window. The police car had approached its turnoff, and a few seconds later it plunged into Gramercy High Street, blocking the vision from view.

McPhee still felt something, though, a piercing joy that was wholly new to him. He didn't know if it would persist, but he hoped it would. No, he hoped it would spread and become the spark for all things new. "Chief," he murmured, but Westlake didn't respond, caught in the skein of his own feelings. McPhee hesitated. He so wanted to ask Westlake if he'd seen any of it—the rearing castle walls, the banners, or the forked white beard flying from the tower window.

POSTSCRIPT

One snowfall couldn't turn St. Justin's into a fairy land. The blackened, tottering walls still looked unspeakably dreary, yet from a distance at least, the massive sloping roofs covered in white were beautiful. They made Sis think of birthday cake. "I suppose we'll just walk back in?"

Tommy nodded. "I don't know exactly how it will work, but they won't have missed us." The high cornices of the main building dripped with swags of new snow, wiping out the grimaces on the gargoyles' faces.

The boys were knee-deep in it. They had crossed the fields bordering St. Justin's Hill, finding it hard to believe that the spring wheat had grown, ripened, and been harvested since the morning they'd left. The December sunset was clear and cold, but ever since the reading of the stone, they had felt warm inside. It had been just past noon when Arthur's group had come to a crossroads, one way leading west, the other back to Gramercy. No one had spoken about it, but there was a question whether the boys should continue.

"There's something back there for you." Derek wouldn't elaborate, and Sis found it hard to imagine anything that could offset the sadness of leaving everybody. The familiar faces meant more even than the circle of peace, and the boys were grateful for a last campfire together. In the glow of the embers the adults had all nodded off, leaving Tommy and Sis to watch the faces they loved fall into repose—Pen, Peg, Derek, Arthur. The next morning Edgerton decided to break off, too, but not to head back to St. Justin's. He wanted to seek the birthplace of Excalibur in the wild reaches of Wales. For him, the song of the sword was still strong. The others would travel with Arthur.

"It's not like walking away," he assured the boys. "That's over with. But I want to feel the land again." Everyone knew what he meant. The court of miracles was no longer in banishment, and the simple joy of being in the countryside felt glorious. A king was reclaiming his own.

So the group parted, leaving the two boys to find their way along the road. They didn't hurry. What kind of reception would they get? After lingering in the fields until dark, they climbed back in the window to Tommy's dorm.

"Who's there?" a sleepy voice challenged as the casement creaked, loud and rusty.

"Just me, I've been into town," replied Tommy.

"Lucky."

"Go back to bed."

The boy gave a token grumble before burying his head in his pillow. Sis waited while Tommy took off his jacket and put it in the tall wardrobe, making sure not to clink the wire hangers. He carefully opened the dividing door to Sis's dorm. The moonlight was strong enough that they could see his bed, neatly made up, his things arranged on the bedside table. Sis hung back.

"What's wrong?"

"I don't want to go in there," Sis whispered fiercely.

"Why not?"

"Because when I go to sleep, I'll forget everything, won't I?"

Tommy couldn't promise him that he wouldn't, but after a moment Sis closed the door behind him and disappeared.

Tommy woke up the next morning to feel somebody shaking him. "What?"

It was McGregor, one of the prefects. "It's Christmas chapel, and you're late."

Tommy struggled into his clothes and ran across the bleak, icy courtyard. The sky was low and gray. He could still see his breath as he ran in the back way of the old Norman chapel where congregations were held. The entire school was sitting, arrayed in pews by form. As Tommy slipped into his seat, he was grateful that the fifth form were nearly at the back.

At a signal the boys all stood up and began singing the hymn, a *Hodie.* Tommy looked up at the pine boughs hung across the rafters with red ribbon. Thick beeswax candles burned at the altar. Was it actually Christmas day? Tommy felt confused. He glanced at the boys on either side, who ignored him. Chapel had always induced a certain protective numbness, but by the time they were all back outside, Tommy began to feel clearer. Yes, he could remember it all now. He smiled, walking across the courtyard under the snow flurries that were beginning to fall.

Some boys in his form almost knocked him down running past. "Come on, Ashcroft," they shouted. "You're missing it." He sped up automatically, thinking they must mean soccer practice, but no, the playing field was frozen solid and white. There was no explaining the clump of boys pushing and shoving in front of him. The pack was swelling rapidly. "You boys there, come back inside," a master called from a door nearby. They ignored him. Tommy pushed his way slowly past the milling bodies until he got up close and saw what it was.

Over the heads of the boys a sword rose, its hilt a good eight feet in the air. The blade had been stuck into an anvil, which in turn rested on a huge stone boulder. "God," Tommy whispered to himself.

"It's because of us, isn't it?"

Tommy looked down to see Sis, flushed and excited, by his side. "I don't know. It happened like this once before."

A light dusting of fresh snow was settling over the stone, but the sword that was stuck in it remained gleaming, pristine. Tommy knew then that it was Christmas morning, the same day when a scorned and unknown boy had amazed all England and won a throne. Only this time there would be no London mob milling about the miraculous apparition. The king had not proclaimed a tournament, and the air was empty of banners and guerdons flying over parti-colored tents. Instead of the hundred knights who wanted to step forward to try to wrest the sword, there was none.

"What are you doing?" Sis asked as Tommy bolted forward, pushing all the boys aside who blocked his way to the stone.

"What do you think I'm doing?" Tommy was smiling, far happier than he had ever been in his whole life. He couldn't fathom why, but he had a second chance to make the web of time tremble. He put his palm to the hilt, then thought of something.

"Sis," he shouted. Unable to push the bigger boys aside, Sis crawled between their legs and made it through. Tommy hoisted him up and placed the little schoolboy's hand around the hilt, just below his. "Pull," he said, and then he braced himself, his face held up to the light of heaven.